# SING

*Also by Lisa T. Bergren:*

**CHILDREN'S BOOKS:**

*God Gave Us You*
*God Gave Us Two*
*God Gave Us Christmas*
*God Gave Us Heaven*
*God Gave Us Love*
*How Big Is God?*
*God Found Us You*

**NONFICTION:**

*The Busy Mom's Devotional*
*What Women Want*
*Life on Planet Mom*

**NOVELS:**

*The Bridge*
*Christmas Every Morning*

The Northern Lights series:
*The Captain's Bride*
*Deep Harbor*
*Midnight Sun*

The Gifted series:
*The Begotten*
*The Betrayed*
*The Blessed*

The Homeward Trilogy:
*Breathe*
*Sing*
*Claim* (Summer 2010)

A Novel of Colorado

**LISA T. BERGREN**

BOOK 2 of THE HOMEWARD TRILOGY

SING
Published by David C. Cook
4050 Lee Vance View
Colorado Springs, CO 80918 U.S.A.

David C. Cook Distribution Canada
55 Woodslee Avenue, Paris, Ontario, Canada N3L 3E5

David C. Cook U.K., Kingsway Communications
Eastbourne, East Sussex BN23 6NT, England

David C. Cook and the graphic circle C logo
are registered trademarks of Cook Communications Ministries.



LCCN 2010920349
ISBN 978-1-4347-6707-3
eISBN 978-0-7814-0437-2



The Team: Don Pape. Traci Depree, Amy Kiechlin, Sarah Schultz, Jaci Schneider, Caitlyn York, and Karen Athen
Cover Design: DogEared Design, Kirk DouPonce
Cover Photos: iStockphotos

Printed in the United States of America
First Edition 2010

1 2 3 4 5 6 7 8 9 10

012710

# For Diane

A woman who picks her children up when they stumble,
turns their eyes ahead when they focus on what lies behind,
and teaches them to sing out with all their heart.

*But I will sing of your strength,*
*In the morning I will sing of your love;*
*For you are my fortress,*
*My refuge in times of trouble.*
Psalm 59:16

# Chapter 1

15 March 1887
Paris

Surely she hadn't heard him right. Moira stared with disbelief at the ledger the bank manager turned toward her. "What do you mean I cannot withdraw this much? I have thousands of francs here."

"You *did*, Mademoiselle. Until this morning, when Monsieur Foster came and extracted all but the last thousand."

"Max? Mr. Max Foster came and withdrew these funds?"

"Oui. It was his biggest withdrawal yet. But as you know, he has full access to your bank account. He makes withdrawals all the time. I assumed this was no, as you say … different."

"Different?" The word emerged from her mouth in a high-pitched squeak. She swallowed hard and looked above that final ledger entry—10,000 francs—to other withdrawals. A thousand. Fifteen hundred. Sometimes twice a week. Her mind raced. Max, her manager of almost three years, paid her servants, the landlord. He paid for the groceries delivered each day. The oilman for the oil that filled her lamps. It took money, a lot of money to pay for all those things. But this much?

"Mademoiselle," the bank manager said carefully, peering over tiny spectacles at her, "has something transpired here that causes you alarm?"

"Non, non," she said, gathering herself. "Monsieur Foster and I merely need to converse. I am certain there is good reason for him to withdraw funds today. I simply have forgotten. Forgive me, Monsieur. My run at the Opera Comiqué has left me a bit … weary."

"I understand," he said, rising with her. "And may I say that your performance has been unparalleled in this city for some time? Paris is fortunate to have you, Mademoiselle St. Clair."

"You are too kind," she said. "Bon jour."

"Bon jour," he said with a nod. But his dark eyes still held the same concern that flooded Moira's heart.

Max Foster would be at Madame Toissette's tea later today—she would speak with him then. But before he took a sip of her fine Earl Gray, he would explain to Moira where her money had gone.

Colorado

*15 March 1887*

*Hoarfrost covers every branch and every bit of every tree within sight. It is beautiful, a sight I always favor, but in this instance, it makes me more fearful than ever. For below it is more snow than I've ever seen. More snow than Bryce or Tabito have ever seen. And while it has ceased for the moment, leaving behind a brilliant blue sky that showcases mountains in bridal white, Tabito believes more is on the way. Tonight? Tomorrow? It would take weeks to melt the snow already here. The men—*

Samuel's cry brought Odessa's head up, and she set her pen aside and went to the babe in the next room. Now seven months old, the child quieted when he spotted his mother, gurgling a pleased coo and wiggling his arms and legs in vigorous excitement. She lifted him and cradled him close for a moment, running her lips over his sweet, soft cheek. She reached for another blanket, frowning at the chill in the room, and returned to the window over her desk, one of only two in the house that were not either frosted or sealed over by the vast snowbanks.

Her eyes traced the channel the men had dug from the bunkhouse to the main house and then over the hill to where the stables and shelters stood. She'd watched them taking turns with the digging until the bank on either side was shoulder high. Against the house, where the wind had driven into drifts, the white piles had been as high as the second-story windows on the western side and not much lower to the south and north. The men had dug them out each day, but each night as they slept through the high, dry wail of the wind, the drifts returned.

"Never, ever, have I seen this much snow," Bryce had said, staring out a whitewashed window as if he could somehow bore through it and see his horses. That had been yesterday, when they wondered if the snow would ever stop. And then this morning it had.

The men were immediately at it, attempting to get to the hundred horses that had been left to battle the elements on their own. Only fifty could be in the stables at a time or sheltered in the corrals that lined it. They had found food and water throughout the storm. But the others? Those who had naught but the small snow breaks that dotted the fields? Odessa shook her head. Judging from the house, they might have all long been buried. *Please, God, please … please let them be all right.*

The passageway through which the men had disappeared remained silent and empty, a yawning chasm of doubt and fear. After a couple brutal years of drought, much of Odessa's inheritance had gone into an extension of acreage that gained the Circle M increased water rights. Could the horses out there even get to water? Were they pawing and digging their way down to streams that were frozen solid?

Odessa blinked twice and turned, deciding to do something rather than stand there and fret. Bread, six loaves, she'd bake. A thick and hearty beef stew the men would love after their bone-chilling, hard work. An apple cobbler from her stash of summer preserves. "Come, Samuel," she whispered, drawing comfort from the weight of him in her arms. She carried him down the stairs and into the kitchen, then set him on the floor atop a thick blanket, near the stove, which she blocked off by turning a chair on its side. It was so dark with the snow that embalmed the windows—despite the bright sun outside—she lit a couple of lamps, stoked the fire, handed Samuel a tin cup to play with, and turned to pull out flour and sugar.

Later, with the bread rising by the stove, she fed Samuel while she sat in her rocker, wondering how much longer it would take for Bryce, anyone, to return to her. She was desperate for word. By now they had surely made it to the snow breaks, assessed the losses—

It was then that she heard the stomping on the front porch, the low murmur of voices. She hurriedly pulled Samuel from her breast. She ignored his indignant cry, her eyes only on the front door as she rushed to meet her husband. He turned to her, and she could see the men walking away with stooped shoulders. But it was Bryce, her dear, sweet Bryce, who captured her whole attention. It was as if he had aged a decade, or suffered from consumption again, so weary and ill did he appear.

"Bryce," she said.

He stepped forward and slowly closed the door behind him, then gradually raised his eyes to meet hers. Tears welled and threatened to roll down his cheeks.

"Oh!" she said, clamping her lips shut, feeling tears clench her throat. "All of them, Bryce? Are they all dead?" She moved forward to wrap one arm around him. Samuel wailed louder than ever, infuriated by the crush of his parents. But the two adults remained there as each gave way to the tremors of sobs.

Her husband wiped his cheeks with the palms and then the backs of his hands, trying to regain control. "Best we can tell, the storm took many of them." He took another deep breath. "Some might have made it to the far side, instinctively heading for the shelter of the trees. But we'll need a week of melt before we can make it across to see. And we can't—" his voice broke and he wept for a moment—"we can't even be sure how many are there, by the snow breaks. They're buried, Dess. Buried. Stood there, waiting for us to save them."

She moved back in to hold him, crying with him again. *Dear God … Please. Please.* The mere idea of it, the overwhelming vision of a hundred horses now dead.… *No, no, no. Savior, please!* What would become of them? The ranch depended on the income of the sale of a hundred and fifty horses each summer. One hundred already dead? And with more snow coming? Her eyes went to the front parlor window, a dark bank of dense snow. *Show us, Lord. Show us what to do. We need You. We need You!*

❦

15 March 1887
Rio de Janeiro

"Come, Son, we have need of your services," said a man gruffly, hauling Dominic to his feet.

Nic winced, both at the rapid motion and the bright light of morning. His stomach roiled and his head spun. Whatever they were pouring last night at the bar was hard on a man's gut, even one used to liquor. He squinted, trying to see the men who were on either side of him as they rushed him down the stairs, out the door, and through a crowded market plaza. "Stop!" he yelled. "Unhand me! What's this about?"

The two men paused, tightening their grip on his arms as he fought back. Two others arrived and lifted his feet from the cobblestones. "Wait! Where are you taking me?" Nic cried, battling both fear and fury now. He writhed and pulled, but to no avail. By the look of them, these four men were hardened seamen.

The leader motioned for the others to halt, and he was once again on his feet. A crowd of curious onlookers gathered, staring at them, but Nic was struggling to steady his eyes on the man. "Where are you taking me?" he repeated. The first relinquished Nic's arm to another's care and turned to face him. "You cost my cap'n a large sum of money last night with your poor fighting."

"The man was twice my size!" Nic snarled, feeling the man's complaint as if it were a sucker punch.

"Yes, well, the cap'n had high hopes for you. Your reputation, up to last night, was … unequaled. He put a fair sum down on you."

"That's a gambler's risk." He pulled again, hoping to get free, but the men still held stubbornly to his arms. If he could get even one fist free….

The leader grinned, showing a mouthful of decaying teeth. "Too bad you didn't win last night. He believes you owe him the money he lost."

"That's preposterous!"

The man shrugged and smiled again. "Be that as it may, we are only obliged to follow our cap'n's orders. And our cap'n is now yours as well."

Nic paused and swallowed hard. So that was it. These men intended to shanghai him—force him to serve aboard their ship. "You're nothing but a crimp! There are laws against—"

"For American ships, sailing under American laws," said the man. He motioned to the others and turned to walk toward the docks, the others following behind, dragging Nic along. "We lost a dozen men here in port to the fever," he said, turning partially toward Nic to speak while they walked. "Now the cap'n is not only cantankerous over losin' them, but also losin' his heavy purse over you. It's your bum luck. Best to accept it and embrace it, man. Six months from now, you'll be set free, in whatever port you wish."

"If I'm not already dead."

The man laughed, a slow, deep guffaw that eventually built into laughter that spread among the others. "Aye, that's the risk of any sailor's life, especially in the waters where we are headed." He looked over his shoulder at his prisoner. "Come along, St. Clair. Cease your struggle. It is of no use. You'll take to the water, you'll see. Yes'sir, gamblers and fighters—they make the best of seamen. You might find you love it as much as the ring."

Cañon City, Colorado

Reid Bannock straightened, groaning at the ache in the small of his back and between his shoulders. He set the pickax against his leg and gestured to the water boy to come his way. He casually met the gaze of the deputy, who watched over the prison chain gang with an armed shotgun resting across his arms. The man gave him a slight nod. They got on, the two of them. Reid fancied the idea that the younger man felt sorry for him even, though the two had never shared more than a few words. Undoubtedly, Deputy Johnson knew Reid's story, passed along more from lawman to lawman than within his files.

The blue-lipped, shivering water boy finally reached him and offered up a grubby ladle full of water. The boy's hand trembled violently, not out of fear but from exposure. In the cold, the top of his bucket kept frosting over and encased the whole thing in ice. He had to break through the top to fetch Reid the water, and it was so cold, it made Reid's teeth hurt as he drank.

It stayed cold, even within him, making him feel as if he swallowed a chunk of ice rather than liquid. He coughed, thumped his chest, and gazed up at the mountains, finally clear after the blizzard. It mattered little, this trial. In a few months he'd be free. Regardless of the sentence, he'd be free. Every morning, he was up and dressed, awaiting the deputy who would chain him to others for the work on the new prison building, whatever the weather. Only the blizzard had allowed them a few days' respite. Each mornin', he greeted the deputy with a friendly word, knowing that consistent good behavior could knock months off a man's sentence.

By his calculations, the county was drawing too many new people, and therefore too many new criminals. The general's propaganda was doing its good work, and Colorado Springs, Pueblo, even Cañon City were seeing pioneers arrive by the thousands, all hoping to make a new life for themselves. After a winter like they'd had, many of them were liable to be desperate, driven to desperate decisions, not all of them on the right side of the law. Already, Reid shared his tiny cell with five other men. Word had it that a sixth would be brought in soon, left to sleep on the narrow space that was currently the only flooring between the two bunks, each with three levels. How long until a seventh arrived? Yes, when number seven arrived, tough decisions would have to be made; the prison warden would have to speak with judges, finding a means to alleviate the pressure before the prisoners exploded.

"Get back to work, Bannock," the deputy barked.

"Yes sir, right away, sir," Reid called back, immediately picking up his ax. He lifted it up over his left shoulder and then let it arc down toward the boulder in front of him, imagining faces upon it, as he had every day on every rock he had destroyed over the last three years.

Moira St. Clair. The woman who had stolen his heart, and then crushed it.

Dominic St. Clair. The man who had stood between Moira and him.

Odessa and Bryce McAllan, the people who refused to give up what was destined to be his.

A chunk of granite fell away with his next strike, revealing a tiny, crooked line of gold that glittered in the sun, too small to warrant the work of extraction, but tantalizing. It was common, these tiny remnants, teasing their discoverers with the idea about where the rock had once stood and what vein had once connected to this small one.… In spite of himself, he leaned forward and traced the line with his finger. Gold. Silver. Treasure untold. Sam O'Toole or his parents had discovered something, up near his mine. Something beyond the few sweet silver nuggets he'd brought out to Westcliffe and sold. Had the McAllans discovered it yet? Had they squired it away for a rainy day?

"The Spaniards, they came up this way, ya know," said an old man, chained to his right leg. He was a chatty fellow, and Reid glanced at him before striking with the pickax again.

"That so?" he said casually.

"Yep. My great-granddaddy, he was a trapper. Ran with Kit Carson and the like for a time. Knew a lot of Injuns."

"And the Spaniards?" Reid asked lowly.

"My great-granddaddy, he was chased right up into the Sangres by the Ute who didn't take kindly to him being—"

"You two!" barked the deputy, frowning in their direction. "Less talking, more work!"

Reid frowned too and doubled his efforts against the boulder. But with each strike, he wondered more about what the old man had to say. A few minutes later, he dared to glance at the old man.

*I'll tell you later,* his eyes said.

# Chapter 2

When it was apparent that Max Foster was not attending Madame Toissette's tea, and she could not find him in any of his usual haunts, Moira returned home, perplexed. She paced the parlor floor and hallways all night, trying to understand what Max's rationale might be, where he might have gone. Come morning, she collapsed into a chair by the entry window, anxiously watching for Francois, the director at the Opera Comiqué, who had pledged to return to her with information, but she could not keep her head erect any longer. She had just closed her eyes when a sharp knock at the door brought Antoinette scurrying from the kitchen.

"Non, non," Moira said in irritation, rising. "I'll receive him." She ran a hand over her hair and smoothed her dress, donned a nonchalant smile and opened the door. But the grim expression on Francois's face immediately shredded any semblance of propriety she maintained. "Francois?"

He wearily shrugged out of his coat and hung it on a peg by the door. "Come, mon ami. Let us sit in the parlor. I have much to tell you." He offered his arm. Moira numbly took it and allowed him to lead her into her own sitting room. Antoinette stood, waiting for her mistress's direction.

"Tea, and plenty of it," Francois said, waving her off. He sat on an ottoman by Moira's knees, so he could take both of her hands in his.

"You are frightening me." Francois was always jovial, a chipper bear of a man, her friend who always made her feel better, brighter, when he was around.

"Forgive me. But it is bad, very bad."

"Quickly, simply tell me. All of it."

Francois swallowed hard and ducked his chin into the folds of fat at his neck. His eyes shifted left and right as he searched for a way to begin.

"Francois—" Moira scolded.

"Max is gone. He boarded a ship yesterday evening, bound for Lisbon."

"Portugal?"

"Portugal."

Moira pulled her hands from his and leaned back. She turned her head to the side, and rested an elbow on the thickly padded arm, knuckles to lips. "He always wanted to see Portugal, wanted me to consider the growing opportunities there—"

"He has a new client. A young thing he discovered in the Moulin Rouge."

Moira dropped her hand from her mouth and let out an outraged laugh. "The Moulin Rouge?" For three years, she had been Max's client; in the last two, she had been Max's *only* client. Why leave her now? For a fallen songstress from the red district? "Were they …" she sputtered. "Were they in love?"

"It appears so."

"So he stole all my money for some tart?"

"It appears so," he repeated. He cleared his throat.

Her eyes moved to him again. "There is more."

"He departed yesterday, because somehow, he found out from Sylvain what I myself did not know—that the Opera Comiqué would be closing immediately."

"What?" Moira rose and paced the Persian-rug covered floor. "Of what madness do you speak? How could … the Opera *Comiqué?"*

Francois grimaced. "The owners … you know how they are, always bickering. Patrice, Roland, Sylvain—are now in legal dispute. Since they cannot agree on a solution, a judge has forced them to close for three months. There is money owed to …"

He went on, describing the foolishness of men that had brought the owners of the opera house to such a grim halt. It would cost them thousands of francs. It would cost Francois a job. And for her … she well knew that every opera house was booked out for a month or more. Some for several months. She could not simply move to another and secure a suitable role. Suitable roles took months and years to procure. Suitable roles were Max's responsibility, planning out her future, their future. She leaned a hand against the wall and covered her eyes with the other. Her heart sank. *Max … not you. …*

Francois came over to her and placed gentle hands on her shoulders. "You need not fear, mon ami. I will take care of you until we find another opera, another stage."

She shook her head and moved away from him. She turned to wearily face him. "No, Francois. I must depart Paris. I'll be a laughingstock. I cannot bear such humiliation. Perhaps in London I can make a fresh start."

"You are leaving? How can you leave?" He stared at her bleakly.

"How can I stay?" she cried out. Antoinette arrived then with a tray in hand. "Please, Antoinette, set it there." The girl bobbed her curtsey and departed, her eyes rife with curiosity over the conversation at hand. She'd have to be dismissed by nightfall. Along with her father, Antoine, the doorman, the cook, and the housekeeper … How much would it cost to pay them all what she owed them? Max took care of all of that, every last detail. How could she function without him?

And yet how could she not? How could she have placed her life in the hands of a man?

"*S'il vous plait*—" Francois said, taking a step toward her, hands outstretched.

"Non, Francois. No, no, no!" she said, putting one hand up. "Please. You will need funds to keep yourself until you find another stage. I cannot be a burden to you."

"You would never—"

"Please. Please. Don't you see?" she dropped her voice and leaned toward him. "Within days, this will all be gone. My house, my lovely things. My creditors will come to collect in vases and glassware. My servants will take their wages in clocks and rugs. I cannot stay here and watch it. I cannot bear it."

"You, you have nothing set aside? Another bank account, investments?"

She lifted her chin. "I have spent my inheritance becoming Moira St. Clair. The Moira St. Clair that so enchanted this city, even you, dear Francois. That was my investment. But now, here I am, and my account has been emptied by my agent. In another year or two I would have…. But not now. And I will not remain here to become the city's favorite topic of gossip. There are people," she paused, "there are people who would revel in my struggle."

"What will you do? What if you reach London, and there is no work to be found?"

She turned away and forced herself to return to her chair and pour tea for her guest. She added a spoonful of sugar and a bit of cream, as she knew he liked it, and stirred, then gently set it on the table to her right. A card, sitting on a small receiving tray, caught her attention, reminding her of another, upstairs. Jesse. Jesse McCourt. He'd escort her to London, help her find a suitable role. He'd understand this. And he'd recently been in London. He knew the right people.

With a surge of newfound hope, she smiled up at Francois. "Come. Come, my friend, and sit. We shall share our last cup of tea, and we will dream of the day we are once again reunited."

❦

*They are gone, all gone. More than fifty of the finest horses to ever wander this marvelous country, and now they lay unbreathing beneath a funeral shroud of snow. I ventured out today to see, in spite of Bryce's objection, wishing to say my farewell to companions that once gazed upon us with wide, wise eyes, laced with long lashes. Companions that once ran across fields of green and through brown brush, as free and powerful and relentless as the trains that rumble down the tracks. I was once accustomed to Death, knew it by sense as clearly as if I could smell it. But now, here, I have been free of his visitations for almost four years. Bryce has not lost more than three horses since my arrival. No*

> *neighbor has perished. Death's return is most assuredly unwelcome, leaving me trembling with sorrow. And seeing these horses, once so full of life, so full of promise—*

Bryce laid a hand on her shoulder, making her jump. She had not heard his approach up the stairs, nor across the floor that led to her desk. "Sorry," he said, sinking wearily into a chair beside her.

"No, it's fine." She stared at him and paused, choosing her words. "Will you burn the carcasses, Bryce?"

"Eventually. But not yet. They're frozen still. And it's snowing again."

Her eyes flicked to the window, hoping her husband was wrong. But of course he wasn't. She held her breath. The gray clouds, heavy with moisture, the fat flakes drifting down. She felt fear she hadn't felt since battling the consumption, or since the night she went into labor. The doctor had told her she was too frail to carry a baby, shouldn't carry a baby. Bryce had been beside himself, so anxious was he that he might lose Odessa as well as their child. But she had waged the battles of labor and delivery with ease, and Samuel, well, Samuel had been perfectly healthy from the start. Memories of that first beautiful night when they were first a family comforted her. Somehow, some way, this chapter of their lives would pass too.

Samuel cried then, and Bryce rose with Odessa. "Stay. I'll get the boy."

She sank back into her chair and dipped her pen in the ink, but she couldn't think of what else to say. All she could see in her mind were the lifeless eyes of the first horse she came upon, a brown beauty that would never carry either foal or rider, never roll in the dust or toss her head as she ran. She heard Bryce pause in the hallway, felt his gaze, and then Samuel's soft baby sounds. Odessa turned and looked over her shoulder, watched her husband kiss the babe's head, leave his lips there and close his eyes as he bounced, as if he was memorizing the feel of the child.

"How do we do this, Bryce? It is so mind-numbingly tragic, so horrific. How can you go on as if nothing more than the average day has transpired?"

He opened his eyes and stared into hers, then gave her a little shrug. "It is life, Odessa. Truly life on the frontier. We have thankfully been free of Death's shadow for some time. But here it is again. The important thing is not to dwell long upon the loss; the important thing is to dwell upon the gifts."

"The gifts?"

Bryce nodded. "We did not lose all the horses. Our finest remain, sheltered in the stables. And some might still be on the other side of the fields, waiting on us."

"If they do not perish in tonight's storm," Odessa said bitterly. She regretted the words as she watched Bryce recoil.

He was silent for a moment. "Some might survive. And we still have those here, in and near the stables where we can better keep an eye on them. And we lost no men in the storm. All are accounted for. In weather like we've seen, men often head out into the white and disappear, their bodies lost until spring, if not forever. We can hope, hope for those horses out there."

"Indeed," she said in a whisper. How did he do that? Manage to comfort her and call her attention to the ways she fell short at the same time? She was grateful for his wisdom, along with a hundred other things that made her adore him. God could not have picked a finer mate for her. If anything happened to him …

She shivered as he coughed, his lungs obviously tight after the exertion outside. For so long they had been well, free of Death. But now, had their luck run out?

❁

A night and two days into their voyage, Nic could still not believe he was here.

"Heave!" shouted Terence Overby, the first mate who had pressed him into service. Together, sixteen men stood amidships and pulled along two massive ropes, edging the main sail up. "Heave, men, heave!"

Nic did as he was told, but his eyes edged past Terence to Ulric Ross, a short, fat, balding man who wielded unmitigated power on this ship. Nic wondered how he managed it, with more than ten men who outweighed him by fifty pounds. It certainly wasn't physical prowess that gained him such power. It was something else, and Nic was determined to find out. *Use your brain as well as your brawn*, his father had once told him.

He'd need both to get out of this mess.

Terence shouted again and the men hauled backward on the rope, fighting the wind to bring the sail fully upright. But with the wind came the swells, and some washed over the starboard edge as they gained speed, then drained out through the scuppers. Upon the first mate's next call, Nic dug in and pulled, but his shoes slipped on the wet planking. He was suddenly flat on his back.

The other sailors roared with laughter and all work came to a halt. Terence shouted, "Turn to!" and some obediently turned away, but two others—Wade and Verne—stayed where they were, seemingly unable to do anything but wipe the streams of tears that left the corners of their crinkled eyes.

Humiliation quickly transformed into fury. Nic pulled in his legs and then leaped to his feet, a trick he had learned in the ring. The two sailors stopped laughing, their eyes widening in wonder. "Oh, oh, look out," cried Wade, "the lubber's beset!" Nic drew back his right arm to punch Verne, but a steely hand stayed him. He turned to attack whoever held him, and almost succeeded in striking the man. Thankfully, his fist stopped just short of reaching Terence's jaw.

"Stand down," said the first mate, never flinching.

Nic dropped his arms and stepped away. To strike the first mate or captain would only lead to lashes or even death. Nic had spent enough time on ships—heretofore as a passenger but paying enough attention—to fully understand this.

Terence stepped forward, until his face was but an inch from Nic's.

"I don't like being laughed at," Nic said lowly, daring to meet his first mate's eyes.

"Sailors laugh, man, every chance they get. If you don't laugh, the elements come and claim you." He narrowed his eyes at Nic. "Move beyond it."

"I see nothing funny. I've been taken, stolen, shanghaied!"

"We've been through this, St. Clair. Accept your lot and get on with it, man."

"Not until I speak to the captain."

"You speak to me. That is as well and good as speaking to the cap'n."

"No, it isn't, since the captain is the one who decided to abduct me. What is he really after? Ransom?"

The first mate let a slow smile edge up his lips. "Someone at home ready to pay to get you back, boy?"

Nic's lips clamped shut, suddenly recognizing his error. The last thing he wanted was to have Odessa, Moira—"No. No! I simply can't spend six months aboard this ship wondering why, wondering if there might not be some other solution. I must speak to him. I must."

"No. Your resolution is to accept your lot and become a good sailor. That is the only solution you need."

"I cannot!" He looked beyond the first mate to the captain. "Captain! Cap'n Ross! May I have a word with—"

The punch sent Nic whirling to the deck again. Two men took hold of his arms and brought him to his feet before his head stopped spinning. He blinked, trying to focus on the first mate, who massaged his right fist. He'd have to remember to avoid that punch again—there was a power there that he'd seldom experienced, even in the ring. Terence leaned in toward him, "*I* am the cap'n, as far as you're concerned, man. You have a concern? You bring it to *me*. Never the cap'n."

Nic studied him for several long seconds. "Captain!" he shouted, looking past Terence. "I must have a word with you!"

He dodged the first mate's next punch, stifling a smile as Terence hit Wade in error. But he didn't anticipate the left to his stomach that came right after it.

"Enough," said the captain, suddenly beside Terence.

Nic looked up at him, still doubled over and gasping for breath.

"It was a punch like that that took you down in the ring, St. Clair," said the captain. "Are you slow? Daft?"

"I don't like to think so," Nic said, still gasping for breath. "It is a desire to become more … knowledgeable, sir, that begs for an audience with you. I must understand some things in order to make my peace in being aboard your ship and in your service."

"I could care less about whether you're at peace. Just do your job. You might or might not get your 'audience.'" He turned to walk away, paused, and then looked to his right. "Lash him to the mast."

"Sir, yes'sir."

❀

The other sailors ignored Nic as the sun set and the chill of night crept over the ship's edges. Nic stared straight ahead. He was furious.

All he had wanted was a word with the captain. A word! He wanted the man to tell him himself why he felt Nic owed him six months of service. He had not thrown that fight. He had lost money on it himself. And the captain must've known that he hadn't lost for weeks, otherwise why would he have made such a bet? What kind of mad thinking was this? Or was it merely a means to populate his dwindling crew? He'd discovered that he was not alone in his predicament—he had seen at least six others dragged aboard. But none of the others spoke English.

He'd been standing for five hours now, lashed to the massive mast with heavy ropes from shoulder to thigh. His feet were numb and he tried to lift them a bit, pushing against the ropes, to allow some circulation to return. But it was to no avail. He turned his head leeward and squinted into the darkness, his eyes hungry for the dim outline of land. They traveled south, and considering the stiff wind and full sails they had enjoyed since embarking on this journey, Nic guessed they were nearing Uruguay. He'd gathered from talk among the crew that they'd seek new provisions somewhere in southern Argentina before attempting to round the Horn.

A man above him in the nest clanged a bell. "Two bells and all is well," he called.

Nic didn't know him. Did he spend each night on watch? It was cold, grim work, shivering in the night wind, trying to see shapes in the darkness until his eyes ached. "Ahoy, there!" Nic called upward.

Silence greeted him.

"Ahoy, mate! May I ask your name?"

In the dim light of the one lantern on deck, swinging before the captain's doorway, Nic thought he saw a head peek over the side of the nest. But then it was gone.

"Is this your watch, mate?" he tried again. "Every night?"

A man's voice hissed down at him from the ropes. "Are you daft?"

Nic turned his head, trying to see him, but failing. The man was too far behind him. "More idle than daft, I hope. What's your name?"

"William. Now cease your chatter and see your lot through. The cap'n will move you from the mast to the bowsprit if you don't."

Nic sighed and stared straight ahead again. The farther south they moved, the farther from his apartments, his possessions, his work he became. It was likely lost by now anyway, his temporary home ransacked as word of his imprisonment spread.

For a while, he had lived lavishly off his inheritance, renting stately homes as he traveled to England and Spain and back. Here and there pretty women had caught his eye, and he kept company with them for a while, but when he grew bored, he left for another city. He was restless, always restless, searching for … something.

His search had brought him back across the Atlantic last year and with his funds rapidly dwindling away, he had once again entered the ring. There, some of the old gratification, release, returned to him with each win. And he followed the invitations southward, from Florida, into the chief ports of the Caribbean—where he seriously considered settling, so transfixing were the trade winds and swaying palms and blue waters—but even they grew wearisome in time. He moved southward again, to Venezuela and eventually Brazil, his white skin drawing record crowds and fat purses.

He had been considering a voyage to California for some time; this ship, the *Mirabella*, was to port in Mexico. So perhaps it was all for the best. His own brand of twisted luck that seemed to follow him like a long shadow.

William, a slender but strong man, suddenly was beside him, lifting a ladle to his parched lips. "Figured you might have a thirst," he whispered.

Nic drank gratefully and considered how the man had crept down the nets again without being heard. Above the wind, he had not heard the creaks of the ropes. "Thank you," he said. "I don't suppose you have any rum in your back pocket?"

William laughed silently, a quick flash of white. "Best be back to my perch."

"Thank you, William."

"Aye."

"And my name's Dominic, Nic to my friends," he whispered hoarsely over his shoulder.

"Hush now, Nic," he returned, so quietly that Nic momentarily wondered if he was imagining a voice on the wind. "Try and catch some winks. It'll make the night pass faster."

# Chapter 3

18 March 1887

A cold bucket of seawater splashed over Nic, and he howled in outrage, sputtering as the water dripped down his face. He had jerked his head up but now he winced, belatedly noticing the mass of knots from his fretful night of trying to sleep while standing up. He squinted and took in the warm golden light of sunrise that surrounded the first mate like a halo.

The ropes about him dropped, and he followed them to the deck, his legs too lifeless to support him. He sprawled out onto the wooden planking and glared at his laughing crewmates, walking aft to receive their morning rations from the cook.

"Pay them no mind," Terence commanded. He squatted down beside Nic. "It'll go best for you if you never brawl with another man aboard ship. The cap'n—and I'll—have none of it." Nic pondered his words, thinking of another man, warning him not to brawl in his town.

Reid Bannock, the treacherous wretch. Murderer.

It all seemed so long ago.

He pushed himself up with his arms to a sitting position. He shivered involuntarily as the pins and prickles of blood flow once again surged through his legs. Was there further damage to his limbs?

"You'll recover," Terence said. "You aren't the first man to spend a night at the mast. But I'd wager you aren't anxious to be the next."

"No sir."

"Good, then. We understand each other. Join Sherman at the aft deck after you eat. You will spend the next three days splicing rope."

Nic grimaced. He'd seen what splicing rope did to even an old seaman's hands. He pictured his fingers and palms, as raw and bloody as freshly butchered meat.

"Agreed?"

"I …" He looked up, saw the determined look on Terence's face, and said simply, "Agreed." There was no way to beat a master; one had to befriend them. Otherwise, no favor would ever be gained. The first mate, apparently satisfied, turned away. Nic used his arms to haul himself over to the mast until he could lean back against it. He massaged his legs, ignoring the pain now, determined to restore them so he could once again rise. He felt vulnerable sitting there.

"Here," said a man, suddenly at his side. "Give it a little time." He handed Nic a tin cup of water and a crude wooden bowl of gruel. On top was a chunk of salt pork. Nic, having been denied supper last night, eagerly accepted and glanced at the young man. "Thank you. I assume by the voice that you are William."

"Not quite as handsome in the light of day as I am at night, right?" William said with a lopsided grin. He had long, wavy blond hair tied back at the nape of his neck.

Nic smiled. "All I saw of you last night was your teeth. And I doubt you have difficulty finding favor among the ladies."

"The ladies?" He arched a brow. "No, I have little trouble with the ladies. It's their husbands that seem to disfavor me."

Nic nearly choked on a thick spoonful of gruel. "You're a rogue, then?"

"I prefer 'a gentleman among rogues.'"

"And far more willing to chat in the light of day."

William leaned one shoulder against the mast, arms crossed, and shrugged. "I was on watch. You were … disfavored. It would not have been wise for me to be found out of the nest or speaking with you."

"Granted."

"Where do you hail from, Nic?"

"I was … *procured* from Rio, where I had been abiding for the last several months. I've been traveling for some time, rarely settling for long. But I consider Philadelphia home."

"My own home was once in Charlotte. And I'm sorry to hear that you joined us by force rather than by choice. It's a difficult way to begin any journey."

Nic chewed on the stringy meat and washed it down with a swig from his tin cup. By William's accent and language, he guessed him highly educated. "How long have you been a sailor?"

"Not much longer than you. I joined the crew in the West Indies. By tradition the greenest crewmen draw duty aloft."

"So I might expect to relieve you up there some eve?"

William cocked a brow again. "It's better than splicing rope," he said as he shoved off, just a moment before the bell rang six times, signaling the crew that it was time to attend to their various tasks. "I'm off to catch my own winks now," William said to Nic, walking backward. "Tear a bit from the bottom of your shirt, and wrap your palms and fingers. It'll leave you some digits to work with."

"Thank you," Nic said, lifting his chin.

William smiled again and turned away, disappearing down the steps that led to the crew's quarters.

❁

Jesse turned to Moira in the carriage to better see her face. The years had been kind to him and a few lines of maturity had only served to make him more devilishly handsome. "Moira, I just arrived. You are asking me to return to London? I need them to beg me to return, not go knocking on their door asking favors. You know how it goes."

"Come now, Jesse," she said, pretending to fuss with the fit of her right ivory glove. "Were you not intending to ask the same favor of me? Did you not intend to use my connections here in Paris to secure a role?" She leaned forward and tapped the handle of her umbrella on the roof of the carriage. "Here, stop here!" she shouted to the coachman.

Jesse looked at her in confusion. "Why? Why are we stopping?"

She ignored his question. "What is Clarence Havender up to?"

"When I left, he was trying to secure a stage and a producer for a new opera, but—"

"There. You see? Clarence always adored me. And together, we could be a very comely duo as his leads. Remember how we sounded together in the Springs? No doubt you've learned as much as I in our years apart." The driver opened the small door and offered his hand to her. "I'll be back in but a moment. Think about what I've said while I'm gone, would you?"

She stifled a smile at his mystified expression. Four years ago, he had been the worldly, knowledgeable man of the stage. Now things were slightly different. She emerged onto the wooden walk of one of the finest Parisian neighborhoods, sparkling after the spring rains, and today under a crisp, brilliant blue sky. She stood in front of her favorite dress shop, considering the words she'd use to convince the proprietress to purchase back some of her gowns to remake into children's gowns. "Please," she said to the driver, "fetch my trunks. I'll be inside."

❁

*And so it has at last ceased. I hold my breath each time I gaze out a window, holding my baby, wondering if the snow will return and steal a bit more of our future. But the sun now shines, warm enough to shrug off my heavy bearskin coat. The men have uncovered the bodies of the horses that perished. Only forty-eight were entombed there, which gives us hope that another fifty-two have managed to survive across the fields. Bryce tells me that horses have managed to survive all sorts of adverse conditions; they will eat bark from trees, if need be, just as the deer do in lean months. But that assumes they made it to the far side of our land.*

Odessa couldn't think any longer about the horses—lost, wandering, waiting for rescue. So she set down her pen and then went to pick Samuel up from his cradle. She laughed at his round cheeks, bright red with sleeping heat. From beneath a furrowed brow, he stared back at her with beautiful sea-green eyes. "A St. Clair you are," she whispered. "I won't tell your papa if you won't." She put on her coat and then picked up the child, stepping outside. After so many days of being sequestered in the house due to the blizzard, it felt glorious to be outside. But soon the smell of burning horsehair assaulted her nose. The men had begun the grisly work; they were burning the bodies of the dead.

She turned the corner of the house and shielded her eyes. There, to the north, five tendrils of dark smoke rose above a bank of pure white snow. It would be better when they were gone, when there was nothing left but ash to gaze upon, rather than decomposing bodies that raised the question *what if?*

Bryce had not slept in a week, entering their shared bed late, rising before she or Samuel woke. She had crept out into the hallway one night to see him sitting beside a blank canvas, brush in hand, paint upon the palette, but doing nothing but stare out the dark window. Morning after morning that canvas remained blank.

*Father God,* she prayed, as she walked toward the stables. *Show me how to comfort my husband. Show me how to maintain faith when I am afraid.* She hoped he was down here, and not with the men burning the bodies. It would be too much, and not good for his lungs. He needed time among the living, the bodies that represented their future, rather than among the dead.

Carefully, she wound her way up and over the slippery, slushy path toward the stables. Outside, in two corrals, Ralph and Dietrich tossed hay across the fence. The horses were agitated, as if desperate to eat, even though they had been well fed throughout the storm. As if they knew death was just a snowstorm away.

"Ma'am," said Ralph, tapping the brim of his hat when he saw her.

"Ralph," she returned. "Is my husband in there?"

"Think so, ma'am."

"Thank you." She moved to the big central door, unlatched it, and let it swing open. After a moment, her eyes adjusted and she spied her husband, chin on folded arms, staring into her horse's stall. Her heart leapt with fear. "Is everything okay with Ebony?"

Bryce straightened and turned toward her and Samuel. "My two favorite people in the world. Sure it's safe, bringing the baby out?"

She smiled and handed the child to his father. "Sure enough. I think he has as bad a case of cabin fever as I today. He's been fussy all morning, until I got him bundled up to go."

"Is that right?" Bryce asked, more to the child than her. He smiled down at Samuel, then turned and lifted him a bit, as if to get him in better light. "Those sea-green eyes just show a bit more of his St. Clair side every day, don't they?"

Odessa moved closer, wrapping her hand around her husband's arm as she leaned in to gaze with him at their baby. "I guess the secret's out. I told him not to tell."

"Not to tell what?" Bryce said, slanting a glance down at his wife. "That he's the son of the most gorgeous woman in the valley?"

Odessa laughed. "That's high praise indeed, considering that there are maybe a hundred of us in the valley, including Westcliffe."

Bryce lifted his chin. "Regardless of the competition, I stand by my compliment."

Odessa smiled. "And I accept it." Ebony moved to the front of the stall, nosing her and taking in big draughts of air, as if she hoped to get to know the baby. "Hey there, girl," Odessa said. "Miss me?"

"I think she's eager for a ride. But there will be no riding for some time, you understand me? The snow's too deep, and there's likely ice in many spots."

"Yes. But can the boys get her out to the corral, give her some room to run around?"

"I'll see to it myself."

❁

Odessa wrapped her arms around his body from behind, and Bryce closed his eyes, relishing the comfort of her slender form. "Are you all right, Bryce?"

He heard the deeper question, what she really wanted to know. She knew his attachment to the herd, the way he nicknamed every horse, even those destined for the train. All his life, he loved spending time with horses, nearly as much as he loved the sea. "I'm as well as I can be. It'll be good to have the bodies gone. I don't want any mountain lions venturing over and then deciding to seek fresh flesh."

He felt her shiver behind him, and he regretted his words. She leaned her forehead against his back. "I love you, Bryce."

"I love you, too." He swallowed hard, wondering if now was a good time to voice his concerns or if he should keep them to himself. Somehow, *somehow*, there had to be a way … "We'll make it through," he said, over his shoulder. "You know that, right?"

"I do. Do you? Or are you merely saying the words a worried wife would want to hear?"

He turned to face her, and caressed her lovely sculpted cheek with his free hand. "I believe it. The Circle M hasn't endured loss like this since the early days, when we'd lose half the herd to rustlers. But if my uncle could make it then, we can make it now." He leaned forward and kissed her, tenderly, and then pulled her close. They stood there for a time, the three of them, a solace to one another in their silence. Even the baby was quiet, staring up at Bryce. But Bryce's mind was filled with memories—of letters of their losses to his father from an uncle. Bryce's father, so far away, blamed him for mismanagement, lack of judgment.... He could still hear the recriminations in his mind, how the man would carry on for hours, how his mother would try to assuage his fury.

Bryce looked up at the stable rooftop. He had failed the Circle M, endangered all they had built. He'd chosen water rights over building snow shelters. At the time it made complete sense. But now ...? He shook his head.

Odessa glanced up at him, eyes squinting with curiosity. "What is it?"

He forced a smile and shook his head again. "Oh, just trying to see my way clear. Figure out our best course now that we're at this new juncture."

"You'll find it," she said with a squeeze, then released him and took the baby from his arms. "You always do."

"Thank you, Odessa. For trusting me."

She looked more deeply into his eyes, and Bryce wondered at the brilliant blue-green of hers, so like the sea ... so like the waters he would soon enter again. "Bryce? Is there something else?"

"No, sweetheart. You be on your way and I'll be on mine."

# Chapter ❁ 4

25 March 1887

"How're those hands?"

Nic looked over to William, who was again sharing a bit of conversation as they ate their breakfast. He swallowed his mouthful of gruel and held up one bandaged hand to show his new friend. "Coming along. I keep breaking open the wounds every time I take up a rope, though."

"You dipping them in seawater thrice a day?"

"'Bout kills me every time."

"Stings like the devil, but nothing will heal them faster. Trust me."

Nic nodded and dug back into his bowl of gruel. At least he was now spared the splicing duty. He had been moved into the ranks of standard crewman. He admitted to himself that he liked climbing to the lanyards, high above the decks, the water racing beneath them, and hauling in sail, lashing them down. The other sailors were easing their jibes and taunts, grudgingly accepting him. They called him "Brawler," rarely using his name, as they had dubbed William "Scholar," making fun of his uppity language. Nic shrugged off their teasing and dug in beside them, doing more than their own shares, making it nigh unto impossible for them to complain about him.

They were worthy workers, even if few educated men ever wandered the decks of a brig other than captains and first mates looking to gain their own commission or ship. The *Mirabella* was a private vessel, a merchant mariner out of Rio. She carried in her belly a wealth of spices and wood and was bound for Mexico, or if the Mexicans couldn't meet the captain's price, California.

Nic's eyes moved aft, to the captain, who paused to converse with the first mate. Yes, he could cope with life aboard ship. But it would never make it right, what the captain did …

"Dominic?" William said, and by his expression, obviously for the second or third time.

Nic jerked his eyes from the captain to his new friend. "When will we port to reprovision?"

"Two, maybe three days. Desterro. Ever been there before?"

"Never this far south of the equator."

"She's a decent city. And has her share of dark-skinned beautiful women."

Nic met his meaningful gaze. "Think the mate will allow me ashore?"

"Not likely."

"No," he said, choking back his agitation. "Thought not. I'll be waiting on your stories."

"Next time you'll go with me." William gave him an encouraging pat on the shoulder and then went to drop his wooden bowl and spoon in the wash bucket. Then he disappeared below decks to catch his measure of rest. The bell clanged, and others hurriedly shoved gruel or salt pork into their mouths, before reporting to their stations. In minutes, all stood where they ought, and the captain strolled out among them. He nodded once, as if in grave approval, and then continued toward the helm, where the first mate was at the wheel.

Never once did he glance Nic's way. Nic's desire to talk with him, to try and convince him to change his mind, remained strong, but as each day passed, Nic accepted this might be a way to reach his own desired next step. It didn't make it right, only somewhat acceptable. He had gone through the monies he had inherited from his father and the sale of his publishing house, the last remnants now behind him in Rio. But even with all he had seen and experienced, his heart still hungered for more, for something else, something ahead of him.

So the captain could keep to himself. It mattered not to Nic. *Let him think it was his choice. His choice can become mine.*

London

"Havender declined our offer," Jesse said bleakly, as he paid Moira's bill at the teahouse and escorted her out. "He was our last hope."

Moira lifted her eyes to meet his in surprise. Impossible. Not after all their discussions, the excitement, the hope. He had said it was as good as done!

"I do not have sufficient funds to remain here in London," he went on. "It is as I suspected. This region is tapped out, hungering for new, unknown talent. You know the Brits—always desiring the next thing. You and I … well, we've been here before. We're known talent."

"Is not experience worth something?"

He tugged her forward, so they could walk, arm in arm, down the street. "Sometimes. But apparently not now."

Moira paused to fish a coin from her bag for a beggar on the street and dropped it in the blind man's tin cup. Jesse hurried her along and pulled her close to his side. "Leave such fellows to the soup kitchens—you'll be needing to hold on to what you have to get you situated."

"There's always enough," she sniffed, "to help someone a bit worse off than oneself." Her mother had always said that, always stopped to help those in need.

"Tell me that again when your last franc is gone."

They continued their walk in silence. Moira was too weary to argue with him and couldn't help but think of Antoine, how sad he and his daughter looked the day she told them that their employment had ended. She sent them off with the finest of recommendations, but she doubted Antoine would ever work again. No one else would hire such an old man, but something about him had pulled at her heart, ever since he first arrived at her door, hat in hand, asking for work. Would Antoinette see to the old man's needs? Moira knew they had no family but each other.

"So we find ourselves in similar financial predicaments. I must return to Paris to secure a role, even without your aid. Perhaps you should return to the States, Moira. Your reputation will secure you a role anywhere you wish—from New York to San Francisco. You can simply pick where you wish to live and settle in."

They walked for some time in silence, Moira pondering her options. It seemed she had little choice. She needed to return to America. The idea of America, home, so appealed, that her hand went to her heart. It surprised her, how she longed for it. Even though she had no desire to return to Philadelphia, there was something about America that was *home*, something that called to her.

"Moira?" Jesse bent to look her in the eye, concern on his face.

"No. I'm all right," she assured him. "I shall book passage to New York."

"And once there?"

"Once there, I had better land work immediately, or I shall be on the streets."

"It's a gamble, Moira." His handsome brow furrowed in concern. "Why not go to your sister?"

She giggled, a giggle that grew into a laugh so deep and hysterical that she drew disapproving glances from passersby. But she didn't care. The idea that she could go to Odessa, live on a ranch! She had to stop and lean a little forward, so hard did she laugh.

"Moira, really." Glancing about, Jesse urged her to stop. "Are you quite all right?"

"Quite," she returned, straightening and hiding her wide smile behind a gloved hand. "It's only the idea of me … Jesse, truly. You think I would fit in on a ranch at this point in my life?"

He smiled back at her. "Better a ranch than the streets." He reached out a sudden, tender hand, barely touching her jawbone with soft fingers. "I fear for you, Moira. I'm sorry I can't see you to safety."

"You've helped me to take a step forward, Jesse, as you did in Colorado. I only regret that we won't get the opportunity to sing together again."

He gave her a sad smile and stood there for several seconds in silent regard. There was much that drew her to him, and obviously, him to her. And yet the timing seemed off, impossible. The barrier insurmountable. "The hotel proprietor plays the piano," he said. "Let us sing a song or two together this night, before we part."

"That would be well with me," she returned, taking his arm. "But let's stop at the rail station to find out about tomorrow's outgoing trains to Dover and what ships are sailing for America, shall we?"

"Indeed." He tucked her hand into the crook of his elbow, patting her fingers. "Moira St. Clair, you are possibly the bravest woman I have ever run across. I am only sorry we do not have more time together."

She smiled back at him but wondered at the darts of fear that entered her heart. Jesse McCourt believed her brave. Inside she was little more than a coward. But she knew her role here, the lines to say, the actions to take. And she would proceed to the next step and the next, pretending all the while if necessary, until somehow, some way, she regained her status, and her wealth.

❁

*27 March 1887*

*Spring is suddenly upon us, the sun warm enough on our skin that we shed our coats and sweaters after morning's chill gives up her task. The snow is rapidly melting, and yesterday, some of our men made it across the field—and returned with twenty-three horses who gladly accepted*

> *copious amounts of hay. The other missing mares and one stallion are gone, either still beneath the snows, or among the forests of the mountains upon escaping through a downed fence. We hope, but not too much. I think we fear further loss; it is almost preferable to believe them dead and move on.*

"Odessa? Odessa!" Bryce called from downstairs.

She looked up from her paper, frowned, and hurriedly set aside her pen. She didn't like the note of alarm in her husband's voice. Odessa rushed to the stairs, pausing when she saw Bryce close the door. Ralph and Tabito were in the front entry area, an unconscious man between them. "Who is this?"

"I don't know," Bryce said grimly. "He came in, driving twenty starved horses, barely keeping his seat in the saddle. Must've been caught in the storm."

"Please, take him to the den. I'll be right there with blankets." Odessa hurried back upstairs and grabbed two thick woolen blankets, then back to the men, who stood in her kitchen with the stranger between them. "Here, lay him atop this until we get him cleaned up," Odessa said, laying a blanket down, in front of the stove. She wrinkled her nose. The man wreaked of sour clothes. He was so filthy, she could barely see the true shade of his skin.

Bryce knelt down on his other side. Tabito reached out to touch his forehead and pulled his hand away quickly. "He burns."

Odessa met her husband's fearful glance and then rose to put some water on the stove. "I'll need you men to clean him up. Bryce, can you fetch a fresh shirt and pair of pants?"

The baby must have sensed the commotion downstairs, because he awakened early from his nap, quickly moving from disgruntled cries to a full-blown wail. "I'll get him," Bryce called from upstairs.

Odessa pumped water into a bucket and then poured it into a massive iron cauldron on the stove. Already hot from its constant perch atop the wood-burning oven, the first of the water sizzled and steamed until she poured the rest in. She took a rag and opened the oven to peer at the fire, and decided to add another log. It was already good and hot; it would only take about half an hour to heat the water all the way through.

Tabito, the ranch foreman, came through the back kitchen door, the washtub on his back. Bryce must've asked him to fetch it. He placed it in the corner and stretched out a privacy screen. "The man might not survive a bath," he grunted.

"He might not survive unless we clean him up," she retorted. She made Bryce force all the ranch hands to bathe at least once a week, preferably twice—they had their own tub down in the bunkhouse—and threatened to not feed them unless they adhered to the rules. "Here," she said, handing Tabito a pitcher and a small cup. "Try and get a little water down his throat, will you?"

"Yes, ma'am," he said, walking away.

She could hear someone running through the slush outside, the splashes beneath their boots, and then there was a quick rapping at her door. Odessa moved to answer it, but Dietrich was already opening it, his face awash with concern.

"Dietrich, I—"

"Sorry, ma'am. Don't mean to go bursting in on ya, but I need to see Bryce or Tabito, right away."

"Certainly," she said. "Come in." She followed the man, choosing not to say anything about the muddy prints he left on her floor. Tabito and Bryce looked up at him.

"Boss, we've got troubles, down at the stables." He rotated his hat between nervous hands, in a circle.

Bryce rose slowly. "What is it?"

"Doc thinks it's the strangles. One of the yearlings that came in with this herd is down. You can see two others are sick. Doc thinks all three will die."

Bryce handed Samuel to Odessa and edged past him. "They're still in the separate corral, right? Away from our horses?" He hurried down the back porch steps, two at a time. Dietrich reluctantly followed behind. Odessa stood in the doorway, bouncing Samuel. Her heart pounded. Bryce's tone told her something was bad, really bad.

Bryce whirled in the snow. "Dietrich, tell me they're in a separate corral."

"Yes, but—"

"But what?"

"They were so hungry, they've reached through the fence and eaten out of our horses' troughs, drunk some of their water."

"And our horses?"

Dietrich was quiet, standing there at the back door as if leaving meant punishment.

"Dietrich?"

"I'm afraid they've shared those troughs, Boss. A few of them anyway," he said in defeat.

Bryce bared his teeth, groaning as if shoving down an oath.

“Come on!” he said, breaking into a run. “We need to get those horses away from the others!”

Odessa turned to Tabito, who placed his wide-brimmed hat atop his head. “Been some time since this ranch has seen a case of strangles.”

“What does it mean? What will they do?” Odessa said.

“Shoot the ill, separate the exposed.”

Odessa’s eyes widened, understanding now. “How contagious is it?”

“Very.” With that, he exited and gently shut the door behind him. Odessa stood there for a minute, thinking of what to do. She wanted to go to the stables, make sure Bryce did not do anything rash, but there was a man in her front parlor who needed tending. The water was boiling atop the stove, but now there were no men left to bathe the stranger.

“We’ll do what we can for him,” she whispered to Samuel. She started to carry him into the front parlor and then paused in the doorway, thinking of the horses and the contagion they carried. What if this man had a fever that Samuel could catch? She returned to the small sitting room beside the kitchen, spread out a blanket and handed the child his favorite tin cup. Then she hurried back to gather rags and water and lye soap to clean the stranger who had brought a plague upon her home.

❧

Apparently the old man wanted to tell his tale to more than Reid, making Reid doubt the authenticity of it. But the monotony of life in prison made him lean a little closer to hear as the man shared the story with anyone in reach of his stage whisper. Reid glanced down the hall between their cells and made eye contact with the guard. The young man looked away, probably as bored as they were, eager to hear any tale anyone wished to tell, even if it was against the rules at this hour.

"My granddaddy, he was runnin' for his life, the Ute tracking him all the way."

"I'd heard tell it was the Apache and Cheyenne a man had to look out for in those days," protested a man in the cell beside him. "Not the Ute. They were peaceful folk."

"They were, unless a man refused to take a chief's daughter as his bride, like my granddaddy did."

The men let out a collective laugh and roar of approval and then settled, waiting for the rest of the man's story.

"Fortunately for my granddaddy, he knew his way about the Sangres and beyond. He moved high and fast, even through the night. He was stumbling forward, aware that a few strong braves still trailed him, but it was the third day, late, you see. And he was plumb wore out. He tripped, and fell down a ravine, rolling and rolling until he came to rest inside the mouth of a cave."

"Did they find 'im then? In that cave?" asked a man.

"No, he holed up in that cave, his gun across his arms, waitin' on the braves to arrive. But after three days, he knew they'd lost his trail, and thirst drove him out." He looked around, as if to see if he still had their attention. "He stood up to go, wobbling on his feet. And that was when he saw it."

"Saw what?" asked a young man, biting at the bait.

"A genu-wine conquistador breastplate. Like what they wore for armor and such? Almost missed it, it was so covered by three hundred years of dust. He blew it off—" the old man pretended to pick up an object and slowly blew on it, and Reid sighed wearily—"and a great cloud of dust set him to coughing. He collapsed and thought he'd take his death right then and there, but in time, he regained himself."

"And?" said yet another man.

"When he stood again, he saw something he hadn't noticed before. Peeking out, behind a pile of rocks, was a stack of gold bars."

The men erupted into a mixed cacophony of disbelief and wonder. Roused, the deputy at the end of the hall came toward them, striking the end of his gun on each bar. Every prisoner scuttled back to his cot, unwilling to pay the price of a lost meal for the story. But when the deputy reached the old man's cell, he paused. "Did he haul the gold out?" he whispered. "Your granddaddy? Did he become rich?"

"Nah," said the old man, leaning back on one arm. "He lost it. Buried them bars again behind the rocks, thought he had the cave marked, and came back months later with men and burros to help get it out—gold bars weigh a bloomin' ton—but he could never find the right canyon again, let alone the right cave."

The men all groaned and turned on their cots, disappointed by the sorry end to the old man's story.

But it took everything in Reid not to sit up straight.

Could it be? Could it be that the treasure old Sam O'Toole had found—and left for the McAllans—was not a fantastic hidden silver mine, but rather an ancient Spanish treasure of gold? One bar, *one bar*, would've been enough to make the man rich. And if this man's story were true, there had been a stack of them.

The McAllans hadn't found them yet. Had they done so, they would not have kept it a secret. It would've made international headlines. So it was still there. *If* it was there, Reid reminded himself sternly.

And possibly, just possibly, he could beat the McAllans to it.

# Chapter 5

Bryce forced himself not to wince every time the men shouldered a gun and put down another of the stranger's horses. He looked over the quarantined Circle M horses in the corral anxiously, studying the tilt of their ears, the way they breathed, any oddities along their mandibles. He entered the corral three times a day to lift their lips, peer into their nostrils, run his hands down the long bones of their jaws, searching for the telltale nodules that swelled with disease, fat bumps that indicated impending doom.

Despondent, he turned and walked out of the series of corrals and up the hill, away from the stables and the house. He could not face Odessa this way. The horses showed no signs of the strangles—yet. But he knew how contagious the dreaded disease was. It would be a miracle if any of them were spared. And he sensed no miracle on the wind. Bryce trudged through mud that coated his boots, ignoring the cold as it seeped in toward his toes. He kept moving until he reached the fence that bordered the first fields, the field where so many had died during that hateful storm.

Bryce grabbed hold of the post and sliced his hand on a hidden nail. He groaned and sucked on the blood that soon dripped down into his palm, but then he took hold of the post again and rocked it back and forth in fury, as if he intended to rip it from the ground.

"The horses do enough of that without you helping them," said a voice behind him.

Bryce groaned and shook his head, not turning. "Go away, Tabito," he said. "I need to be alone."

"You will be alone for a long time to come. Have you told the missus yet? What you are considering?"

"Not yet."

"It isn't wise, keeping secrets from your wife."

"She won't understand," Bryce said, looking up the slope of the field, then higher up, into the mountains that bordered the ranch.

"No, she won't," Tabito said quietly, moving to stand beside Bryce. "Send some of your men instead, to Spain. You should not go, Bryce. You should not risk it."

"It is I who should go," Bryce gritted out. "I've made some foolish decisions, Tabito. I didn't build the snowbreaks. I put too much money into getting us more water. Now … we're cash strapped. Banks won't be lending, not after all that everyone has lost through this storm. They'll be skittish, and it won't change before fall's harvest."

"What will you do?"

"I don't know. If I don't have more horses, I can't make my payments to the bank. If I can't make my payments, they'll come collecting parcels of land. I can't let that happen, Tabito."

"You can't or you won't?"

Bryce stared at him. Tabito looked back to the mountains and was silent for a time. "Think like the river, Bryce. Seek wisdom, the right route, rather than an end to the journey."

Bryce let out a breath of exasperation. "Don't all journeys come to an end?"

"Sometimes. Most times, the river only becomes the sea."

Forgetting the cut, Bryce ran his hand through his hair in agitation, winced and then stared at the slice on his palm. He leaned forward on the post and watched the blood drip down and then onto the fresh, white snow below. Tabito watched it too, saying nothing more.

"This ranch has demanded sacrifice after sacrifice," Bryce said slowly. "I will not be the man who loses it. Not after everything my family has put into it."

"Your family would not wish to sacrifice you for it."

Bryce looked at him and then smiled, without humor. "Maybe. Maybe not." He shook his head and began making his way down the hill, toward the house.

"Bryce," Tabito called.

He turned and looked up at his foreman, his old friend.

"Sometimes the river disappears on one side of the mountain and appears on the other. Sometimes the river goes deep."

❧

*29 March 1887*

*My patient cries upon hearing each shot, each one signifying a partial death to a dream. Harold Rollins is a Texan. He was driving his herd north to his new spread near Fort Collins. A young wife and three children anxiously await his return. He swears he had no idea that the herd carried the strangles, and by the time he noted the yearling was ailing, he was terribly ill with pneumonia himself. God saw fit to save him by bringing him here; one more night of exposure would have likely killed him. But will his arrival be a death knell for us?*

Odessa heard several horses pull up outside the front door, and she scurried downstairs to open it. "Sheriff Olsbo," she greeted warmly.

"Mrs. McAllan," he said with a smile, then dismounted and tied his horse to the front post. Two other men beside him did the same. "Bryce around?"

"I expect him momentarily for noon dinner. Care to join us?"

"I don't know about you boys," said the burly sheriff, looking at his men, "but I could use a bite or two. Sure you have enough, ma'am?"

"Enough for you three. Please, come in."

"These here are my deputies, Lance Rudell and Ernest Newland," the sheriff said, pausing at her door. "Deputies, this is Mrs. McAllan."

One younger deputy mumbled a shy greeting, and the other one smiled. "We've met before …" she said, suddenly remembering the tall, lean man.

"Yes'm," he said, clearly reliving that day at Sam's cabin in memory along with her. "You're looking well. Much better than last I saw you."

"Thank you. Life has been good for me, here on the ranch." She took their coats, remembering that fateful day in full, that day when she thought they were soon to die at the hands of Reid Bannock and Doctor Morton. Sheriff Olsbo and his men had narrowly saved them.

"What do you hear about Mr. Bannock?" she asked, trying not to tense up. Harold was resting in the other room, where it was warmer, and Samuel was napping. She gestured toward the chairs in the formal parlor and the men took their seats.

"Got off way too easy, if you ask me," said Lance. "Fancy lawyer from Denver did none of us any good, helping him off that murder charge."

"He'll still be in prison for a few more years," Odessa said, taking a seat too.

The men were silent. The sheriff coughed as the deputies shifted in their seats uncomfortably.

"Sheriff?" she asked, glancing from one face to the next.

Sheriff Olsbo tucked his head to the side and fiddled with his hat in his lap. "I, um … Odessa, you see …" He paused, seeming as if he was making an effort to choose his words. "The prison's getting a bit crowded. They're building another one, but they can't keep up with the pace. All the newcomers Colorado has seen … it was bound to push the prison population too."

"Wh-what are you saying?"

"Now, Mrs. McAllan," he said, leaning forward and reaching out a bouncing hand as if to settle her. "I don't want you to fret at all about Reid Bannock. I saw to it when he was released that it was a part of the orders: If the man dares to set foot in my county, I'll string him up myself."

"When he was *released?"* Odessa repeated, considering his words for a moment. *Reid Bannock. Free.* "It's a big county, Sheriff." *And Reid thought they knew the way in to Sam's old mine—*

"Yes, but there's little that goes on in these parts that I don't know about. Take, for instance, your visitor."

"Mr. Rollins?" Odessa asked distractedly. Who cared that Harold was here? Reid Bannock might soon be upon them! She lifted a hand to her forehead, suddenly feeling woozy.

He nodded. "That's the rancher driving horses north?"

"Yes."

"There are some rumors, Mrs. McAllan. Rumors of strangles in the herd."

She let out a humorless laugh. "Wish you had heard those rumors several days ago, Sheriff, and come to tell us *before* he arrived."

"I should've known better," Bryce said, from over her shoulder. "You'd think I was green in the saddle."

Sheriff Olsbo looked up in surprise, and all three men rose to greet her husband. He had entered the house quietly, as was his way. Now she heard the ranch hands, stomping off mud on the back porch, removing their boots before coming inside to eat. And she had nothing quite ready to serve … "Pardon me, I'm late in getting the food out," she mumbled toward her guests, and then turned to her husband. "Sorry, love," she said lowly, "I was embroiled in this conversation."

"No worries," he said, holding her hand and gazing meaningfully into her eyes. He knew. Knew about Reid. From the expression on his face he had for some time.

Odessa frowned in confusion.

"I'll be back to help you in a minute, Odessa. All right?"

She pulled her hand from his and hurried to the kitchen, sudden, hot tears in her eyes. How could he know about Reid's release? And not tell her? Her! It was too much, too much after all that had happened in the last two weeks. But the low rumbling of the hands' conversation in her kitchen pulled her attention away. She had to maintain some decorum. Get this meal served then excuse herself to go upstairs. Then she could cry. She swallowed hard against the lump in her throat.

The men were taking turns at the washbasin, rinsing their hands. She pulled three loaves of bread from the cupboard and placed them at intervals down the table beside bowls of rich, creamy butter. From the oven she pulled a fat rolled roast, still sizzling in its juices. Her hands shook, but she moved on to the mashed potatoes, transferring them into several serving bowls. There were no vegetables to be had, but she opened three precious jars of preserved apples and poured them into three more bowls.

"Dess?" Bryce said, suddenly at her side. His voice was tense.

"Can you slice the meat?" she asked, her voice trembling. She dared to look at him, and he frowned at the tears in her eyes.

"Yes," he said. "Are you—"

"I need to go and rest," she said, hurrying out of the kitchen as tears slipped down her cheeks. She just made it up the stairs and into their room, burying her face into a pillow before the sobs broke free from her throat.

❀

"I thought it best to wait," Bryce said, slowly shutting the door behind him.

She turned around. "Until when?" Odessa asked, dipping her pen and placing it to her paper. She'd been madly writing, consumed by the emotions roiling within her. "Until Bannock showed up here again? Until he came and threatened Samuel and you and me and the men again? He nearly killed us, Bryce! Intended to kill us, all because he thought we knew the way into Sam's mine. He'll come again, Bryce. He'll come after us again."

"We've been through this, Dess," he said, walking across the floor to stand beside her. She saw then that the baby was in his arms. She hadn't heard him wake. "It would be suicide to come here. I've told every man on this ranch to shoot the man on sight if he dares to come near. And that mine is a fiction! Sam made it up. We can't give him what we don't have. Bannock'll move on to greener pastures."

"It wasn't a fiction. Samuel O'Toole showed up in town with fine ore. Had money to spend. Most miners live hand to mouth. Sam did not."

Bryce sighed and sat down on the edge of the bed. "Maybe he found a trace vein, as his neighbors did. Maybe his mother left him a small fortune. I've told you before, Sam liked a bit of mystery. But the fact remains—Sam left us nothing but land."

Odessa turned back to her desk and tapped the end of her pen on the wood. "But Reid does not know that."

"Reid Bannock has no job. He's been stripped of everything but time. He'll want to get on with it—on with life."

"You forget his ways. He'll have money, when and if he needs it. And you don't think he'll consider it worth his time to come here to torment us? Retribution for sending him to prison?"

"Bannock's mean, but he's not a fool. There's one of him and twelve of us. Trust me, he doesn't have the resources to hire help like he did the first time he came. He's done, Dess. It's over." He lay back wearily, bringing the baby to his chest.

Odessa closed her eyes and set aside her pen, then cradled her forehead, elbows to desk. She sighed heavily. "It was just too much, finding out about that threat, on top of all we've encountered over the last weeks," she said.

"I know it. I'm sorry I didn't tell you. I didn't want you to fret."

She longed for him to rise, to come to her, but he stayed where he was, separate. "You put down so many of Harold's horses," she said, barely stifling her anger, wanting him to relive the pain of it again, wanting him to take some of the pain from her shoulders.

"I had no choice. All those horses were exposed and showing the signs. Swollen mandibles. Coughing."

"Why not wait, to see if they might recover?"

"Because I couldn't!" His voice rose, impatient. "Nine times out of ten, they die anyway. I couldn't risk it, Dess!" He got up and handed her the baby. "Don't you see? Strangles has a way of spreading. It puts ranchers out of business—small and large. We can't … we've already lost almost a hundred …" He shook his head as if exasperated and turned away.

"Wait. Where are you going?"

"Out. I told the men to tend to their own supper dishes, that you were feeling poorly."

"Out where?" she called to his retreating back, as he hurried down the stairs.

"Out!" he yelled. After a moment, she heard the front door open and then slam shut.

And never had Odessa McAllan felt more lonely.

❁

Moira turned to resume her walk around the leeward side of the ship, out of the sea's spray. A small umbrella, held at an angle against the wind and light rain, served as her remaining defense against the elements. Despite her best efforts she could still feel her hair pulling out from the tight bun, the tendrils curling in the moist air. But for the first time in a week, she felt as if she could take a deep breath. She knew it wasn't fitting, a woman alone out on deck, but she had pointedly refused several gentlemen who had offered to accompany her. She only wished to be alone. And not indoors another moment.

She passed the bank of cabins, all with tiny windows in a neat line, then turned to lean against the rail, ignoring the shiver that ran down her back from the cold and damp. She was determined to stay out here as long as possible before returning to her cabin to snuggle beneath the blankets for a nap.

She closed her eyes and listened to the whine and thump of the steam engines, the thump of each blade as it dug into the waves, propelling them forward to America, sweet America, still weeks away. It was an act of endurance, she decided, travel overseas. Moira took a deep breath, smelling the brine of the wash beneath them and a hint of … pipe smoke. She turned and looked over her shoulder.

"You might have announced your presence, Mr. Adams," she said with a haughty sniff. The enigmatic man she'd been introduced to that morning was sitting under the small roof of the cabins, atop a crate.

"I might've," he allowed. His eyes steadily met hers. "But you seemed as intent as I for a moment alone. Figured you'd move on soon enough."

She lifted her chin and resumed her moody stare out to sea. He wouldn't chase her away, despite his rude behavior. She had as much right to be here as he.

"Beg your pardon, Miss St. Clair," he said, suddenly beside her at the rail. He looked down at her out of sad, dark brown eyes and she noticed for the first time how frightfully handsome he was. Not with the dapper, smooth looks of Gavin Knapp—a businessman who had caught her eye and flirted with her mercilessly—but with the rugged strength of a man used to hard work. There was something of him that reminded her of Bryce, her brother-in-law, but he was taller, broader. Wide at the shoulder, narrow at the waist. His black hair had a wide curl to it, so it framed his handsome face with waves. Strong chin, nice nose. But it was his eyes … they had an intensity to them she hadn't encountered before. Dark pools that seemed to capture and hold a woman.

"Miss St. Clair?"

Moira started and focused more clearly on his eyes, embarrassed to be caught in reverie. Had he said something else? She felt the slow burn of embarrassment crawl up her neck. He pulled his head to the right, nodding toward the crate. "Please. Take your ease there. You'll be shielded from the wind."

"Oh no, I couldn't," she protested. "You were first to stake your claim," she said, shooting him a flirtatious smile. "And I'm no claim jumper."

He didn't smile back. "Please," he said, gesturing toward the crate with his head.

"Well, then, if you insist," she said. She moved forward to the crate, then once there, hesitated. "It's most kind."

"Here," he said softly, reaching out to take hold of her small waist and easily lifting her to a seated position atop it. He was right; here the wind was practically nonexistent. She shifted to the right a few inches and after a second's hesitation gestured to the spot beside her in weak invitation.

He stared at her, his big brown eyes searching hers. "You do me an honor with your invitation, Miss, but I'm about to head in." Again, he gestured with a wave of his head behind him. He hesitated. "You'll be all right, on your own?"

"Well of course, Mr. Adams," she sniffed, feeling the burn of irritation now. "I am no young twit." No man had ever turned down an offer from her! Who was he to do such a thing?

"Good," he said softly, and moved away, out of sight within a few long, easy strides.

Moira only sat there for a few minutes longer, her mind embroiled in unraveling the mysterious Mr. Adams. Who was he? He wore no wedding ring; perhaps he had a girl waiting for him back in the States. That was it. That explained him turning away from her; he was simply honorable. She lifted a hand to her forehead and chastised herself for her idle imaginings. What did she care, really? The last thing she needed at this moment was another man in her life. She needed to concentrate on her career, her future. Men had brought her nothing but heartache and trouble.

But her eyes lingered on the empty area that Mr. Adams had so recently occupied. Something told her that his reasoning wasn't as simple was a girl at home. And why did she keep thinking about his big sad eyes? She much preferred to think of Gavin Knapp and his bright, blue eyes, glinting with mischief. She smiled. Yes, that man was far more exciting …

❀

Moira arrived at the captain's table that night dressed in one of her finest Parisian gowns with a tiny feathered cap to match and a net that descended from it to capture her mass of blonde curls. She had always created a stir in Paris when she wore the dress; the reaction from the men around the table who rose in respect told her a man was a man was a man in any locale, be they on the street or at sea. The lone other woman at the table, the dowager Mrs. Jones, perused her with cool eyes and then looked to the captain, a married man of about forty with a trim brown beard, who flashed her a polite smile and then waited for someone to seat her.

Gavin Knapp, as was quickly becoming his habit, had saved the last chair for Moira, and he graciously helped her into her seat. He was as smooth as Jesse, like a dancer in his movements, and she found comfort in his attention. It felt like a bit of home, normalcy, after the upheaval she'd experienced of late. The seas were mild tonight, but still the water and wine in the goblets before them rocked back and forth—or rather the goblets rocked and the liquid within remained level. She reached for her wine as the captain raised his own for a cheers, and that was when she noticed Mr. Adams directly across from her.

Mr. Adams's expression was more kind than it had been that afternoon, his lips even tilting a tad in a smile as he raised his glass an inch higher in her direction. But his gaze did not linger upon her as the others' did. He looked down the table to the captain, as if eager to look anywhere but at her, and then he leaned toward Mrs. Jones to hear a word from her that Moira couldn't make out. His movements said, *I'm not interested; leave me alone.* No doubt, he'd prefer a transatlantic voyage on a sailboat by himself, rather than in the company of all of them.

Well, Moira thought, a ship was no place to hole up, withdrawing from others. One could take their ease for a time, on their own, but a voyage was all about getting to know one's shipmates. Servants arrived, placing heavy plates loaded with lovely roasted chicken, hearty mashed potatoes, and cinnamon apples before each person at the table. But Moira barely glanced at the food; her eyes were upon the man across from her.

She cleared her throat and smiled. "Mr. Adams," she said pertly. He looked at her and frowned slightly, but she ignored it. "I do believe we've heard from everyone at this table about what occupies them day to day except for you."

He took a sip from his goblet and stared at her. "What is it you wish to know, Miss St. Clair?"

"Please, everyone calls me Moira. We're all on a first name basis after a week at sea, aren't we, Captain?"

"Yes, yes—" the man grinned—"by all means. We leave only the most necessary of social contrivances dockside, I believe."

The others smiled around the table, each eating, but their eyes drifted between Moira and Mr. Adams. "What is your given name, Mr. Adams?"

"Mr. Adams is good enough for me," he said, a hint of an impish grin soon hidden behind a napkin.

Moira ignored the small slight. "Oh dear, Mr. Adams, I don't suppose you are ashamed of your name? Is it something frightful, such as Horace? Or Archibald?"

"Thankfully, no," he said, retreating, now clearly wishing the attention off of him and on to other matters. "It is Daniel. So please, Miss—Moira," he said her name slowly, and Moira found herself thinking only of the low, mellow timber of his voice. A baritone, she imagined. "What is it you wish to know?"

Moira ignored Gavin's irritated shift beside her. He clearly didn't like her attention on anyone but him. But she stared across the table. No man ignored her. Why was this one so different? "Your occupation, please. Let us begin with that." She looked down the table. "Among the gentlemen here are three seamen, three bankers..." she smiled at Gavin as she continued, "a commodities broker, a politician, and a real estate tycoon." She looked back across to Daniel. "Please tell me you have a career of interest."

Daniel swallowed and tried to smile. It was a lopsided, awkward thing to behold, but oddly endearing. "I am simply a man sent to procure a shipment for my employer from London and see it safely to his new hotel in Leadville, Colorado."

Moira sat up a bit taller, in spite of herself. "Are you a hotelier, then? Or a barkeep?"

"Both, at times. For now, I suppose I am an importer if I expect to sit at this table for much longer," he said, looking around to the others.

The others smiled and raised their glasses in salute. "Are you at liberty to discuss what it is you are importing?" the captain asked. "Rarely have I seen crates that large loaded upon my ship."

"It is a large, quite beautiful bar of pure mahogany," Daniel returned. "My employer paid a handsome price for it and had it built exactly to his specifications. The bar itself runs twenty feet in length, and there is fine carving beneath the top. The mirror that sits behind it runs the same length, and the woodcarvers outdid themselves in showcasing it with a fine border." He shook his head in wonder. "I work for a clever man; many will enter the hotel solely to see such a beautiful piece in the wilds of Colorado."

The men asked him about Leadville, about the mines that had been exhausted years ago, but how people continued to arrive, intent on claiming their own bit of mountain paradise or digging for a bit of still-undiscovered silver. Daniel answered every one of them, but his replies were short and to the point, as if he was hiding something, longing to return to the shadows.

"So how long have you been a hotelier-barkeep-importer?" Moira casually asked.

"Quite some time," he said, his tone clipped, brooking no further query.

*Why the secrecy?* Moira wondered.

"Do you have a family, back in Leadville, Daniel?" the captain asked, coming to his rescue.

Moira studied the man, and didn't miss the shadow that crossed his face. "No," he said simply.

"I've heard there are twenty men to every woman in those regions," Gavin said. He leaned forward and looked at Daniel, curiosity live in his bright blue eyes. He truly was amazingly handsome, elegant.

"Sounds right," Daniel allowed, jerking Moira's attention back across the table. "Saying goes that any woman who comes our way has ten marriage offers before she steps off a stagecoach. And singers … why they're as popular as a cold well on the hottest day of summer." He did not look at her, but folded his napkin and said quietly, "That reminds me … would you kindly grace us with a song after supper, Moira?"

All eyes were suddenly upon her again, and she saw the glint of pleasure in Daniel's eyes as his finally met hers. He'd found the way to shift the topic of conversation at last. So he was more clever than he appeared. She felt a smile on her lips. "I'd be honored," she said demurely.

Later after supper, they all assembled in the large parlor, where they spent most of their days. In the corner was a small upright piano, and happily, one of the bankers proved to be a decent accompanist. Moira sang a lovely tune, one of her favorites, but as she looked into the eyes of every person present, she noted with some dismay that the man with sad brown eyes was not present.

*No matter,* she thought, dismissing him. She focused on Gavin, with his keen blue eyes, who smiled constantly and engaged everyone he met with ease. This was the man she needed to think about. Not some other who clearly didn't care a whit for her—or even getting to know her.

❧

Nic stared up into the starlit sky, wondering what William was up to in port. As a more junior crewman, William had been given less time ashore than some of the others, but he shoved off in the last rowboat at sunset, giving Nic a flick of his finger to the brim of his hat in farewell. "I'll bring you back a spot of rum," he said lowly.

Did the captain intend him to stay aboard ship for the length of the entire voyage?

Nic'd go mad if that was the case. Even now, he found himself pacing like a caged cougar, back and forth atop the deck on watch—but more on his own hopeless watch than any serious care for the *Mirabella.* And why did the captain not head for port himself? Terence had shoved off with William, but the captain stayed. Did he so love the sea that he—

The captain opened the door of the lantern, lit a bunt, and then closed the small glass door. He placed the bunt in the bowl of his pipe, sucked on the stem, trying to get the tobacco to light.

"Cap'n," Nic said in surprise. Rarely was the man on deck when the first mate was not. But perhaps this was normal protocol in port.

The captain grunted and walked toward him. Nic stiffened as he leaned at the rail and puffed at his pipe for several minutes. The sweet smell of the tobacco wafted over them both. Nic inhaled, the smell casting him back to smoke-filled fighting rings, and further back, to his father and grandfather, who often used different tobaccos, particular favorites, to stuff their pipes. At last, the small man turned toward him in silent regard. "You hate me, don't you, Dominic?"

"Hate?" He swallowed a laugh. *Hate* had become a tender word compared to what he felt for the man. *Loathe? Abhor?*

"It matters not," the captain said, with a wave of his pipe. "Are you missing the ring? Please," he gestured to the rail beside him, "take your ease for a moment, watchman."

"Not until tonight," Nic said. He eased his stance but did not lean on the rail as the captain did. "Up to now, I've been too tired to think of fighting."

"And now?"

"Now, here, I feel the pull of it," he admitted. "The ring."

"And so if you were in port, now, you'd find a fight?"

"Or a willing woman," Nic said evenly.

The captain grinned. "Sounds like you're already a sailor to me."

"A sailor by force," he dared.

"Yes, well there is that. You lost me money, St. Clair. I intend to make it back in labor. Round the Horn with us and I'll begin paying you."

"And you think that is fair?" Nic sputtered. He could feel the heat rising up his neck, tension making his arm muscles taut. "To kidnap a man, force him to leave behind everything he owns? Should I work for everyone who made a poor bet on me? Perhaps there are some racehorses you can saddle and put to work in your stern too!"

"Fair enough," said the captain in casual regard. "Keep in mind I could keep you aboard for the duration and pay you nothing for six months. This ship is my own kingdom, and I am free to do as I please within it. Consider it largesse, St. Clair, on my part, this offer." He straightened, stared at Nic a moment, and then slowly turned to walk away.

Nic turned back to the rail, breathing rapidly through his nose, forcing himself not to run after the captain and tackle him to the ground, beat him.

"St. Clair?" called the captain.

He could do nothing more than raise his chin to mark the fact that he'd heard his captain call. To turn toward him would undoubtedly mean losing control.

"Life is not fair, St. Clair," said the captain lowly. "Life is life."

❁

Reid Bannock accepted his funds from the begrudging banker in Cañon City, who clearly knew who he was and why he'd served time. It mattered little to Reid. He smiled at the banker and placed his hat atop his head again as his eyes met the blessed, clear spring sun outside.

*Free. I'm a free man.*

He stood there on the street of the small town, considering his options. A wise man would head far from here, take a new name, reinvent himself. A wise man would bury the past like a dead neighbor and move on to stake a new claim.

He remained there a long time, feeling the weight of his decision shift within him, like fluid in a jug, from one side to the other. It was powerful, the desire to get even with the McAllans, Moira, Nic, as was the desire to begin anew, to be free of the past, to make better, wiser decisions in the future. He wasn't old; at forty-two, there was still time to take a wife, have a family. And the stakes were high. Sheriff Olsbo would be watching for him.

Reid stood there for many long minutes afterward, asking himself the same questions, over and over.

At last he moved. There was a time for wisdom, the time to withdraw, seek safety. And there was a time to gamble it all.

# Chapter 6

6 April 1887

Bryce picked up the telegram and then closed his eyes and took a long, heavy breath. He was coming; Robert was coming here, to the ranch, to survey the disaster. He hadn't enough to do, back at the shipyard—he had to meddle here too! Bryce shook his head slightly. Always the older brother …

"Bryce," Odessa said, from over by the sink where she was washing dishes. "What is it?" she asked tentatively. "You barely touched your breakfast. Are you feeling all right?"

"Fine, fine," he mumbled. He hated the tone in her voice, the distance between them, but could not seem to find the way to bridge it, not with what he had to do still before them.

She turned around and dried her hands on the towel. "Tell me. What does the telegram say?"

"It's Robert," he said.

"Your brother? He's well?" She sat down beside him, around the corner of the table.

He forced a small smile to his face as he dared to look at her. "Well enough to come for a visit."

Odessa smiled, her eyes widening. "That is wonderful news!" Her smiled quickly faded. "You are not … pleased he is coming?"

He rubbed his temples. "Dess, there is something I need to tell you. Something I've been considering."

"Then tell me. Out with it. No more silences, no more secrets, Bryce. There's been enough of that lately between us."

"My brother is coming, but I might be gone."

She lifted her chin a bit, as if bracing for what was to come. She was so strong, his wife. Maybe strong enough to endure this—

"I must go to Spain, Dess, and bring back a hundred head of horses—fifty to sell at a profit and fifty to strengthen the herd and breed for next year."

She stared at him with those lovely blue-green eyes for a long moment and blinked slowly. Above them, they could hear Samuel begin to stir from his morning nap, but she ignored it.

"We've lost too many, Dess." He reached out a hand to cover hers, but she pulled away. "The blizzard. The strangles. There is no way to recover. Our cash is all in the land. Your own inheritance is in the new land … I won't see it sold. Any of it." He shrugged. "And we can't make it through another winter. There's simply not enough." He rose and paced alongside the table. "Robert will review our books. He'll want to see how the family's investment is faring, and he'll see the errors I made. Buying that land last year instead of investing in snowbreaks." He ran a hand through his hair in agitation. "I need him to see that I'm rectifying the problem, not ignoring it."

"Sell the land," she said, looking up at him. "I don't care if it was my money or yours. It's ours, together. Sell some of it."

"No," he said, shaking his head. "It's unwise, Odessa. There isn't a man in this valley who could pay us half of what we paid for it a year ago. Everyone's lost too much this past winter. That's how things work."

She searched his face, desperation making her own look drawn and weary, and Bryce felt another pang of guilt. "There are years of plenty and years of famine," she said. "I am willing to accept that risk, as a rancher's wife. But I am not about to risk your life." She rose and walked to him. "Think about it," she said, putting a hand on his forearm. "It was your voyages to Spain that first brought you low with the consumption. We've been without disease for three years, Bryce. Breathing free." Samuel's full-blown wail brought her head up and around. "I have to go to him. But please, think about it."

"You think I haven't?" he said. "You think I've made this decision lightly?"

She turned on the stairs to face him again.

"Everything I do, I do for you and Samuel, Dess."

"Not this," she said, shaking her head and crossing her arms. She pointed at him. "This … this is something different. Pride? Fear? What is it? You can't face your older brother in the midst of a hard year?"

"Stop, Odessa," he warned.

Samuel coughed, he was crying so hard, but Odessa still stared at Bryce, now shaking in anger. Never had he seen her so furious, until just a couple of nights ago when she learned that he'd known Reid Bannock had been release and had not told her. "You would leave us here? To run the ranch—"

"Tabito can run the ranch."

"You would leave us here, when Reid Bannock might show up again? How is that caring for me and Samuel, Bryce?" She shook her head. "No, this is not about us. This is about you."

"Regardless, I must find a way to supplement the herd and help us through the year. You don't seem to understand that there is not enough to make it through."

"Can we borrow from the bank?"

He shook his head. "Not this year."

"Maybe … maybe your brother can lend us money."

He looked up at her and frowned. "You know how it is with us. I don't want him in my affairs any more than is absolutely necessary."

She looked to the window, arms crossed, thinking for a moment, then back to him. "Then cash in on the gold bar we found in Louise's cabin."

His frown deepened and he brought a finger to his lips, shushing her. Harold Rollins was sick in bed, in the parlor below them, but the man still had ears. "We agreed to not speak of it again," he whispered.

"No, that was how you wanted it, and I went along with it for a time. Since we couldn't find the rest, it hardly mattered. But Bryce, that bar could see us at least partway through another winter, help us get our feet under us again."

Bryce rose and walked over to her. "You're the one who fears that Bannock will return. If he hears we have conquistador gold, he *will* find a way back to us, Dess. And he won't be alone."

She lifted her chin and her eyes grew more defiant. "Then let's melt it down here so there are no markings and divide it into smaller, less obvious pieces. You can take them to California, if you have to, to exchange it for cash. California won't kill you; Spain might." Her eyes softened and she came over to him. "Don't you see, Bryce? This could be God's provision, His way of seeing us through a trying year. Why not utilize what He has given us?"

❦

*8 April 1887*

*Our visitor, Harold Rollins, has moved to the bunkhouse. The men are under strict orders to treat him with respect, but none can avoid the fact that he remains only because Sheriff Olsbo has forebade him to leave; he must remain three more weeks to make sure that his remaining eight horses are free of disease and will not infect any other ranchers as they have ours.*

*Three of our yearlings and two mares are showing signs of the strangles. I can feel the swellings along their jaw lines. Bryce is beside himself, since we must begin the breeding process, and yet he hesitates, not wishing to risk the health of either dam or foal if strangles occurs. But which to breed? Which to segregate? Put down the ill or hope for recovery? I notice he is not as eager to put down our horses as he was Harold's, and this seems to trouble him too.*

Odessa walked with the baby down to the stables, intent on looking in on the twelve young foals that had managed to survive the blizzard. Not one of them showed signs of the strangles, and she had taken to looking in on them each day, finding hope, vision for their future, every time she gazed at them across the stable doorway. They were already bored, seeking to leave the close confines of the small stalls they shared with their mothers, but Odessa knew it would be some time before Bryce risked their tender lungs. As it was, he only allowed the hands to take them out once a day, to the farthest corral, for exercise.

She looked about, wondering at her nervousness at the thought of encountering her husband. Odessa didn't know what to make of this new mood in him. And she alternated between frustration and fear. Was this to be their relationship from here on out? Why could they not draw together to fight this new battle? Why did it seem to divide them when they needed each other most?

Odessa smiled as she spied the first foal, a lovely chestnut colored imp that tossed his head when he saw her, as if in greeting. She lifted Samuel up to get a better look, and the baby gurgled and kicked excited fat legs in pleasure. She moved on to the next stall, glimpsing Bryce approaching them, but ignored him. She felt too angry, too hurt to speak to him. He'd left without waiting for her to retrieve Samuel, left without even trying to find resolution. The ranch hands all appeared to be elsewhere this morning; at least none were inside at the moment.

"Odessa," he said, from over her left shoulder.

"Bryce," she said, not turning.

She stiffened as he wrapped his strong arms around her waist and leaned his head in to kiss her shoulder and then her neck. They stood there for a minute in silence. To Odessa, it felt strange, almost as if she were getting to know her husband again. "I need to tell you what is on my mind," he said.

"I've been waiting for that …" She turned to him and he took Samuel from her, bouncing him in his arms for a moment. "Is this about why you seem so … distant?"

"Most likely," he said grimly. He lifted his free hand up to pinch his forehead, as if massaging away pain there again. Together, they walked to an open window, one that gave them a view of an empty corral and beyond it, the wide fields and towering mountains that bordered their ranch. "I was already worried, before the strangles. We were late in breeding."

She nodded. She knew there was always pressure to breed sooner rather than later. The earlier a future racehorse was born in the spring, the better chance he had in his age group. The better he performed, the better his breeder did in future sales. While none of the ranch's horses had gone to racehorse buyers recently, in years past up to a third had. And that third was so valuable; it doubled their annual income. This year the yearlings, having been born late, would not be as highly sought after, and they'd lost half of them in the storm. Another two were now quarantined for strangles. And they were already a month behind in breeding for the next year's sales due to the blizzard.

She wrapped her hand around his waist. "We are not God, Bryce. Only the Lord controls the weather. The light. The mares will not begin their cycle until there is enough light."

He swallowed hard and stared out. "Last fall Robert suggested I build the snowbreaks, and also three new barns and stable units, dividing the men to care for subgroups of the horses through the winter. He asked me to do it, outright. He'd read about breeding operations that bring their breeding dams in early, and light many lanterns throughout, day and night, so the horse thinks it's later in the spring than it really is."

"You thought it foolish," she said quietly.

"I thought it meddlesome. I told him to mind his own business, to pay attention to his ships rather than my horses. I thought, *Why do mechanically what God does naturally?* We've done well in the last decade on this ranch. The expense of those new barns and stables, let alone the increased number of hands we would've had to hire, feeding them—and you with a new baby—I thought it ludicrous. Greedy. And the new land … we'd already pushed as far as I was willing to go."

Odessa sighed heavily. She leaned her cheek against his shoulder. "You made the best decision you could with the information you had at the time. I know how it must feel, how you are beating yourself. But what if you had agreed to it? Undertaken the task, the expense? We might have only had ten, twelve mares already impregnated? That wouldn't put us so much further ahead."

He lifted his chin and stared up at the roof of the stables. His demeanor was easing, his shoulders more relaxed as he shared his burdens with her.

"Will I like your brother, Bryce?" she asked carefully.

He laughed then, a quick snort of air through his nose. A mare edged her nose over a stable stall and he stepped over to give her a good rub. Samuel closed his eyes and opened them wide in surprise, then turned his head away as if it were all too much to take in. "You'll like him. Most everyone does. Truth be told, I do too."

She moved over to him. "I want us to remember where we've been, Bryce. Four years ago, standing here together, just holding our child would've seemed impossible. Ever since that day with Reid, I committed to trust God, with whatever breath I had left, with as many breaths as I had left. He holds our lives in our hands, Bryce. Our past. Our present. Our future."

Her husband nodded. "I know it."

"And this has been a terrible month. We've suffered terrible losses. But we are here. We are alive. We are healthy. Think of it! Neither of us has even had a consumptive attack since we left the sanatorium!"

"It's you," he said softly, wrapping an arm around her shoulders and pulling her close. "You are my medicine."

"Love has done us both good," she whispered. "But it is God that grants us life. We must praise Him, Bryce. Even when it's hard. Even when all seems dark. We must remember what is good, what is true, rather than believe fears and half-truths. That is how we cope with the day. That is how we keep living our lives the way He would have us live them, embracing them rather than just surviving them."

"Amen," he said, leaning back to look her in the eye.

She laughed through a big sigh. "All right, I'll quit preaching. But I'm right, aren't I? Come what may—even if we lose all, we always have our God, our hope."

"And each other," he said, kissing the top of her head.

❁

"How is it that no man has claimed your heart, Miss St. Clair?" Gavin asked as they strolled around the deck of the steamship. Both were wrapped in heavy coats, the spring sea barely hospitable for a walk outside, but neither could tolerate another day without at least a few moments in fresh air.

"I will not allow any man to ever claim my heart," she said, glancing up to measure his reaction.

He laughed, lifting his chin upward, and then tucking it again. "You are quite original, aren't you?"

"I like to think so."

"Rest assured, you are." They tried to stroll, but the heavy sea made it a bit of a challenge. "You do not wish for children?"

"I will leave the breeding to my sister. She has had a child. While I wish to visit her, see my nephew, there is nothing in me that wants one of my own. I want the stage. I want a career. That is my child. And you, Gavin? Are you in pursuit of a suitable wife?"

He slanted a glance down at her from the side. "My parents would like that. But I am not much tempted toward life at home. While I find distinct pleasure in the company of women, I fear that I would be a despot of a husband, always away." He shook his head. "No, a marriage would only be a strain on both my wife and me. She would feel forgotten, ignored. And I know enough of women to understand that is never a good thing."

"You are wise, accepting the truth of your life. And you are right. Not many women could tolerate such a marriage. How often *do* you get home?"

He pursed his lips, considering. "In the last three years, I have been home no more than three months."

She leaned closer to him. Any man who spent that much time seeing to his business was bound to be quite successful. Success would explain his air of confidence, his fine clothing, his casual references to the exotic. "Tell me about some of your adventures, Gavin. Where have you been? What have you seen?"

He smiled. "Let us go inside. If these waves keep up, we're liable to be tossed overboard." He opened the door to the large central parlor room, where many already sat, huddled in groups around pot-bellied stoves, trying to get warm, swaying with the deep waves. He gestured toward a small settee in the corner, and she fairly fell into it with the motion of the ship, pulling a woolen blanket around her shoulders while he went to fetch some tea. A few ladies glanced her direction, narrowing their gazes judgmentally. But Moira couldn't care less. Her business was none of their concern. Gavin returned with two tall cups of steaming tea on a small platter and placed one before her on the table. The cups were wider in the body and smaller at the rim, allowing seafaring passengers to keep more inside and spill less. On the saucer were two rectangular shortbread cookies, her favorite. "You remembered."

"Ah yes. I am making it a point to commit to memory everything about you, Moira."

"You flatter me." It was reassuring, familiar to have a man's complete attention again, and particularly enjoyable that it was a man as dashing as Gavin Knapp.

"So … you wished to know of my travels. I have been to every continent and many countries in each. Of which region do you wish to hear?"

Moira took a sip and considered him. She imagined him in his travels around the world, much like an actor in one of her plays at the opera house. What costume would suit him best? Should she dress him in the soft, flowing desert costume of a sheik, riding a camel?

Or in the light, flowing silks of the Burmese atop an elephant? Or the crisp-shouldered jacket of the Japanese? All at once, she could imagine this man everywhere, 'round the globe. He seemed to fit anywhere she imagined him, a chameleon of sorts. "Have you been to the Great Wall? I've yet to meet anyone who has been to China, or Mongolia."

"Please, call me Marco," he said with a twisted grin.

Her breath caught. "As in, Marco Polo?"

He took a sip of tea and then set his cup down on the saucer. "I made it a point to trace as much of his route as possible while in the region. I stayed in foul-smelling tents they call *yurts* in Mongolia. Walked miles of the Great Wall—you'd be amazed at how much still stands, and disappointed at how much has been carried away to erect new buildings. In one region, they have these most remarkable cliffs that rise from the sea like massive monoliths, green and foreboding. The natives sail among them like innocents ignoring sea monsters about to strike."

Moira clapped her hands in delight. "Tell me more! What of the people? Did they welcome you? How did you capture the language? Did you have an interpreter? How did you manage to conduct business in such a foreign land?"

Gavin laughed and made a motion with both hands to try to settle her. "It was marvelous. I look forward to the day I can return. Perhaps you can accompany me," he said casually. "The Chinese would be quite fascinated with an American singer. And you, my dear … would be a veritable phenomenon."

She smiled. "Let me endure this voyage and then we shall speak of travel again."

He nodded. "And yes, I was properly welcomed, and my interpreter most likely was the one to thank for that. Business is conducted as it has been done for a thousand years. If I want what another has, I am willing to pay for it. And undoubtedly, I have what someone else is willing to pay for. It's rather simple, really, trade. Straightforward. I like that aspect."

Moira spotted Daniel, who had just entered and appeared to be pulling on a coat for a walk outside. "You'll need a scarf and gloves today, Daniel," she called gaily. "It's much colder than yesterday."

He lifted his chin in recognition of her words, glanced her way as if he wished he didn't have to, then, spying Gavin beside her, quickly looked away. Strange man, that one. Was he interested or was he not? She shook her head and focused on her less mysterious, more forthright companion, sitting beside her. "And so, Gavin, after all your travels, all you've seen of the world, and the little you know of me … do you think New York will welcome me as Paris and London did?"

He squinted his eyes and peered at her. Then his eyes lit up. "The city will undoubtedly bring you the patronage you seek. But why not head toward Adams's Colorado? Or Nevada? Are you so well mannered and of society that you cannot see the coin to be made in the frontier?"

She frowned, trying not to shake her head at the thought. It would be rude.

He stared at her and laughed, a pleasant, low rumbling sound. "Now, hear me out, Moira. Take the Chinamen of which we just spoke. You made what in Paris? Twenty, maybe thirty francs a night?"

She did the math in her head, exchanging English pounds for French francs. "About that."

He nodded appreciatively. "A decent sum for a young opera star. But what if I told you that in China, you could command triple what you were paid in Europe?"

It was her turn to raise a brow. "It might be worth a voyage."

"And what if," he said, leaning a bit closer to her, "I told you that you could sing in the mining towns of Colorado and earn quadruple what you were paid?"

Her hand went to her chest. "You jest."

He smiled and leaned back. "No. I tell you the truth. It's all about trade. You want to sing. They want to hear a singer. For some, they just want to lay eyes on a woman. And when the woman is as handsome as you—"

"I can't return to Colorado. There are people … people who don't wish to see me return and prosper."

"So steer clear of them," he said with a shrug of his shoulders. "Change your name."

"You do not speak of opera houses."

He paused. "No. Entertainers in those regions … they take any stage they can. Sometimes it's the top of a piano. Sometimes it's a bar."

"A bar!"

He smiled. "Are you so provincial that you've never set foot inside a bar?"

"Well yes, I suppose I am."

"Then, Miss Moira, I submit that you are ignoring a valuable trade opportunity. Take it from me. If you traveled from town to town in Colorado, you'd be a sensation. I've been there, on other business. I can see it, plain as day. They would throw money at your feet."

"And sing what?" she scoffed. "Something from *La Traviata?* Mining towns hardly draw the caliber of patron who would appreciate such songs."

"You judge them prematurely. The lure of gold, silver, has made many a man in established professions depart for unknown territory, all on the promise of potential, no guarantees. There are attorneys, accountants, professors out there, laboring over sluices, as we speak."

"And failed farmers or day laborers," she added.

"Them as well. But collectively, they care not what you sing. You may well sing of Verdi's fallen woman, or a satire, or a saloon belle's song."

She choked on her tea. This man knew opera. A layman. A businessman, who knew opera!

"Are you quite all right, my dear?" he asked, frowning and leaning toward her.

"Fine, fine," she said with a strangled voice, blushing with embarrassment.

"These men only wish to see a beautiful woman singing beautiful music," he went on. "It helps some of them to remember where they began, helps them remember home. Perhaps in doing that, Moira, you would find your sense of home as well."

"Do you have the impression that I am missing home?" she said, surprised by his insight. And yet she couldn't really argue against it. A part of her did miss family, yet a bigger part still longed to make a mark in the world. She had just begun to feel that in Paris....

"Moira, you might love it, out there on the frontier."

She set down her cup. "Love it? I've lived in Colorado before. We went to seek the cure for my elder sister, Odessa."

Gavin blinked in surprise but remained silent as she went on. "I love that the mountain air cured my sister, but I didn't love living on the frontier."

"Where did you live?" Gavin asked.

"I was in Colorado Springs. And I heard the only way to get around in the mountains is in a rickety carriage, traveling among horrible, mud-soaked roads. That hardly speaks of any kind of home that I might be longing for." What did this man know of her, really? He didn't know of how hard she had worked to get this far, to achieve what she had. And now he suggested she relinquish her hard-won reputation for … what, exactly? He didn't even know!

"Of course there might be risks, challenges. But think about it. We began this conversation speaking of trade. And I see significant opportunity here. A singer without a stage. Many stages without a singer. You've made one of the finest stages in the world—Opera Comiqué—your own. Why not carve out yet another niche for yourself?" He rose with her, sensing her irritation. "If you dare."

"If I dare!" she sputtered.

"If you dare," he said with a grin.

❀

The storm had been building for days. Daniel knew after a turn around the deck and from the gruff expressions of the sailors he passed that it would be a rough night. He turned into his tiny private cabin several hours later, eyeing the door five down that he knew was Moira's. For all her worldliness, the girl was young and somewhat naive. Did she fully recognize the dangers of being at sea—and from men such as Gavin Knapp?

He stood there a moment, wondering what it was about the little spitfire that so intrigued him. Perhaps it was that she was so utterly different than his wife … Shannon had been quiet, almost stoic. They could spend hours in companionable silence, communicating at times with a single look or gesture. Theirs had been the most peaceful relationship he'd ever known, and yet deeply passionate.

Daniel looked down the hall again, imagining Moira inside. That one wore her passion on her sleeve. He closed the door, deciding Moira St. Clair was no concern of his. He was to look after his boss's shipment and return to his quiet life in Leadville. That was his only charter.

He climbed into his bunk and rocked against the side panels, so heavy were the seas. He forced himself to think of Shannon, finding comfort in familiar old sorrow rather than the agitation of new intrigue. Shannon, dear God, Shannon … more than two years ago now …

❦

Daniel awoke when a wave hit the ship with such force that he rolled over the barrier bar and onto the floor. He blinked, trying to see anything in the India-ink darkness and make sense of where he was. The wave passed and he rolled back again, hitting the bunk with a grunt. He grasped hold of the wood and hauled himself upright. Outside in the hallway he could hear faint calls for help, moaning. Were people injured?

He found his trousers and fell into his bunk to put them on, leaning against the next wave, swiftly buttoning them with one hand and holding on to the far side panel as the boat rocked to nearly a forty-five degree angle. If this kept up, they would be in danger of capsizing. They needed to get upstairs, to the parlor, all the passengers. Somewhere they'd have a chance of escaping.

Daniel tried to move cautiously to the door, but was again thrust to the far side of his narrow room. He grimaced and felt for the knob, found it and pulled it open. In the hallway a lantern swung from a central hook, confirming what he already knew. The ship was in trouble. Ten passengers were already in the passageway. "Get upstairs!" he barked. "To the parlor! If we go over, we need to be up there to escape!"

A woman, still in her nightdress and cap, covered her mouth in horror at Daniel's words, but her husband emerged from their room, wrapped a blanket around her shoulders and then led her toward the stairs. Others followed them. How many were left?

Daniel made his way to the end of the hallway and began pounding on each door, shouting at the occupants to rise, make their way upstairs. He opened each one, surprising an elderly couple, but finding the rest mostly empty. He got to Gavin Knapp's room and heard moaning inside. He quickly entered and found the man on the floor rolling back and forth, his head bright with blood. He frowned and picked up the man and placed him on his bunk again, tying a shirt across the top of him to keep him somewhat in place. He'd come back for him once he knew everyone else was out.

The next two cabins produced two more men, one a merchant, another a banker he'd met at the captain's table. Both had managed to don jackets and trousers, although neither wore shoes. They nodded at him in grim greeting and, with hands out to either side of the passageway to brace themselves, made their way to the stairs.

Daniel hesitated at Moira's door. Then, irritated with himself, knocked sharply. "Miss St. Clair! Moira! We need to get above decks!"

"I cannot!" she called back. "I'm trapped. A trunk slid sideways and it's jammed against the door."

Her tone denoted fear, but not panic. "Shove, Moira. With your shoulder. You must get it clear."

Another wave hit, making the ship groan, as if every plank wished to crack in half. Daniel crashed against the door across the hall from Moira's, but it held. He looked down the hallway to the lantern, his eyes narrowing in concern as it was again at nearly a forty-five degree angle.

"Daniel!" Moira called. "Daniel!"

"I'm here! When the ship rights itself, get away from the door!"

"All right!"

They seemed to be hanging on the edge of this giant wave for a terribly long time. How big were the swells? But then they were past it, coming down the far side, and Daniel used the momentum of the shift to crash to the other side, shoulder first, breaking through the top of the thin wall of her cabin door. He peered inside, trying to see her in the deep shadows. "Moira?"

"Here!" she called, and suddenly he could see her slender fingers reaching for his. He grabbed hold and, going to his knees, pulled her up and through the hole. The wave released them and they crashed across the hallway. He held on tight to the woman, fearful she would be hurt, but then found he was fighting for breath.

"Daniel?" she edged off him and to his side. "Daniel?"

He turned toward her, noting her pretty wide eyes were now under the eave of a furrowed brow. Heavens, she was a sight. Mass of blonde curls about her shoulders. White nightdress with soft ruffles at the neck. An angel. So like—

The boat rocked again and he grabbed hold of her forearm and braced himself against the far hallway wall, easing them both across the way. "We have to get out of here, Moira. Go, up the stairs to the parlor. If we capsize, being down here will be our doom."

"I want to stay with you," she said, suddenly a frightened little girl in a grown woman's body.

"No, I have to go and get Gavin. He's been hurt."

"Gavin? Let me help."

"No!" he said sharply. He pointed down the hall. "Go! Now!"

She stared back at him a moment, fury making her defiant, then she turned and made her way in the direction he had pointed. Daniel watched her for a long moment, then turned to get Gavin.

❦

Moira sank down into a corner, knees before her chest, and looked around in terror. Women screamed with each new wave, and men grunted or groaned. Light from the few lamps in the room cast eerie shadows across them all and glittered on the stream of water that leaked from under the door and across the parlor floor.

A man outside shrieked and then a massive wave hit, sending many of them tumbling down to the other side of the room. Moira clung to the deck doorway, where water was pouring in from all sides. Would it hold? Or would the very sea soon pour in upon them, filling the ship until it sank to the bottom? Water sprayed downward, drenching her, and the ship hung for so long, at such a terrible angle, she feared it was the moment of demise.

What had happened to the sailor who had called out before the wave hit? Was he gone? Overboard, drifting, calling, helpless?

*Alone. Mama, I'm so alone.* It pierced her, the thought, stole her breath. *I don't want to die alone.* She wished her mother was here now, huddled with her, cradling her head to her chest.

*You're not alone, Moira.*

*I am. I need to get to someone. Someone who can save me … or die with me.*

The ship groaned and creaked, sounding as if it might break in two, and then slowly rocked back. Moira used the momentum to stand again and move as quickly down the stairs as possible before the next wave hit. In seconds, she was down in the sleeping quarters. But it was terribly dark.

"Daniel! Gavin!" she called. "Daniel!"

Water dripped down from above from every hole and crevice between the planks. How much water had they taken on? She was drenched and cold. Were the men underwater? Trapped?

"Daniel!" she cried, making her way forward, hands out to keep her from crashing into either wall. "Gavin!"

Daniel swung partway into the hallway then, lantern in one hand, Gavin to his side. For but a portion of a moment, Daniel's eyes locked with hers, intense, as if he was silently communicating with her. He was angry, furious, frustrated, but conversely glad to see her, glad she was all right. She could see all that in his eyes. Moira held her breath, waiting for him to speak again to her, speak without words. "I told you to stay above, Moira," he ground out, breaking their reverie. "If we go over, I don't want you to—"

But then the momentum of a smaller wave brought both men fully into the hall, side by side, and it was Gavin who captured her attention. Gavin's arm was stretched across Daniel's back and blood flooded down his handsome face. He lifted his head and grinned, staring at her. "Do my eyes deceive me? Look, Adams, the storm has brought us the most beautiful mermaid of all. Heavens, Moira, if a stage director could capture you, like this, there would be no end to that opera's production."

"Shush, Gavin," she said, making her way to them. The passageway was too narrow to help them, to slide under Gavin's other arm, but she waited until they were near. She lifted a trembling hand to push back a shock of wet blond hair from Gavin's brow, studying the gash.

He took her hand and kissed it. "I'll be all right, beautiful. We only have to survive this storm and we'll have a tale to tell, won't we?"

She glanced at Daniel, but he was already moving his eyes from her and hauling Gavin forward.

Apparently, he had nothing left to say to her, spoken or unspoken.

❦

"Keep your eyes open for phantom ships," William said lowly.

"No pirate would dare attack us," Nic retorted. But still he ran his fingers over the hilt of his revolver, tucked into the back of his waistband. The Falkland Islands were rumored to be rife with pirates, intent on capturing any merchant daring to round the Cape Horn en route to the West Coast of America or onward to the Far East. He couldn't blame them, really. This was a solid trade route. The *Mirabella* held a wealth of her own in the hold.

"The British privateers keep most of them at bay, but word has it the brigands favor fog such as this."

"Nothing but the ghost stories of idle sailors." Nic raised his fingers and widened his eyes, feigning fear a moment, then letting out a scoffing sound. "It makes no sense. If we can't see where we're going, how would they find us to attack?"

William pursed his lips and lowered his voice. "They say they know these waters as a blind man knows his own street. They're able to sail sightless."

"But if they were sailing, they'd be dead in the water in this soup," Nic retorted. "We would have to assume they were powered by steam, as are we. And we'd hear their approach."

William narrowed his eyes, barely covering a grin, and straightened his jacket. "Would we? Or would our own steam engines block the sound of their approach?" He clapped him on the shoulder as he departed. "Don't let them kill you if they come."

Nic resumed his pacing along his portion of the steam clipper's deck. This was the first time the captain had elected to fire up the steam engines, since a steady wind had accompanied them from Uruguay on. But here by the islands the wind had abruptly stopped, an odd occurrence this time of year. It had set all the sailors on edge. The engine made a terrible racket, and they missed the soothing rush of wind and water.

Nic didn't care one way or another. He only wished for them to return to eating up the miles that lay between him and his life. His life … what was that? Where would he go? What would he do with his time? How would he make money? He leaned against the rail and stared into the dense fog, the passing ship sending it swirling into forms that would make many a sailor believe in ghosts. He shivered, but forced himself to remain where he was. He had to admit that while he missed the release of the ring, it was a relief to not be constantly healing. Life aboard ship was strengthening new muscles, and once his hands healed from that first encounter with splicing ropes, he had had no other injuries.

He rolled his left shoulder, feeling the familiar ache of an old boxing blow there. By the time his father was twenty-seven, he had taken over the helm of St. Clair Press and seen Nic born. He was settled, a success. Happy, at peace. Why couldn't Nic find the path that would take him to such a position in life? These last years had been a relief—the new towns, new women, new fights an escape, a diversion. But standing here, preparing to round the Horn and make their way toward North America again, Nic thought he felt much the same when he stood on the bookshop's stairs for the last time in Colorado Springs. He'd experienced much, but little had changed inside. Would life always feel unsettled for him? Would he always have this constant need for something *else* inside? What food would fill him, what liquor would ease him, what woman would soothe him? And why couldn't he discover it?

# Chapter 7

By the pale hours of the morning, the seas eased, like a spent monster at last taking slow, steady breaths. The weary passengers fell asleep against walls in the parlor, huddled together—depending on one another to sound an alarm in case the monster regained its fury—and they'd secured Gavin and another injured man to two settees, tying them down with long strips of old cloth to keep them from rolling off after they'd dressed their wounds.

Gavin was sitting up a couple hours later, complaining of a headache, but jesting with Moira and others around him, when the captain announced they were clear of any further danger, and they could all return to their cabins. Daniel rose to go, without looking Moira's way.

"Daniel," Gavin called.

The man stopped in the doorway and then looked over his shoulder. He was plainly weary, as they all were, but Moira wondered what else was behind the sorrow in his eyes.

"Daniel, thank you for getting me—and Moira—up here," Gavin said. "We are indebted."

Moira shifted under the inference of Gavin's statement—that they were a couple—and watched as Daniel looked from Gavin to her and back again. He gave him a slow nod and then disappeared into the hallway.

"We're all indebted to him," said a man to Moira's right. Another woman murmured her agreement.

Moira thought back to the dark cabin, being trapped, and what might have happened if the ship had indeed capsized.

"My men will have your door repaired in a quarter hour, Miss St. Clair," said the captain, patting her shoulder in a fatherly way.

"Thank you," she murmured. But inside, she trembled. Entering that cabin, and closing the door behind her, would take an act of courage in itself. Her eyes shifted to the empty hall doorway and she found herself wishing—

"Will you be quite all right, Moira?" Gavin asked, slipping his warm hand beneath hers. "You must've been terrified."

"Oh, I'll fare all right, I'm certain. I'm more alarmed over you. Are you certain your head is quite all right?"

He smiled and knocked on the other side of his head, the side that wasn't injured. "Hard as rock, this one. I'll be up for ballroom dancing on the morrow. Care to take a turn?" He grinned and she couldn't avoid matching his smile. He was so charming, even in the midst of trauma.

"I'd be delighted, Gavin." And in that moment, she could see herself in his arms, gliding across a parquet floor. The image of being on shore, in her finery, at his side, restored her confidence, focus, and she rose, shoving thoughts of Daniel to the back of her mind. "Will you be so kind as to escort me to my cabin?"

"Indeed," he said, rising slowly. He straightened his shirt and offered his arm.

"Should you be taking my arm instead?"

"Most likely," he said with a small laugh. "Most likely."

❦

Nic thought he had his sea legs, thought himself utterly comfortable atop the lanyards, until the *Mirabella* attempted to round the Cape Horn. After three days of fighting thirty-foot swells, the steam engine quit, and the crew was called upon to lash sails, unfurl sails, and lash them again in the midst of forty-knot winds and driving wind so hard it stung a man's cheek as it landed. Weary sailors began to make mistakes, and men fell to the boards again and again as the waves washed across the deck.

Two were washed overboard that morning. One had lost his footing and then was washed over the rail. While he clung there, his mate tried to pull him in. Another wave, a monster, came and pushed them both into the frigid seas. Nic had watched it happen from across the deck, as if it were a dream. He could barely see between the rain and the wave spray streaming over his eyes. But he had seen the men, struggling there. And then the wave. And then the empty deck.

He'd rushed over, intent on tossing the sailors a line, but all he could see was dark, roiling seas, as if she had sucked the men under immediately, giving them no chance to call for aid, no hope. He was so stunned by the sight, another wave took him by surprise. He was only glad that he had been clinging to ropes, rather than the slick rail, when it came.

Nic followed William up the ropes as the first mate called, a bare whisper over the whistling wind, asking for a second sail. He was obviously trying to stabilize the ship's progress, aid her in exiting this storm rather than languishing in its eye, where the storm would slowly, methodically tear the *Mirabella* apart. And yet it was a delicate dance, for if there was too much sail aloft, with this much wind and such odd swells, she could list too far, too fast for the crew to right her. They'd end up capsized, and Nic was sure, no matter how hard he could swim, eventually, the seas would drag him down too. He'd disappear, just as his mates had disappeared that morning.

The ship crested a giant wave and then heaved to her starboard side. Above him, William shouted as he turned in the air, following the ship's progress. He held on to one rope with his left hand, but then he was spinning, his legs flayed out, the rope arcing farther. His body slammed into a mast and he lost hold, slipping several feet, before gaining his grip again. He swung back toward the ropes where Nic clung. "Here! William, give me your hand!" Nic screamed above the wind.

William reached for him as he neared, but their fingertips only barely touched before the ship swayed again and his friend was swinging back toward the mast. He rammed into it, lost hold of the rope, and fell to the deck, twenty feet below. Nic lost sight of him as another wave washed over the deck and the whole ship tilted, threatening to capsize. Had the bilge pump failed? Weren't they riding lower in the water now, plowing through waves rather than sliding over them? Or were the waves simply growing larger?

"Belay the order! Belay the order for second sail!" called a man from beneath him on the nets. The wind had increased to such a keening wail that they could no longer hear captain or mate from the bridge. They were down to passing along orders. He looked up to the three sailors ahead of him, two already clinging to the second lanyard, high above. "Belay the order!" he screamed. "Belay it!"

The man ahead of him nodded and appeared to shout to the two up top, but Nic could hear none of it. He took a step down, pleased to be heading toward relative safety. Up on the higher lanyards, in seas like this, sailors talked of being "shaken loose like a monkey out of a tree." He glanced through the holes of the net as he climbed and at last saw William, cradling his knee, his face contorted in pain. But then there was another wave.

"Dear God!" Nic screamed at the sky. "Enough! It is enough!"

He paused a moment, as if hoping his furious words might be heard by the Almighty, but only the continued sounds of wind and wave greeted him. No sudden calm. No beam of light from between parted clouds. He laughed at his foolishness, tasting the salt of the sea on his tongue. After all, he'd sworn off God years before, when "the good Lord" had seen fit to take one brother after another, and then his sister and mother. Why would God listen to him now?

"Fine!" he shouted upward. "Let me have it! You've never held back before!"

"St. Clair!" shouted a man above him. "Move! Go!"

Nic glanced from the black skies, still streaming with rain and wind, to the men above him. He was blocking the way.

"You want us all to meet our death?" shouted the man. "Go!"

Nic hesitated and then mechanically moved down the ropes. Did he want to die? Was he really ready to die? Disappear beneath the waves this night? Never see his sisters again? He shook his head, as if there were water in his ears and he couldn't hear himself think. He reached bottom, and the other crewmen passed him by, the first angrily shoving him aside. But Nic just stepped to his left, one fist full of net in case another wave came, as he stared at the deck. Men were striving to keep their feet, stay alive, while the sea seemed intent upon taking them down.

❁

Bryce sat down heavily at the kitchen table. Odessa was asleep, as was Samuel, and a full moon shone through the window. To his left was the conquistador gold bar, found in Louise's cabin several years ago, and to his right was his brother's letter. He cradled his head in his hands, trying to figure out what was the best route. He had to have a plan, answers to Robert's questions before he asked them.

If he cashed in the gold, he might stave off financial disaster for a time, but it didn't resolve his ongoing problem of having too few horses—the only way to fix that was to bring in more Spanish horses, fresh bloodlines, at the lowest cost—and have cash to sustain them on the ranch while he rebuilt the herd. The gold bar was likely to bring him a huge amount of money.

And yet if he left Odessa to go to Spain, he might indeed be risking his health. If he suffered a consumption attack and died while abroad, what would happen to Odessa and Samuel then?

He sighed and put his head in his hands. "Lord, I don't know what to do," he whispered. "Show me. Please show me the way I'm supposed to walk. Help me provide for my family and keep them safe. Help me, Jesus, help me."

A knock sounded at the back door, and Bryce opened his eyes in surprise. Swiftly, he stashed the bar on the couch and casually threw his coat across it. Then he went to the door and peeked outward.

"Tabito," he said, opening the door for his friend.

"Saw your light. Knew you must be troubled, to be up this late."

"Come. Sit." He moved into the kitchen and gestured toward a chair for Tabito. "I don't know what's right, Tabito."

"You told her, then?"

"Yes. But it's confusing for her, for me. And with Bannock out there now. . . ."

"You hired the man? To follow him?"

"The detective, yes. We should receive a telegram several times a week. And if anything is alarming, he's to come here to report to me … or you."

"Sell the gold, Bryce. Go East, but only to sell the gold and return. That far away, Bannock won't learn you had it."

"It will hold off the bank, see us through a winter. Not purchase new stock."

"Then hold off the bank. Let the stock do as it may. You never know what the new year will bring. Wait. Trust. Hold."

Bryce rose and ran a hand through his hair in agitation. "I cannot wait … It's not the McAllan way."

"It was your uncle's way."

"But not my father's."

"You do not fear Bannock's return?"

"What does he have to gain? It's very public that we have not mined any of the O'Toole property. If he asks anyone, he'd know that. And he knows nothing of this bar of gold—only you, Dess, and I know of it. Even I think it's the only one, a bar that got separated from the rest at some point. We can't make any sense of the marking in Louise's Bible—she might have been as mischievous as her son, trying to lead us on some wild-goose chase."

"Or not."

Bryce shook his head. "No. I can't follow that faint trail, Tabito." He put his hands out as if holding a large ball. "I have to move forward with what I know, what is real, known to me *now*." He paced back and forth, chin in hand, thinking. "Maybe you're right. Maybe I ought to go East, see if I might sell the gold, see if there is enough to purchase at least some stock from a breeder. It will be more expensive, but if the gold is worth enough, I could pay the bank what I owe and even gain eight mares, maybe a stallion ..." He cocked his head to one side and stared at his friend. "We'd be ahead."

"But you'd leave one very angry wife behind."

Bryce stilled and stared at him. Then he nodded. "I would. She'd be furious. But it's for our good, all our good that I must do this."

"Send me. I'll take the bar, buy horses if there is enough."

Bryce hesitated. It was a good solution, wise. But Indians, even in a white man's clothing, were notoriously taken advantage of. There would be no way he'd get a fair price.

Tabito, obviously reading his look, sighed and rose. "Then send Doc and Dietrich, men you trust, and who know a good horse when they see one."

"Maybe." Bryce looked up and smiled. "Maybe." But even as the word left his mouth, he felt a shudder of doubt. What was the right course? And why was God being so silent?

❦

Moira and the others settled back into life aboard ship, eager to forget the trauma that lay behind them. Five sailors and one passenger had died that night, all but two of them washed overboard. All six were remembered in a brief ceremony, and the remaining two bodies were buried at sea. *To fight that night only to be relinquished to the waters,* Moira thought, as she heard the splash below and closed her eyes.

She opened them and found herself looking into Daniel's deep brown eyes. Even though she stood beside Gavin, it was as if Moira and Daniel were the only two on deck. He had avoided her since that night. Was he angry, jealous? She knew not what drove him, but at this point in her life, she preferred the clear, aboveboard communication that Gavin offered, rather than the mysterious, silent ways of Daniel. There were enough questions ahead that she didn't need a man raising more for her.

She ripped her eyes away from him and back to the captain, who was completing his brief eulogy. Her gaze moved to the wall beyond him, where planks had been replaced, new bright-gold pine against a plane of gray, weathered wood. In three days they had repaired the ship and buried the dead, put everything back to rights. Sailors were nothing if not efficient.

Mrs. Olsen came up to them, smiling demurely at Gavin across from Moira. "We think it would be good to hold an Irish wake this night. Three of the sailors were Irish, and I do believe it will lift all our spirits. The captain has approved. Will you join us?"

"Certainly, certainly," Gavin said. "Exactly what we all need to break us from this gloom and doom." He moved off with Mrs. Olsen, chatting about the plans, but Moira turned to look for Daniel. Perhaps he needed a party too, to lift him from whatever darkness had descended upon him that night of the storm. Parties did good work on such a front. She knew this from experience.

But he was gone. In seconds the deck was empty, everyone hurrying inside to avoid the cold.

Moira blinked in surprise.

"Moira?" Gavin called. She turned, to see him standing beside Mrs. Olsen, both of them looking her way. "Are you coming, darling?"

Moira smiled. "Coming," she said with a nod, staring at Gavin, so bright, so dapper in his crisp clothing. Even the healing gash at his head made him appear more gallant, intriguing. She pushed Daniel out of her mind, intent on the man before her.

If Daniel wished to live his life in shadow, that was up to him. For Moira, Gavin's light was too bright to ignore.

# Chapter ❁ 8

19 April 1887

Practically everyone aboard was gathered on deck the day they sailed into New York Harbor. Despite the cool weather, Gavin had encouraged her to don her coat and come outside a good hour earlier than the rest in order to secure their place at the rail. "You'll wish to see the great lady. She's new since you left America's shores."

He spoke, of course, about Lady Liberty, a gift from the French, who couldn't seem to cease talking about it in Paris—never mind that Americans had had to raise funds to build a base in order to raise her. But when she came in sight, a glorious copper woman, stately, hopeful, Moira's breath caught. Atop her pedestal, she was taller than Notre Dame's bell towers and far more grand. She represented freedom for the thousands who continued to pour into the United States, all hungering to achieve, succeed, prosper—and believing that here, nothing could stand in their way.

And here, more than anywhere else in the world, they did have that opportunity. Moira had that opportunity. She wore a fine gown worth a hundred dollars, but she had precious little cash left to her name. How many others had arrived with but a few coins in their pockets only to find their way to independence, even wealth? America, land of opportunity. Would Moira find her opportunity here now? An opportunity denied her almost four years ago?

Gavin edged an arm to her right, resting it on the rail, standing close to her, as if protecting her. And she drew comfort from it. No, the man wasn't interested in finding a wife. He'd made that clear. But the two of them weren't so different. They wanted the same things, independence, to use their abilities to their fullest. He pulled a tendril of curling blonde hair off her shoulder and tucked it behind her ear, a forward action, but welcome now after their two weeks of nonstop camaraderie. Moira shivered in delight at his touch. There was something about him that soothed and yet entranced her at the same time.

While her plans were to get to the train station as quickly as possible and begin seeking out a suitable Broadway agent, Gavin's lingering questions about the wealth to be made out West kept echoing through her mind. Was she doing the right thing? She stared back at the statue as the ship moved by. In minutes, it was behind them. Others turned to leave, to go and gather their things, but Moira and Gavin stayed where they were.

"May I ask a favor of you, Moira?"

She glanced over her right shoulder, up at him. His sparkling blue eyes stared back at her from under the brim of a bowler hat. "You may."

Gavin wrapped his other arm around her, a hand now on either side of her at the rail, his body precariously close to her own. He leaned his head around hers, his mustache tickling her ear as he said, "Can I convince you to not rush off? Would you dare to give me three days to convince you that I might be right?"

She smiled and moved slightly away from his face. "Convince me of what?"

"That you have more opportunity than you can imagine."

"I'm quite capable of dreaming up my own dreams, thank you."

"But what of our … friendship? Are you so anxious to be rid of me?" He was moving quietly, seductively. *My, was he attractive …*

She turned to face him. He made no move to release the rail. She glanced one way down the deck and then the other, surprised that they were so quickly, utterly alone, and that she felt no fear. A lifeboat hid them from view from anyone inside the main parlor. "I confess I am not anxious to be on my own. I believe a part of me shall miss you, Gavin."

A tiny smile lurked at the edges of his lips. He moved his left hand to her neck, and she obediently bent it backward, preparing for the kiss she'd seen in his eyes for a week now. He leaned in slowly, hovering a hair's breath from her lips. "Moira St. Clair," he murmured, "are you possibly as innocent as you seem?"

A whisper of alarm went through her mind, but then he was kissing her, pulling her closer.

A man coughed, and Moira broke away. Gavin laughed and glanced guiltily in Daniel's direction. "Lady Liberty inspired me to take my own liberties," Gavin said with a roguish smile.

She felt the heat rise up her chest and neck, knowing she was blushing. How long had it been since a man had made her blush? It had been months, no years! But it hadn't been Gavin's forward ways … it was Daniel's discovery, she realized.

"Yes, well …" Daniel said. He tentatively glanced their way. "I only wished to say good-bye. Forgive my intrusion."

"No forgiveness needed, friend," Gavin said, stepping toward him. "Perhaps our paths will cross again someday. Does your employer ever hire singers to entertain your constituents?"

Daniel's eyes flicked to Moira and back to Gavin. "All the time."

"Excellent," Gavin said. He reached forward a hand. "We may find a way to repay you someday for coming to our aid."

"No need."

"It's been a pleasure."

"For me as well. Godspeed, Gavin. Moira."

"Daniel," she said with a nod. She stayed beside Gavin, but wished she could go after the other man, say a more proper and thorough farewell, but for once she couldn't think of a single thing to say. Nothing seemed right, adequate. After three weeks aboard ship, what they had survived, shared—not shared?—there was a connection that was something akin to family. And yet Daniel had made it clear he wished them all to stay at arm's length.

"Gavin, what do you think Daniel's story is? Why is he so sad, so secretive?" She glanced up at him, glad for the moment breaking the heat between them.

"Who knows, darling. The man is a mass of secrets, for certain. I'm more interested in unraveling yours." Gavin took her hands in his, pulling her attention toward him. "My sweet, give me three days. Let me show you this city. And let us speak of what might be ahead of us." He shook his head. "I have much business to attend to. But nothing could be more important to me than spending another minute with you. Shall you give it to me? Three days?"

Moira paused, unsure. Yet his blue eyes tugged at her. "I … I really shouldn't … Gavin, to be frank, I really must use my time to secure my next role."

"Think nothing of it," he said with a flick of the hand. "Hold on to your precious savings. I have an apartment on the East Side … completely furnished. And utterly empty."

Her hand went to her throat. "I couldn't, Gavin. Stay with you?" What kind of woman did he think she was?

"Oh, darling, of course not! I will not be there. Unless, of course, you mean to forward an invitation," he said, speaking in seductive undertones again and pulling her a bit closer. He abruptly took a step away, leaving her slightly dazed. Was she relieved? Or a bit sad that there was not to be another stolen moment? She could not see her way clear.

He reached a hand to his head, as if it ached. "Come, we must see to our trunks." He reached out a hand. "You will do this, for me? Give me a few days? I cannot bear to say good-bye to you yet, Moira. Say you will."

She paused, glancing down the gangplank. Daniel left, never looking back again.

The future seemed daunting. Perhaps a few days of rest would do her good, help her see her way clear. "All right, Gavin. I will stay." But as she placed her hand in his, instead of the comfort she longed for, she felt a small tearing inside.

"You all right, darling?" he asked, giving her a quizzical look.

She turned away from him, facing the harbor, watching the people below. She would be. Somehow. Some way. She had to be.

"I'm fine, Gavin." She glanced back up at him, over her shoulder, and smiled as he nuzzled her ear. "I'm fine."

But as he continued to kiss her, growing more forward, Moira couldn't keep her eyes from the tall, broad, dark haired man who shouldered a trunk and moved through the crowd, without ever looking back.

Daniel. Would she ever see him again?

❁

Moira awakened in the middle of a massive, sumptuous bed and shivered as she realized how cold her nose was. She opened her eyes and gazed about the room. Gavin had hired a carriage to take them from port, up through Wall Street, which was silent on a Sunday, past St. Paul's with its historic old bell, paused at a favorite restaurant to treat her to lunch, then up through the lovely lanes of Central Park, where he had opened a bottle of champagne and poured her a glass, and then another. The trees were budding, some already in full spring flower. "Just awakening to the edge of possibility, as you are, darling," Gavin had said.

He'd dropped her off here, before nightfall, the perfect gentleman, along with a wedge of cheese, a vine full of grapes, and a long loaf of bread, purchased from the baker on the corner of the Italian district. He'd seen her in, helping her stow her things and then pausing in the doorway to kiss her softly on the lips.

"I feel terrible," she said, as he slowly leaned away, "edging you out of your own apartment."

"I have another," he said.

"Who has a spare apartment in the city?" she asked.

"Anyone wealthy enough to wish it," he said. Then with another kiss, he left her.

She had eaten and then fallen into his big bed covered in smooth russet silks. It was bound by four massive posts, hand-carved by some East Indian laborer, undoubtedly. Above, flowing, shimmering golden fabric undulated over cross bars and down the end, giving her the fanciful idea of sleeping beneath a mosquito net. It had been deliciously enticing last night as she slipped beneath the covers, but now, in the brisk chill of morning, she felt alone. For years she had had a servant to light a morning fire, fetch her tea and a robe. Even aboard ship, where there were no personal servants, the cook still lit fires and heated water for coffee and tea.

Oh well, she decided. If she was to be an independent woman she would have to do some things for herself. She cast aside the covers and scurried to her trunk, hurriedly donning a dress and her mink wrap, then slipping her feet into a delicate pair of slippers. While the shoes didn't warm her feet, at least they kept them off the cold marble floors. She moved around the room, looking more carefully at the books and pictures on the wall, each testifying to Gavin's mysterious past and experience, making Moira long to know more of him.

There were woodcut prints and metallic etchings from far-off countries, mostly of women. She studied their gowns, tucking details into her memory to pass along to costumers in future operas. She had made her way into the hall, still studying each item as she moved, when a swift rap at the door, followed by a key in the lock made her gasp. She took a step back and then sighed in relief as Gavin came through.

He was impeccably dressed, from head to toe the dapper gentleman. But his eyes were on her, slowly moving from her feet to her hair. He shook his head slowly and gently set down his cane. "Never, Moira, never," he said lowly, moving toward her, then wrapping a wide hand around her lower back and easing her toward him, "even that night aboard ship when you were a soaked siren," he whispered, studying her face, then lifting another hand to finger a coil of her hair, "never … have you looked more enticing."

She laughed at him and tried to step away, reaching up as if to try to straighten her morning-mussed hair. "Really, I must look a sight."

"A most delicious sight," he said. "Tell me, darling …" he pushed her gently backward, step by step, until her back hit the wall. He ignored the way his pictures moved, precariously pushed off-center by her hair, for his eyes were only on her. "Tell me, did you just rise? Out of my bed?"

She tried to swallow, but her mouth was suddenly dry. All she could do was give him a quick nod, feeling a bit like a schoolgirl in the arms of her first lover. She shook her head, ashamed at her stupidity. How many times had she played a lover on stage? She knew the signs, had played the part of seductress. But this, in real life, had crept up on her. She had not recognized it, had not wanted to recognize the signs that she was being seduced.

"Ah yes, you have realized it. The lamb in the wolf's lair," he said, easing back a bit. He gestured toward the front door and then straightened. "You are free to leave, Moira, at any time. I will not chain you here. I am not your keeper. Only your admirer. Only a man who would like to open your eyes to things you seem to have missed."

She paused, confused. She sensed the truth of it—he'd let her walk away. How long had she kept men away, because they wanted her, wanted to control her, wanted to own her? But this man offered her nothing but opportunity, adventure, kindness. Wasn't that what she wanted, really? Care without commitment? Companionship? And this spark between them, this pull … she edged across the hall toward him and lifted her chin. "I am not going anywhere yet. I promised you two more days."

"Three," he whispered, leaning down to barely edge her lips with his own. "Yesterday did not count."

And in that moment, as he kissed her neck, slowly, softly moving downward, Moira St. Clair knew she'd promise him anything.

❁

Odessa carried a tray down to the bunkhouse and strode to the end, where Harold was sitting up, reading. "You're looking like you have more color," she said, handing him the tray, full with a hearty breakfast. "Soon you'll be on your way, back to your family."

"Thanks to you, ma'am."

She could feel his heavy gaze upon her but ignored it. She paused at the end of the bed, turning back to force a smile. "Can I fetch you anything else?"

He smiled shyly and then glanced at an old, worn copy of Longfellow's poems beside him. "I don't suppose I could trouble you for another book? Perhaps some more poetry?"

She looked down at her boots and smiled a little in return. "I imagine I have another volume or two. I'll bring you one from the house."

"Thank you, ma'am."

Odessa turned to go, but he stopped her with a tentative "Ma'am?"

She glanced at him over her shoulder. "Yes?"

"I know I brought you an extra share of heartache, with the strangles and all. I'm right sorry about that. Had I known—"

"I know," she said quickly. "You were sick, Harold. Nothing you could've done differently. Our call is to deal with what is, rather than what might have been, right?"

He gave her a sad smile. "I'll do my best to make it right, ma'am. Once I'm home. Once I get some money, I intend to send some to you and Mr. McAllan."

She nodded slowly. When would that be? Two, three years down the road? What would become of them in the meantime? She forced a smile. "I'm glad to be of help to you. Please, give it no more thought."

But as she turned and walked down the center of the bunkhouse, her boot heels clicking on the wood, she could think of nothing else. Bryce was clearly worried. What *would* become of them? The ranch?

✿

"Why are you doing this?" Moira asked, as he tucked her hand around the crook of his arm.

"Doing what?"

"Taking me about. Introducing me. Showing me this … underworld?"

"Underworld?" Gavin laughed, laughed so hard he had to stop midstride and bend partially over.

Moira was not amused. She folded her arms across her chest and looked from under heavy-lidded brows in one direction and then another. He was drawing the eye of every passerby.

He finally got a hold of himself, straightened, and then covered his smile with a gloved hand. His blue eyes twinkled with mischief. If he wasn't so devilishly handsome and intriguing, Moira would've turned and walked away from him right then. "Forgive me, darling. That struck me as …" He gave in to another laugh but quickly regained his composure. He waved in one direction and then another. "Look about you, Moira," he said softly. "Tell me what you see."

"A street filled with the poor. Factory workers. Women hanging laundry." She wrinkled her nose. "Far fewer street cleaners than this number of horses warrant."

Gavin smiled benevolently, but shook his head. "Have you not listened to anything I've taught you?" He moved behind her and placed relaxed fingers on either of her shoulders. "Look, darling. Look again. How many people are on this street versus those that you would typically frequent?"

"Many more," she said.

"Exactly," he whispered in her ear, his breath sending a delicious shiver down her neck. "And what is that called, when there are more people in one place than another?"

"Potential revenue," she said.

"Yes!" he said, smiling and taking her hand and tucking it back around his arm as they resumed their walk. "Think of it, Moira. More than a quarter of these people will stop by at their corner tavern to knock back a pint. And the wise saloonkeeper will bring in entertainment to make sure he gets more of the what?"

"A bigger piece of that market," she answered.

"Perfect," he said, patting her hand. "You are as smart as you are beautiful, Moira St. Clair."

"And you really and truly believe," she said, pausing to make her way around a pile of garbage, "that I belong here, rather than—"

"Where? Where, Moira? Considering your current place of employ, it seems that market is saturated. There aren't enough high-brow consumers to sustain so many performers. In order for one to succeed there, they must essentially drive out the competition. But here … look again at this street." He waved down the avenue and then came behind her to stare out with her—at the masses of people, many in drab, poor clothes, but all hurrying onward. "All these people desire is a little diversion," Gavin said in her ear, "a little beauty. They're hungry for it. And no, they don't have as much to put down for a seat in a theater. But look, Moira. Look how many there are!"

She brought a hand to her throat. The throngs parted and moved about them like a river around a rock.

"Listen, might you not consider this as nothing more than a new role to accept, adapt to, absorb so you can convincingly play the part? One that could make you more famous within a new arena than anything you've ever dreamed about? Is it so impossible to consider conquering a different world than that you originally dreamed of?"

Moira tried to swallow but found her mouth dry. "Papa … My father would not have approved."

Gavin gave her a curious look. "Didn't you tell me he wouldn't have approved of you on any stage at all? That hasn't stopped you yet. Why let it stop you now?"

"I-I wouldn't know where to begin. And you—you'll soon be off to look after your own business, not some girl you met on the crossing."

He paused and turned to her. He moved his gloved hand under her chin and lifted it until she met his smoldering gaze. "You, Moira St. Clair, are not some girl. You are extraordinary. A bud waiting for the sun. I intend to open that curtain, let the sunlight flood over you, and see you in full bloom." He smiled and raised one brow. "You just might represent my greatest business opportunity yet."

She held on to his gaze, staring impudently up at him. "So … you propose yourself as my new manager? Someone to guide me in this dark and unknown world?"

His smile grew wider. "Oh my darling. With me as your guide, you have no idea just how delicious this journey shall be." He bowed slightly. "Will you accept my humble services?"

She smiled as she sashayed past him. "I'll give you your remaining two days. We'll see where that leads us."

"Forty-eight hours," he said, catching up with her. "Much can transpire in forty-eight hours."

❁

Reid rose several times a night to walk, solely because he had the freedom to do so. It felt grand to be out, free to do what he wished, when he wished, where he wished. Two former prisoners traveled with him—Garboni and Smythe—men who knew how to play the game, work hard, and get to the payoff.

Stefano Garboni appeared from the trees now, making Reid shift his hand to his holster until he knew the man was one of his. The tall, thin man's eyes moved toward his hand and then met his eyes. "That Sheriff Olsbo and his deputy are following us. They're still a half day's ride away, but they haven't lost our trail yet. And they have a third with them—someone I don't know."

"We'll shake them," Reid said, looking down the mountainside. "We need to ride above the snow line. We're making it easy on them to track us. Another day's ride and we'll make the cabin."

Garboni came around to face him, his features just discernible in the pale moonlight. "Why, Bannock? Why are they dogging us?"

Reid met his gaze a moment before answering. Garboni needed to know Reid was in charge, sure of himself. "He told me specifically to stay out of his county."

"And yet here we are," Garboni said, throwing out his hands. His eyes narrowed as he pointed toward Reid's chest. "You lookin' to get thrown back into prison?"

"The people who live at the Circle M hold the key to the treasure."

The man turned away slowly and looked down the valley too. "You sure they know the way? To the treasure?"

"They know something that can get us closer at least. Chances are, it's not easy, or they would've found it themselves."

"What makes you suppose you can find it, if they haven't?"

"I'm a driven man. I have nothing but time and dedication on my hands. They have a ranch to run, a baby, if Anthony is right. They're distracted."

Garboni thought on that a minute, then said, "I'll have to shoot them. I don't like having a lawman on my trail. Not after just finding my freedom again."

"Fine by me," Reid returned. "But you will wait until I tell you it's time. And now is not the time. We take those men down, we'll have more lawmen on our trail. And that will not further our cause. You understand me?"

Garboni turned back to him and nodded once, then walked away.

Reid stood where he was and smiled.

It was good, so good, to be back in charge.

❀

"I can't endure another day of this," Nic muttered, hauling in rope at the first mate's call. Fifteen-foot swells pitched the ship up and then down. They had narrowly survived the harrowing Drake Passage, only to encounter storm after storm as they struggled to make their way north, past the coast of Chile. So far, the South Pacific seemed dead-set against them.

There was little concern that another would hear him and report him to the first mate. The howling wind made it nearly impossible to hear. William was three feet away from him. Terence Overby kept them both on the same shift, and on the same task, because they worked so well together. "If you want to sign on for another voyage after this—" William had suggested the day before.

"Not on your life," Nic said, cutting him off. "I've paid the captain back for his imaginary debts. He said once we passed the Horn, I collect pay, just like any other. I'll take my earnings when we make port in Mexico, then I'll make my way north via railroad. I don't care if I ever set foot on a ship again."

Nic hauled again beside William, quickly wrapping the rope around the first aft mast sail, lashing it to the lanyard. It was a tricky business, not losing his footing, but with the swells and the constant rain—

At that moment a terrible sound of breaking wood cut the howling wind, and at the same time, the ship pitched hard to the right, as if digging down into the wave. His eyes scanned the water, barely settling on the horrifying glimpse of rock and reef, before the ship shuddered and pitched again. Nic lost his grip and hurtled over the lanyard, and he just barely grabbed a second rope, the action sending him spinning and swinging beneath the massive crossbeam. He reached up and got another handhold, and coiled it around his leg, desperate not to slide until he could see if he had the length to reach the deck. He looked left and right, trying to peer through the rain, back to where William was last. But he wasn't there.

Nic looked about, watched in horror as the deck planking began to pop, first one board at a time, and then in terrible rows of three or five and eight. Men were screaming, scurrying about in no semblance of order. He watched as one, a man he knew could not swim, jumped off the edge. The ship was going down. The *Mirabella* was lost. Every man knew that to stay aboard a sinking ship meant death; one could become trapped in the wreckage and drown, or get sucked down with her in the final moments, or die when a mast or lanyard came down on his head.

There. He caught sight of William, cradling his leg, his face awash in pain. Blood spread out from him like a slowly creeping red tide. Nic had brief thoughts of sliding down his measure of rope, reaching his friend. Saving him. But then the cracking planking and buckling ship reached the mast that held the lanyard from which Nic dangled.

The mast tilted, sending Nic swinging forward to the main mast. He barely had time to suck in a breath before impact. So startling and stiff was the blow that Nic splayed his hands and immediately fell from the rope, too stunned to even grasp for it again.

He fell, fell toward the cracked and broken decking, staring up into a sky filled with rain, rain, and more rain. It seemed to take forever, this hurtling through the air.

And yet he had but two thoughts as he waited for the pain of impact. *This will be the end. I am to die.*

# Chapter 9

Nic came up out of the depths from his plunge, gasping for air, and circling, trying to see anything, or anyone, about him. Ten feet off was a large chunk of the *Mirabella*'s side wall, and he swam toward it. Wearily, he hauled himself up and onto it, half submerging his raft with the weight of his body, but it was something solid, some comfort in the midst of the rolling water. Dimly, above the staccato beat of heavy raindrops pelting the water around him, above the wash of waves as they crested and rolled on, he could hear the cries and screams of men in the distance.

So he wasn't alone, wasn't the only survivor. He cupped his mouth with one hand and yelled out, "William! William!"

But there was no answering call.

"Can anyone answer me?"

Again there was nothing but the wash of the sea, the splattering of raindrops about him. He heard another man cry out in the distance one more time, and then … nothing. Had they all been carried out and away? Or drowned?

Nic shivered uncontrollably and tried to haul himself farther up on the makeshift raft so less of his body was submerged. He was weary, weak beyond any measure he could remember. He stayed where he was, willing the minutes to go by, for the storm to let up, for night to relinquish its hold on today.

At some point, he dozed off and when he awoke, Nic winced. It pained him to open his right eye, and he carefully tried the left. Bright sunlight blinded him and he quickly closed the lid, but he had seen enough in that brief glimpse.

He had washed up on a beach, broken timbers from the disintegrated *Mirabella* all around him. He managed to raise himself to his elbows and dig his right and then left arm into the coarse, tawny sand, and then again, and again, until all but his legs were free of the nagging waves. *One more time*, he told himself, panting from the effort, recognizing the cold had made his legs so numb that they were useless. It was as if he had sprouted a long tail and was beached. And yet deep inside, he knew that the cold would eventually kill him. More than one sailor had survived a shipwreck to succumb to the sea's frigid, deathly intent. He had to rise once more and dig in, pull with his right, then with his left.

At last, his feet were clear of the water.

The sand here was dry. Warmed by the sun. He collapsed into it, took a deep breath, and let the dreams spirit him away.

❁

It had begun with the saloons. Gavin brought her to one, and Moira stood in the corner aghast, watching as the men drank, many of them until they were inebriated, and then women used their charms to seduce them. A distant part of her kicked herself for not doing the same sort of research prior to playing seductive roles on stage. She watched in wonder as a woman passed a man and slowly traced her pinky finger up his arm, from wrist to shoulder, and he immediately rose and followed her from the room as if he were a hooked fish on a line.

Gavin watched her absorb all of this, this overt physical but silent communication between a man and a woman. He grabbed her wrist. "So innocent, darling. How could all this have escaped you? I want you to practice all of that. Your feminine wiles. The role, darling. On me. Consider me your free-for-all. There is nothing wrong. Nothing bad. All is somewhere on the target. All is acceptable. You can practice on me and learn. It's the only way to succeed. Agreed?"

Her eyes widened in surprise. After she nodded, he placed his hands on her waist and lifted her to the corner of the piano. "Ladies and gentlemen!" he shouted. "I give you … Moira St. Clair!"

The crowd erupted in applause and Moira immediately warmed to them. She leaned down and whispered the name of a tune to the pianist. The pianist frowned in confusion. Moira looked to Gavin, and he smiled and shook his head, and then leaned toward the pianist and whispered as well. Then, as the man ran his fingers along the keys, Gavin moved toward Moira, took hold of her heavy skirts, and slowly tucked the excess material up beneath her knees, revealing the tops of her boots—and even a bit of her calves.

She gasped and reached out to stop him. But he looked at her and mouthed the words, "Trust me."

Moira looked about the room, noticed that every man and woman had their eyes on her, and slowly she let go of Gavin's hands. The worldly song's introduction filled her head, called to her with its easy, enticing notes. She slowly looked around the room and felt an impish smile pull at her lips. Could this crowd truly be her new audience? The pianist paused when she failed to sing, and then did his introduction again. Moira sang, sang as if she was meant to be in this saloon, on top of this piano, with her body exposed to the world as if it was the most natural thing in the world. As if she belonged.

As if she couldn't hear her mama whispering to her. *Moira, Moira, what are you doing?* She shoved the voice away, finding glory in the wondering glances of those far and near in the room, warming her. Was it her slim skirts drawing the admiring gaze of every man in the room, or her voice?

Gavin moved in closer, turning toward the room with arms crossed, as if he were her personal bodyguard. But as Moira sang, all she could think of was the feel of his hands upon her body, so steady, so calm, so sure. And later, it was all she wanted to experience again.

Because never had a man made her feel both mastered and masterful at the same time.

This was what Moira remembered the next morning, as she awakened in his arms, slightly groggy, slightly aghast, slightly elated. Her virginity was gone. She was a woman, in every sense of the word.

But then, why didn't she feel … satisfied?

❀

Odessa checked and rechecked her hair, properly wound and tucked, in the mirror. She could hear the men downstairs speaking to one another in deep, masculine tones, muted through the floorboards. What would Robert McAllan think of her, his brother's wife? Would he deem her worthy? Or would he question Bryce's choice?

She shook her head and stared at her image in the mirror. "You have traveled across America to chase the cure, Odessa McAllan. You have found health. You have birthed a baby, the first in the McAllans' next generation, despite a doctor's firm warning against it. You are a child of God. If Robert doesn't care for you, then … well, let him not care!"

She lifted her chin and allowed a small smile, then she turned and lifted Samuel from his bed, moving without hesitation down the stairs to her husband, who was calling to her.

Robert McAllan, easily recognizable as Bryce's brother—but slightly shorter and more solidly built—turned toward her as did Bryce. He had blue eyes like his younger brother, but his were a darker hue. They twinkled in a familiar way, as they moved between her and the baby. "Odessa," he said, moving toward her. "At last, I meet my new sister. If only Mother could be with me." He offered her a warm hand and a slight bow with a smile, and then looked at his nephew. "May I?" There was a tender, tentative plea in his voice.

"Certainly," she said, immediately placing Samuel in his arms. The child squirmed and then studiously stared at his uncle for a long moment. Robert laughed, a deep laugh from his belly, and Odessa was moved to see a tear run down his cheek. He looked from the baby to Odessa, then over to Bryce. "Your wife's more beautiful than even you could boast," he said, raising a brow.

Bryce smiled and moved a step toward his wife. "Only God could orchestrate such a feat," he said. He wrapped an arm around Odessa and an arm around his brother, and looked from one to the other. "Do you know how many times I dreamed of this day?"

She looked up at Bryce in curiosity. He had seemingly set aside all his fears and concerns for the moment in the midst of the joy of reunion with his brother.

"Do you know how many times I dreamed of you marrying a good woman, carrying on the family name, taking the pressure off of me?" Robert returned. Odessa smiled and pulled away to take Samuel from Robert when the child began to fuss. Robert moved off with Bryce, the two in immediate, animated conversation.

Odessa sat down on the settee to watch her husband of four years, reunited with part of his family. The men laughed and teased and laughed again, boisterous, alive, connected immediately. She was fascinated. He was clearly happy to be near his brother again, but there was an edge to his voice, an undertone of fear that she hoped his brother wouldn't notice. They talked about family members and friends, catching up on years' worth of news not worthy of a telegram or letter, but both carefully steered clear of mentioning what had transpired of late on the ranch.

Odessa decided that Robert was nothing like she imagined, an overbearing older brother, belittling her husband, ignoring her. He included her, filling her in on the background of one person and then another, so she could be a part of their talk of Maine and beyond. He told her of their mother, Mary, and how she longed to hold her grandson, but poor health kept her from traveling. "The ague, you know," Robert said, the only grim note in his entire evening of conversation. "Maybe someday you could come East to us." Robert produced a fine bottle of scotch. From then on the conversation only grew more animated and easy.

She wondered at this sense of family, something she had not known—although the ranch hands had become a sort of family to her—since her brother and sister had left and she'd married Bryce. Odessa wondered where they were, what they were doing now. If they were safe. Well. If they would ever be together again, having the kind of conversation that was unfolding before her now.

Because there was something about being with people who had known you your entire life. Seen you in your unbecoming moments and in your glory. Walked beside you through dire times. Shared in the victories. Loved you through it all. Knew you through it all.

Odessa moved Samuel to her shoulder, finding comfort in his small, warm body, the smell of him as she patted his back. She moved her nose across his cheek and ear, felt his smooth skin, and eyed her husband. Bryce and Samuel were her family now. And Robert … was her brother.

# Chapter 10

Nic awakened when the waves again surrounded him. He coughed and sputtered and then forced himself to his knees, and then to his feet, reaching forward as he stumbled out of the surf. He had not far to go to gain the beach. He was on a tiny island of sand and rock, still a good swim yet from the coastal beach. To his left was William, passed out in a nook of the rock, his left leg hanging at a grotesque angle. To his right was another mate, still on his belly in the surf. The waves washed up to his waist. Dead? Perhaps.

But what dumbfounded Nic was the view beyond their tiny island, a vast, empty beach, sweeping up to a high, barren, tan mountain, some ancient volcano that even the trees had not bothered to conquer in its dormancy. Brown and more brown, as far as the eye could see.

He looked left and right. To the right, perhaps a mile or two distant, he thought he saw several figures. But they were tiny and possibly moving away from him. Other members of the crew? After a moment, he could no longer make them out and wondered if he had seen the heat waves emanating off the sand as human forms. He spun around and shaded his eyes again. There. The remnant of the *Mirabella*, only a fragment of the prow and half a water wheel visible over the green waves. Slowly, his eyes scanned the water, looking for more bodies. Had the sea sucked most of them down? Battered them upon the rocks? Were he and William the sole survivors? Where was the captain? The first mate?

Nic moved to the right, wanting to know if the one man was alive before he checked on William. The thought of losing William … He tried to swallow, but all he felt was his swollen tongue and the dry, sandy taste in his mouth. It had been late afternoon when they wrecked in the storm. Had they been washed ashore a day ago? Longer? Nic knew that a man could last days without food; fresh water was another matter.

Slowly, he knelt and reached a shaking hand to press into the cold, waterlogged man's flesh at the neck. He leaned a little farther over. Jerry Kester, of Livermore. Father of two. By his own account, husband to a shrew who drove him to sea, but a man who was expected to come home. Provide.

He was dead.

Slowly, he lifted his eyes across the rocks and up to where William had dragged himself. If Jerry was dead, there was little chance that William now lived. Not with that injury to his leg.

Briefly he considered leaving this small isle, swimming for the beach a hundred yards distant, without knowing if William lived or was dead. If he lived, how would he get him across to the mainland? But as he took a step away, he knew it was impossible. He could not leave his friend behind. On leaden legs, he moved toward William. He imagined his friend dragging himself to safety in the dark hours, to the rocks that would certainly make it through high tide. He might've seen Nic, wished he could help him, and then gave in. That giving in to unconsciousness brought Nic a brief reprieve from the guilt. He reached the man's side and quickly, before his hand could shake, felt for a pulse. Grimly, he glanced from William's pale face to his leg, where red seeped into the sand in a frightfully broad arc. The man was cold.

But then William said, without opening his eyes, "I'm not dead yet."

Nic jerked his hand away, frightened for a moment, half to death. "William! William! Where are we? Do you know where we are?" He sank to his knees, so thankful to hear the man's voice again, as scratchy and faint as it might be.

"Atacama … Coast," the man said, taking a breath between each word. He peered at him through a narrow slit in his heavy lids. "Chile. Head south. I'd wager you'll hit Antofagasta. Port … town."

William passed out then and Nic whipped away from him, hands on head. He let out a long and harrowing scream of frustration. A dead man to one side of him, a dying friend on the other. On a tiny outcropping of land that was a swim away from a beach that would lead … possibly, to a dimly remembered port town. William had only passed this coast once? Twice? Nic struggled to remember his stories, where he had sailed, what he had spoken of seeing. How reliable was a man who had lost most of his blood, a man who should not be alive?

Nic let out another cry of frustration and fear and bowed his head. If he hadn't been so dehydrated, he guessed he would be crying now, but no moisture leaked from his eyes. He knelt down to the sand and his stomach clenched, but then he stopped, panting as he stared at the sea's foam, edging in curving waves toward him in gentle washings.

Then he looked up at the sky, such a high, light blue this day. Where was that sun the day before? Where had the wind gone? "Is this all You have?" he cried upward, to the God of his father, his grandfather. He laughed without humor. "Is this all You have? Is this Your worst?" He rose to his feet. "Do You not have anything more? You think this can best me? Do You? Do You?"

He turned then, with his thoughts crystallized in his mind. He moved to William, ripped a strip off the bottom of his shirt and tied it as tight as he could at the man's thigh. The man was as good as dead, but he wasn't dead yet. Nic would see him to safety or hold him when he died, but he would not leave him here alone. He would not.

❀

"There's one thing I said I'd never do," Moira said, tucking her hand in the crook of Gavin's arm as they walked down the street.

"Ah. And what was that, darling?"

"Let a man master me. I fought too long, Gavin, too hard to get where I am." She pulled him to a stop and he faced her, in front of the dress shop. They had less than twenty-four hours left together, thirty-six, if one counted the night. Would it bother her, Moira mused, to leave him behind? She was unsure, confused. But she tried not to show it.

Gavin laughed. "I am not your master, darling," he said, lifting her hand to his lips. He raised one brow. "You are certainly mine. Never before have I been so captivated by a woman."

"By an opportunity," she corrected lightly, moving through the door.

"By both," Gavin said simply. They paused by a gown on a mannequin, then approached the counter. He smiled at the dressmaker. "We seek a showgirl costume. But not just any showgirl's gown. Something tasteful. Something suitable for an opera singer trying her hand on the common stage. Something that sets her apart, but not too far apart, if you know what I mean."

"But of course," the dressmaker said, as if this request was common. He looked from Gavin to Moira and back again. "Right this way. We might be able to modify one of two dresses I have in back for the lovely young miss."

They emerged three hours later with both dresses across Gavin's arm. "Come, darling, there's a restaurant around the corner that I think you would very much enjoy."

"So now we have the costumes. You are confident of my decision, aren't you?" she laughed. "Are you intent on me rehearsing this potential new role tonight?"

"Why not? You saw how people responded to you last night. Can you imagine what will happen if you return in one of these fabulous new dresses?"

Moira smiled. The crowd had been drawn to her last night, just as he said they would be. But she still felt separate, like an interloper. Gavin was right. She had to find the way to let the role settle on her shoulders, become the saloon singer if these people were to adopt her. If she wanted them to …

She wondered about her own hesitation. Why not take this new path? If it was more profitable than the life of an opera singer, why not try it? "I'd need a new name," she finally said.

Gavin grinned at her.

"I'd need a new name if I was to try this path for a time. Then I could return to my own name if I wanted to return to the world of opera."

"I've thought of that," he said, waggling his eyebrows. "What do you think of Moira Colorado? It's worked well for Emma Oregon to take the name of her home state."

"My home state is Pennsylvania."

"Yes, yes, I know. But there is little romance, little intrigue with anywhere along the East Coast. People are intrigued with the West."

"Even if we—I—end up in Colorado itself?"

"Even if we end up there," he said with a smile spreading across his face. They reached the restaurant, and the maître d' led them to a table for two in the corner. The man pulled Moira's chair back and then swept a large cloth napkin across her lap with a flourish.

Gavin seated himself and accepted his own napkin. "So ..." he said, "You are seriously considering this, then? I could be your manager and see to all your bookings and business."

Moira paused for a moment. It was right, this, she was sure of it, but she had learned her lesson. "I'd be happy for you to take care of all such arrangements, Gavin," she said. "But I've been taken once. It will not happen again. I'd have to be privy to all pertinent conversations, and you can't get your feathers in a ruffle if I ask to see the books."

"Done."

"And what of ..." She leaned closer and lowered her voice, glancing to a nearby table full of gentlemen. "What of our living arrangements? I told you aboard ship, Gavin, that I am not seeking a husband."

"And I am not seeking a wife," he returned, delight in the glimmer of his eyes.

"So this would be entirely a business arrangement?"

He cocked his head and nestled his chin in hand. "Now, Moira, surely you know that once a man samples a woman's wares, he feels the urge to sample again and again."

Moira's eyes widened in alarm. She looked to the other tables and was relieved to find them absorbed in their own conversation. She returned her gaze to the handsome man across from her, his eyes smoldering with desire. "Gavin, now really—"

"Really. It is the truth of it. You might as well admit to it, Moira. This is a fantastic new journey for both of us. Think of yourself as enlightened. Emboldened. Enhanced. The perfect specimen of modern womanhood." He leaned forward. "You may take me as your lover when you want me. You make the decisions, you choose. I only offer you the opportunity to be worshipped as you ought."

Moira paused and smiled. "And the spoils of war?" she asked, licking her lips. How did he manage to draw her with every word? "How would we split the profits of this venture?"

"Out of your earnings, we would cover two hotel rooms—we must maintain some semblance of propriety—food, travel expenses, costumes. Although, these first two are my gift to you. After that, the profits would be split fifteen to eighty-five, to your favor, of course." He reached out and took her hand. "I would need to see to my ongoing business every morning and possibly explore new opportunities as we travel. But the afternoons and evenings?" He picked up her hand and kissed it lightly. "They'd belong to you, darling."

She slowly pulled her hand from his, as a waiter came to take their order. Gavin glanced at her, and swiftly ordered something he knew she'd love. This man couldn't wait to see her on the stage. Relished the opportunity, along with her. "What is in it for you?"

"A portion of your proceeds, as your manager. And the ability to spend every minute possible with you, of course." He reached for her hand and lifted it to his lips to kiss again.

"What of your other business dealings?"

"What of them?" he asked, casually setting down her hand and covering it lightly with his own.

"I'm well aware that you would need to tend to them as well, Gavin."

"And I shall, from wherever we are," he said. He gave her a small smile but lifted his right hand to massage his temple.

"Headache?"

He shook his head and seemed to force a smile. "Just need my supper, I think."

"Would you wish for me to accompany you on your business dealings, Gavin?"

"A beautiful woman's company always enhances any table, business or pleasure," he returned easily. "If you would care to accompany me, I'd be delighted."

"But would you expect me to be there?" she asked carefully.

"Moira Colorado, there's only one expectation you'd face in working with me."

"And what is that?"

"That you sing, sing with everything in you. That you meet the gaze of every man and woman in every hall that you sing in, so they remember your gorgeous green eyes for weeks to come. You are magic on stage, Moira. Do you know that?" He paused, waiting for her to nod. "That is all I expect of you. To make the most of the gift that has been given you." He smiled.

He winced suddenly, his hand going to his head, his eyes squinting shut.

"Gavin?" Moira asked in alarm. "Are you all right?"

"Fine, fine," he said, another quick smile on his lips. "Just this headache. I need to eat, I think." Just then, the waiter arrived with their soup, and Moira sighed in relief. Hopefully it would alleviate Gavin's pain. Moira dipped her broad soupspoon into the crab bisque, and her mind shifted from her concern for him to wondering at the turn her life was taking. She thought of her parents and imagined how they would have taken to the idea of her taking a stage name. Moira Colorado, she mused. It sounded wrong—and yet right at the same time. Her eyes flitted up to Gavin, so handsome, so confident. He so clearly understood her and her needs. Her desire to be free, to explore. With him as her manager, she could let go of her fears, this instant, of running out of cash. He'd see to her welfare, make certain she had what she needed.

A man had stopped at their table to talk to Gavin, shaking hands. He rose and slid a smile in her direction. *Mama,* Moira thought, talking to her mother as she used to. *How can I refuse him? Look at him. He's liquid; he's so smooth. Surrounding me. Lifting me. Drenching me. Refreshing me. Is this how you felt about Papa*?

She took a quick sip of water, and then a gulp of wine. Why on earth was she correlating what she felt toward Gavin with the love her mother and father once shared?

❀

Nic left William on shore in the meager shade of a boulder. He figured he had several hours before the cold of night replaced the heat of day, potentially stealing whatever breath his friend had left. William was unconscious and shivering, a terrible shade of gray that spoke of death approaching.

Nic moved away, wincing as a thousand coiled shells, some odd species that obviously favored this God-forsaken coast, cut and poked at his bare feet in the sand. In another time, another place, he might have considered them beautiful, with their swirls of amber and coal and coral and ash. Finally he cleared them, but hopped from one foot to another as the hot beach burned his bare soles. He set off southward, as William had directed, running from one shady or damp spot to another, heading toward a hill that marked a turn in the coastline.

He tried to ignore the pain of his lower lip, cracking for want of moisture. Tried to forget the now enticing brackish taste from the ship's water barrel. He only had to reach a town, a person, and beg someone to help him return for William. That was all he had to focus on now. After that, water, food, sleep would come.

In an hour he reached the hill and struggled up the loose dry sand to the top. What he saw made him close his eyes in defeat, but the image was burned in his mind. The coast went on for miles. There was no boat. No house. No gathering of shipwrecked mates around a fire. Not even a goatherd with his flock.

He turned back, gasping for breath, and saw the sun was low on the horizon, the sky already holding the first vestiges of pink. What was over the mountain? A verdant valley? Farms? Villages? It was impossibly high, and looked to be largely made of crumbly dry sand that might collapse with each step. Would he perish simply trying the ascent?

He closed his eyes again and covered them with his palms, wishing he had tears to shed. Never had he not been able to see another human being on his horizon or at least known there was one around the corner. His eyes scanned the beach, toward the boulder where William lay. Was he already dead?

"A minute spent doing is a minute not fretting," Nic muttered under his breath, repeating a favorite saying of his mother's. He stood and haphazardly made his way down the hillside, sliding partway. What would his mother and father think of his being here? Now? Would they be proud of him, venturing off to explore the world? Or, more likely, horrified that he'd gotten himself into this situation? He grimaced, imagining his father learning that he had spent his inheritance. Frivolous investments with high promises and low returns. A good portion on high-society travel. He'd gotten as far as Italy and Greece before he turned back and spent time among the islands. There, the rum and dark-skinned women had sucked many a money pouch dry. Soon after that, he'd moved on to South America, intent on regaining a portion of his funds before returning to the United States.

He hadn't even sent Odessa a letter in six months, wishing to be on his feet again before he told her where he was. Shame, he admitted to himself, forced him to hide from her. *Coward*, he berated himself. *Able to face any man in the ring, but not a girl who has her mother's eyes, a bit of her father's concern about the mouth. Coward!*

How was she? How was Moira? Would he ever see them again?

The sun reached the horizon, sending warm peach hues across the skies. He neared William, so still, so deadly still. He knelt and felt for a pulse. Faint, but there. The man was shivering, freezing although the air was quite warm. Nic settled in beside him, wrapping a leg and arm across his body to try to lend some heat. He grimaced as William trembled so hard it sent tremors through his own body. "Hold on, William. Hold on," he whispered. "Don't die. Not here. Not now."

But as the sun gave way to stars, Nic wondered if he spoke to himself more than to William.

❀

*Bryce and Robert have settled into an easy camaraderie over the last days, a connection only born by kin. All was going well until this afternoon, when Robert asked to see the ranch books, to review what had transpired this last year. He says he only wishes to help, but Bryce bristled and moved away from the table, instantly defensive. But it wasn't the fear of what is to come that bothered me the most—it was the evaporation of that familial companionship. Before Robert arrived I didn't know I had been missing—*

A soft knock sounded at her bedroom door, and Odessa turned in her chair to see her brother-in-law. "Oh, Robert. Are you in need of something?"

"No, no," he said, giving her an awkward smile. "Bryce is off to check on the horses in the stable and I thought I'd turn in. But I wanted to thank you for dinner. It was delicious."

"Oh," she said, giving him a small smile. "You're quite welcome."

"Odessa, in asking for the books, I didn't mean … I only wanted …" He paused, sighed, and ran his hand through his hair, just like Bryce did when he was agitated. "As much as the Circle M is your business, yours and Bryce's, there's still a family stake in it. It's just the way it has to be."

"I understand, Robert. I'm certain you and Bryce will work it out." *But to what end?*

He took a tentative step and cocked his head. "May I ask what you're working on?"

"Working on?" she repeated blankly. She glanced to her desk. "Oh. This. It's only my diary."

"Only a diary? Bryce told me that you hoped to become a published author at some point."

She gave him a rueful smile. "I fear that is an old dream for me. I'm fortunate to get a few thoughts down each day, an account of life here on the ranch."

Robert stepped back and leaned against the doorjamb. "For whom to read?"

She lifted a brow and shook her head. "I do not know. Me? Samuel, someday?"

"Come now, Odessa," Robert said. "Think. You come from a publishing family. The nation is fascinated with life here in the West. Why not turn your journals into a book?" He put two fingers in the air and waved across the air, like it was a newspaper headline. "'*Journals of a Frontierswoman*,'" he said, "'best-seller.'"

She smiled. "Right. I highly doubt that others would consider the day in, day out of ranch life riveting reading."

"You never know," he said. "Look at what happened with books about the Oregon Trail. Or for miners. Even new territories. For all intents and purposes, Colorado is still new territory, even though it's been a state a while."

"I suppose that's true. You never know." Her father had always said publishing was a gamble. And that invariably, his favorite books sold few volumes and the books he rather disliked sold in the thousands. *There is no accounting for American reading tastes,* he'd say, shaking his head.

"Well, good night, Odessa," Robert was saying. "Thanks again for supper."

"Certainly, Robert." He left her doorway and disappeared behind the door of his room, closing it softly so as not to disturb Samuel.

Odessa stared at her journal. Might there be a chance that a publisher would be interested in her writing? She smiled and looked down to her lap. The slow turning wheel of publishing would take years to generate any income, if she could find a publisher …

She shook her head. She wouldn't pester old friends and acquaintances of her father's about her little book. It wouldn't be proper.

No, her writing was for her benefit alone. Her family's. That was all there was to it.

# Chapter 11

Moira glanced up to the great glass ceiling of Grand Station and reveled in this lovely moment. Such potential, such interest, such hope. Who would have thought it possible, with so little of her inheritance left in her bags? But fortune had smiled. She gave Gavin a secretive grin as he approached across the train platform, two tickets in hand. Never had she felt more alive, and part of that feeling was most assuredly due to this man, her new friend, partner, lover. She flirtatiously cocked one brow up at him. "So … tell me. Where did you decide we should begin?"

"I'm impressed," he returned. "I didn't think we'd make it to the train station without you choking that out of me."

"I can be patient …" she placed a gloved hand on the curve of her hip, adding, "when inspired. But now I'm done. Where are we going?" She plucked the tickets out of his hand before he could react. Her eyes scanned the words, once, then twice. "San Francisco," she said. "I thought you said it was—"

"I said it was saturated. The market potential largely gone. Your audience is farther afield, darling. But you wanted to see it, and see it, you shall. We'll move on from there, directly to Gunnison, to where the first front of your market lies in wait. In the meantime," he said, putting a gloved finger beneath her chin to lift it, "we'll dally … and explore … and learn what we need to in order to succeed."

"So that is it?" she asked, pulling away slightly. "You can walk away from New York, all your business, and focus solely upon me?"

"For a time," he said. "For the next few months my goal is to see Moira Colorado become the most famous woman in America."

She eyed him from the side. "You can do that? You honestly believe you can make me famous?"

He smiled. "Darling, we've already begun. Come now. Let us explore your new kingdom together."

❁

Helpless, Nic held William. The man shivered so hard he shook them both. For a while, Nic hoped to bring heat back to his friend, give him a fighting chance to live. But as the hours passed, he hoped only to lessen William's discomfort, ease his transition into death. He'd long been unconscious, but still seemed to suffer. His teeth were chattering and Nic thought they might soon break and fall out of his mouth, but he supposed it didn't really matter. Where he was going, teeth weren't really necessary. Were they?

*Just take him,* he said to God, holding William tight, hoping to lessen his tremors. *Be done with it. You're intent on it, right?* "Just take him," he ground out. He couldn't stand it, seeing his friend suffer any longer. There was no hope here, in this godforsaken land. There would be no healing, no recovery. He didn't even know William's next of kin, so there was no way for him to tell them that William was gone.

*Failure upon failure. I fail everyone. Over and over again.*

"It's all right, William," he said. "I'll find my way. Don't worry about me, man. You can be done with me, if you're hanging on for me. I'll be all right. Always am. Somehow."

He thought he'd have to keep talking to him, giving him permission to die.

But then William stilled in his arms.

The chattering of his teeth abruptly ceased.

He felt William's heart thud to a final thump and then fail.

He breathed in, once, but did not breathe out.

It was done.

Nic let him go and scrambled away. The cold chill of death was upon him, thicker than the layer of shells that stuck to his arms and legs. Nic crunched away across the shells, panting, hands on knees, staring at his cold, still friend.

He looked around. What to do, what to do now?

He'd bury William, give him a proper burial. And then—

Nic looked northward, up the beach, then out to sea.

He would never set foot on a ship again, not if he could help it.

He'd walk, all the way back to the States, if necessary.

❁

"You can't put those up," Moira said, ripping a poster from Gavin's hand.

"Why not?" he asked.

She stared down at the poster and struggled to answer him. It had her stage name, Moira Colorado, emblazoned across the top and a drawing of her in the middle, above the Gunnison Opera House, along with the dates and times of her appearances. The opera house was nothing like the Opera Comiqué of Paris, or even the opera houses of New York, where fine and upstanding men and women produced lovely stories and song across the stage. It might have been built to accommodate a minor show, even a true opera, at one time—like General Palmer's opera house in the Springs—but like so many other boomtowns that had gone bust, the owner had given in to the will of the masses and now booked much bawdier entertainment. *Whatever brings 'em in the door,* he'd said.

"It's … it's in two weeks. We'll never be ready in time."

"Come now, darling. Trust me. You've watched the girls in San Francisco. You have it in your mind, this role. I've seen it in your beautiful eyes. It's taking shape. You know the songs, we've hired the musicians, even your opening act."

"This poster says I've appeared from coast to coast."

Gavin smiled without showing his teeth. "You have. I've escorted you from East to West myself. Simply not on stage."

"It is a falsehood, Gavin. And what is this, 'Thousands of admirers'?"

"Darling, you do have thousands of admirers. Think of how many came to hear you sing in London and in Paris. They were in the thousands, if not more."

"Not more," she said, shaking her head.

"But thousands is accurate, right?"

She sighed. "It's only that—"

He wrapped an arm around her and walked her down the wooden boardwalk. "You are ill at ease. I know. This is so new for you. But trust me. Allow me to do my job. You've always let word of mouth do the work of bringing people to see you. Why not sell out every seat from opening night? I want people standing in the street in front, vying to get in because they're dying to see you, frustrated, because they can only hear rumors about how terrific you are."

Moira couldn't help but smile at the image. He reached to tuck a stray hair behind her ear.

"We'll stay here for a bit," he went on, "until word spreads, out to the smaller towns and camps. And then when we reach those towns, we'll stay only a few days, with but one or two appearances." He laughed under his breath. "Trust me, darling. You'll never feel more desired and sought after than once we begin to tour."

"Mister!" a boy called behind them. "Mister!"

They turned to see three children of about nine years in age racing up the walk. "A friend said you were paying a nickel to paste up those posters across town."

Gavin grinned at them and then at Moira. "Do you trust me?"

She nodded and looked into his bright eyes. "I do, Gavin," she said.

Gavin handed a stack of posters to each of the boys. "Now I don't want any merchants angry with us for putting posters on their storefronts. Keep 'em to the alleyways, understood? But then I want at least one on every wall from one end of town to the other. Put two on the alley walls near the saloons and cathouses." He dug into his pocket and pulled out a handful of coins. "Here's a nickel for a bucket of paste and a brush, and a nickel for each of you. Come find me at the Worthington Hotel when you're done. If I look around and see that you boys have done a good job, there'll be another dime for each."

The boys stared with wide eyes and then broke out into grins, nudging each other. In seconds they were running down the street, leaping in the air, whooping at their good fortune. Gavin was smiling as he turned to look at her again. "They understand how it works. They can provide something I need, and if they do it well, I will pay more for it." He reached for her hands. "And you, my dear, will take the stage and be the best thing any man or woman has ever seen on this side of the country. And they will pay handsomely. You'll see." He waved one hand in the air, and at that moment, Moira wondered if he were more magician than man. They resumed walking. "You'll begin with these camp songs you've been learning, taking them high and then low and then high again, building, building. And at the end, I want you to sing an aria."

"An aria?" she asked in confusion, pulling him to a stop.

"An aria. Something in Spanish or French so it sounds all the more exotic and sophisticated. Your audience will leave feeling cultured solely from having heard it. For some it will be the first fine music they've ever heard. For others it will hearken back to their best theatrical memories, if not surpass them. But you will have become their friend through the course of the evening, almost one of them with the more simple songs, so you won't be such a distant star that they can't think of reaching out and touching you. We want them to reach, darling. Long for you. Hunger for you."

Moira looked up into his eyes and saw the familiar desire in them. She sensed that he no longer spoke of the audience to come, but of his own wanting. They had checked in as Mr. and Mrs. Knapp, so they could share a room without scrutiny as well as save on the expense. It was foolish, really, to book a second room when they spent every night together. Gavin had even bought her a gorgeous yellow diamond and slipped it on her finger with the whispered words,

"Our little, delicious secret." And it was delicious. Moira loved the shiver of excitement she got passing by the hotel manager at the front desk. Did they really fool the man? It mattered little, only that she, Moira St. Clair, chose how she ordered her days and nights and with whom she spent them. For the first time since she found out Max had stolen all her money, Moira felt masterful. In control.

But as they moved inside the sumptuous hotel lobby, her eyes caught a familiar figure and face. She paused, watching the woman until she turned.

Gavin looked down at her and then over to the woman in curiosity. "Moira?"

Moira stared at her for a moment, even after the older woman fully faced her. It was not her mother. But she looked hauntingly like her.

"Do you know her?"

"N-no," she said, turning at once to resume their climb up the stairs. But the thought of her mother here, watching her, knowing what she was doing immediately robbed her of any glory she had felt. In its place was a sense of foreboding. Her stomach pitched.

"Are you all right, Moira?" Gavin asked. "You're suddenly flushed."

"I'm only a bit weary. Do you think you might leave me for a bit, allow me to rest? I have a sudden headache."

"Certainly," he said. "I'll go and fetch some ice from the barkeep, so you might have a cool cloth upon your forehead. It is a bit warm for the end of April. More like summer, I'd say. Perhaps you got a bit overheated?" They moved into the room and he threw back the covers, then moved to help her undress, slowly unlacing her corset.

"Mmm. Are you certain you have a headache, darling?" he asked, kissing her shoulder and then her neck.

"I'm afraid so," she lied. "Forgive me." Moira knew Gavin would respond to her complaint of a headache, since he so often suffered from them himself. She moved away from him and slid underneath the covers. "That cool cloth? It would be divine," she said, raising the back of one hand to her forehead.

"Of course," he said slowly, giving her the impression he did not believe her act. But as he slipped out the door, quietly closing it behind him, she had difficulty caring whether he believed her or not. Because all she could see was that woman in the lobby, the cut of her nose, the hollow of her eye, all so hauntingly familiar. *Mama, I miss you.*

She shoved away the thought of her mother seeing her here, in this hotel room shared by a man who was not her husband but masqueraded as such. Her mother and father were long gone. Her family—Odessa, Nic—were far away. This was her life now. Hers to make of it as she wished. She grasped for the fleeting glory she'd felt that morning, the brief respite of power, but failed to find it again. All she could feel was a burning in her chest, a burning that took her a while to name.

Shame.

Shame? She let out an unladylike snort through her nose and threw back the covers, just as Gavin arrived with his small towel and chunk of ice. "Thank you," she said, lifting a hand to her forehead again. "Honestly, I can't tell if I need to rest with the curtains closed and that atop my head, or to get out again under the bright sun. I'm so antsy, and yet weary too."

He sat next to her on the bed and handed her the towel and ice. "That woman downstairs … did she remind you of someone?"

Moira paused and glanced nervously his way. "She … she reminded me of my mother."

"Ahh." He lifted his chin and then dropped it. "I see. How long ago did your mother die, Moira?"

"Five, almost six years ago now."

"And your father?"

She pushed back the covers and rose, striding to the window to peek out the narrow slit to the street below. "I'd really rather not talk about it."

Gavin came up behind her and wrapped his arms around her torso, kissing her head. "Then we shall not discuss it. I could take your mind off of—"

She squirmed out of his arms and turned to face him. "Gavin, perhaps I do need that nap. Forgive me for being so discombobulated. Could you do me a favor and give me an hour alone?"

Gavin straightened his shoulders and jacket. "But of course, darling." His words were smooth, but his tone was sharp. She had hurt his feelings, the first time she could remember doing so. But before she could make amends, he strode over to the door and snapped it open, then closed it behind him with exaggerated care.

# Chapter 12

Robert climbed up the fence of the corral to sit beside Bryce. They remained in companionable silence for a while, watching the men work a few of the mares. Bryce was considering his stock, which mares to breed with which stallion. But now that his brother was here, he could think of nothing more than the day before, when he pored over the ranch ledgers. And then said nothing.

"You're in some serious trouble," Robert said at last.

"That and then some," Bryce returned, his eyes still on the mares before them.

"I don't see how you'll make it, Bryce," Robert said. He turned and stared at him, but Bryce stubbornly refused to meet his gaze.

"I'm still thinkin' on it."

"You have to go to Spain. Pick up new stock, enough to sell some for profit upon return, and enough to replenish the herd. Even then, it'll be lean for a few—"

"You think I haven't thought of that myself?" Bryce cut in, looking at his brother then, eye to eye. "You don't know anything about ranching. What makes you think you should come in here, tell me how to run the Circle M?"

Robert stared at him a moment, then turned back to the corral and licked his lips. He tucked his head and glanced at his hands, then back to Bryce. "My business is shipping. Yours is ranching. It's been the way of it for years. But the family still has a stake in the Circle M, just as the family has a stake in my shipping yard."

"And you don't see me out there in Maine questioning you about your next keel, right?"

Robert sighed. "If you had only listened to me last fall, Bryce. Built the snowbreaks, the extra stables. Given up the added water rights …"

Bryce shook his head. He pulled off his hat and looked over at him again. "I don't see a way out. I go to Spain, I'm bound to get sick again. And I can't leave, not now. Not after all that's happened, not with Bannock anywhere near Colorado, let alone stateside. I won't leave Dess, Samuel alone. I can't." He shoved his hat on his head and looked to the mountains, a brilliant blue line in the near distance, capped with receding white snows. "And yet if I don't …"

"Sell some land."

"Sell it? At a loss? That makes no sense."

Robert eyed him. "You have to do something. You're not going to make it through winter."

Bryce let out a scoffing laugh. "I lose if I do, I lose if I don't … I didn't need you here, brother, to tell me what I already knew."

❁

*23 April 1887*

*I know Bryce longs for the sea; he has longed for the spray upon his face, the rhythm of the waves as long as I have known him. And yet his paintings have become more monochromatic over the last year, as if he's forgotten the stormy gray azure of the Atlantic, the unique green of the Caribbean, the same green that he claims he remembers every time he looks in my eyes.... In the last months he's not painted at all. We've had the storm and the losses with which we've had to negotiate, and it's also been foaling season and then breeding season, keeping him busy, but we have fewer horses than at any time in our marriage. So I can only think that it is the longing for the sea that dampens his spirit, mutes his palette.*

*Might it be a good risk for him to take, to go to Spain to replenish our stock? It would give him the plan he needs to assure his brother he has things in order despite our current troubles, as well as give him a dose of the ocean he so loves. And yet it would leave him exposed to the consumption and me exposed to an attack from Reid. Try as I might, I cannot find the answer. I only know that something must be decided soon, for we are like three dancers, all without a partner.*

When they reached Westcliffe the next day Bryce accompanied her into the General Mercantile, and Robert went off to explore the town. He was intent on finding a pram for Samuel, regardless of Odessa's protest against the unneeded expense and the fact that the mercantile didn't have one. "Do you really see me pushing your nephew around the ranch in a pram?" she asked wryly.

But he was adamant. "Mother would want to know Samuel was in a proper carriage," he said. "Indulge an uncle, would you? And his grandmother from afar?"

"Oh, all right," Odessa said, throwing up her hands and letting out an airy laugh. "Do what an uncle must."

They purchased flour and sugar and several flats of canned beans and carrots and berries. "Oh, I cannot wait to add these to our normal fare," she said to her husband. "I'm sick to death of roast and potatoes!"

He smiled at her and loaded in three crates of chickens to supplement their own flock. "Summer's around the corner, darlin'. And with it will come a harvest from our own garden!" He dropped a sack full of seed packets for that garden—rhubarb, cabbage, carrots, peas, beans, potatoes, corn, and even some flowers like hollyhock and larkspur. Most crops only did modestly well in the Colorado extremes, but they'd take what they could get. The men took turns aiding her in the garden, weeding, watering, harvesting. It was one of the things Odessa liked best on the ranch. And after running out of canned vegetables in April, she was anxious to expand it this year.

"We should plant a few fruit trees too, Bryce," she said, eyeing the tender young saplings at the corner of the mercantile. "A few peach, apple, and plum."

He cast a doubtful glance in the trees' direction.

"Just to see," she added. "You never know."

He moved around the corner of the wagon and edged near her. "You never know." He reached up to touch her cheek and then bent to kiss Samuel's back. He was asleep on her shoulder. "That's one of the things I love about you, Odessa McAllan," he said, "you're always so full of hope."

She smiled and lifted a brow. "Does that mean we can try it? A little orchard?"

He gave her a wry grin. "We can try. But I'm betting those little saplings will be next winter's kindling." He shook his head. "This just isn't fruit country."

"It works in Penrose. And on the Western Slope."

"Different conditions, temperatures. But you can try it if it'll make you happy."

"Oh! Thank you!" She reached up on tiptoe and kissed him on the cheek.

"Heavens, Mrs. McAllan, what will all these fine people say?"

"They'll say 'those McAllans must be a happily married couple.'"

"They'd be right," he said, smiling into her eyes. "I'm proud of you, Dess. It's come to my attention how much you do at the ranch, for our family, for the boys. I see you, Dess. I know what you put in, day in and day out. And I appreciate it."

She hovered there for a moment, relishing his kind praise. "Should we go, then? Grab those saplings?"

"Sure," he said. "Sure."

❁

Bryce, Robert, Odessa, and Samuel were eating at Fanny's Restaurant, enjoying a delicious dinner of roast chicken and new potatoes with a healthy portion of early peas—"just came in on a train from California," the waitress announced proudly—with Samuel happily asleep in the new large pram perched beside their table. Odessa had no idea what she would do with the pram once they returned to the ranch, but it satisfied her brother-in-law to have accomplished what he set out to do.

They talked of life in Bangor, of the family's shipping business, and new trade routes that were opening around the world.

"Deciding to take part in some of the trade, rather than simply build the ships, was some of the most clever advice I ever took," Robert said with satisfaction. "You would not believe the loads of Victorian nonsense we're importing from China—shiploads of furniture, bolt after bolt of silk fabric … I tell you the truth, we could keep ten more ships busy full time, simply on that venture. And thank God for it! After losing those two ships this winter, we'd be in dire straits ourselves, had we not expanded in such a fashion."

Odessa studied him as he spoke, waiting for him to broach the subject of the shipping business success versus the ranch's struggles, but then Robert asked Odessa about growing up in Philadelphia. They realized they knew a couple of the same families, connecting them, albeit loosely, but connecting them all the same. Robert told a hilarious story about his friend trying to woo a girl that Odessa once knew, all to no avail. But the story amused her, bringing back happy memories of Philadelphia society. It all felt like so long ago …

Odessa sat back against her chair, uncomfortably full after a slice of apple pie, but completely satisfied. It felt so grand to be out, away from the ranch for the day. Most times when she came with Bryce to Westcliffe, they bought their supplies and made their way home. It never occurred to them to eat a little early and head back using the last of daylight to reach the ranch. "I love this," Odessa said to Bryce. "This is the ultimate luxury, not cooking—having someone else feed us for a change."

He smiled over at her. "You deserve it. We'll need to make it a habit, every time we come to Westcliffe." A shadow crossed over his face. Money. He was thinking about money again, the future.

Robert paid the bill, and they rose to depart. But as they were pulling on their jackets, Sheriff Olsbo and his wife entered the restaurant. The sheriff glanced over to his wife and said, "Would you mind if I take a moment with these folks?"

The short, well-rounded woman waved him onward as she followed a waitress to a small table for two in the corner. Odessa instinctively knew she didn't want to know the words that would come from Sheriff Olsbo's mouth. But Bryce reached out a hand to her, and Robert was already proudly pushing the pram out the restaurant door.

"Come, Dess," Bryce said, reading the hesitation on her face.

Together, they walked out the door and Odessa pulled her coat a little tighter around her. The evening still held spring's chill. They gathered together, and the sheriff eyed Robert and then glanced at Bryce.

"It's all right," Bryce said. "This is my brother, Robert. There are no secrets between us."

Odessa wondered, wondered when he had told his brother about that hateful day when Reid and Doctor Morton came to the ranch, murdered their ranch hand Nels, and kidnapped her.

"Reid Bannock's been sighted in the county." The sheriff's voice was low, gentle, his eyes on Odessa.

Her breath came out in a swift whoosh, and she was glad that Samuel was safely in that ridiculous pram, because suddenly, her legs felt weak. Bryce wrapped an arm around her waist. "You all right?"

She ignored his question, straightened, focused on her anger toward Reid, and stared at the sheriff. "When? Where?"

"We trailed him for two days and lost him this morning, just over the pass. He was instructed to stay away," he rushed on, his big hands bouncing in the air. "If I get a hold of him, I have the right to jail him immediately."

"Where was he heading?" Bryce asked.

"Hopefully, he's on his way West. Just took a shortcut to tell me he's man enough to taunt me."

"No," Odessa whispered. She glanced at her husband. "He knows, Bryce. He's found out about the gold bar … or he's coming for us."

The sheriff glanced around and then leaned in. "There aren't but a few who know about the gold," the sheriff said, doubt lining every word.

"But the legend is well-known around these parts, and Cañon City isn't far away. If he caught wind of it, wouldn't he come to the same conclusion as we did? That the treasure Sam was trying to direct us to was not a new treasure but rather an ancient one? And that bar might be just one of many more?" Odessa said.

She grimaced as both Bryce and the sheriff shushed her. In her agitation, she hadn't realized how her voice had risen.

"All I know for sure," the sheriff returned in a hushed voice, "is that if he dared to come 'round, he'd come up against Bryce's shotgun, with twelve men to back him up. And I'm sayin' I wouldn't question a man who shot a trespasser like that on his property."

"*If* Bryce is home," Odessa ground out. "And what if word has reached Reid that we found that gold bar in Louise's cabin? Reid has always thought we knew the way into Sam's mine. He'll find us even more irresistible if he thinks we know the location of conquistador gold, that he could simply lift and load."

“What do you mean by ‘if Bryce is home’?” the sheriff asked, eyes narrowing in confusion. “You mean if he’s not in the house?”

“No,” she said, barely shoving back tears. “If he’s in the country. If he’s in Spain.”

The sheriff glanced from Odessa to Bryce. “You thinkin’ of takin’ a trip?”

“Thinking about it,” Bryce allowed.

“I’m thinkin’ you ought to consider different options,” Sheriff Olsbo said carefully, gesticulating with his big paw of a hand. “As I said, I don’t expect Bannock will come this way. But if he did … I don’t want your wife and child at home alone.”

“They wouldn’t be alone. I’d have the hands rotating watch.”

Sheriff Olsbo raised one doubtful, bushy brow. He shook his head. “How ’bout you take the missus with you to Spain? That’s a six, nine-month trip from here.”

Odessa’s eyes lifted in surprise. Hope surged through her. It was better to take the risk and be together than—

Bryce was already shaking his head. “Impossible. The consumption makes it too dangerous for Odessa.”

“Haven’t you struggled with bouts of consumption yourself?” the sheriff pressed. Bryce glowered in his direction, and the sheriff immediately backpedaled. “I’ve said enough.” He raised both hands. “Sorry to be the bearer of bad news, friends. Let’s hope Bannock’s simply on his way elsewhere. I’ll let you know if I catch wind of anything about him. And you let me know if you head East, all right?”

Bryce took his outstretched hand and shook it, carefully avoiding Odessa’s gaze. The sheriff shook Robert’s hand too, then tipped his hat toward Odessa. "You need anything, ma'am," he said, "you come and find me, understood?"

"Thank you, Sheriff," she said. And as she turned away, she tried not to think of a reason she might need to find him.

❁

As the McAllans and the sheriff parted ways, a man bent to light his cigarette, right around the corner from them all. He grinned up at the moon. He'd been following the McAllans all over town, even sitting at a table near them through dinner, but this, this was exactly what Reid Bannock had been after. Confirmation that the McAllans had the gold bar and had not yet retrieved the rest. It sounded as if they were unsure where the rest might lay, but if Bannock was right—he'd find a way to help them figure it out.

And then the treasure would be theirs.

❁

"Bryce, what are you doing?" Odessa said, hating the high pitch of her tone. She bounced Samuel, who had been fussy since their return.

He paused as he put on his chaps and glanced toward his brother. "Now, Dess, you know I need to do this."

She shook her head. "No. No, Bryce. You can't mean to go after him."

"I'm taking Tabito with me." He reached out to her, but she took a step backward, still shaking her head. He bit his lip and looked down at the floor, then back to her. "Robert is here with you. You and Samuel will be safe with him."

"You are going after Bannock?" Robert asked calmly, from the chair.

Bryce reached for a bag and tossed it over his shoulder. "Tabito's the best tracker around. Chances are Bannock's moved on, but I'm going to make certain he has. If he's hanging about, he's after me or mine. Best to meet him head-on."

Robert rose. "Why not bring four men in here to guard your family? I'd like to come along."

Bryce cocked his head and rubbed his neck. "I'd feel better knowing you were here with Odessa and the baby. Bring in as many men as you feel necessary to back you up." He straightened and looked to Odessa. "We'll be back within a week's time. If not, send for the Sheriff."

"Why not go for the sheriff now?" Odessa said, hearing the fear in her own voice.

Bryce shook his head. "We won't know anything more than he told us!" He clamped his lips shut, frustrated by his own sharp tone. "Look," he said, raising a conciliatory hand, "no one has attacked this ranch in years, other than Reid Bannock. I'm not about to sit here and allow it to happen again."

He stepped toward her and wrapped an arm around her and the baby. "I'll be back as soon as I can."

She said nothing, only stiffened. He released her and didn't look back as he walked away. When the door shut behind him, she looked to Robert. Inwardly she was lamenting letting Bryce go without a proper farewell. What if something happened to him?

"He had to go. You see that, right?" Robert said.

"I suppose," she said, bouncing Samuel in her arms. She knew her tone was unconvincing.

"This Bannock clearly concerns you both." His brow furrowed in worry for her.

She looked her brother-in-law in the eye. "He meant to kill me and Bryce, in his effort to get Sam's treasure. We are responsible for him spending these last years in prison." She shook her head. "I wouldn't doubt that he would shoot us at a moment's notice. So yes, I am *concerned*."

"Please, Odessa, sit with me."

She ceased her pacing and looked at him. After a moment's hesitation, she did as he bade, taking the chair adjacent to his.

"There's no way I'm going to let Bannock through that door," he said quietly. He nodded toward the back porch door. "I'll stay up all night if I have to, to keep you and Samuel safe."

She returned his even look. "And I appreciate that, more than I can say. But Robert … my husband is going out to track Bannock. What if he is here? What if they come face-to-face? I have no doubt that Reid would kill Bryce. Without hesitation. I—" Her voice broke. "If he's going to risk his life, he might as well go to Spain for those horses!"

He rose and opened his arms to her, and she did the same, weeping. "I couldn't take it, Robert. We've lost so much already … to lose him …"

"You're not going to lose him, Odessa. Bryce is a great shot—so is Tabito. They'll be all right. But he couldn't sleep through the night, thinking Bannock is here. He had to be certain he was no threat to you." He pulled back and lowered his head to get her to meet his eyes. "Look at you," he said tenderly. He brushed a strand of hair off her forehead. "This is what he didn't want you to endure. He wants you to be free, at peace."

“I know it,” she said with a quick nod. “Thank you for being here, Robert. For standing with us through it.”

“I am with you, Odessa,” he said, rubbing her shoulders and then dropping his hands. “One way or another, we’ll get through this. Together.” He led her to the stairs and nodded up them. “Get some sleep. My nephew is liable to wake you far too soon.” Robert went to the front door and slipped the rifle from its perch, then turned back to stare in her eyes. “I’ll be right here, Odessa. You sleep. No man will get past me.”

There was something about him that made Odessa believe him, trust him. Bryce’s fears that he might press them, punish them for his decisions, were all for naught. This man was family. And having him here, particularly this night, calmed her heart.

# Chapter 13

Robert lingered at the table after breakfast, apparently none the worse for wear from sleeping in the chair downstairs. Odessa glanced at him from the corner of her eye, appreciating the similarities between her husband and her brother-in-law—a grin that made the corners of their eyes wrinkle when they smiled, their even white teeth, and a calming manner about them that put everyone at ease. The ranch hands warmed to Robert. He was clearly a man used to the ways of hardworking men, easily asserting himself when necessary. In minutes he had organized them into teams of two to serve as guards at the front and the back of the house for two-hour shifts, allowing them to get their other duties done between times.

Odessa's eyes went to the window again and again. She hoped to see Bryce and Tabito across the field. But there was no sign of them. As the last of the men filtered out the door, mumbling their thanks for the meal, she stood at the counter, eyes searching the bright-green grasses that signified spring, wishing it would come for her and Bryce. That they could rediscover their daily cadence, their hope, their confidence. Everything felt … off.

"Mrs. McAllan?"

Odessa turned in surprise, "Oh, Harold. Yes?"

The tall, gaunt man held his hat in his hands. "My three weeks are up here, ma'am," he said. "I'll be heading off today with my horses."

"Oh yes. Of course. We'll pack you some provisions for the road." She forced the words from her lips, what was right, what was proper, what was expected. But inside she could not match the fact that Harold Rollins was leaving the ranch a month after he had arrived, and her husband was not home. Somehow it seemed he couldn't leave while Bryce was still gone.

He seemed to sense her hesitation. "Ma'am? Would you rather I stay around until Bryce gets back?"

"No, no," she said, feigning confidence. "We're more than fine, Harold. You need to get to your wife and children."

He took a step, paused and looked back. "You sure, ma'am? I owe you such a debt, I—"

"No, no. I insist. You get ready. I'll get a sack ready for you with food." She forced a smile. "Soon you'll be home. And seven horses is better than none. It's a start," she said, quickly nodding. "A start."

"A start," he repeated. He nodded again. "Yes'm. And it's thanks to you and Bryce I have one at all. I'll never forget it." With that, he turned and walked away, leaving the doorway empty, a chasm, a portal she wished would magically fill with her husband.

"Odessa?" Robert asked, gently touching her arm. "Are you all right?" he asked, his brow furrowing in concern.

She pushed aside her hair and nodded, glancing furtively into his eyes. She was embarrassed that he had caught her in her reverie. "I'm well," she smiled. "I only wish Bryce would return."

"I understand." He moved past her to stare out the window too, crossing his arms. “He’ll be coming across that field sooner than soon, hungry as all get-out for your delicious food.”

She hoped he was right.

And that it wouldn’t be Reid Bannock instead.

❁

Tabito and Bryce ran across the ridge, hunched over, rifles in hand. Bryce was glad that the spring heat had continued, melting much of the snow from the rocks. Near three trees, they crouched, panting. Tabito reached for his canteen, took a long, deep drink and then handed it to Bryce. Bryce shook his head as he stared at the men below.

“They head to Leadville,” Tabito said. “Just as they did yesterday. And the day before. And the day before that.”

Bryce frowned at him. “I have to be certain.”

“You’ll be certain tomorrow, when we reach town?”

“Or the day after, when he remains.”

“Odessa, she will be worried if you are gone more than a week.”

“She’ll be glad to know that this threat is past,” he returned. “We will stay on this man’s trail until I say we are done.”

Tabito grunted and looked down the valley to the trio making a fire. He watched them for a long moment, took another drink from his canteen, and then glanced at Bryce. “A man such as that … he is only with others because he needs them for something.”

“I thought the same,” Bryce said. “Until I know his plans, I can’t rest.”

“Then let us learn of his plans,” Tabito said.

❁

Samuel began to fuss and Odessa finally pulled the roll of blanket away so he could turn over. But once on his stomach, he continued to cry. Wearily, Odessa opened her blouse and put him to her breast. Even the feel of his warm body against hers, his soft baby skin, his contented snuffling sounds, failed to comfort her.

She heard the creak of the stair and two doors shut, telling her that Robert was turning in for the night. She burped Samuel and placed the sleepy boy in a small bassinet, wanting him near, and stared at her bedroom door, wishing Bryce would walk in. But he did not.

After an hour, long after Samuel had fallen asleep and the sounds of her brother-in-law's snores rumbled across the hallway, she crept down the stairs for a glass of milk. Six days, Bryce had been gone now. No word. Robert had the men scout the perimeter of the ranch twice a day, and there was no sign of either Bannock or her husband. Bryce had said he'd return within the week. What if tomorrow came and went and there was still no word?

Numb, she set down her empty glass and went to the hall and took her coat from the peg. She pulled on gloves and a scarf and eased out of the house. Doc, sitting in his chair, which was tilted against the house, roused and took a moment to understand it was Odessa before him.

She waved her hand at him when he started to pick up the rifle across his lap. "It's just me. Can't sleep. I'm heading down to the stables."

He pushed to his feet. "I'll escort you, ma'am."

"No. You stay here. I need you to listen for the baby. And Robert needs his sleep tonight. He was up all last night."

"Then Ralph can see you down there," he said, brooking no argument. He rose and went to the kitchen, where the other man was watching over the back door. In minutes, they were back and Odessa and Ralph padded down to the stables in silence.

She glanced at the short, strong man beside her. He had a broad face and wide-set eyes. "Do you mind waiting out here, Ralph? I could use a little time alone."

"No problem, ma'am," he said. He held the door for her and then quietly shut it behind her.

Odessa looked around, only the light of her lantern illuminating a ten-foot circle about her. She moved to Ebony's stall, finding comfort in the horse's presence, the warm smells of the stables—fresh hay and manure and wood. She made her way down the central aisle, lighting a few other lamps, until the whole stable glowed with light. The horses nosed out over the doorways, wondering who was here, if it was morning, if there was more hay for breakfast …

"No, no," she murmured. "I'm just visiting. You all go back to sleep."

How could Bryce stay away so long? How could he consider ever leaving her for weeks, or months, when a few short days were torture? The questions whirled through her mind, round and round like a whirlpool over a washtub's drain. She was so tired, so weary of the same questions, questions with no answers.

She moved back to Ebony's stall. Her horse had been sorely neglected of late, and she wished to brush her down, maybe even braid her mane. Odessa needed to do something with her restless hands. She entered the stables quietly, relieved to find all the men away at the bunkhouse.

She grabbed a bucket full of oats and unlatched the stable door. Ebony greeted her, rubbing her nose on Odessa's leg and, as she turned, all the way up her back. In spite of herself, Odessa smiled. The horse whinnied, and Odessa rubbed her behind the ears, where she liked it best.

Placing the feedbag over the animal's head as she munched contentedly, Odessa began to brush her. Fine dust and hair filled the soft orb of lamplight as she worked, moving from the mare's head backward. Ebony seemed to appreciate the attention, especially with the added treat of oats. She stood fairly still for a good hour while Odessa worked. In the end, she took a pair of shears and trimmed the horse's mane rather than braiding it. It felt good to have a task, space, something to calm her swirling thoughts and concerns.

When she heard the creak of the stable door, she assumed it was Ralph, peeking in to check on her. She heard his footsteps stop at Ebony's stable door, sensed him lean over it.

"It's a little late for working with the horses, isn't it?"

Odessa glanced in surprise to the doorway. It was Robert, not one of the others. She clamped her mouth shut, suddenly aware it was hanging open. "Couldn't sleep," she said. She picked up the brush and resumed brushing the horse, over areas already covered, wishing Robert would go away. She needed more time alone.

"Me neither. I heard you go out and when I didn't hear you return right away, I thought I'd check on you."

She stilled and stared at him from across the horse's back. "Bryce thought looking for Reid was the wise thing to do. But I … " She glanced away, embarrassed by her fear and the tears that were immediately rising in her eyes again.

"You're afraid," he said simply. "You think he should be back by now?"

She nodded. "I'm caught between fear and fury. Bryce promised …" She paused, wondering if she should really share all. "Bryce once left me at the sanatorium to return to the ranch. He said he always regretted it. Then when Reid came here …" She shook her head. She'd said enough. Her words were best left for her husband, not his brother.

"He went for you and Samuel. To protect you. To make certain Bannock wasn't coming."

"I know it," she said, but her voice cracked. She turned away.

He opened the stable door when tears began to slide down her face. "Odessa—"

"No, don't," she said, holding up her hand. If he came any closer, aiming to comfort her, she was liable to start weeping in earnest.

"Odessa," he said, taking another step. "Please, come here."

Odessa moved around her horse, closer to him. He opened his arms to her and she tentatively stepped forward. He gave her a long, brotherly hug, and she cried harder. How long had it been since she had been held by a man other than her husband? It made her hungry to see Dominic, made her long for her father, now passed on. Robert was sturdy and strong like Nic.

"I'm sorry this pains you," Robert said, taking her shoulders in his hands and lifting her away after another minute. "I should've gone instead."

She smiled through her tears. "Bryce knows this territory and Reid better than you do. It's only right that he went."

"But you shouldn't have to suffer so." He reached out and gently pushed some hair off her face.

Robert stared at her for a long moment, his familiar eyes taking her in as if she were a wondrous creature. For the first time, Odessa realized what a sight she must be. She'd let down her hair when she went to her room and hadn't put a brush to it in hours. She moved a hand to it, as if to wind it upward, but Robert grabbed her hand gently. "No, don't. You're beautiful."

His hand remained on hers, warm.

"I better get back," she said, turning to the gate. She moved out of Ebony's stable, not waiting for Robert to follow or offer to walk her back. It was best they separate now, discern what was flowing between them. And then figure out how to set it back on course.

Ralph glanced at her as she hurried out of the stables, then followed behind her in silence.

❀

It was Gavin who decided on her costumes, changing his mind about the two they had purchased before. Three dressmakers arrived and draped them over Moira as she stood on the ridiculously tiny stage. Gavin deemed one after another too risqué, too common, too uppity. He told them to set aside anything with too high a neck, and then to set aside anything that was too low. "Moira Colorado," he said, "is not a showgirl, but any showgirl would want to be like her. She is an opera star who has descended from the heavens to bring light and beauty to a world in need of it."

The dressmakers both blinked at him in confusion but continued to try to please. Finally, they agreed on two gowns—a deep russet dress that dipped daringly in back and just enough in front, and a teal dress that clung tantalizingly at the very ends of her shoulders. Both had full skirts that dragged a bit when she walked, something Gavin said appealed to men. It drew the eye upward as she walked away, to the gentle curve of her hips and her small waist, then up to her neck and head. “They’ll be praying you turn back around, look upon them once more. Because they’ll want to see your face again—it’s a face they’ll never forget,” he said, tenderly rubbing his hand beneath her jaw.

“Wear the red gown tomorrow night,” he said. “We’ll find a black lace fan, and a comb for your hair. We’ll draw thick kohl lines about your eyes. You’ll remind them of the little they know of Spain, of passion, the exotic, but your blonde curls and green eyes will remind them of home. Make certain the pianist has the music for your Spanish aria today—you’ll bring the house down. This town won’t be able to talk about anything but you.”

“Nothing but me?” she said, arching a brow.

He smiled in her direction. “It’s already happening.” He nodded to the saloon-keeper who was wiping down the bar.

The fat man smiled but managed to hold on to his cigar. “Hiring six other men today. From the talk around town, I’d expect we’ll draw twice as many as anything we’ve seen before. After the first night, I’ll charge to reserve a table.”

“And we’ll get a cut of that,” Gavin said.

The man nodded once. “Fifty-fifty, as agreed.”

“Good,” Gavin said, turning back to her. “So tomorrow is the night we lay the bait. The next we begin to reel in the fish. And the third night, we sink the boat with the bounty. Then we move on.”

"If it will be that good of a run, why leave?"

"Because you always want them hungering for more, Moira. Trust me. I've seen this process unfold before. I'd wager we'll have some who will follow you for miles just to see you again." He rubbed his temples, obviously suffering from one of his headaches. Moira frowned. He never had a headache on their crossing. Was this too much? Too trying?

"That's the kind of excitement we need," he went on finally. "The kind of word that will spread like wildfire, so that in the next town, we'll be reeling in the fish from the first night on. Once we've been to two or three towns, I'll hire some men to go ahead of us, secure the right spot for the show, place the posters."

"It is an ambitious plan," Moira said.

"It is a profitable plan," he said with a wink as he pulled her to his side. "You, my darling, are about to be the belle of every county we enter."

❀

Moira watched from behind the curtain as the saloon filled with men, and some women. They flooded in, filling every corner of the floor, and cheered the three girls that Gavin had hired to sing a few songs to warm up the crowd. They were a sassy trio, with heavy makeup, and when they danced, they lifted their skirts as high as their knees. Sometimes higher, bringing hoots and hollers from the male onlookers and shrieks of laughter from the women. It was the epitome of the type of performance Gavin did not want her to give, and she was thankful for that.

But they did serve to loosen up the onlookers, and the contrast between what they presented on stage and what Moira Colorado presented was bridged, but clearly separate. They were showgirls; Moira remained a lady. They were crass; Moira was class. As they departed the stage, they reached out to touch the hands of those in the front and kiss a few men of the audience, blowing out every other lamp as they moved toward the curtain.

When Moira entered, carrying a lone candle that cast a warm glow on her face and singing a low and lonely tune about a girl longing for the husband who had left her for the mines, the audience hushed into a reverent silence, practically holding their breath as they waited for her to sing the next lyric, to tell the story. The song ended with the girl giving up, giving in to death, and as she sang the last note, she allowed a tear to fall down her cheek. When it dropped, she looked down with heavy lids, sighed, and then blew out her candle.

The saloon was eerily silent for several seconds before one man—Gavin—stood and began applauding. A few seconds later, every man and woman was on their feet, cheering her as well. Then she smiled and the girls emerged to light more of the candles in the lanterns, as the pianist turned to a more buoyant tune, telling the story of happier times, of the ways of a maid with a man. The music lifted into an arc and sashayed down, lifted again and hovered, showing off her broad range, trained by years of opera. But the song was written for the common man, and the common men, judging from their faces, loved it.

So did Moira. In the opera houses, people remained somewhat distant, reserved. To be certain, they rose to their feet in a standing ovation at the end of her task, but here, now, these faces showed every emotion—sorrow over her brokenhearted portrayal, delight in the flirtations between a man and woman, hope. If she moved a step, every head followed her. If she lifted her arm, they looked to where she pointed. They were raw, untried, and extremely malleable, all of which Moira decided made them thoroughly delightful to entertain.

She finished with the Spanish aria that pushed her to the very limits of her range. It emerged from an opera about a wealthy lord who enslaved the poor people of his land, forcing them to work in his fields and orchards for very little money. Moira sang the part of a young woman who was in love with a young man of her village, but an evil man came and squired her away. The majority of it was a pining, aching song, but at the end, the evil lord died, and the lovers were reunited, allowing her to relax and spin and smile, which in turn, allowed her listeners to relax too.

All of it was in Spanish, of course. There might've been one or two present who spoke the language, but the rest were no doubt following her visual cues and the story told by the musical notes themselves. The showgirls had offered to act out the brief scenes behind her as she sang, but Gavin immediately said no—there would be nothing resembling pantomime behind Moira Colorado. So they elected to risk it, gamble on the fact that most men preferred to be seen as educated, and that opera was at its core entertainment.

She never expected them to be transformed. But they were. By the time she whipped her black lace fan into its lovely arch and peered out at her audience over it, they were again on their feet, clapping and whooping and hollering for more.

But with a brief, dignified curtsey, Moira Colorado left the stage, more confident than ever that her people only wanted more of her.

❁

Gavin entered their room that night and found her standing by the window, watching the flood of people disperse from the saloon below. He was smoking a cigar and grinning widely. He cast out his hands, "Did I tell you or did I tell you?"

"You told me," she said, moving toward him and kissing him deeply.

"Moira, Moira," he said, cradling her face, "you were perfect. You played it perfectly! I couldn't be more proud of you." He kissed her again, pulling her close, seductively. But then he abruptly broke away and playfully sat her down on the edge of the bed. He reached inside his jacket pocket and puffed on his cigar, grinning again as smoke emerged from his nostrils in twin streams.

He tossed a wad of bills on her lap and Moira stared down at them in wonder. "Our bonus for the night. Saloonkeeper figures he tripled his earnings with us here." He knelt on the bed and kissed her ear and then her neck as she counted the money. Hundreds, hundreds of dollars! She hadn't seen this much money since Paris! She laughed then, and accepted him pushing her flat atop the bed, kissing her ear, sending shivers of delight down her spine. Briefly, she thought of the woman she had seen downstairs, the one who reminded her of her mother, but then cast the memory out of her mind.

It didn't matter what Mama would say now. Moira was a woman, in every sense of the word. She was free to experiment and travel where she wished. She controlled her destiny. It was good she had gone through her inheritance, really, gotten rid of the ties that were binding and foreboding and shaming. Her inheritance had afforded her the privilege of training, giving her the foundation she needed—for that she was thankful. But now she was free to do with her talent as she wished. No strings attached. And here, in the arms of Gavin, her brilliant new manager, an entire new horizon had been opened to her, as if it had been hiding behind a curtain the whole time.

❁

Odessa didn't pause when she saw Bryce and Tabito making their way across the field astride their mounts. She called something to Robert about watching the baby as she flew out the door. She ran to the fence, ducked through it, and tore across the field, crying as Bryce at last swept her into his arms and slowly turned her around. He kissed her cheek.

Dimly, she saw that Tabito had moved on, giving them their privacy, but she could only look on Bryce. She put her hands on his hairy face and looked up into his eyes, her own blurry with tears. When she couldn't say anything, so thick was her throat for the want of crying, he simply pulled her close. "It's all right, Dess. It's all right. He's gone."

"Gone where?" she croaked.

"To Leadville."

*Leadville, at least a three-day journey.*

"Looks to me like he intends to settle in there. He and his cronies separated once they made town. But our man will watch Bannock every day, for as long as we like, and report back to us via telegram, three times a week, just to be sure." He shook his head once. "He's gone, Dess. We can let go of fearing his return—if he was coming after us, he would've done so by now."

She cried again, from relief, clinging to his sweat-soaked collar, "Please don't leave me again, Bryce. Please don't go to Spain."

He hesitated and then kissed her head softly. "We'll figure it out, Dess. Together."

# Chapter 14

Moira eased into her role as Moira Colorado with such ease, it seemed like a sleight of hand, such as the magician who sometimes preceded her on stage performed. In Telluride, she paused by a poster outside a hat shop, and her eyes ran across the name, Moira Colorado, over and over. It seemed good, right. Fitting. In Colorado she had learned what freedom, what being a woman, really meant. In Colorado, she had spurned two men who fought to claim her. In Colorado she had been given her start, that first night on stage.

"There you are," Gavin said, pausing in the alleyway and doubling back to meet her. "You really shouldn't be alone here, Moira."

"It's midday. I'm perfectly fine."

"But these people have been waiting for Moira Colorado to sing for them for over a week. If they knew it was you, here ..."

She gestured toward the illustration of her on the poster—a mysterious, delightful drawing Gavin had had done of her. It showed only the top of her fantastic teal gown, her long neck, chin, and full lips, and then delicate fingers pulling the brim of a dainty hat downward, keeping her eyes hidden. It spoke of intrigue and class and ... dare she think it? Seduction. Moira Colorado was swiftly finding the power and art of it, learning from the master, Gavin Knapp. More and more she could see how he slowly drew her in, eased into her life, and filled her needs as they emerged, making her think it was what she wanted all the while. It was masterful, godlike. And she was using some of that knowledge in seducing her audience every night, making them love her, making them want her, cry out for her return, mourn her departure.

Leave them wanting more, Gavin always said. And with a start, she realized that he always made her feel the same way about him. She hungered for another moment, another conversation, another kiss. Never, when he walked in the room, did she groan inwardly, wishing to be without him. Gavin took her arm and steered her back into the flow of the busy downtown, chattering about their venue for the evening, sure to draw more than three hundred.

She couldn't imagine this life without him, her manager, her partner. For the first time, Moira wondered if they could continue like this forever. What would it be like if he left her? Returned to his world of business? How could she hold onto him? Make him feel as intrigued with her as she was with him? He loved a puzzle to unravel, a problem to fix. He was in the process of launching her, Moira Colorado, in a new field of theater, giving him endless puzzles and problems. What would happen when those riddles were solved? Would he tire of her?

She'd simply have to come up with some new way to entice him if that happened. Because a month and a half after she met him, the thought of living without Gavin was suddenly equivalent to losing an arm. The idea of it brought her up short. She hesitated, and he peered down at her, eyes narrowing in concern. "Are you all right?"

"Quite," she said, and nudged him forward.

"Good," he said, from the look on his face not quite believing her, and then adding, "I need to stop up here. Send off a few telegrams and make sure all is well back in New York. Do you mind? Waiting?"

"Not at all," she said, adding a smile. She paused outside. "I'll stand here, in front," she said in a low tone. "I want to watch the people, get a sense of them."

He quirked a smile. "Very good."

Moira lowered her parasol and then wound its fabric tightly around the rod. Then she stood there, hands perched atop it, watching the throngs of people pass by. This was largely a mining community, but there appeared to be a good number of gentlemen. Several eyed her as they passed, tipping their hats. Moira smiled demurely in their direction. After about ten minutes, a handsome one hurried by her, turned fully around to smile, walking backward, and then resumed his path down the street. After another moment, he rotated on his heel and returned to her.

"You new in town, Miss?"

"Fairly new," she said, sliding her eyes down the street.

"You need some assistance?" He raised a brow and crossed his arms, looking her over as if she were a pastry in a baker's window.

"She's with me," Gavin said, suddenly at her side.

"I thank you, sir," she said, sliding her hand through the crook of Gavin's arm. "You are most kind. If you'd care to come to my aid, please … attend my show this evening." She slid a flyer out of the cuff of her dress, handing it to the young man, whose eyes widened in surprise. He glanced from the flyer back to her to the flyer again.

"May I take it as a personal invitation?" he dared to ask in front of Gavin.

"I fear it is a most *public* invitation," she returned. "Come now, Gavin, we must be off, yes?"

"Yes," he said, but his eyes remained on the young man as they turned.

She wrapped her arm through the crook of his. She could tell by the clench of his jaw he was still irked. "Gavin, I was only doing as you taught me … encouraging the audience."

He looked down at her and studied her for several long seconds, then returned his gaze to the walk. "I want you to engage the audience corporately, Moira. The only man I want you to engage alone is me."

Moira doubled her steps. "Can we slow down a bit, please?"

He did as she bade but remained silent.

"Gavin, the only man I wish to entertain alone is you," she said softly. Did he have no idea how much she cared for him? None at all?

He slid a look at her from the corner of his eye. "Good. Good," he repeated. "So? An early supper?" He gestured toward a small restaurant.

Smoke poured out of a chimney and the street smelled of freshly baked bread, making Moira's stomach rumble. She looked to Gavin again. There was something off, different about him, as if his mind was on other things. "Gavin, is everything all right?"

"Fine, fine," he said. "Shall we?" He gestured toward the door.

Moira, giving up on understanding the current that flowed just beneath the surface, sighed and turned inward. She'd need some food before that night's performance.

Reid Bannock was striding down the street of Leadville, enjoying the high spring sun and his new town. To his left was an impressive ridge of mountains, with a new wave of miners still exploring them, seeking their fortunes—all potential customers in his newly purchased mercantile. He had stashed away enough cash to last him a while, prior to his unfortunate imprisonment, and had easily obtained it after he was freed. Now all he needed was a home, a home fit for a successful merchant. Everyone knew that such things got around—if it came to be known that Leadville Merc was owned by a well-to-do man who knew how to run a business, turn a profit, then they'd want to be seen shopping there. It said something about a man or woman.

He glanced at several posters, lined up, one atop another on a wall as he passed. Then he stopped, doubled back and ripped one down.

"Moira Colorado, Singing Sensation of the West, Coming to Leadville, Three Nights Only, May 10–13."

He laughed softly, staring at the line of her profile, remembering just that expression in real life. His index finger touched her lips, remembering the sweet taste of her. She had nearly been his. Nearly.

And now she was coming to Leadville. To a town that was rapidly going to be his town, even more clearly than Colorado Springs had once been. Right into the devil's lair. It was unbelievably perfect. Divine.

A man fell into step beside him. Dennis. "I have received a report on the McAllans, sir," he said in a quiet voice.

"Good. What do you have?"

"They suffered a terrible winter. There was a blizzard that killed many of their horses and an outbreak of strangles took out some others. Also, Mrs. McAllan has a son, an infant of about eight or nine months old."

"I see," he said, carefully keeping any glee at their misfortune from his voice. "What of the O'Toole mine? Or the gold bars?"

"That appears to be a dead end. May even be rumor rather than fact. They've not touched the O'Toole land, nor have they brought any bars to the county assessor. They seem to be pursuing ranch life as if that is all that is ahead of them."

"Oh, they know where it is. I'm sure of it. They're just biding their time, deciding when to let the world know where the gold is and how much they've found."

"I think not," the young man dared. Reid shot him a narrowed look and the man quickly amended. "There's something else. There is some speculation that Bryce McAllan might head to Spain to secure new horses to supplement his herd."

Reid paused and stared down at the man. "Are you certain? He would consider leaving his wife and child alone on that ranch?"

"Well, yes, other than the twelve ranch hands and foreman. McAllan's brother is there visiting. Perhaps he'd stay on."

Reid looked to the mountains and let a low, small laugh emerge from his lips. "That is too perfect. She and the gold'd be there, ripe for the picking." He lifted the poster in his hand and glanced at it again, then folded it into a tidy square and pocketed it. First Moira, then Odessa. If only he knew where Nic was, he could complete his three-act play of revenge, one after another. The St. Clair siblings would know, once and for all, that they had messed with the wrong man.

They continued their walk to the store. "There is one other thing I need you to see to immediately," he said. They paused, tipping their hats to a lady and gentleman passing by, and continued on.

"What is it, Boss?"

"There is a man following me—don't turn around—as he has ever since I arrived here. I believe he must be a detective, hired by the McAllans to keep tabs on me. I want him to disappear as soon as I give you notice. Get Chandler, Abercrombie, whoever you need. But get the job done. And I don't want him to turn up. When the time comes, make sure he's disposed of properly. Understand?"

"Yes."

"Then ransack his hotel room and find any telegram he's received, as well as any receipts of those he's sent."

"Done." Dennis peeled off from his side and disappeared down a side alley. Reid could feel the detective shadowing him, about fifty paces back. Who did he think he fooled? Maybe he didn't care. Maybe he wanted Reid to know he was there, hovering, watching. It mattered not.

Reid pulled the poster from his pocket and looked it over again as he walked. In a few days the detective would be gone.

The man would never have the opportunity to warn Moira that Reid lay in wait. And the man would continue to send the McAllans—or whoever had him watched—telegrams, lulling them into a sense of safety. And then, only then, would Reid strike.

Reid pocketed the poster again and whistled as he continued down the street, to a house newly for sale, on the corner, just three blocks off of Main. It was a fine house built for a miner who had gained much and then lost it all, such a common story in these mountains. He could relate to the story, but his fortune was about to turn again. Because Reid Bannock would inhabit and make fine use of the home. It was a merchant's house, a wealthy man's home.

It was the house of a victor.

❀

Bryce heard Robert and Odessa laughing as he came downstairs with the baby. It still surprised him, that his brother and wife got on so well, but it pleased him. When he arrived though, their banter stopped and all was quiet. Bryce frowned. "Something going on here I need to know about?"

"No, no," Odessa said, turning toward him and giving him a kiss on the cheek before taking the baby from him.

Deciding to look beyond whatever secret they shared, Bryce sat down at the table and gestured to both of them. "While I was out there, tracking Bannock, I had time to think some things over. Having him so close to the Circle M," he paused, tucked his chin, and grimaced, "reminded me that I don't want to ever be gone from this place again if he chooses to visit." He looked directly at Odessa and reached out to take her hand. "He might come back, Dess. I can't promise you he won't. But I don't think he will. If he does, we'll face him together."

There was such relief and gratitude in her pretty blue-green eyes that Bryce nearly wept at the sight. But when he glanced at Robert, his brother was leaning back in his chair, arms folded, chin down.

Robert looked up at him. "How will you make it through, Bryce?"

"I'm well aware of how I've endangered my family, the future of this ranch," Bryce said, holding up a hand. "I don't need you to remind me."

Robert's lips pressed together in a grimace. "My intention is not to remind you of your failures but to help you figure out a solution."

"Right, right," Bryce said, laughing without humor, "you're always there to help, aren't you?" He shook his head and leaned forward. "Fact is, Robert, you've never trusted me. You've always thought you could run this ranch as well as the shipyard. Certainly better than I."

"Now, hold on!" Robert moved his head back and forth, as if thinking of a retort, but disagreeing with his words. "In a different world, you might've spent your life as an artist. Your paintings are among the finest I've seen." He leaned forward too. "I've always been a businessman, always had an interest in the family businesses. Bryce, we both know that. It's fate that made you ill, forced you from the sea, robbed you of your subject matter. Not me. But even as a boy, you had a gift with horses—there are none better than you. Father saw that. I see that. Are you so prideful that you cannot accept some simple business advice?"

Bryce shrugged one shoulder. "What would you suggest?"

"Send me to Spain," Robert said.

Bryce let out a guffaw. "You? You hate being at sea with a load of horses. Their fear drives you mad."

Robert gave him a rueful smile of agreement, and Bryce felt a bit lighter, sharing in it. "Then send Tabito, and two of your men who know horses well. Dietrich. Doc."

Bryce sighed and sat back. He needed his foreman here.

"All right, all right," Robert said, both hands up. "At least hear me out. Long term, this ranch can't succeed unless you supplement periodically with fresh blood. Isn't that what you told me? Now I don't care where you get that blood—stateside or directly from the Spanish breeders you so favor—but someone has to go after them. Given your consumption and your desire to be here with your family," he said, nodding toward Odessa and Samuel, "I'm thinking you're not liable to go anywhere they can't go too, and those places are fairly limited."

Bryce raised a brow and nodded slightly, bringing a hand to his chin as he thought through his brother's words.

"Now's the time, Bryce," Robert continued, "to train some others to do what you cannot. At least to try. But Bryce—Tabito, Doc, Dietrich, they're men who've worked these horses with you for years. I'd wager they'd make their way and do well by you."

"If you could get Tabito to leave the Circle M," Odessa said with a warning look. "I don't think he's been farther than Westcliffe all the time I've been here."

"All right then, some other man is likely more than willing to take his place."

"There's still the problem of cash," Bryce said, forcing the words out. "We have none set aside—all our money is tied up in the land and horses."

"And I don't have much to lend, after losing two ships this last year. It's not fair to the shipyard for me to risk my margin here. I hope you can understand that."

The three sat in silence for some time, thinking.

"What about the gold bar?" Robert asked, leaning forward. "Isn't this a wise time to cash it in?"

Bryce looked at him, then to Odessa. She gave him a small nod. "It'd get us started. But it wouldn't come close to buying the horses we need. I was thinking we'd use it to see us through the winter, as we rebuild the herd."

Robert nodded, still thinking. Then he took in a quick breath, eyes wide. "I've got it."

"What?" Odessa asked.

"Your paintings, Bryce. Conner sold that one you painted ten years ago to a friend for a handsome profit. People love how you capture the sea, and ships. Do you have any others?"

Bryce looked at Odessa, and she smiled at him. "I have about twenty or thirty upstairs."

"Twenty or thirty?" Robert asked in a voice tinged with excited surprise. "That's grand, grand, brother." He sat back, obviously calculating in his head. "For what I can sell them for back East, that'll come close to buying thirty horses."

"You're joking." Bryce looked to Odessa, and she obviously shared in his surprise.

"I'm not. Listen," he said, gaining momentum, "we'll organize an auction. I'll invite every art collector I know. You pay a bit to the auction house, but they'll garner far higher prices, in a far more efficient manner, than I might ever hope to attain."

"Which would be terrific," Bryce said, "but I still think we'll be short of cash, come winter."

Robert sighed and leaned back. "Right." After a moment more, he said, "So … tell me more about what you know about old Sam O'Toole's treasure."

# Chapter 15

Moira and Gavin made their way through the best towns of Colorado, carefully chosen for their distance from major cities but still prosperous base. Gavin quickly groomed three young men to go ahead of them—and they plastered every upcoming town with posters, talked to newspaper editors, chatted up barkeeps and hoteliers alike. In each of those towns, Moira stayed only two to three days, meeting and charming the leaders of each community and singing in the largest venue available in each. In some towns, it was a local saloon. In others it was an "opera house"—sad comparisons to those in which she once sang. But Moira grew to not care; the money she was making each night was triple what she made in Paris, and she had few expenses, other than the "poster boys," as Gavin called them, Gavin's cut of 15 percent, and hotel and food and travel and her warm-up acts.

She moved down the street of Telluride on Gavin's arm. He wore a dapper new suit and hat that perfectly complemented her new ruby gown. This one had a slightly longer train than the previous dress, which she wore tied in a bustle during the day. It was of an exquisite Oriental silk, with tiny covered buttons on the bodice, and a daring dip to the center of her back that made the men howl when she lowered the shawl that covered it, like a secret that she held until the end of each show—Gavin's idea.

Gavin tugged on her arm and pulled her to a stop, staring in the window of a photographer's shop. Moira moved to stand beside him and looked upon arresting images of Indians and pioneers, children and old people. "This man has an artist's eye," Gavin said with glee. "Come."

They moved inside, a bell tinkling overhead, but no one appeared to be there. "Hello?" Gavin called.

"Hello?" Moira added.

"Just a moment!" called a muffled voice.

"Darkroom," Moira guessed. It reminded her of Odessa and her friend with the camera in Colorado Springs. Was Odessa still making any pictures these days? Or was she too busy as a rancher's wife and mother? Not since Paris had Moira been in a place long enough to receive word. Perhaps here, she could send off a telegram, let her sister know she was so close—but a few days' journey away—and request a response in Silverton, their next stop. She was curious about her sister. And maybe Odessa had heard from Nic.

"Look here," Gavin said, gesturing to the downward cast of a woman's eye. "And look at this one," he said, hovering over a smiling woman's portrait.

One never smiled in pictures. Did they?

"He'll be just the one," Gavin said. "He'll create a stunning portrait of you, my dear, that we'll use on every poster for the coming year. It will be phenomenal."

"You think it wise?" she asked doubtfully. "There is something about photography that is even more intimate than portraiture. It's so real."

"Exactly," he returned. "It will be titillating, eye-catching. No one will be able to resist looking upon your visage."

"What exactly—"

The photographer emerged then, from the darkroom, smelling heavily of developing chemicals, odors that again brought Helen and her sister to mind. Had it only been a little over five years since that day she and Odessa visited Helen for the first time? That seemed preposterous, with all that had transpired since then. The proprietor, lanky and tall, peered at Gavin and Moira over a pair of half spectacles. "May I help you?"

"Yes," Gavin said. "This is Moira Colorado. Perhaps you've heard of her?"

The man looked down at her, studied her a moment, and then shook his head. "Forgive me. I have not."

Gavin shoved down his bit of irritation and moved on. "The lady is an entertainer. A singer. And we are in want of a portrait for a new poster to advertise her coming appearances. You seem to be able to capture the unique, sir, and we wish to hire you to do the same for her."

The man came out from around his counter and looked at Moira. "Very well," he said with a sigh, as if his vocation wearied him. He edged to the side of her and directed, "Chin up, my dear." After studying her a moment, he walked around her, analyzing her from behind. "You have lovely posture."

"Thank you," she returned.

He moved on to her other side, still perusing her, like a sculptor studying his model. It appealed to Moira, reminded her of artists in London and Paris she had once known … and after several weeks in the intimate venues in which she did her shows, she found that she was comfortable under the intense scrutiny of his gaze. He moved back behind her. "Miss Moira, would you feel comfortable dropping your shawl?"

"But of course," she said, slowly sliding it around her shoulders and into her hands. She started to turn, but Gavin halted her.

"No, no, stay where you are." He looked to the photographer and motioned him over. "Look at her from this angle," he said to the photographer. To Moira he directed, "Look over your right shoulder at us."

The photographer nodded. "Yes. That would be perfect."

The man walked several paces to her right. "Now look up here." He pointed to the top right corner of the showroom ceiling. "Good. Don't move." He returned to Gavin's side. He was shaking his head. "I'm sorry but this is far too suggestive. Do you see that when she looks back at us, she is a seductress. I assume you are not marketing a whore's services."

"No," Gavin conceded before going on. "But don't you see—there is a touch of innocence that is equally enticing, yes? She is innocently seductive, as if caught unawares."

The photographer was deep in thought. "I shouldn't agree to this," he said. "I have a reputation as a decent businessman, a—"

"And as an artist," Gavin coaxed. He waited for the man to take the bait. Moira watched it unfold, had seen Gavin manage to get his way in similar situations countless times, though she was as amazed at his gift as if this were the first "negotiation."

Finally the photographer arched a brow. "Very well," he said.

"Grand," Gavin said. He barely could keep the glee from his voice. He looked back at her, and Moira shivered in pleasure. She felt more beautiful and daring than she ever had before. "Can you do the portrait now?" Gavin pressed.

"But of course," said the man. He quoted Gavin a price. Gavin quickly laid out the cash on the counter. "Let's get several renditions," Gavin directed, laying another bill on the counter. "I want it to be perfect."

"Done," the photographer said, scooping up the money and placing it in his small register.

❁

They conquered Silverton and then Ouray, and the new poster photograph accomplished what they intended—crowd attention. It was eye-catching, evocative, and yet innocent and hopeful. It elicited gasps and whispers, but over and over, they saw people stop and peruse the poster as if trying to decipher what caught their attention.

After a long train ride to Crested Butte they met with the proprietor of the opera house, Andrew Wiman. He was young, as handsome as Gavin, and terribly debonair. Moira moved toward the tall, sandy-haired and blue-eyed man. He looked down at her and slowly kissed her hand. His eyes traveled up the length of her arm to her face. "You are as lovely as your posters promised, Miss Moira," he said.

"You are too kind," she said, flattered by his attentions.

"Not kind, simply honest," he returned. He looked to Gavin, then to Moira, then back to Gavin again, clearly assessing them both. "I assume you travel as man and wife to cover your affair," he said in an even, quiet tone. "But I would be most appreciative if I could steal Miss Moira away for a dinner alone this night. She is an entertainer in my opera house. I always consider it a privilege to be privately entertained before opening night."

What did the man intend? Moira looked with alarm from him to Gavin, but Gavin was staring solemnly back at him. "I assume you speak of supper only, nothing more."

Andrew smiled impishly. "Why, Mr. Knapp … of course that would be all. I simply love the company of a beautiful woman and am in the position to request it. Do you mind it, terribly?" He turned his gaze on Moira. "Or do you, Miss Moira? I shall immediately rescind my request if I offend."

"No, no, of course not," she said, immediately sliding a dainty hand into the crook of his elbow. She glanced Gavin's way. He was silent, considering, playing the game—and she assumed he wanted her to do the same. "But Andrew, I shall expect the finest supper this town can offer."

"Of course," he said. "And I always insist on champagne. I'll have her back by seven," he tossed over his shoulder at Gavin, not waiting for a response.

Moira glanced again at Gavin and smiled her farewell, covering her shiver of glee. Gavin was seething, clearly jealous. It was just where she wanted him, again thinking solely of her and not of business affairs in New York as he had been that morning, sending telegram after telegram.

❀

"I didn't need your front men to tell me I wanted you in my opera house," Andrew said once they'd finished the main course. He leaned over the table as if sharing a secret, "I knew I wanted you here from the first time I heard your name. Moira Colorado. You are on your way, miss."

"My success is largely Gavin's doing," she said. "I was preoccupied with opera in Paris. It was he who showed me that if I simply modified my goals I could find a much broader audience."

"Much. He's a smart manager. He gained a mistress and a moneymaker in one move."

Moira frowned. "Please. Lower your voice."

"You are ashamed that he is your lover?" His brow lowered as if he was laughing at her.

"Andrew, I must insist," she hissed. "Please. Lower your voice."

He picked up her hand, looking at each finger. "I figured you as a cultured woman, a woman of today. But you have a streak of innocence that is terribly provocative." His eyes moved to hers, and she pulled her hand away. "Do you wish to leave your partnership with Knapp, Moira?" he asked, leaning back in his chair. "There are other opportunities, you know. Other men of substance."

*Like me,* he was saying. She was flattered and yet flabbergasted by the man's forthright manner. But Gavin promised her a future, new adventures, not a dull life stuck in a town destined to fade in time. And yet this man owned the opera house in which she was to sing. She could not offend him or close this door yet. As if reading her mind, Gavin arrived at their table then, and Moira breathed a sigh of relief.

"Finished, darling? I thought I might escort you home."

Andrew covered a smile with his hand and then looked up with a sober face. "It was kind of you to see to us. Yes, we're quite finished. Although we just had the most illuminating discussion. I believe that

Miss Moira might be up all night, thinking about it. Forgive me for getting her mind on other things besides the show. We all know how important it is."

Gavin looked down at her, a slight frown in his brows. Did he have another of his headaches? "Come, Moira." He reached for her hand. "You need your rest before tomorrow. Andrew is quite right about that."

Andrew rose with her. She offered her hand and he kissed it, elegant and smooth in his movement. "Until tomorrow."

❁

Nic made it through thirteen days and nights, steadily making his way north via the narrow, winding trade roads, before the smell of roasting meat brought him to the edge of a village. The abuse from outsiders in these high mountain towns had made many a villager leery of newcomers, more apt to strike with an arrow than offer a cup of water. After two such experiences, Nic decided he was better off not encountering another.

He hid in the brush watching a native family preparing a meal. At the smell of roasting meat his stomach rumbled. He pressed a hand to halt the sound and his eyes widened, fearful that his body would betray his hiding place. After a few tight breaths, he watched in relief as two village women came to turn the goat on the spit. They moved on, back to tiny huts, apparently to tend to children whose voices he could hear.

The meat cracked and sizzled. Downwind, so the smell wafted over to him. His stomach rumbled again. Weeks aboard ship, well fed but constantly at work, had left him lean, taut. Nearly two weeks on this trail had him starving, on a diet of berries, leaves, and as of yesterday, bark he'd seen the green-faced monkeys eating. He had to have something more, something of substance, if he was to make it. He was slowing down, nowhere near his prior pace of twenty miles a day. He was lucky to make ten miles now.

*I must have some food.* He rose dizzily from his squatting position in the brush and looked, as if in a dream, left and then right. No men were in sight, just a couple more women. *Just that leg from the charred side. I'll leave the rest.*

He moved forward on stiff legs, drawing very near one of the huts. A small child with big eyes came to the doorway and watched him, hand in mouth, as if Nic were some sort of exotic bird, landed among them.

Nic brought a finger to his lips and winked, hoping to keep the child in rapt, silent attention.

He was a foot away from the fire when the boy child looked over his shoulder and said something to his mother.

Too far from the forest for safety, too close to the meat to give up, Nic stepped forward and grabbed the hoof of the goat and yanked. But the meat was still partially raw and didn't release in the moist, succulent manner in which he had fantasized, popping at the joint, tearing neatly away …

He frowned and tugged again, even as a woman screamed in outrage. He could sense others emerging from their huts, adding their cries. And that was when he heard the answering call of the men.

Grieving his loss, but certain he would be killed if caught, Nic turned and ran. He dived into the jungle and moved downhill. The one time he stopped, an arrow came whizzing through the trees, striking a trunk three inches to his right. Poison darts.

Nic ran until nightfall and the dense canopy above him kept him from navigating by the stars. Frightfully dizzy and with his knees collapsing beneath him, he edged under the wide, umbrellalike leaves of a low-hanging bush and curled up as tightly as possible.

He slept until the screech of monkeys and cries of the birds edged him awake. He knew he couldn't keep on, couldn't make it all the way up and out of Argentina, let alone through Central America and Mexico. Distantly, he considered the desire to allow himself to remain right here, to go to sleep to the jungle's lullaby and never awaken.

*Odessa. Moira.*

*Look after them. Make certain they are all right.* His father's voice echoed in his ears, years after the fact. Nic opened his eyes and stared at the spine of the broad leaf above him, now illuminated by the meek sunlight that infiltrated the canopy. He hadn't written in months. Hadn't been long enough in one spot to hear from Odessa in a year. What had happened with them? Were they all right? What would it be like for them if he disappeared? Would it be a relief? Or would they forever wonder about him?

He closed his eyes and sighed deeply, thinking of his sisters' faces. He couldn't stand the thought of them, either of them, fretting over him. Moira was likely busy with her own life, but Odessa would be wondering, wishing for a word. He'd doled out the inheritance from their father and walked away, only able to see his own path. But that had never been his father's desire; his desire for Nic and the girls was that they might somehow, some way, remain connected. Family.

And Nic and Moira had run as far away as possible.

*Failure upon failure.* Dominic St. Clair could not allow it, could not allow himself to die with such a word ringing in his ears. He was a fighter. A fighter!

Wearily he rolled to his knees and forced himself to his feet.

In a day he made it to the coast. Half a day after that, he made it to a small port and begged for a small bowl of gruel. An hour after that, he grimly signed his name to an Argentinean captain's log on a ship bound for California. He laughed at himself for going against his promise to never again walk a ship's gangplank, but if he was to reach America, he'd have to trust his life to the frail confines of wood and steel and sail and steam. His clothes hung on him. He stared down at arms and legs wasted by lack of food and chronic dysentery. He ignored the taunts that came in Spanish and Portuguese in his direction, words easily translated by tone alone, even if he didn't know the languages. *Ghost. Dead man.*

He trudged down the ladder to the hold, found an unoccupied cot, and pushed aside an insect-infected mattress stuffed with hay, preferring the hard, clean wood below. It seemed as if he had just drifted off to sleep when a man was shaking his shoulder, shouting to him in Spanish, obviously telling him to get up, to meet the "Capitan" above. The man turned at the door and then tossed a biscuit to him.

Nic, groggy from lack of food, barely caught it.

"Put some muscle on that skeleton," he thought the man said, loosely translated, "or the captain will toss you overboard."

# Chapter 16

For the third time in as many days, Odessa, Bryce, and Robert talked over what they knew of the clues Sam O'Toole had left behind. "We find the treasure, it resolves our cash crisis and saves the ranch," Bryce said, hands on his head, thinking.

"It's a long shot," Robert said. "If no one's found it by now … think of all the shepherds that have wandered those hills and caves for decades now, to say nothing of prospectors. Seems as if that gold wants to stay hidden."

"If it's there at all," Bryce said.

"May I see it? Sam's Bible? The gold bar? For myself?" Robert asked.

Odessa and Bryce shared a look, silently asking if the other one agreed, and then Odessa went to fetch the Bible, while Bryce went to the door and locked it. After glancing out the window, he pushed the kitchen table to the side and lifted a floorboard. He pulled out a cloth-covered bundle, about the size of a brick.

Robert smiled and waggled his eyebrows. "There's a bit of this that makes me feel like a boy playing pirate."

Bryce smiled. "Me, too. That's why I don't want to get too carried away with it." The three of them sat down at the table.

Robert finished unwrapping it and set it before him on the table. It was a dull color, and there was clearly a Spanish cross on the top, along with roman numerals, apparently denoting date and weight.

"It might be the only one," Bryce said. "For all we know, Sam cashed the rest in, maybe even melted them down. He always seemed to have plenty of money. Or maybe it was his father who had found it and hidden it away for a rainy day. Maybe Sam never laid eyes on another gold bar himself, other than this one."

Odessa unfolded a piece of paper. "This was the poem he left for me. He referenced 'treasure that burns, and that which is eternal,' which we assume refers to some sort of real treasure here—whether it is this one gold bar or a stack of them—and here, here's Louise's Bible." She turned it toward him and slid it across the table.

"Gaelic?" Robert asked, flipping it open.

"We believe so. You'll see seven bookmarks inside—I've been through every page. And it's the only thing I could see that might be a clue for us."

Robert went to the first, then the others, seeing the hand-drawn symbol of a cross with three small drops beneath each arm.

"Sangre de Cristo, blood of Christ," Bryce said, tapping on one. "It's why we believe it's in our mountains, rather than in the Wet Mountains near Sam's claim."

"It was our thought, anyway," Odessa said with a sigh, sitting back in her chair. "But it could take twenty years to check each of the caves up there. And when you find a cave, how far do you go back? It's rather dangerous."

"I would imagine," Robert said.

"And there are many that are overgrown with shrubs, even trees,"

Bryce said. "You could pass within three feet and never know they're there."

"You'd need quite a few men searching," Robert mused, scratching his chin, "in an organized fashion."

"My thought too," Bryce said. "But I just can't justify tying up my men on such duty, not on top of all the duties down here ..."

Robert turned back to the old Gaelic Bible and randomly opened it. "*Anns an toiseach bha am Facal agus bha am Facal Maille ri Dia ...*"

"Do you read Gaelic?" Odessa asked, hope surging in her heart.

"I can read it," Robert returned ruefully. "I just can't translate it."

"We compared it to our Bible in English," Bryce said. "We're reasonably sure that every cross and blood drop mark is near a reference to the word *gold*."

"Okay, Mr. O'Toole," Robert muttered, looking from one reference to the next. "What were you trying to tell us? Genesis ..."

"The first book?" Odessa put in, standing to pace. "Meaning, 'Begin here'?"

Bryce went to the corner of the den and fetched their English Bible. "Here are the verses we found," he said. The pages were still marked. He read them all aloud to Robert and Odessa. But the words gave up few clues. Most had to do with jewels and gifts of gold.

Robert blew out his cheeks and leaned back in his chair. "Go back, Bryce. Read that second reference."

Bryce turned several pages back. "The name of the first is Pison; that is it which compasseth the whole land of Havilah, where there is gold," he read.

"Start earlier," Odessa said. "Maybe we need more context."

He looked to the previous verse. "And a river went out of Eden to water the garden; and from then it was parted, and became into four heads." He looked below the reference. "And the gold of that land is good; there is bdellium and the onyx stone." Odessa moved to the window, ignoring the sounds of Samuel waking from his morning nap.

"What's bdellium?" Robert asked.

Odessa moved back to the bookshelf and pulled out a dictionary and read the definition. "It's a plant, producing a gumlike resin." She lifted her head. "Ever seen anything like that?"

"Seen anything like a river, parting in four?" Robert asked. "High up, where you take the herds in late summer?"

Bryce pressed on either side of his head, as if he intended to squeeze out a memory. "No," he said, shaking it. "I've been all over the place up there, and I can think of places the river divides into two or three, but not four." He rose and padded off to his study.

Odessa turned to the definition of *onyx*. In mineralogy, it referred to straight, parallel bands of alternating colors. It also meant a pure black, ebony. "Have you seen any black rocks or bands of rocks?" she asked.

"No, I don't think so," Bryce said. He unrolled a map of the Circle M atop the table. It was old, but fairly comprehensive.

Odessa thought back to rides through high canyons and over ridges. No, most of what they saw was iron-rich granite and limestone. Hues of rose and salmon and sand, but no black.

She sighed, then spoke reflectively, "Sam, what did you want to tell us? How to discover the treasure or focus on the treasure we have here, now? Or both?" She stared up toward the mountains. Maybe the notations were his mother's.

Louise. She'd been a sheepherder over in the Wet Mountains, but they had brought their sheep west, through what was now the Circle M, and high up into the Sangres during late summer. It would've been thirty, forty, even fifty years ago, back when they were the only white people for miles, fighting off Indians and loneliness.

Odessa studied the map that showed the high meadows Bryce and the men favored for taking the horses for summer grazing. "Bryce … read that second reference again, would you? The one about Havilah and something?"

Bryce turned the page in the Bible and read, "'The name of the first is Pison; that is it which compasseth the whole land of Havilah, where there is gold.'"

Odessa smiled and tapped the map. "Havilah—could that not have become Avilla Canyon in time? And look—No Sip Creek. What's No Sip backward?"

"Pison," Bryce whispered. He grinned and then came around and picked her up. "That's it, Dess! That's it! The clue we needed!"

Odessa blushed, embarrassed under Robert's warm gaze. "Put me down, Bryce. We have plans to make!"

But Bryce was already ahead of her. "I'll set off at sunup. Nobody knows that high country like Tabito and Dietrich—I'll take them with me." He looked to Robert. "I'd feel better if you stayed here, to watch over my family. Bannock doesn't appear to be turning our direction again, but I don't like the idea of them ever being alone again."

Odessa let out a little sound of frustration. "I want to go with you! It will be the death of me, sitting here, wondering if you've come upon it!"

"Don't get too excited," Bryce warned, sobering. "I still doubt it will be easy. We only know we're bound to be in the right canyon. We still could be searching a hundred caves."

"We'll hope there aren't as many," Robert said. "And that you'll see black rocks or odd plants that help you find your way."

Bryce smiled. "I'll go talk to the men now. And ask to see if any of the others have seen anything like it."

"Just make sure you don't make them suspect what you're up to," Odessa said.

Robert laughed. "If you do, you might have your own gold rush right here on the ranch."

❀

After supper Odessa settled on the settee with a cup of tea. Bryce was down at the stables, due back any moment. She drew her afghan across her lap and looked over to her brother-in-law, who held Samuel, smiling at him, trying to get him to smile back. The baby only stared dolefully back at his uncle. He held him up so Odessa could see, and they laughed together. "So … you're the eldest. Expected to carry on the family name. Why haven't you married, Robert? Had a family?"

He paused for a long moment, as if frozen.

She instantly regretted the intimate question, was formulating a polite way out, when he said, "I never met the right woman like Bryce did. Thought I had once, but …" He shook his head, letting the words trail away, as he looked her way.

Odessa shifted in her seat, uncomfortable under his intense, longing gaze. She had to get his mind on something else. "Care to tell me about her?" she asked lightly. "What kind of woman steals Robert McAllan's heart?"

Samuel began to fuss, so Odessa reached for him. Robert's fingers were warm as they touched. He stayed where he was, leaning forward, and rested his forearms on his thighs. "She looked a bit like you, and she had the most marvelous laugh.... There was much I enjoyed about her."

"So?" Odessa probed gently. "What went wrong?"

"She fancied herself in love with my best friend."

"Oh," Odessa said quietly. "I'm so sorry."

Robert forced a smile and looked into her eyes. He shrugged his shoulders. "As I said, just not the right woman."

Did his eyes linger on her just a little too long? Odessa frowned, at a loss for words. She longed for an escape.... Oh, why couldn't Samuel choose to cry now, demand his mother put him bed?

He smiled then, breaking the tension in the room. "Take your ease, Odessa," he muttered. "What am I going to do, snatch you from my brother's arms? I think not."

Her eyes moved back to his. After a moment, she gave him a slight smile, as if she were in on the game from the start. But it wasn't a game. There was something real, moving in a swift, warm undercurrent, sending a shiver up her spine....

He took another sip of tea and regarded her. "Dess, as lovely and enticing as you are, it is foremost in my mind that you are my brother's wife. I will always treat you as a sister."

"Thank you for that." *Dess*. No one called her that but family.

But Robert was family. Her brother. Trustworthy. It was all right, was it not?

She rose and went toward the kitchen. "I'm weary, Robert. I think I'll turn in."

"I've upset you."

She turned to look at him. He remained seated in the chair in the corner. "No, not upset. Unsettled." She lifted a weary hand to her head. "I just need a night's sleep. It's been a long day." She could see from the expression he wore that her words were not enough, that he wouldn't allow her to depart with this between them. "I asked you a direct question, Robert. You gave me a direct answer. All right?"

"All right. Good night, *Odessa*." So he had noticed how his use of her nickname unsettled her.

"Good night, Robert." Quickly, she made her escape, not breathing easy until she was up the stairs, Samuel in his crib, and her back against her closed bedroom door. She looked to the moon, streaming a pale, early light across her desk and floor.

She unbuttoned her gown, then turned and stared at her bedroom door. She frowned at the thought, but then moved and slowly slid the bolt across it. She never locked her door when Bryce was home. She did not fear Robert.

Or did she? Not in the way that Reid Bannock induced a wave of terror. But in a scalp tingling, shiver-down-her-back way. She shrugged off the thought as she pulled off her dress and pulled on a night shift, and then crawled beneath the cool sheets, waiting for her body to create a cocoon of warmth.

She'd have to rise and unbolt the door when she heard her

husband come in downstairs. But for now, she only wanted to feel … warm.

❁

Today was the day. Moira St. Clair, now called Moira Colorado, was arriving in his new town. Reid leaned against the front wall of his store, one foot propped against it, and took a long pull from his cigar. Pretty Miss Gorder and her mother walked by, and Reid lifted his hat and nodded at them with a smile, but there was another woman on his mind. He watched the road for a while, then lifted his pocket watch out. Stage was still fifteen minutes or more out. Half the time, coaches were delayed by mud or broken wheels, what the locals claimed was a springtime malady that summer would soon cure.

Dennis arrived and stood beside him, perusing the street. "I have good news."

"What is that?" Reid asked, still staring down the street.

"The McAllans appear to be searching for treasure."

Reid eyed him. "Are you certain?"

"Certain as can be. Read it for yourself."

Reid took the telegram from his hand, sent from the Circle M man he was paying handsomely to betray his employers. *Weather better here—STOP—sun shining all day today—STOP—No rain yet.* It was unsigned. But Reid lifted his chin and grinned. "Telegraph operator was probably looking at our man cross-eyed for sending such an odd note." *Sun shining all day* meant the McAllans were on the move, searching for old Sam's treasure again. *No rain yet* meant they hadn't yet found anything, at least as far as his man could tell.

Reid looked back down the road, wondering when the stage would arrive. All was coming together beautifully. Simply beautifully. He glanced at Dennis. "You'll need to take care of Bryce's detective immediately. Let him send one more telegram tonight, to buy us the most time." He turned toward the man and stared at him intently. "But he must not recognize our visiting songstress as a St. Clair before he does so."

"How would he, given her new name?"

"Chances are, he wouldn't put two and two together, but I'm not taking any chances here. You understand?"

"I understand, Boss." Dennis departed then to see to Reid's errands.

Portly Henry Colvard, the opera house owner, came down the boardwalk, rubbing his hands. "You as excited as I to meet this Moira Colorado, Bannock?"

"More so, I'd wager," Reid allowed. "But I'll wait to see her sing to introduce myself."

The stage turned the corner then, for once right on time. And as Colvard scurried across the street, Reid moved into the store, content to watch from the hidden shadows of his window as she emerged from the stagecoach. He feared for a moment that she would know he was here, be forewarned, but then realized that as far as she knew, he was still in prison. Surely, if she was communicating often with her sister, she would have been warned not to come to Leadville. Her very presence meant she was ignorant of that fact.

He smiled and could see his thin-lipped reflection in the window. But then there she was, as stunning as he remembered, if not more so, her features now slightly more rounded, mature. His eyes narrowed as a thin man dressed as finely as a banker offered her his arm and paused before Colvard to introduce him to Moira. Who was her escort? A beau? Husband? Or merely a manager?

It mattered not. Soon she would be his.

Or she would die.

❁

After agreeing to meet Mr. Colvard for supper, Moira climbed the stairs beside Gavin. "Do you think we'll come across Daniel Adams here? This is his employer's hotel."

Gavin appraised her. "Perhaps," he said, offering nothing more. He had been acting increasingly cold to her, saying little to her other than curt responses to her questions. Was it all due to Andrew Wiman's flirtations? He had clearly been jealous and protective, but as they moved out on the morning train from Andrew's town, something had also clearly slipped between them. In fact, there had not been one easy conversation or loving word between them for days.

He opened the door for her and then turned to make sure a hotel servant was bringing in their six trunks from the coach. Moira glanced around, patting her hair, when her eyes rested upon the man behind the bar.

He smiled at her, gently, the sadness in his eyes lifting for a moment.

"Daniel," she said, trying not to rush across the saloon floor. Only a few patrons were at tables, the afternoon not yet done.

"Moira St. Clair," he said, coming around the bar to greet her. He took her hands in both of his, which felt oddly warm and encompassing, and smiled down at her. "When I heard you and Gavin were coming, I could hardly believe it," he said. "It seems a year ago that we were passengers aboard that ship."

"It's not been even two months," Gavin said from over her shoulder. He reached forward and Daniel shook his hand too.

"And yet you've managed to launch Moira's new career," Daniel said in gentle admiration. "Have to hand it to you, Gavin, you must have the touch. Men have been talking about Moira's arrival for weeks now."

"He is marvelous at this," Moira enthused, anxious to seize any opportunity to bridge the gap between her and Gavin. She took his arm and smiled up at Gavin. "I'd be lost without him."

"I see you got the bar installed," Gavin said, pulling away from her and going to the counter. Was it her imagination or was he eager to be away from her? He ran his hands down the smooth, highly varnished surface of the mahogany, shaking his head in admiration as he studied the back wall that was covered by the largest beveled-glass mirror Moira had ever seen outside a major city and flanked by massive, intricately carved columns. "It's as beautiful as you claimed."

Moira smiled at Daniel and then realized he was staring at her hand, at her ring finger with the yellow diamond, not listening to Gavin. He started, suddenly recognizing both she and Gavin were looking to him, waiting for him to respond. He gestured toward the staircase, to a matronly woman awaiting them there. "Mrs. Duven will be happy to escort you to your room," he said. "I'm certain you are weary after such a long coach ride."

Moira paused. He'd said, "room." Did Daniel already think them married? Did he know of their falsehood? That they were sharing one room? Or did he think it was truly what it seemed? She hid her ring with her other hand, shoved down the agitating thoughts, turning toward him and forced a bright smile. "We will see you again, Daniel?"

"I'm hard to miss, 'round here," he said, giving her his own sad-eyed smile. What were his big brown eyes saying to her? Did she mistake the welcoming pull of them as a beseeching, encompassing note?

Gavin squeezed her elbow then, and Moira turned, to follow him upstairs.

Halfway up, she looked back, and found Daniel staring after her. What was it about him that made her feel known, cared for, protected?

Daniel was the first to break their reverie. "Good night, Moira. Welcome to Leadville." His smile was thin. His eyes said more.

"Good night, Daniel. Fancy this, meeting you a couple thousand miles from where we first met."

"Fancy that," he said drily, his eyes not leaving hers.

❁

"The show is tomorrow at eight?" Moira said, peeling off her light jacket.

"Eight sharp," he said, turning over in their shared bed. Not even a kiss good night.

Moira turned her back to him too, minutes later, and shivered under the thin hotel blanket. Gavin afforded her little warmth, making no move to touch her since they left Telluride. She stared out into the dark night, watching as the moon slipped behind swiftly moving clouds and then out again. Gavin was snoring softly behind her. How had he fallen asleep so quickly? She shivered again.

She was losing him. Her plans to draw him closer had backfired. His mind was occupied with other things, his head constantly in the ledger that contained his other business, not her. How to bring him back? Close again? He was dear to her, his mind as engaging as his other delightful attentions. But he seemed to regard Andrew's favor and her brief flirtations—even her friendly, chaste reunion with Daniel—as an egregious affront. Not that she could've done much to dissuade Andrew. He was, after all, the owner of the opera house. Had she offended him, he might have sent them on their way and not allowed her to perform at all! And had it not been Gavin who chose her gowns as "innocently seductive"? He traded on her flirtation! No, there was something more, something deeper shifting here …

Moira looked over her shoulder at his sleeping form. Perhaps she had erred, opting to become entwined as his mistress. Perhaps she should have kept him at arm's length, hooked on her pinky, as she had all the other men in her life. But there was something heroic about Gavin to her, beyond her ken, knowledgeable, enticing on a deeper level. She cradled her hands beneath her head and stared out at the moon again and again, watching as it crested and sank in the Western sky, then at the empty chair beside her. She wished her mother or sister were here, someone she could talk to. No, not Odessa. She'd lecture Moira. At least she could talk to her mother.

*Mama, I've made a mess of things.*

*There's always a way to clean up a mess.* She could hear her mother's voice, as clear as the day she left them.

*Not this one. I love him, Mama. Love! I never thought it'd happen to me.*

She imagined her mother looking over at him and then to the window, disappointment edging her lips a bit downward. *This isn't how I raised you, Moira. You've gone far astray. You're off the path. It's time. Come back to what you know is right and true.*

*It's not your path. I know that. But can't my path be my own? Things change between generations, values—*

*Values never change.*

*My life is so different from yours. My world is—*

*You live in the same world I lived in. God's own. You are God's own.*

*God. I never had the faith you possessed. It was an heirloom, a tradition. No, I need to make my own way.*

*Make your own way, dear daughter. But you'll find it is much more painful and difficult if you ignore the God who walks the path with you.*

Moira closed her eyes, and when she opened them, she could not summon the voice of her mother again. She rolled onto her back and pushed her knuckles against her eyes, trying to ease the ache behind them. It was just as well. *Mama will not tell me anything I wish to hear.*

Mama and Odessa had oft seen things the same way. There was much in her older sister that reminded Moira of her mother. Odessa adopted her parents' faith. Moira increasingly thought it antiquated, a means to keep people in line, organized, accountable. Such things did not apply easily to the arts. The arts demanded freedom and flow, not formality and function. She turned again, and a moment later, again.

"Are you ever going to go to sleep?" Gavin asked in a mumble, shortly before dawn.

"I cannot."

He sighed. "You need your rest, Moira. It will affect your performance. And my head is throbbing."

A rush of anger washed through her. She sat up and leaned against the headboard, staring at him. "I can't sleep because I am thinking of you."

He leaned a little her way and put a hand to his head. "Whatever you think of me, can we speak of it come morning?"

"No, Gavin. I don't believe we can. Something is wrong between us. Dreadfully wrong. What's happened? A month ago, we were in love, the world before us!"

He looked over at her and then sat up, leaning against the headboard too. He took her hand, and by the way he did it, Moira was cast between hope and horror. Slowly, he looked from her hand to her face again. "Moira, I've been infatuated with you since the day we met. But I have never professed love."

She pulled her hand away and folded her arms before her. "No, it has not been spoken between us. But what do you call this?" She lifted a hand to their shared hotel room.

"Convenience. A logical next step. We are adults, living in an age of propriety. If we wanted ultimate access to one another, we had to pretend we were man and wife."

"Or we could become man and wife."

He scoffed and moved to face her. "Is that what this is about, Moira? You want to be married?"

"Not to you," she bit out, rising from the bed and pulling on a robe. She strode over to the window and stared outward. No, she would have to be honest, if this conversation were to get her anywhere. She took a breath. "I confess … I've imagined …" She looked over her shoulder at him. "Are we not quite well suited?"

He stared at her, and his eyes softened as they used to when she first thought it love. He rose and came to her, wrapping his arms around her shoulders and kissing her head, softly, slowly. Her heart lifted, thinking he would recant his hurtful words, confess how he had erred. But then he said, "Moira, we are well suited. But I cannot marry a woman of the stage. Especially the common stage. My friends, my family—well, it would not be accepted."

Bewildered, Moira turned. "You … your family?" She frowned and whirled, sputtering in fury. "You have made me into … *this*. You *made* me Moira Colorado. You launched *this* career."

"And it is delightful. But this is what I do. Launch a business or career and then move on. I'm a builder, not a maintenance man. And you are well on your way, Moira." He reached out as if to cradle her cheek, but she moved away.

She could barely breathe. He was leaving her. She knew it now, rather than merely suspecting it. He was biding his time, searching for his opening to go. And now she had given it to him. She was merely a *maintenance* project to him.

"Come now, deep down, didn't you figure our alliance was temporary? A delightful sojourn shared. You must admit, it has been mutually profitable. You found a new chapter of your career, and I—"

"Gained a mistress. A woman to put food on your table as well as warm your bed."

"And I learned much," he corrected her gently, "about an area of commerce I knew little about, and about a woman I care for deeply."

"But do not love," she said steadily.

"No, Moira. I do not love you. I have yet to find out what that means."

She stepped forward and took his hand, lifting it to the center of her chest, covering it with her own. "But I do. This cannot be a mistake, Gavin. It cannot. I have felt the sparks of love before, but nothing like the sparking flames I've known when it comes to you. Perhaps it will only take a bit more time for you to understand what I already know. That we are meant to be together."

His face grew more troubled. "I see now that I have let this go on too long. Forgive me, dearest. For a time you saw it as I did. I'm certain of it. When we first shared a bed, we were quite clear on things. Remember? You wanted to answer to no man. When did that change?"

She paused. He was right. She had insisted on that. Why did it feel like such a long time ago that she dictated thusly? "Slowly," she said carefully. "Over time. Day after day, the more we were together, the more I came to respect you, love you. We've been working together, dreaming together, building together."

"We're building a *business* together," he said ruefully. "The business being 'Moira Colorado.' Our intimate associations are simply a side benefit of that enterprise."

"A side benefit," she whispered.

He stared at her for a long moment. "I guess it is true. That all women eventually equate the body with the heart."

She released his hand, the shadow of devastation closing in. "No. I equate sharing a life with love, whether as a friend or a lover."

"Then I beg you to consider me friend, as well as lover."

She turned away, rubbing her temples with her left hand. "That is how my mother once described my father in her journals. Friend. Lover. Spouse. That is where I have erred. You have never been my friend. And never truly intended to be my spouse."

He was silent for a long moment. "I will pack my things and be off in the morning. I can hire a man to be your bodyguard."

"That is what you want, isn't it, Gavin? To be able to say I sent you off? So you can shrug off any guilt?"

"I assume no guilt, Moira," he said, straightening his shoulders.

"No, of course you don't."

He moved across the room and opened a trunk.

"What are you doing?" Her voice rose several notches.

"Packing. I'll catch the first train out of here so my presence does not torment you any longer. I'll depart, and you can take the day to collect yourself before your performance."

Her performance? Walking onto the stage was the last thing she could think of. "I will send word that I am ill and incapable of singing tonight."

He paused. "Tonight. But not tomorrow. You must find the strength to do what you do best. To further your goals."

"What do you care? You are leaving on the morning train."

"But I have not invested in you to see my investment languish."

Her eyes narrowed. She remembered signing their agreement. Gavin received fifteen percent of anything she made. "Of course not. You have, what, another year of profits to collect? From afar?"

"Three years," he said calmly, as he folded a shirt, "from the time we dissolve our association." He stared at her. "Which I assume we are doing right now."

"Three years?" she sputtered. "I would not have signed such a document." *Unless I fancied myself in love ...*

"But you did, Moira. And I would not have agreed to this without it. I was clear with you from the beginning. I wanted to invest in this business, explore it. But I would not have done so without some assurances to compensate me for my time."

Slowly, she sat down on the edge of the bed, dimly listening to him pack, her mind racing with words and promises that might entice him to stay. But she swallowed each one like bitter spoonfuls of lemon. Nothing would change his mind. She listened to him wash his face and wet down his hair, lather and shave, familiar morning sounds for her now. Sounds she would not hear again. She listened to him dress, pulling on his trousers and shirt. A belt, a vest, a tie.

She wished her mother were here. To hold her, keep her upright when she felt as if she were about to disintegrate into a pile of ashes. She imagined her mother in the chair beside the bed again, her face awash with love and concern, reaching out to hold her hand.

*He's leaving me, Mama. He never intended to stay. I was a fool.*

She wished she could feel the warmth in her mother's hand, a gentle squeeze. *Let him go.*

*But I want him to stay.*

*I know. Let him go.*

*But I can't do this without him, Mama. I don't want to do this.*

*I know. Let him go.*

And within minutes, she did.

# Chapter 17

What Moira couldn't get out of her mind was how easily Gavin walked out the door without a backward glance. Hidden by the curtains, she watched him leave the hotel and walk down the street, a satchel in one hand, a man carrying his trunk behind him. He turned the corner, apparently on his way to the train station. And never once did he look back. It was his way—ever forward-thinking. It was part of what had attracted her to him. But it burned, to know that even she couldn't make him think twice. Or indeed, even pause.

She sat down heavily upon the bed. For hours.

Moira felt dizzy, but not faint. Hungry, but with no desire to eat. Sleepy, but unable to doze. She was lost. Adrift. Spinning. Empty. *What to do, what to do …* She alternated between fury and indignation and a heartrending agony she'd never before experienced. *What have I done?* she wondered, running a hand over his side of the bed. How could she have allowed him to so completely own her, envelop her? Was she not Moira St. Clair beneath the Moira Colorado facade? Was she not more than this? A whimpering woman, a mistress tossed aside? She would not allow him to reduce her to such a shell, the mere shadows of a life she desired, no, *claimed.*

A knock sounded on her door. "Miss Colorado?" asked a deep voice.

Moira frowned and pulled her robe tighter. But she walked over to the door without opening it. "Yes?"

"It's Daniel, Moira," he said lowly. "Can you come out for a moment?"

She frowned, not liking the tone of his voice. Slowly, she unbolted the door and pulled her dressing robe closed at the neck and peered out.

Daniel looked at her, taking in her stricken appearance, then glanced down the hall, both ways. "Get dressed, Moira. I need to talk to you, but you need to come out here, properly dressed."

"What is it?" she said in irritation. "Out with it." The last thing she needed right now was a lesson on propriety—

"It's Gavin," he said miserably.

"Gavin?" Slowly, her eyes moved to Daniel's big hands, hands that held his hat solemnly before him. He didn't worry the hat, circling it around and around, but there was something—

"Moira, Gavin's dead."

Her eyes slowly moved up his torso to meet his sad brown eyes. Surely she had misunderstood him. Gavin was liable to be turned around by now, seeing the error of his ways, formulating a proper apology to her—

She shut the door and dressed, as woodenly as a puppet upon a puppeteer's strings. Surely she had imagined what Daniel had said.… Surely …

Moira came out into the hallway, her hair down, her dress haphazardly buttoned, but her eyes were on the tall man before her.

"He didn't make it as far as the next town on the train," Daniel said miserably. "He stood up, complained of a headache, then crumpled to the aisle. Passengers said he was dead before he hit the floor. Doctor said it must've been an aneurism."

"Aneurism," she repeated dully. The headaches, the constant headaches, ever since he was struck on the boat in that storm, when Daniel had come to their aid and—

"No one could have known, Moira. Even Gavin—he never sought a doctor out, right?"

"No," she said, shaking her head, her mind cascading through every town they had traveled through. "Maybe that was part of why he was going though, part of his need to return to New York. Maybe he wanted to see a proper physician...." She lifted a hand to her head, feeling dizzy again. "I should have seen it, Daniel. Noticed. But all I could see was my—"

Her knees gave way then, but he caught her, easily lifting her into his arms. Dimly, she recognized that he carried her to the bed and gently laid her atop it. He was backing away, moving toward the corner chair when she recovered from her faint. She stared at the wall, afraid if she looked into Daniel's compassionate eyes she'd begin weeping again. "He never loved me. I trusted him, gave him everything, and he still didn't love me."

Daniel hesitated, then, "Did you love him?"

"I ... I think so. Yes." She lifted a hand to her head. "But I do not know if I know what love is."

"You will know what it is, in time. At the right time, Moira. You'll know."

She shifted her eyes slowly to him. "Have you ever been in love?"

"Once," he said. He rose, rubbing his palm on his denim pants as if it was sweaty. "A long time ago. A lifetime ago."

"You are not that old, Daniel. Just a few years older than I."

"Old enough to have lived through much." He looked to the ceiling and then back to her. "Moira, I'm sorry for your loss. You need to know that before he left, Gavin hired me to escort you anywhere you want to go. Said he wouldn't trust anyone but me to watch over you, which I'd take to mean he cared, even if he didn't love."

"Gavin," she whispered.

There was a pause before he returned, "And he left something else for you." He pulled a thick leather wallet from an inside pocket of his jacket.

With trembling hands, she reached for it.

"I'll be downstairs if you need me—" He moved as if to leave.

"Thank you," she said, seeing nothing but the leather wallet he had handed her. It filled both her hands. She sat up and flipped it open, gasping at the stack of bills on either side. In the back of her mind, she heard the door close behind him.

There was a brief note with the bills.

*Moira,*

*Thank you for sharing your life with me for a time. Regardless of what you think of me, I have enjoyed being with you and seeing you flourish. Please know that I am not to be compared to your ex-manager in Paris, about to rob you blind. In here you will find more than enough cash to see you through Leadville and beyond, if you keep to the schedule. Also enclosed, please find your account information on the two bank accounts we opened while in California.*

*By contract, I will look for your account information each month. Please send it by the fifth day. If you can see fit to look beyond your fury, I would appreciate a brief word on your itinerary and how you are faring. Even though I could not profess the love you seek, I do care, Moira, and always will.*

*Gavin*

She set it aside and glanced in at the coin and bills that covered the depth of the chest. She'd been bought off like a high-class whore. She let out a humorless laugh. She deserved it, she supposed. *Act like less than who you are or who you want to be,* her father always said, *and that's how others will treat you.*

❁

*10 May 1887*

*Bryce, Dietrich, and Tabito are off to Avilla Canyon again today in search of something recognizable in Sam's clues. They go under the guise of seeking new summer feeding grounds, but I wonder if the men suspect Bryce's true motive. Meanwhile, I am home with Samuel, and I find that I am making myself scarce, dodging any further intimate conversations with Robert. Was it all in my imagination, his longing glance? Hope in his eyes? That would make a fine mess of things, considering all that is a mess already.*

*Perhaps I am simply discombobulated, confused, unable to think straight with all that is transpiring around me.*

Samuel coughed from the nursery, and Odessa looked up with a frown. He had been uncommonly fussy today, unhappy in her arms or in his crib. She had attributed it to him waking early from his nap. She listened closely as he coughed again, but then was quiet. He hadn't nursed well before he went down, constantly pulling off the breast as if he was as agitated as his mother. Odessa paused for a moment, holding her breath in order to better hear, and then he coughed again and began to cry, a sleepy, frustrated sound.

She rose, unlocked her door and went across the hall, pausing to see if he would settle without her picking him up, but instead he found steam to fuel his little engine. "Oh, Samuel, Samuel," she said soothingly, moving over to touch his back. She pulled her hand quickly away, trying to make sense of the heat. It was early May, and the house was chilly at night. But then she knew. She picked him up and cuddled him close, his smooth skin as soft as a peach against her jaw, but as hot as a boiled potato.

Odessa paced back and forth across the nursery floor, patting his bottom, talking to him in a low, soothing voice, trying to ease his agitation. All the while, she was thinking through what she remembered of babies, of her mother caring for her younger siblings. "Are you teething, sweet pea?" she asked Samuel, holding him out in her arms. He squinched up his face and cried harder, as if frustrated that she wasn't figuring out what he wanted to tell her. She sat down in the rocker and tried to put him to her breast, but that made him so angry that he began to cough again.

"Oh, sweetheart, Samuel, Samuel, where did you pick up a fever? She held her breath when he cried so hard he couldn't seem to gather a breath, scaring her to pieces. What if … what if it was … no. She refused to even entertain the thought. It was the teething. Or some other illness. Not the consumption.

Odessa buttoned her nightshirt and tied her robe as best she could. His diaper was dry. He wasn't hungry. She cast back through the week, of people who had come through the house, none of them sick. But three days ago, a neighbor had come by with a basket of biscuits and mentioned her youngest had the fever. He'd recovered, but he was an older child, not a baby.

The fever. *Please God …*

She turned to the door, longing for Bryce to come through it, and at the same time remembering he wouldn't be coming home for a couple of days.

"Bryce. I need you," she whispered. She walked to the top of the stairs and looked down, wondering if she should trouble Robert. She gasped when she saw he was sitting on the bottom step, head in his hands as if praying. "Robert?"

"Dess," he said, looking up the stairs at her and the baby. "Is he all right?"

Holt, the hired man assigned to guard the door, rocked forward from his position—leaning against the wall on a chair—down to four legs. Together, he and Robert stared upward.

"I-I don't know. I'm afraid he has the fever. Mrs. Teller was here a few days ago. Her son had the fever and she held him. Do you think—"

Holt rose and put his hat on his head. "I'll go for the doctor, ma'am. We don't wanna take no chances."

Odessa breathed a sigh of hope. "Thank you, Holt."

"Ma'am," he said with a nod. In a blink, he was gone.

Robert climbed the stairs and looked down at Samuel, whimpering in her arms. "Think a cool cloth might help?"

"Of course." Why hadn't she thought of the same? A cool cloth, a doctor … a surge of gratitude and hope went through her. "I'm … I'm glad you're here."

He gave her a slow smile. "Glad I can be. I'll go out to the icehouse. Meet you in the kitchen?"

Odessa returned to her room and hurriedly pulled on a day dress, ignoring her cold, bare feet. On the bed, Samuel was crying so hard he was turning purple. She lifted him in her arms, cooing, bouncing him, trying to soothe him any which way she could. She heard the front door open and close.

"Ma'am? Mrs. McAllan?"

She moved to the landing. "Trace," she greeted the tall, thin man.

He pulled his hat from his head and rested it on his chest, watching as they came down the stairs. "Holt said he was goin' for the doctor in town. Asked me to take up his post on guard."

"Fine, fine," Odessa said distractedly. She moved past him, her eyes focused on Robert as he came in the door, a kerchief filled with ice in his hands. She went to a cupboard and pulled a towel from it.

"Here, let me do it," Robert said. He was just over her shoulder, peering down at the babe in her arms. Odessa shivered at his proximity and hurriedly handed him the towel. She moved to the other side of the table, hoping it wasn't obvious that she suddenly needed some sort of barrier between them.

Robert peered at her with compassionate eyes. "Where are your raisins, Dess?"

"Raisins?" she asked blankly.

He lifted a small cloth bag in his hand and came around the table toward them. She forced herself to stay put. "I have some dried lime peel," he said, as if that explained everything. "It's a remedy our mother used when we were children. Raisin tea. Worth a try?"

Odessa raised her eyebrows. "Couldn't hurt, I suppose."

Robert did not wait for her response, just turned and walked around the kitchen, assuming she trailed behind. "Where are your raisins?" he repeated.

Odessa inwardly shrugged. If tea would help little Samuel, she was willing to try. "Lower left shelf in the cupboard," she said..

He pumped some fresh water into a bowl with the ice, wrung out the cloth and handed it back to her. She gently dabbed it at Samuel in her arms. Surprisingly, he didn't wail in protest. Perhaps it felt good to him. "Poor baby," she cooed. "Poor little baby. It'll be all right. Mama has you." Robert pumped more water into a bucket and then poured it into a kettle on the stove.

She sank into a rocker by the adjacent den's wood stove and rocked the baby back and forth. Thankfully, Robert stayed over by the stove. "I didn't know you were a medicine man," she said to him.

"Not a medicine man," he said with a slight smile. "Only a man with some medicines."

In a few minutes, the water was boiling and Robert added the raisins and lime peel. It filled the kitchen with a warm smell that reminded Odessa of Christmas. "So how do you propose we get tea down a baby's mouth?" she asked.

Another small smile. "I'll show you." He used a ladle to put a small portion in a tin mug, then reached for her potato masher and pressed down on the mixture. He glanced over at Samuel now and then when he let out a particularly loud cry. "Do you have cardamom? Sugar?" he asked.

"Lower right side of the cupboard," she directed, her eyes on Samuel. He was quieting a little, not because his fever was abating, she knew, but because he was terribly tired. She rose and went to the bucket, wringing out the cloth with one hand to get rid of the access moisture.

She settled in again, trying to help her baby get comfortable. He shifted repeatedly and then let his arm hang listlessly from the side. She frowned, watching as his little rib cage rose and fell so rapidly, as if trying to wave off the heat roiling inside of him. Robert appeared at her elbow and leaned over them both. "Give him to me a moment, will you?"

Reluctantly, she let him take the baby from her arms. He moved to the small settee and unwound Samuel's twisted nightshirt and lifted it away. "Please, the cloth?"

Obediently, Odessa handed him the ice wrapped in the towel. Samuel, startled by the sudden cool, stretched out his arms and widened his eyes but then settled immediately. Robert spoke quietly to the child, using low tones to sooth him. He looked at Odessa. "Come, sit beside him a minute while I fetch the tea."

He padded over to the kitchen and poured a bit of his raisin tea into a heavy cotton bag. Cupping his hand beneath it, he came over to them and asked Odessa to open the baby's mouth.

He let a few drips fall in. The baby frowned and then his tongue moved in and out of his lips as if he were tasting it. And liking it.

They repeated the action over the next quarter hour, until Samuel had ingested several teaspoons. "Good baby," Robert soothed, stroking his fuzzy head. "Good, good baby."

Robert left to put the cotton bag in the washtub, then returned to sit in the rocker across from them, his eyes never leaving the baby. She watched the baby too, waiting for the miracle that she had been praying for in snatches over the last hours—that the babe's fever would break, that the doctor's visit would be for naught.

Samuel drifted off to sleep and Odessa shifted in her seat. Her shoulder ached from sitting too long in one position.

"I can hold the baby," Robert offered. "Why don't you try and rest a little?"

"Oh, that's all right," she said. "I want to stay with him." It was sweet of the man to offer, but she couldn't. The only one she'd leave the child with at such a frightening hour would be Bryce. *Oh, Bryce, why'd you have to leave?* She knew she was being selfish, that he was out searching, hoping to find a way, a future for them all, but she couldn't help but feel sorry for herself, for Samuel. They needed him here. Now.

She ran her hand over the baby's head. Was it her imagination or did the child feel not quite as hot now? Robert saw the hope in her eyes and ran a hand over the baby's head too. "Ah yes. The raisin tea always seems to help."

"Should we give him more tea?"

"No. Let's wait for the doctor. The tea always helps ease the fever, but it never takes it away completely. At least the little guy can get some rest."

"I'm grateful for even a temporary reprieve. Where did your mother learn to make it?"

He shrugged. "I suppose from her mother or grandmother. I often return to her remedies for such things. That's why I had the lime peel with me." He studied her. "Here, you take the rocker again, at least. Your arms are obviously aching."

She tried to smile at him through her worry after switching chairs, but then she closed her eyes and rested as she rocked the baby, attempting to settle again, to sleep. With luck, Holt would be back soon with the doctor. It reassured her that he would be here, as Samuel began to whimper again. She wouldn't rest until a physician came to examine Samuel and pronounced him out of danger. It was just too close to what she had experienced with her little brothers … watching them struggle against the fevers of consumption, each finally succumbing.

Robert stretched out on a long settee on the far wall, intent on waiting it out with her. "He'll be all right, Dess," he said.

For the hundredth time that night, Odessa was thankful that her brother-in-law was with her, if Bryce could not be. But staring down at her baby, listless, still burning with fever, she wished she could believe him.

❦

Holt and the doctor finally arrived sometime after midnight, just as Samuel's fever was spiking. Doc Murphy immediately took the baby from her arms and laid him on blankets on the kitchen table to examine him. "Sorry it took so long, ma'am," Holt whispered. "I had to wait for the doc to get back from another visit."

"No, no," she said, giving him a grateful smile. "I'm glad you're back at all. I worried you wouldn't get back until sunup."

"Is Bryce back?" he asked.

She shook her head, paying attention to the doctor's movements and expression now. Holt quietly slipped out the back door. Samuel started to wail as the doctor unswaddled him and took off his gown, pressing on his belly, first one side, then the other. He looked her way. "How long has he had the fever, Mrs. McAllan?"

She stepped forward. "I noticed he was fussy all afternoon. But it was evening before the fever came on."

"This as hot as he's gotten?"

"No, he was much hotter. Robert gave him some raisin tea that seemed to ease it." She slipped down the bench on the far side, so she could stroke the child, trying to calm him as the doctor continued his exam. He turned Samuel on his side toward the lantern to look down into his throat.

"Know anyone else who's been ill?" he asked.

"No one on the ranch," she said, shaking her head. "But Mrs. Teller stopped by a couple of days ago and said her son had been sick."

He nodded and then sighed. "She should've known better. Probably held the baby, right?"

"Right," Odessa said ruefully.

"There's a fearsome case of the influenza that's been going around the valley," Dr. Murphy said. "Haven't seen it in one this young—that's what concerns me."

Odessa's eyes narrowed, and she looked again to her baby. "What can we do for him?"

"We wait it out. Get as many fluids as we can down him. Is he nursing?"

"Fitfully."

"Wetting his nappies?"

"Not for the last couple of hours."

"Hmm," he said, wrapping the baby up again and handing him to her. "We need to get anything we can down him, to give him what he needs to burn off this fever."

"He seems to like Robert's raisin tea," she said, moving to the cup and cheesecloth. "It brought down his fever for a time."

"Anything in it but raisins?" Dr. Murphy said, eyeing the cup and then her brother-in-law.

"A little cardamom and sugar, and some lime peel."

"Sounds fine to me." He packed his things back in his bag. "Try and get some rest. I'll come back by tomorrow afternoon to check on the baby."

"Thank you, Doctor," Robert said, reaching out to shake his hand. He showed him to the door and then returned to Odessa's side. He stroked Samuel's head as the baby squinched up his face in a weak wail again. He put his other hand on the small of Odessa's back, as if comforting her. "You look like you're about to faint, Dess. Can I take him for a while? You can go and rest upstairs, or here, on the settee, if you prefer."

Now that he'd said it, it was all she could feel, the sheer weight of exhaustion. "Maybe … maybe just a short rest over there. Are you sure you don't mind?"

He reached for the baby and said, "Not at all. You go. He seems bent on crying no matter who's holding him." She nodded and moved toward the settee, intending to sit a while, catch her breath. Maybe close her eyes for a moment. Blinking heavily, she watched as Robert walked the baby, patting him, murmuring to him in low, calming tones. She wished Bryce were here. *Bryce, come home … I don't care about the treasure. Come home. Lord, bring him home to us.*

And yet just before her eyes closed, she watched Robert's hand, patting the baby, reassuring him, and thought about how that was the same hand that had rested on her lower back. Holt came in then, to fetch a glass of water. She leaned to her side, caring not for the impropriety of falling asleep in the company of men who were not her husband. She was too weary to care.

*Thank You, Lord, for Robert. For bringing him here to us. For the help he is to all of us.*

❁

*11 May 1887*

*Doctor reassured me that as long as Samuel continues to improve day by day and will nurse a little so he doesn't become dehydrated, he should fully recover. I will keep this entry short, since I yearn to be with him, even as he naps. I—*

"Watching him every moment won't hasten his recovery," Robert teased her quietly, arms crossed, watching from the doorway.

Odessa started and then smiled. "I simply feel better, being near him," she whispered.

Robert moved as if to go, then paused, apparently searching for the right words. "Bryce said you lost some little brothers to the consumption."

"Four of them. Those were horrible, horrific days."

"I can only imagine."

"It meant a lot to me, Robert. That you waited it out with me. Thank you."

"Please," he said, holding up his hands. "Anytime, Odessa."

"Still," she insisted. "Thank you."

He gave her a tender smile. "I'll get a start on supper for the men."

"Oh! Supper! I hadn't a thought."

"Don't," he said with a smile. "Owen and I have a plan. We'll feed the men down in the bunkhouse, so the house can stay nice and quiet."

"Oh," she breathed. "Thank you." As he turned to go, Odessa hesitated a moment, still wanting to say more, and then frowning, she turned away. What was this desire within her? The desire to keep him around. Not to talk. Just to be present. She sat back down in Samuel's nursery and rocked, harder and harder. She was a mass of emotions—relief, angst, frustration, fear, bravery. What was the matter with her anyway? Perhaps she was just weary.

She glanced down at her sleeping son. By God's grace, both Samuel and she could get a good night's sleep.

# Chapter 18

Daniel paced back and forth, using a cloth to polish a glass that had long been dry. He glanced upstairs, wondering about what he had signed on to do for Gavin, for Moira. And yet deep down, he knew he would've done it anyway. There was something about Moira that pulled at him, something that made him want to protect her, heal her, try to fill the bottomless need for approval he sensed in her. She appeared shallow, absorbed in the surface of life, but once in a while, in those deep green eyes of hers, he glimpsed depths, like the pools in a slow moving river. When she allowed him to see into those pools, he knew she was more than she appeared.

He was alternately intrigued and aggravated by her, just as he had been on the ship.

Daniel set down the glass and took to straightening the rows of glasses on the bar shelf. Even if one took Moira St. Clair on a surface level, any red-blooded man could to see that she was everything a man could want. Curvaceous yet slim, blonde curls, long neck, rosebud lips. He was thankful that Gavin had been on board the ship, that he had gone after Moira in such an overt way, because something had been building quietly between Daniel and her—something Daniel wasn't ready for. Daniel had stepped aside, knowing Gavin was more her type anyway …

But he had been wrong about Gavin.

Daniel glanced up the stairs, feeling a pang of guilt. Knapp had used Moira and tossed her aside like a common whore. Set her up to earn him money and eased his way into her bed. Their "marriage" had been a sham, simply a cover to allow the rake complete access to her.

Daniel set down the mug, hard, on the bar and leaned against it, head down. His heart raced. Had he known they were not truly married, had he understood it right away, he would've punched Gavin Knapp so hard he would've flown across the room.

But he hadn't. And it wasn't his place. Moira had not asked anything of him, yet. It had been Gavin, who had come downstairs, bag in hand, and convinced him to watch over Moira "while he saw to business." Daniel had been too slow figure out what he was really saying, that it was over, that he was leaving her forever. He still couldn't believe it, really. Even if he only saw her as a mistress, why would he leave her? Had she pressed him, pressed for a real marriage?

It hadn't been scruples that had driven Gavin Knapp away; Daniel was sure of that. They'd never know, really, what drove the man. But Daniel knew that he had been wrong, wrong to not step between them aboard ship, wrong to not stop him the day he left, wrong to accept the duty of Moira's care. Who was he to take on such a task? What woman would want him around? Not after she found out who he really was, what he had done …

No, as soon as Moira St. Clair knew who Daniel really was, she'd toss him aside as easily as Gavin had tossed her.

❧

Moira dressed and put on her makeup as if she were a marionette, doing only as her puppet master directed. Daniel had seen to notifying Gavin's family; the railroad had already shipped his embalmed body East. She sank into a chair before her dressing table, fighting the urge to go back to bed, wishing she might have seen Gavin one more time, to say good-bye, say good-bye forever …

Dimly, she recognized someone was pounding on her door. Henry Colvard, the opera house manager had accepted her claim of illness yesterday, but would hear none of it today. "Get on that stage, or get out of my town," he said from the other side of the door. "I have men and women here who have come for miles to see your show. If you don't appear, they'll never come to my establishment again. Can I count on you to be there?"

She'd agreed, as if in a fog. At least she thought she agreed to it. She felt as ill as she sounded. What was this terrible tearing inside of her? This loss? Gavin was a fine man, the most intriguing she'd ever met, but in the end, he was but a man. She set down her pot of rouge and moved over to the bed.

Moira had thought she was acting like a woman of today—free. Unconfined. A modern woman. But where had it gotten her? Was this who she wanted to be? Alone, in a two-bit hotel in a fading mining town? She'd always been comfortable alone, because she was always surrounded by people. Until Gavin. He had given her a sense of partnership and companionship she hadn't known was possible.

But it had all revolved around her career. Moving forward. Expanding her fame. In retrospect, Gavin had asked few questions about who Moira was; most of their conversations had revolved around who they wanted Moira Colorado to become.

For the first time, Moira wondered if her vision of Moira Colorado melded with who she was inside. She had excelled at promoting the image, the role. People loved her as Moira Colorado. But was it … her? Who she was meant to be?

A knock sounded at her door. "Miss Colorado?" It was Mrs. Duven. "I have an early supper for you here."

"I'm not hungry," she called. She grimaced at the thought of food. "Please, take it away."

"Are you certain?" asked the woman after a short pause. "Mr. Colvard, he doesn't take kindly to fainting singers."

"I'm certain!" she replied, more sharply than she intended. Thankfully, she could hear the woman trudge away from her door and down the hallway. But then Moira started crying, and when she remembered she would be destroying her makeup, she couldn't find the resources to care. All she could do was give in to the tears again.

Thirty minutes later, she had only an hour to get to the opera house. She forced herself to rise and go to her trunk to fetch some candied ginger. It never failed to ease her upset stomach. Gavin had introduced her to it. She wished she had at least kept the tea that Mrs. Duven had undoubtedly had on her tray. That sounded somewhat good to her too. Moira sat down at her dressing table again, and with a cloth wiped away the dark smears her tears had produced. Her eyes were puffy, but there was little she could do about that. She reapplied powder and eyeliner and shadow and rouge, finishing with more powder and some lip coloring. She didn't look her best, but at least she resembled Moira Colorado.

She glanced at the clock. Fifteen minutes until her warm-up act went on stage. She rose and paused, shoving back the bile in her throat and reaching for another piece of ginger, then she picked up her bag and hurried out the door. Downstairs, Daniel met her at the stairs and visibly pulled back. Did she look so terrible?

He seemed to catch himself and offered his arm. She took it, clinging to it as if she could absorb some of his strength. All she could think about was getting to the opera house, making it through her songs, and returning to the hotel room to sleep. Sleep. All she wanted to do was sleep for hours. Days, if she could.

She hesitated, all at once very dizzy. Daniel paused with her, one hand under her arm, the other at her lower back. "Are you all right?"

"Fine," she said, brushing him off in irritation and moving down the sidewalk again, pretending she wasn't lying.

"You aren't walking as if you were fine. Moira, have you been drinking?"

"Drinking! No, I am simply feeling poorly. Were it up to me, I'd be skipping tonight's performance again and resting in my room." She paused. She needed someone. She couldn't do it alone. Not really. "Please. Daniel, help me get there, and get me back. That's all I can think of right now. Forgive me for being rude. I hope you can understand."

"I'll be right here, every step of the way," he said, looking down into her eyes. The kindness in his gaze nearly broke her. "I'll carry you back if I need to."

"Thank you, Daniel. You truly are a fine friend." She took a firmer grip upon his arm, leaning heavily against him as they made their way down to the opera house and in through the back door. The showgirls who opened for her lifted eyebrows in relief when she appeared, as seemingly unified in their thoughts as they were on the dance floor. They rushed to her, inquiring as to how she was feeling, but Daniel, bless him, moved them aside, telling them she had to get to her dressing room to rest.

Daniel settled her in a chair, and she was just allowing herself to nod off to sleep, so enticing, so dear, when he was back. "Moira, you're about to go on. They're calling for you." Gradually, Moira's ears focused on the familiar call of a hall full of men, all come to hear the famous Moira Colorado. The opera house manager had undoubtedly whipped them into a frenzy, as was his job, anticipating her arrival. She could hear the end of the showgirls' song, and knew that right now, they were dimming the lanterns, setting the stage for her arrival.

"I can't do it," she said.

A shadow washed over his face. "You must," Daniel said not unkindly. "You have obligations to a man who has obligations to others."

"I must," she muttered. When had her life become a series of musts? As if in a dream, she rose and took his large hand, following him out of the cramped dressing room, down a dark hallway, full of props and people, to the stage. The roar of the crowd became louder as she neared. She paused and Daniel looked back at her worriedly. "I can't," she whispered, shaking her head. "I can't." She barely saw him, only felt a sudden panic. She couldn't remember the words. The music. All of this seemed foreign. Wrong.

"You can do this, Moira," he said, frowning. He walked around to the side, so she could see the stage before her. She was trying to remember her opening line, decipher the notes of the music as it began. A girl—did she know her?—pushed a burning candle into her hands. Was this her prop? The curtains pulled aside, and she was alone on stage. Logically, she knew she had sung this song twenty times on twenty different stages. But at this moment, in this place, she couldn't remember a bit of it. It was if it had been erased as clearly as a teacher's marks from a blackboard.

The pianist glanced up at her, frowned, and then repeated his introduction. A glimmer of hope lifted Moira's chin. The opening line. A half note late, she began to sing. There was no passion, no power in her voice, but at least she was singing. The words unfolded from her mouth. She did not move, unable to think of anything but the next phrase, the next obvious musical note. But she did begin to make eye contact with the people in the room, all sitting in neat rows, in fine, red-upholstered chairs. The men purchased beer from a bar at the back, but at least they were sitting in rows—more like the opera houses in which she had gained her fame in Paris. It comforted her, calmed her, and her voice gained in strength.

She took a step forward and moved her hips in time with the next stanza, still touching each person in the crowd with her eyes, as Gavin had taught her. She could do this, even without him. Her eyes moved through the second row and then on to the third, brushing past the men but then faltering.

The words faded from her mind. Her eyes moved to the left again and hovered over an empty chair. She searched the aisle to the left and studied the large back of a man who was walking out, leaving.

Her eyes had deceived her.

Reid Bannock could not be here. He was in prison.

She glanced to the left, backstage, where Daniel watched her, his brow furrowed.

The pianist, throwing up his hands, began the song again, hoping to aid her.

But she could not remember the next line. Or the next. After a couple of measures, the pianist quit playing and the crowd was silent.

Then the first man booed. After a moment, another shouted, "Get her off stage! We want the real Moira Colorado!" Others shouted for their money back. One cried out to fetch the sheriff.

Daniel appeared beside her, but Moira felt frozen in place. It was then that a man threw his glass mug at the stage. The glass shattered all around her, and the beer made a terrible arc, certain to stain, over her beautiful silk skirt. A second mug was thrown at the stage. The crowd was in a frenzy. Several men were fighting. The girls stared at her with horrified expressions as she passed. But she didn't care.

It was over. Done with.

She shook the image still in her head. Reid was not here; he was in prison.

This performance was an utter failure, but there would be future performances. Other opportunities.

All she needed was a little sleep.

❧

Hidden now, Reid leaned against the back wall of the opera house auditorium, in deep shadows, watching Moira fall apart before him. It was perfect, really. Shock and terror had registered on her face as he exited his seat. He could've chosen to pick her up and carry her off stage, protect her, as he once yearned to do, before her betrayal.

He could've claimed her as both victor and lover, if she came to her senses and begged his forgiveness.

Perhaps someday soon he could convince her that his actions on the McAllan ranch had been justifiable, necessary. Things had simply gone awry. It had been Doc Morton's plan; he'd convinced Reid it was the right way to go. But he could see now how wrong it all was. After all these years of telling the same story—the last time, to the parole board in Cañon City—Reid almost believed the story himself.

"What's the matter with her?" he asked the man to his right, while still staring at the empty stage.

"I don't know, Boss. But I do know that the ranch is expecting some rain."

Reid looked at him sharply. "Rain?"

His man smiled and tucked his head. "Prospector's been out, looking for storm clouds."

Reid smiled and stared again at the empty stage. "Find out about the man who is with Moira now."

"You anticipating moving on that front, Boss?"

"Not until you tell me it's pouring down there, Dennis, not till we know for sure. In the meantime, I believe I have some work to do here."

# Chapter 19

Moira stirred in her bed as Daniel knocked again. "Moira? There's a doctor here to see you."

"I told you," she muttered, "I don't wish to see a doctor." Her voice was feeble in her own ears. She undoubtedly needed to see a doctor—something was unaccountably wrong—but she didn't feel like seeing anyone right now. All she wanted was rest, blessed sleep, escape. But instead she heard the key scratch into the lock, turn, and the door creak open.

"Daniel, I told you—"

"No arguments, Moira," he said sternly. He looked at her then. "Something's wrong. Something … more. Doctor Beason will figure it out."

She tried to focus on the man whom Daniel admitted to her room. A kindly looking man, far too young to be a doctor of any worth, pulled a seat next to her bed and smiled gently. "Hello, Miss Colorado. Please tell me what is troubling you."

If Moira was to endure this, she wanted the doctor of her youth, old Doctor Smith.

"Miss Colorado?"

"Moira," she said wearily. "Please call me Moira."

Daniel slipped out the door behind Doctor Beason and quietly shut it behind him. She imagined him wincing when it creaked again. But in a moment, she was alone with the young doctor.

Moira dragged her eyes up to meet his. "Ever had your heart broken, Doctor? That is all that ails me. Do you have medicine to treat that?"

His gentle eyes studied her, and he reached down into his black satchel to pull out a stethoscope, probably to give him something to do. "I've had a measure of heartache, yes. But broken? No." He put the ear pieces in his ears and leaned closer. "May I?"

Reluctantly, she folded down her blanket and looked toward the ceiling as he carefully moved aside her blouse and listened to her heart and then her lungs.

After a moment, he sat back and put the stethoscope into his bag. "Heart sounds steady, broken or not. Lungs too."

She gave him a small smile for his attempt at humor. He picked up her wrist and held his pocket watch in the other hand, timing her pulse. "Hmm. Your pulse is a bit slow. When'd you eat last?"

"I don't remember. I confess I have no desire to eat."

"Common, when ailing from heartache," he said sweetly. His eyes were quick, light gray. "Your man said you've been nauseated over the last few days."

*My man.* Daniel, he meant. "Constantly."

"Hmm. It's difficult to manage a meal if one is purging. Forgive me the intrusion, Moira, but I need to do an abdominal exam." He pulled down the blanket, and she looked away. It felt like a hundred days since a man had touched her. The doctor's fingers were mechanical, purposeful, not the hands of a lover. "Any pain?"

She shook her head.

"Here?"

Again, she shook her head.

"How 'bout here?"

"No."

He paused and then sat down in the chair again. "Moira, have you had your monthly time yet?"

She frowned, thinking back. "No, not yet."

"How about last month?"

Her frown deepened as she concentrated. She'd had it right before they reached New York. But since? She gave her head a little shake. "I've been traveling constantly. Perhaps that's upset my cycle."

"Perhaps," he returned, no belief in his voice. "How long? When was the last cycle you remember?"

"Two months past."

He nodded, chin in hand. "I'm sorry, Moira, but a doctor must sometimes ask painfully personal questions." A blush grew at his jaw line and spread up his lower cheeks. He refused to meet her eyes. "Could it be … is it possible that you are with child?"

"With child?" she repeated blankly. She knew how babies were made, of course. It was possible, considering her relationship with Gavin. She shook her head. "No. No, no."

"No, it isn't possible? Or no, you hope I'm incorrect in my potential diagnosis? Your uterus is enlarged and hardened, as is common with pregnancy."

"No, no, no," she whispered. Tears dripped down her face, into her ears.

She could almost feel his eyes on the false wedding ring she wore. "Your husband … Daniel told me he passed on. I'm so sorry for your loss."

That made her giggle, slightly hysterical. "My husband? Passed on? I supposed that's right, in a manner of speaking."

He frowned and put his chin in his hand again. "Do you have people you could go to then? During this time?"

People. People, yes. But people she could go to? How would Bryce and Odessa, the perfect, proper Christian couple, receive her? Who knew where Nic was; it had been a long time … And Gavin was dead. No one in his family would ever acknowledge the responsibility of his estate to provide for his child, born out of wedlock. It was impossible.

"Can you get rid of it?"

His eyes widened and his mouth fell open for a moment. "I hardly think—"

"I've heard … there are methods. Ways to be rid of an unwanted—"

"No. I would never be a part of such a thing." He shoved back his disgust and leaned forward. "Moira, despite your sorrow, could this not be a good thing? A blessing?"

She laughed in his face. "A blessing? A blessing! I will be ostracized. No one will hire me for the stage, unless I become a common showgirl. 'Moira Colorado' is not, she's not … someone who becomes pregnant without being married."

"Apparently she is," the doctor said drily. "Moira, the mirage that is Moira Colorado is quickly evaporating. You need to decide who Moira the woman—the mother—will be." He buttoned up his satchel. "And it's imperative you eat. If not for you, for the child. I'm leaving this tonic for you. Take a spoonful three times a day. It will calm your stomach. I'll be back tomorrow to check on you."

"Don't bother."

"Doctor's duty," he returned. "Give it a night's sleep. What might seem the darkest news possible might be what ultimately brings you light."

"Are you a philosopher or a doctor?" she asked wearily.

"Both," he said with a small smile, "on occasion."

"I might leave town this very night. I'm in no condition to sing."

"No, I agree on that count, but I advise you to stay right where you are. Gain your strength. Gather your thoughts. Come up with a plan. It will all work out. It always does."

"Not always—"

"Not always the way we planned. But somehow, life has a way of righting itself, even when it's been put at odds." He turned away and walked to the door. "I'll come back tomorrow at the same time."

"Suit yourself. I may or may not be here."

"I hope you are, Moira."

He put his hand on the knob.

"Doctor!"

He looked back at her over his shoulder.

"Not a word about this, to anyone?"

"Of course not."

"If anyone asks, tell them I'll make a full recovery, in time. That's true, isn't it?"

"Perfectly."

❀

"It is too perfect," Reid said to Dennis. They watched as the young town doctor shook hands with Moira's guard—Daniel Adams—and walked down the street. "Judging from their faces, Moira will not be singing again tonight. The opera owner will be beside himself with rage." He looked to the man. "You took care of the McAllans' detective?"

"He will no longer be sending them further word of your whereabouts."

"You have all his telegrams?"

"I obtained them last night from his hotel room."

"Excellent. And his telegrams to the McAllans?"

"Your funds secured copies. You can easily emulate them." He reached inside his jacket pocket and pulled out a leather folder. "You'll find everything in here. He's been sending a telegram every three days."

"Easily replicated," Reid said, clasping his hands together. "Who knows better than I what I am up to? This will be rather enjoyable, keeping the McAllans busy with news, until we are directly upon them."

# Chapter 20

Bryce had returned from his search with the men. She could tell by the stoop of his shoulders, the way he hung his head, that they had not found success. Quickly, she told him of Samuel's illness, and he listened with concern. He pulled the baby into his arms and stared down into his eyes, then softly kissed his forehead. Then they sat down on two porch chairs and he looked her way. "It's a ruse, Odessa, a myth," he said. "We found the canyon, the canyon with a layer of black. It ran ten miles along No Sip Creek. We searched a hundred caves. There's no treasure, Dess. We must face the moment at hand, rather than what might be. And this moment," he said, taking her hands in his and looking to the mountains, then back to the ground. "Dess, I don't see a way out." He dared to look her in the eye. "Something must give. Robert will auction off my paintings, and we'll sell the gold bar and send the men to Spain, but in the meantime—Dess, there's no way to make it. I've reviewed the ledgers again and again. We'll starve before they return. We have to sell off some of the land."

Odessa considered his words. She knew why he was loathe to take this path. There was a cattleman to their north who would undoubtedly be pleased to pick up their land, but what would happen next year, when they needed it as their own herd returned to normal? Every year, even as remote as they were, this valley was becoming more populated.

"We have to pray for direction," she said, lifting a hand to her husband's cheek. "This desert place, this feeling of being lost? Let's ask God to show us how to go." She gave him a little shrug. "Because surely, I am as lost as you."

He slowly brought his eyes to meet hers. "We could sell it. Sell it all. Live off the proceeds for decades, even after Robert takes his cut."

She stared at him. She could not imagine him, her husband, without a ranch, without horses. She could not imagine herself anywhere but here, under the shadow of Eagle Peak. This was home. Theirs. Core. And yet, she bit her tongue. Who was she to say this was not the way in which God was leading?

"Can we pray about it?" she asked, her voice higher than normal.

He gathered her in then, into his arms. "We'll pray about it, Dess," he said, kissing her forehead. "I know this place means as much to you as it does to me. But all things are temporal, right? Could it be that God has something different in mind, even far better than we imagine?"

"Perhaps," she managed to whisper, nestled beneath his chin. But she longed for her heart to believe what her lips were speaking.

❁

Odessa picked up the baby from his crib and moved to the window where she studied their ranch. It was a spectacular afternoon; brilliant white snow still clung to the tips of the mountains, but below them, the valley was a riot in glorious spring green. New wildflowers had emerged this week, sprinkling the canvas with drops of bloodred and tropical orange and lemon yellow. "We must get out into that,

Samuel McAllan," she said to the baby. "It will clear our heads, allow God to speak directly to us, I'd wager."

He looked up at her as if startled she was speaking to him, then smiled and cooed his approval of her plan. She was so glad to see him well again; no trace of the fever lingered.

"Your father doesn't want me going anywhere alone, but he's occupied elsewhere." She thought a moment. "Come, let us see if your uncle cares to join us." She hurried down the stairs and into the kitchen and stopped short, when she saw Robert was again pouring over the ranch ledgers. "Oh," she muttered.

He looked up at them and then down to the ledger. "Bryce asked me to take another look," he said, explaining. "He told me he's thinking he might have to sell a portion of the property to see you through—and wondered if I might be able to see another way."

She hesitated, feeling the shift within her from defense to partnership. He was looking for a way to help them. Help them all. "Well then, I won't bother you."

"No, no," he said, "you're never a bother. Please. What did you need?"

"I didn't need anything. It's only that it's so beautiful … I wondered if you'd care to go on a ride with me. Bryce is up in the north forty and isn't due back until sundown." She sighed. "Even though he's hired a man to watch Reid Bannock, he's a little overprotective. He'd be very angry if I set out alone. But I fear if I don't get out of this house, I just might scream. And I know my horse needs it as much as I. But if you're too busy, I can talk one of the ranch hands into it."

He gave her a wry smile. "It might be good for me to clear my head—might give me some new ideas on how to help." He reached over to stroke the baby's head. "You think Samuel's well enough for it?"

"Tabito taught me how to make a sling to strap him on. He'll probably go straight to sleep with the rocking motion. And the fresh air will do him good."

Robert smiled again and lifted a brow. "I'd be happy to escort you."

"Marvelous!" she said. "I'll just pack a bag with some water and food and supplies for the baby and we can be off—if you'll see to our horses."

"I'd be glad to," he said with a mock bow.

She smiled and turned from him, thinking again how much he resembled Bryce. She wished Bryce was here to take the ride with her, but in his absence, his brother was a fine stand-in. She'd been silly, worrying over what might be transpiring between them. Since Bryce had been home, Robert had been nothing but proper. She shook her head. Her imagination was taking her places she didn't need to go. Bryce would be glad if she showed Robert the other side of the ranch, and the overlook that they both so loved.

Soon enough, they were riding across the fields. Samuel was so firmly strapped to her torso, he moved right along with her. At first, Odessa thought her plan would not work after all, because Samuel began to get fussy. But the momentum of their ride did the magic she expected, wooing him to sleep within minutes. The only bad thing was that with the baby's small body so close to hers, she was unbearably hot under the sun that was rising high in the sky. By the time they entered the forest on the far side, she could feel the sweat dripping down her neck and chest underneath her sleeping babe.

She led the way to the overlook, pushing Ebony up the steep trail, and she sighed in relief as they finally reached the flat top of the boulders. She turned Ebony to the side and looked back for Robert. In seconds, he joined her.

"Didn't realize this was a race," he said. But then he frowned in concern. "Are you all right?" He dismounted and hurried over to her, reaching up his hands to take her waist and help her down. It was a bit awkward, with the bulk of the baby in front of her, but they managed.

"I'm all right, only terribly hot. Your nephew is like a small heating oven."

"Shall we get him off of you?"

"I don't know. If we take him off, I'm not certain I can get it back on without Tabito."

"Surely it isn't too complex," Robert said, looking down at the straps of cloth and how the man had tied it. He walked around her several times. "I think I can do it."

"Bless you," Odessa said, suddenly incapable of thinking of anything but setting the baby down for his nap on a blanket. She lifted her arms, as she had for Tabito, and Robert went round and round her, winding the cloth strips around his arm in orderly fashion.

"Be you woman or be you mummy?" he asked with a grin.

"Both, in this instance," she said. In a minute, she was free, and she gleefully lifted Samuel off her chest and onto her shoulder. Cool air blew across her torso as she pulled the sticky, wet fabric from her skin again and again, hoping it would quickly dry.

Robert had turned from her, hands on hips, as he surveyed the valley. "This certainly is one of the prettiest places I've ever seen in my life." He crossed his arms and looked over his shoulder at her. "And this is the perfect overlook."

"It's my very favorite," she said. She settled Samuel into the blankets. Thankfully he stayed deeply asleep through it all. Then she reached for another blanket from behind the saddle on Ebony and spread it out on the rock. "Bryce and I think it the perfect picnic spot. I'm happy to share it with you." She looked out, northward, wondering how Bryce and the men were faring. This morning, Bryce had been downtrodden, so worried was he about what was to come. Could he really sell the whole thing? Cash out? A part of her thought it might be lovely to purchase a small cottage somewhere. He could paint. She could write. But deep down, she knew he'd be terribly bored …

Robert went to his horse and pulled down the bag that contained their water and food. He knelt across from her and pulled out a couple of apples, imported from California, and ham nestled between thick slabs of bread baked that morning, wrapped in cloth. "Looks wonderful," he said, handing her one. "I'm famished."

"Me, too," she said, unwrapping her sandwich and taking a big bite.

"So do you still think the conquistador gold is hidden in these hills, despite Bryce's pessimism?" Robert said.

She smiled and swallowed. "I don't know. That legend has been told for some time."

Samuel stirred and, in seconds, built up to a full wail. "Guess he's hungry too," Robert said. He jumped up to fetch the child and then returned him to her. "I'll just go over to the other side; give you two some privacy."

Odessa smiled her appreciation and once he was a distance away began to unbutton and untie undergarments to feed her son. She draped a blanket over her shoulder, in case Robert forgot himself and returned too soon, but he stayed on the other side until they finished and she called to him. "I better get back. I need to start supper."

"Hate to leave this place. It's truly beautiful."

"Me, too."

"So, you ready to get mummified again?" he asked, reaching for the long strips of cloth.

"Only way to get the boy back," she said with a shrug. She'd have to remember to take early morning or late evening rides if she was going to take the baby along, especially with summer's heat coming on.

"Let's see," he said, hovering behind her, hesitating.

She bit her lip, realizing that this might become very awkward. Why hadn't she just settled down in the shade for a moment? Why had she rashly decided to detach Samuel as quickly as possible?

He reached both arms around her and pulled the strip straight in front of her waist, then brought it in back to tie with a quick knot. "There, I think that's how he did it. Now we wind you up."

"The trick is holding the baby as you wind," she said. She turned and lifted an elbow and then did another half-turn and lifted the other. She did several more rotations.

"It's rather like a dance," Robert said, blushing. They came to the end of the first strip and he carefully knotted a second at her hip and they continued to wind around, fastening Samuel to her chest again. The third strip ended by the baby's neck and Robert's brow lowered in concentration as the child voiced his frustration. "Almost done, little man," he said. He was fumbling with the knot, struggling to find another strap loose enough to fasten it.

"Here," she said, "let me." She took the end from his hand, and then she dropped it as soon as their hands touched. His eyes immediately met hers and for the first time, they both realized how close they stood together. Only little Samuel was between them.

He searched her eyes, his own rounding with desire, hope. She could feel her lips part as she took a slow, labored breath, her chest suddenly heavy for reasons beyond the babe atop it. He reached up, and she thought he was coming to himself again, realizing they were on dangerous ground, reaching for the strap to finish the knot and be out of here, but instead he touched her cheek.

"Robert, don't do this," she whispered.

"I can't help it. God help me, I can't help it."

"No, Robert," she said, shaking her head and edging away. "No."

He took a hold of her hips and Odessa couldn't move, feeling as if she were indeed in some sort of mad dream. Dimly, she realized Samuel was quiet, sucking on his lower lip, but still, settled. Did he not know what sort of madness his mother had entered? Robert leaned closer, over Samuel's head, waiting for her to look up, welcome his kiss, join him in this exploration. "One kiss," he pleaded in a whisper, so close she could feel his breath on her forehead.

"That will lead to what?" she said, looking up at him. With each word, the fog receded, clarity returning. She pulled his hands from her and backed away. "Think, Robert. I am your brother's *wife*."

He closed his eyes and ran both hands into his hair, his face awash in agony. "Forgive me, Odessa." He opened his eyes and shook his head. "I am weak." He attempted a smile as he dropped his hands into a gesture of defeat. "Can I be blamed for sharing my brother's taste in women?"

Odessa did not smile back. Fury made every nerve taut. "Yes, Robert. I believe you can." She moved over to her horse, eager to get back to the ranch now, away from him. But when she reached Ebony's side, she realized she couldn't mount without his assistance.

"Here," he said, reaching for her waist.

"Try it, and so help me, Robert, I will punch you with everything in me."

"Dess, I'm just helping you mount."

"And I need assistance. But you have to swear to me you'll be a perfect gentleman, or I'll walk Ebony all the way home. And then you'll have thirteen men ready to build a gallows for you." She realized she was advancing upon him, pointing her index finger into his chest.

He grabbed hold of it and wrapped both hands around her hand, bringing her to a standstill. She paused, awestruck at the emotions that swept through her. The thrill of being admired, sought after … heavens, did she *share* his forbidden attraction? She looked up at him and he looked back at her, his face a picture of misery. "I deserve the gallows, Dess. But what does it say that I'd risk them for you? Don't you see? Can't you feel—"

"No!" she cried, turning away and reaching for Ebony's reins. The horse pulled against her, irritated at being yanked away from the tender green shoots that sprouted from the rocks, but she held on. "We have a choice, Robert! Regardless of any feelings we might share! I love your brother. Your brother! We must come to our senses and walk away." She realized she had hot tears running down her face.

He stepped forward but she frowned and turned away, hurrying down the path.

"Dess! Odessa!"

She ignored his calls and hurried onward. She wiped her eyes with the back of her hand and tried to focus on the path. If she lost her footing and fell … *Lord God! This is terrible! Please, help me! Help us all!*

There. Two ledges pushed into the path, like two stairs up the side. She quickly climbed them and then straddled her horse, sliding her boots into the stirrups.

"Odessa, wait. Let's talk this through." He was right behind her, already astride his horse. Calm had returned to his features.

But she was taking no chances. She turned Ebony halfway around so she could face him. "No, Robert. We'll speak at home. On the front porch. And only in the light of day. We'll need to send a man to town to purchase a ticket."

"A ticket?" he asked blankly.

"A ticket on tomorrow's train. You, Robert McAllan, are heading home. Figure out your excuse for Bryce. But you are leaving. Do you understand me?"

He regarded her solemnly. "I do."

# Chapter 21

Moira was failing, Daniel knew. She was suffering from some terrible ailment. And there was a lost look in her eyes, as troubling as a canoe drifting down a river with no one at the paddle. He'd done his duty, seen to it that the doc came by. The rest was up to the others, and to God. He was getting too involved, letting his heart get too wrapped up in this girl. Again.

He sighed and padded down to the end of the hall to look out upon the street. That new merchant, Bannock, stood across the street, leaning against a post in front of the law office there, smoking his cigar and studying the hotel. Daniel frowned. What was he watching?

Bannock took another draw from the stub of his cigar then dropped it to the dirt of the street and ground it in with his heel. He set off down Main in the direction of his mercantile and Daniel shrugged off the dislike he felt for the man, along with his aimless suspicions. In a town this size, it never was good to make enemies. His goal was to get along with everyone, be neither friend or foe to anyone. That was how he liked it. That was how life had become manageable these last three years.

Henry Colvard, the Leadville Opera House owner, barreled past Bannock and across the street. Daniel walked to the top of the stairs and saw him pull open the front door of the hotel with such force it banged against the wall. Daniel grimaced and a shiver of anger ran through him. A girl not singing was no cause for damaging another's prop—

"I will see Miss Moira immediately," he said, looking up at Daniel. He immediately began climbing the stairs.

Daniel raised his hands. "I told you, Mr. Colvard. She's not up to it. Go and ask the doc," he said, pointing back down the staircase. "Ask him yourself. Miss Moira is poorly, so poorly she'd faint dead away if she got up on your stage. You saw how it went two nights ago."

Daniel thought about Moira. The way she was acting … it was as if she didn't even want to get better.

Colvard shook his head in rage. "Do you know what it's like to turn away two hundred men who've traveled a day or more to see her? *Two* nights in a row?"

"Can't say as I do," Daniel said. They had entertainers from time to time on the tiny stage in the saloon, but no one half as grand as Moira Colorado. "You're lucky she's sticking around. She told you she wouldn't leave until she fulfilled her obligations." He ducked his head to one side. "You're not the only manager who will be wrestling an angry mob if she can't get moving again. Miss Colorado understands that. Her intention is to make things right, as quickly as possible. But Colvard," he said, putting up one hand, cutting him off as he tried to pass him, "If the woman's too sick to sing, she's too sick."

"I was fortunate they didn't burn me out last night! I had to promise them a free drink tonight if they returned. What will they do when I fail them again?" He paced back and forth and shook his head, his jowls following a half-second behind. He raised a finger at Daniel. "No. No, I said that last night was the end of my patience. Giving her another night to recover was beyond gracious. No other stageman I know would tolerate this. Every entertainer in the business knows the show must go on … even when one is feeling poorly. If I don't see Moira Colorado—"

"You shall see me on your stage tonight, Mr. Colvard."

The men turned to see Moira standing in the hallway. She was dressed to perfection, even with a tiny hat perched on her head. Colvard sputtered and turned to her, all his fury spent like butter on a hot stove. "Miss Moira! Oh, am I relieved to see you up and about!"

He didn't seem to notice that one of Moira's gloved hands clung to the doorjamb without moving, as if it were the only thing keeping her upright, or that while her makeup was perfectly applied, beneath it she was still the pasty girl Daniel had glimpsed inside her room.

It was all an act. He was witnessing an act. She purred and murmured to Henry with aplomb, reaching out with her left hand to graze the man's shoulder and then forearm as she spoke, reeling him in like a fat trout on the line. But she'd soon need to cut this fish loose. She couldn't stay on her feet much longer.

Quickly, he poured a glass of water from a center hall table and casually walked over to the duo. "Glad to see you up and about, Moira," he said. "You must be dry as prairie grass in summer."

"Bless you, I'm parched," she said. She accepted the glass and drank half of it down, then handed it back to him. All done up or not, she was truly beautiful. While she'd pulled her blonde hair up into a tasteful knot, curling tendrils escaped around her neck. A China doll, with those rosebud lips and wide green-blue eyes. He saw, then, a thin rivulet of perspiration running from her temple down her neck and into the bodice of her fine gown.

Again, he wondered how long she could manage this charade and silently he urged Colvard to leave, as if he could will the man out of the hotel.

"I confess I believed the worst, Miss Moira," Henry said with a bow of his head. "I thought you might be an addict, or worse, simply reneging on your contractual obligations. As I'm sure you understand, I cannot tolerate either. It would be to the ruination of the opera house."

"I understand," Moira returned sweetly. She raised one delicate, arched brow. "Until tonight, then? I shall be backstage by five o'clock, ready to go on at six."

"Perfect," Henry said with a sigh. He placed his hat atop his head, a rather smart top hat that made his round face a bit less round, and gave her a small bow. "Thank you, Miss Moira. I look forward to hearing you sing tonight." Moira gave him a wave, and then he was back out on the street.

Daniel looked around and saw that Moira was again in a swoon, falling in an arc. He narrowly caught her up in his arms. Up close, he could tell she'd dressed hurriedly and she needed a bath. Daniel sighed and lifted Moira higher in his arms and entered her room to lay her on the bed.

Then he sat in a corner chair to wait.

She roused in a minute, looked around groggily, then seeing him, tried to sit up.

"Whoa, whoa," he said, lifting his hands, but remaining in his seat. "It's all right. You just fainted."

"Oh," she said, lying back. She laid a delicate hand on her forehead.

"Moira, what is the matter with you? Did the doc say?" He paused and waited, but she remained silent. "Is it … is it, Gavin?"

"It's nothing," she said, obviously lying. "I'm simply exhausted. Gavin and I …" Her voice broke. "It was the constant travel, I'm certain," she said, gathering herself. "Our transatlantic journey, then my life seems to have been one train or stagecoach ride ever since." She looked at him and smiled. "Give me a little time. I should recover soon."

He sat back in the chair, arms folded, wondering if he should confront her now or later. She had a show to do tonight, and she was plainly grieving Gavin. But he knew what it was like, running from the truth. You could never get far enough ahead of it to make it worthwhile.

"Moira."

Slowly, she looked his direction. She looked so young, so frightened, so weary, Daniel had a hard time keeping his seat, not going to her. But he sensed that would overwhelm her, send her into hiding rather than drawing her out as he wished. "Tell me. As fast as you can. Without thinking about it. Just tell me." He paused. "You can trust me."

She waited as if weighing his words, then blurted, "I'm pregnant." She stared at him as those two words left her rosebud lips, as if shocked she'd actually let them out.

He sat back for a moment as the ramifications of her declaration settled on him. The terror for her, to be alone—"Congratulations," he said softly.

She gave him a scoffing laugh. "Congratulations?" She shook her head once, then turned to look at the ceiling. "It was a farce, Daniel. A convenient lie. We were never married. He never loved me. Never intended …" Her voice broke then and she tucked her chin, blinking rapidly.

Fury surged through Daniel. *Gavin.* He'd suspected the man was using her. Taken advantage of his position. And yet Moira was a woman grown. Responsible for her own decisions. He looked to the window and then down to his hands. He was in no position to judge.

"Daniel." She was looking at him with those gorgeous green-blue eyes, beseeching him. "Say something."

He stared back at her, knowing he couldn't be near her. Not now. Not yet anyway. "Moira, you are not alone. I promise you that."

❁

Moira sank gratefully into the warm bath that Daniel had had two maids bring up. It wasn't too hot, which would sap her, and not too cool. She had opened her trunk and lifted a small chest full of aromatics—a bit of mint to invigorate her; a touch of lavender oil to soothe. She was shaky, but after closing her eyes for a while and choking down a half cup of chicken broth, she managed to get to the tub and into it unaided. She held her breath and went all the way under, letting the water seep into her scalp, and then resurfacing, eyes still closed, breathing in the lovely smells.

She wiped her face with a small cloth, washing all her makeup off, intending to begin again. Then she reached for a luxurious, rich shampoo that she lathered in her hands before rubbing it through her hair and rinsing. She had to see tonight's performance—and tomorrow's—through, then escape this town. She would send word to the opera houses on her schedule that she would have to postpone, in plenty of time to avoid the ire of the last three of four. That would give her three to go back to when she was again ready to take the stage. If she would ever be ready …

She rubbed her hands over her belly. There was no telltale curve there, no fluttering within. How had the doctor known? She pressed down, wondering if she could feel a small baby there, and discovered a hardening, the size of an apple. Her womb. Now carrying a child. "Oh, Mama, what have I done?"

She looked to the empty chair beside the tub, wished her mother were perched there, ready to help her sort it out. Had her parents been alive back in Philadelphia, with her still at home, they would have sent her away to quietly have the baby. They would have helped her find a good home for it. She'd heard whispers … of how it was done. Then a match would have been made, to a less-than-desirable suitor, who would not hold it against her that she had been deflowered before their wedding night. It was the common penance for a fallen woman of society—life without love, now a life negotiated. But she was not a girl under her mother's wing or her father's roof. She was a woman grown. And she had to figure this out herself.

She nervously glanced to the empty chair, her last question echoing in the air. *Mama?*

*You are well aware of what you have done, child. Now the question is, what will you do?*

Moira closed her eyes and listened to her mother's reasonable, measured tone. There was no condemnation in it, only a demand for her to think responsibly now. What to do, what to do.... She knew she needed to, first, get through tonight. Salvage her reputation. Preserve it for the future. Then set it aside like lovely summer preserves on a basement shelf while she negotiated winter. And Daniel ... Daniel had promised her she wouldn't be alone. What had he meant by that? He would see through his obligations to protect her, watch over her as a hired guard? Or something more?

*Isn't that enough to figure out, for today?*

*You are dodging the baby.*

*I know it. But, Mama, I can't think about it right now. It's too much, too overwhelming.*

*Just remember, Moira, you were once as small as that child within your womb. She will one day reach for you and you will smile with gladness, happy she is yours.*

*That isn't helping, Mama. Please, stop ...*

*The only way through difficult times is to put one foot in front of the other. Lift that St. Clair chin. Throw your shoulders back. Move, and the rest will come.*

Moira shook her head and then went back underwater, as if she could muffle her mother's voice in her ears. She knew it was all a figment of her imagination, but she felt powerless to stop it. A phrase kept ringing through her mind: "Happy she is yours." *Yours. Mine.* Hers. She didn't want a child. A child was the last thing she'd ever wanted. Odessa was the natural mother, the ideal mother, the meant-to-be mother. Not her.

*But you have been given a child. God does not make mistakes.*

"But people do," she whispered back. She rose and reached for her towel.

❁

Two hours later, she was dressed in a fresh gown, her makeup reapplied. She pushed down another half cup of broth that Daniel had brought up. *You can do this. You are Moira Colorado. Show them what that means.*

She moved to the door and found the hallway empty, then went down the stairs and finally spied Daniel, talking to the front-desk girl in hushed undertones. She wondered at the wave of irritation she felt, seeing the man pay attention to another, but then she shoved the feelings away.

Daniel followed the desk clerk's gaze to Moira, letting his sentence trail off. "Moira," he said, moving over to her. "You look … fine."

"I'm much improved," she lied. Hopefully, if he couldn't see the fine sheen of sweat along her hairline, others wouldn't either. "Are the girls over there? The pianist?"

"Everyone," he said, still studying her with eyes filled with concern.

He really was handsome, a bit of a Greek god in his looks. He looked her over and lifted his chin. "Are you certain you're up to tonight's show, Moira?"

"Absolutely," she declared, doing as her mama suggested and lifting her chin in response.

A tiny smile edged his lips at her answer. "Glad to hear it."

She took his offered arm and moved forward, concentrating on walking as if she were floating. "I thank you for sending the bath water up and for the broth. I believe both will help me see this through." They moved past the mousy front-desk clerk who busied herself with the sheaf of papers before her.

But by the time they reached the corner, Moira was shaking.

"Moira?" Daniel asked in concern, pulling her to a stop.

"Just get me to the theater, Daniel," she said in a whisper, wiping her forehead with his handkerchief and praying she didn't vomit right here on Main Street. "I'll rest there, and discuss with the girls how to manage this, with me … in recovery."

❀

Daniel's eyes settled on Reid Bannock, who sat alone at another table, over to the left of the stage. Reid was staring at him, over a full glass of whiskey, and when their eyes met, he raised it, as if in salute. It was not odd for a well-to-do merchant to come to a well-known performer's show, Daniel supposed. But he couldn't shove away the shadow that he felt creep across him, especially after seeing the man out on Main today, staring at the hotel. He stifled a groan when Bannock rose and made his way over to him.

"You're Daniel Adams, aren't you?" Reid said, reaching out a hand.

"I am."

"I'm Reid Bannock. I think we've met before, over at your saloon. You work for the hotelier, tend the bar, right?"

"On occasion," Daniel replied slowly, as if just remembering their meeting. "But my time here has come to an end. I've given my notice and am on to new things."

"So, what brings you out tonight? I've never seen you at the opera house before."

Daniel studied him. Just what was he asking? Again, the cool shadow crossed over him. This man was dangerous. No need for him to know his role in Moira's life at the moment. "Thought I needed a night out," he said casually.

"All men do," Reid said with a wink. "Does the missus know you're here?"

"I don't have a wife."

"Hmm," Reid said, as if absorbing the information like it was some great secret. He raised an eyebrow. "Neither do I." He gestured toward Daniel's empty table. "Say, can I buy you a drink?"

"No, thanks. I don't partake."

Reid frowned, puzzled and took a chair across from him. "Now that's a story I'd like to hear. How does a barkeep not partake?"

Daniel smiled gently and put out his hands. "Maybe it's a story I'll tell you someday. When we're better friends." Blessedly, the music began then, indicating the show was about to start.

"Fair enough," Reid said, reaching out to shake his hand again. "Enjoy the show," he whispered.

He left, but there was something about his last words that troubled Daniel, as if he meant something more.

The showgirls came out and did their opening act. Daniel crossed his arms and looked down at his table while they danced, judging from the hoots and hollers around him that those skirts were lifting far too high. Being a gentleman, he refused to look. In his opinion, women need not show their legs to garner attention. But as the women withdrew, blowing lanterns out as they went, and the music slowed in pace and tone, he looked up.

Moira, at last. Could she make it through a whole song, let alone several, given her condition?

But she entered, each step smooth, assured, looking hauntingly beautiful. His thoughts came to a standstill when she sang her opening note. It was almost immediately drowned out by the cheers of the people in the audience. Daniel fought the urge to rise and tell them all to be quiet. They remained in an opera house in a West barely settled, and the rowdy crowd in attendance was a prime example of it. He clamped his teeth together and forced himself to remain still, watching as Moira emerged from behind the curtain in her lovely deep russet gown. She sang with such clarity, such depth of emotion, that he doubted anyone knew she was suffering. She moved in time with her song, emphasizing high and low notes with the lantern in her hand, and slowly, ever so slowly, she got up and made her way to the end of the stage, near him.

He watched her make eye contact with every man in the room, beginning in back, drawing them in. He could see that she had made this an art, captivating everyone she sang for in some deep, visceral manner, but he couldn't summon the will to be jealous. All he wanted was for her to sing, keep singing. Sing bar songs, sing children's ditties, sing hymns, but just sing, because surely, this was a gift from God on high!

She built into the crescendo of the song, then slowly wound toward the end. Her eyes were just behind him now, moving left to right, as she had that first night. The effect was mesmerizing. He finally saw what Gavin had immediately seen … Moira was a sensation with foundation. A legend about to be born.

There. Her eyes reached him. He didn't know whether to smile or nod. Instead, he shifted uncomfortably. Her blue-green eyes hovered upon him, made him feel seen, known, and then she moved on to the man at his left.

❁

Reid's heart pounded with anticipation. In a moment, she would know her eyes had not deceived her, that he was really here, right before her. Tonight, Moira would again be in his arms, one way or another. And she would serve as the key to unlock the McAllan fortune. And as they made their way to the Circle M, she could find a way to make things right for him, pay him back for all the ways she had robbed him.

Moira stopped singing, staring at Reid as if he were an apparition.

Daniel came to his feet. The pianist started round again, urging her return to the song, but Moira appeared frozen, staring at Reid.

And Reid stared, a slow smile spreading across his face. "Hello, Moira," he said, so lowly that only a few around him could hear.

Moira screamed and dropped the lantern. Oil spilled across the stage and the fire ran behind it, as if lapping it up. Some spilled on her dress, and it immediately was aflame. She ran, down the stage, backstage, as chaos erupted throughout the hall. Daniel ran after her. Men and women charged for the exits, panicked by the fire that spread impossibly fast. The front stage was a wall of flame in under a minute. Reid slowly rose and looked around. Only a few others remained, beating at the fire with their jackets. But with the base of oil, it was hopeless. The entire building would be engulfed in minutes.

Backstage, he could hear women screaming.

And Reid smiled.

# Chapter 22

Daniel made his way around the side of the stage to the very back and climbed atop. At one side, the curtains were burning and reaching to the ceiling. The building was surely lost. Daniel hoped it wouldn't take most of the city. Fires could devastate a town, take months if not years to recover from. "Moira!" he yelled. The fire was growing in noise, beginning to breathe, as if panting in anticipation of its next bite. Crackling wood, falling timber and objects added to the clamor amidst the screams of the fleeing crowd. "Moira!" he yelled.

A man ran by, calling for another girl. "Moira!" Daniel yelled, grabbing the man's arm. "Have you seen Moira?"

"Back there," he yelled, squinting against the smoke. "In her dressing room!"

Daniel pulled a handkerchief from his pocket and covered his nose and mouth. It did little to help, but something was better than nothing. He opened one door after another. Two women ran by him, holding hands and crying. Daniel yelled Moira's name over and over. Perhaps she'd gotten out. Escaped.

But then he got to a door that was locked. "Moira!" he shouted, pushing at the door with his shoulder to no avail. "It's Daniel! We must get out of here!"

There was no answer. But he could hear crying. She was behind the door, he was sure of it. He looked left and saw the fire race up an arc of cloth as if it were paper dried in a kiln. The man he had seen before came running toward him, dragging a coughing woman by the hand. Both were soot black and had singed hair. "Get out, man!" he yelled to Daniel as they passed.

"Moira, I'm coming in!" Daniel shouted. He backed up and rammed through the door with his shoulder, wincing at the pain of the breath-stealing blow.

A man emerged through the smoke. Reid Bannock. "Get out, Adams!" He shouted. "This whole place is coming down!"

Daniel hesitated. "She's in there," he said, nodding toward the door. "I have to get her out."

Reid's eyes widened and he said, "We'll do it together. On three."

After his count, they burst through, Daniel falling in front of Reid.

Moira screamed. "Help!" she shouted. "Help!"

Daniel frowned. "Moira," he said, shaking her. The left shoulder of her dress had burned and was practically falling off. He winced to see that she had suffered burns to her skin there, up her neck. Half her hair was singed away. "Moira, it's all right. We're going to get you out."

"No!" she said, scrambling backward, as if she wished to sink into the corner of the room. "No!" It was then he noticed her eyes were not on him. They were hovering behind him.

He turned slowly, the hair on his neck standing on end, and saw Reid Bannock, his pistol drawn and pointed at him. Behind the man, up higher, the room was billowing with dark, choking smoke. The roar and heat of the fire was very near.

"What are you doing, Bannock?"

"I'm rescuing Miss St. Clair," he said. "You, sadly, must perish here." He squeezed the trigger.

"Wait—"

The bullet pierced him and sent him whirling.

Moira screamed.

And Daniel blacked out.

❁

Daniel was coughing so hard he thought he'd never catch enough oxygen to gather another breath. He opened his eyes, but they immediately stung so much that he shut them. He winced and rocked his head back and forth, trying to make sense of the pain, pain like he hadn't felt in years. A bullet. Panting, he reached toward his shoulder and felt the familiar ooze of a wound.

His eyes opened again, wide. *Moira.*

"Moira," he said, rolling to his knees. Flames were licking inside the room, darting in and out like a dragon's tongue. "Moira!" He gagged on the smoke and began coughing again.

His only chance—and maybe hers—was for him to escape this inferno.

And find Bannock.

❁

Moira awakened in excruciating pain. She opened her eyes and cried out in terror. It was almost completely dark.

"Shh, you'll wake the neighbors," a man said, opening a wooden door. She could see a bright starry sky behind him.

"D-Daniel?"

"No, Moira, it's me," he said, moving to the center of the room.

Moira held her breath, hoping she had misheard. He turned up the wick of a lantern and then bent to put wood into a stove. Then Reid turned to her. He paused a couple feet away, as if understanding her fear, confusion. "Do you remember what happened?"

Moira lifted a shaking hand to her forehead and found it sticky and wet.

"Don't do that," he said, raising a hand in her direction. "You'll want to leave that be."

He moved to the stove, picked up a kettle, and poured a cup of tea. Then he brought it over to her. Peppermint, she decided, by the smell of it. It hurt to move her mouth to drink, but she was so thirsty, she had no choice. She lay back against the pillows and fought the desire to scream—both from the pain and from her fear. What was he doing out of prison? And here? What did he intend to do with her? Casually, she stole a glance beneath the covers. Still in her russet gown. He'd cut away the fabric over her burned shoulder and upper bodice but left her corset in place, keeping her modesty intact. The bottom of the dress was cut to her knees, and as the covers settled again, she winced at the pain, especially in her calf. "How bad are my burns?"

"Your leg's pretty bad," he said evenly. "I've seen a man die of burns like that, and they weren't much worse. Infection sets in. Your neck, face and scalp—" He shook his head. "I'd say your showgirl days are over, Moira."

She sat up, unable to say anything before she vomited her tea on the blanket. She lay back, her stomach relieved, but her heart and mind in upheaval. She could not stop the tears, but as they flowed down her cheeks, she winced. The salt cut through whatever balm he had put on her face and irritated the burns, which only made her cry harder.

Grimly, Reid gathered the blanket together and took it outside. Where were they? Where had he taken her? He returned after a moment.

"Daniel, he—"

"He's dead. Left him behind in the opera house, and I doubt there's much left of him but cinders now."

Moira moaned, feeling so ill she wished she could vomit again. *Daniel.* She remembered now. "Why, Reid? Why are you here? And why have you taken me?"

He smiled. "You are the key in the lock of my treasure chest."

"What are you talking about?" she asked, wiping away her tears.

He sat back down beside her and picked up her hand. On it was the wedding ring that Gavin had slipped on her finger. "Here's the deal. Your husband is dead. And now your guardian is dead. I'm your only hope at survival, Moira. And I'm taking you home to Odessa, to the Circle M," he said, as proudly as if he were escorting her to a county picnic.

She shook her head. "There is no mine, Reid. Old Sam … it was all a ruse. They haven't found anything."

"You've been gone a while, right, Moira?" Reid leaned closer to her. "So I'd wager I have newer information than you. I'm not after the mine, anyway. There's something more, I think. Having you with me will force them to hand over what they've discovered." He rose and placed a hand on either side of her and looked her over. She couldn't bear to watch him. Did he intend to rape her now too?

"Moira Colorado." He shook his head. "You had to go and chase that dream of the stage, didn't you? Where has it gotten you? Burned and scarred for life." He rose and walked away, as if disgusted.

Scarred. Again, she reached up and dabbed at her face and up into her scalp. Then down to her neck and shoulder. Was she burned everywhere? Or just one side? The only good thing about it was that it might keep Reid at bay. She glanced his way.

He regarded her coolly from across the room, reading her thoughts. "It's mostly your neck. Hair must've caught fire. Someone must've gotten that put out backstage before I found you."

She looked up to the ceiling, thinking. "Yes. Matthew, a stagehand. He got it out, but then a curtain was on fire, and then my hair and my dress …" She reached up and felt for her hair. Her eyes widened in alarm.

"Half of it's gone," he said calmly, as if describing a storm already passed. "If we tend to the burns on your scalp, there's a chance it'll come back." He glanced over at her again. "Quit your weeping, Moira. It'll sting the burns on your face."

❦

Daniel awakened again in Dr. Beason's office. He blinked hard against the bright light of eight lanterns surrounding him. Then screamed out in pain, all of a sudden remembering what had brought him here in the first place.

"Hold him still," the young doctor said firmly. Several people took better hold of him as the physician dug into his flesh, making Daniel scream again. "There, we have it," said Dr. Beason, holding up a bullet to the light and dropping it into a pan with a clank.

Daniel panted hard, trying to focus, remember what had happened.

"You were lucky," the doctor said, moving into his line of vision. "All that soot on you, it took us a while to figure out someone had shot you too."

*Moira. Bannock.* Daniel's vision cleared and he sat up.

"Whoa, whoa, whoa!" Dr. Beason cried. His assistants rushed back toward their patient.

Daniel brought his legs around.

A new man entered the room—Sheriff Chambers. "You in a hurry to go somewhere, Daniel?"

"I have business to attend to," Daniel said, reaching for his shirt, which was covered in soot and blood.

The sheriff gave him a rueful smile. "Think you'll want a clean one. You're lucky to be alive, Daniel. Who shot you and left you for dead?"

The doctor and his assistants forced Daniel to stay still as they began to bandage up his shoulder.

"It was the same man who took Moira Colorado," Daniel said, wincing as they wound the bandage around him. "Reid Bannock."

The man's eyes narrowed. "Bannock? And Moira Colorado is alive?"

"Yes, and somehow she knew Bannock. She was afraid of him, looks like for good reason."

The sheriff thought over his words. "You're not the only one who got shot. There was a man in town—a detective—who was shot and left for dead in an abandoned mine. We just retrieved his body."

"Think Bannock shot him, too?"

"Could be," he said, tucking his chin down. "The question is, why?"

Daniel stepped off the table and winced, blinking rapidly, hoping to keep from blacking out. "I need to help you find them. Moira's in danger. And I was charged with her care."

"You just leave Miss Moira to me," said the sheriff. "We'll find 'em."

"Did anyone see which direction they were heading?" He reached out and steadied himself against the wall, then, after a moment, grabbed his jacket. It was burned full of holes.

"I'm afraid not."

Another man peeked in the doorway and caught the sheriff's attention. "Excuse me," the sheriff said, moving into the hallway to speak with the man. Daniel wished he could get past the doctor and nurse and follow him out. Had they learned something more about Moira?

"Sit down, Mr. Adams," said Dr. Beason sternly. "You're liable to pass out. You need to give that shoulder a few hours before you even think of moving."

"Sorry, Doc," Daniel said, pulling on his soot-soaked shirt. "I have to be on my way." He ignored Beason's angry retort and left. Fortunately for him, the doctor had many other patients awaiting him; people lined the hallway and waiting room. He threw up his hands at Daniel's stupidity and moved on to the next one.

Daniel walked directly over to the sheriff and deputy. "Listen, Sheriff, I have to help you find her. It's my duty."

Sheriff Chambers regarded him and then reached for the paper in the deputy's hand. "Looks like Reid Bannock has been a bit of a nuisance down near Westcliffe." Daniel's eyes scanned the wanted poster, detailing Bannock's history as a freed prisoner who had violated his parole.

"How could this have happened?" Daniel asked. "How was it that he had enough money to come here, buy the merc and the house?"

"I intend to find out," the sheriff responded. "There's more. The telegraph operator identified the detective who was shot as one who had been sending a telegram every other day to a couple near Westcliffe."

"Westcliffe?" Daniel repeated. Bannock had been wanted down there. "I think Moira said something about having a sister thereabouts. On a big spread not far from Westcliffe." He remembered her going on and on about it aboard ship one day, how her sister had become a rancher's wife while she felt more at home in a city. She had a brother, too, somewhere.

"You said Moira appeared to have known this Bannock?"

"Yes."

"It all has to be tied together somehow."

"Yes," Daniel agreed. "It does. Bannock is after something, and he's using Moira to get it. Those people at the ranch, they clearly feared he was coming back and wanted to make sure he stayed put. We have to warn them."

# Chapter 23

Nic liked the sultry, slow-paced rhythm of Central American ports as the ship made her way northward. He even settled into the cadence of being aboard ship again, appreciating things he hadn't before—the rations of fresh water, two meals a day, tasks to complete, and then falling into his hammock for a night's rest. Slowly, he gained a few of the pounds he had lost, but never had he felt stronger, physically. He could endure a six-hour shift of hauling up and belaying sails or six hours before the yawning mouth of a coal-burning stove, fueling the fires that emitted the steam that helped him inch his way back to America. The combination of both steam and sail made the ship one of the fastest he'd ever sailed on.

He did not know what he would do once he reached her shores, but he knew he wanted to get back to the United States. He daydreamed of sourdough bread and pot roast, of pie and ice cream, straight off the paddle. He thought of Moira and Odessa, hungry for word of their well-being. His father's voice echoed through his dreams at night, urging him to see to his sisters' welfare, make certain they—

Nic fell from his hammock, groaning on the floor. He looked up and saw that he was surrounded by shipmates, and they were laughing. It was Alejandro who had his hand on Nic's hammock—he had dumped him. He gestured toward Nic and said something foul in Spanish. The man had been taunting him from the day he first crawled aboard, starving to death. Up to now Nic had ignored him, but this, this was too much.

Nic jumped to his feet and edged toward the man, ignoring the alarmed delight of the other men. "Stay away from me," he warned Alejandro in his own tongue. "Trust me," he said, switching to English, "I could pound you to a pulp."

The man sneered at him and spit in his face. Nic waited no longer. He pulled back his fist, looking forward to seeing Alejandro spin away from him once the punch landed, when a strong arm held him back. He whirled, ready to hit the man who held him.

Manuel, the coal boss. Nic lowered his fist.

"You wish to make it to California?" Manuel asked.

"I do," he ground out.

"Then, no fighting. The capitan, I've seen him toss brawlers overboard for the sharks." He tapped Nic on the chest. "Make certain you're not the next."

"Manuel, you can't expect me to ignore them?" Nic said, gesturing in exasperation toward the retreating backs of Alejandro and his companions.

"I expect you to think only of California and how you get there. Right now, this ship is your fastest way there, no?"

Nic didn't answer. He clenched his hands and slowly flexed them.

"California," Manuel said again, one eyebrow arched meaningfully. "Say it."

"California," Nic whispered.

Nic knew it would take another twelve days to reach California's border, another two to reach Los Angeles. Fourteen days. Could he make it fourteen days without fighting? *California,* he repeated silently. Just the name of it stirred him, buoyed him to belief that there he could make a new start, make a name for himself as … what? He did not know how he would make his way back to Colorado, to Odessa, only that California was the bridge that would get him there. And once there … perhaps Odessa could help him figure out what to do next.

If he couldn't even reach the States—if he was thrown overboard for fighting—he might not see his sisters ever again.

Alejandro, the leader among six men who seemed to delight the most in his slow torture, edged past him as he emerged on deck, hitting his shoulder so hard that Nic spun halfway around. Nic paused for a moment and closed his eyes, feeling the shiver run up his neck and over his scalp, back down his shoulders and to his fingertips, now wrapped in a clench. Alejandro moved on, tossing his hand in the air and laughing, calling Nic several foul names, recognizable in any language. He took several deep breaths, repeating, "California."

His captain whistled and lifted his chin in Nic's direction when he opened his eyes. He gestured down, toward the steam room, and Nic turned immediately to obey. It would be a relief to be down there for a while, to shovel the heavy coal, to sweat until he felt weak, then eat, drink, and fall into his hammock. It would be another day down, another day closer to home. He rushed down the ladder. Manuel, already at his post, watched him with wary eyes as he entered, and before he could say a word, Nic picked up the shovel and began shoveling the irregularly shaped, dusty bits into the wide mouth of the stove, already making his face burn with heat.

He liked the crunch of the coal, the grinding slide of the shovel, the cadence of *dig, lift, toss*. He worked furiously for a while—at double the pace of the two men who stood on either side of him—fueled by thoughts of the sneer on Alejandro's face, how it would feel to slap him with the flat of this broad shovel or cut into his nose bridge with the edge.

*Use your brain as well as your brawn*, his father's voice echoed through him, seeming to emanate from the heat waves dancing off the coal before him.

*I am learning, aren't I?* Granted, he longed to use his muscles to end this silent war with Alejandro, once and for all, beat him until he backed off and left him alone forever. All his life, he never tolerated bullies, jumping to take on a fight before it was ever brought to him. But what had once driven him to fight was slowly fading, still there, to be sure, but not so vivid in his chest, his jaw, his fists. He paused, panting, and stared at the fire, then over to the coal boss, who gave his nod of assent over a brief respite.

The coal boss took the cigar he had been chewing on, brought a lit torch up to the end and puffed on it until it drew smoke, as craggy lines of fire lit the tobacco leaves inside. Nic looked away, but could still feel Manuel's gaze. After a moment, he glanced back to him, and the coal boss pulled his head right, beckoning him to come and stand beside him.

Nic did as he bade, aware that the other two men, using slow and steady movements, would soon be through with their piles. He tried not to let it annoy him; after all, they had arrived earlier than he, been at it longer. But a shift was five piles long. One could do it fast or slow and steady, but when a coal digger was done, he got a full barrel of seawater dumped over him as he exited, and then a bucketful of freshwater. The other sailors had to wait a week between baths.

And after that, he was free to do as he liked. It was what made it good to work a shift in the coal bins. "Sit, sit," Manuel said, gesturing to a stool beside him.

He lifted his cigar toward Nic, offering him a puff, but Nic shook his head. "No, gracias."

"Dominic," the coal boss said in Spanish, "what burns inside you?"

"Uh … por qué?" He had no idea if he was understanding the man correctly. He understood the words, but the question made no sense.

Manuel repeated it. "What burns inside of you?"

Nic frowned. "No comprende."

The coal boss smiled so that folds of fat at his neck grew deep with wrinkles. "You understand me fine. You are an intelligent man, a man who sees much around you. But the anger you feel is rotting you away from the inside out. Anger is hot; it burns. Like that coal there." He nodded to the fire, and Nic followed his gaze. What was so special about Nic that would draw this out?

Manuel allowed him a moment to think. Then he continued, "I see you, day in and day out, and you are like a large piece of coal. On the outside, you are dark, silent, still. But on the inside you are burning away, your heat expanding. Look to the coal. What happens to those pieces, once they are consumed by the fire?"

"They disintegrate," Nic muttered. He knew Manuel knew no English, but the man obviously understood what he was saying. He switched to Spanish and said, "But I am changing … if you could've seen me a few months ago … the burning has lessened."

"Ah no," said the man, laying a rounded paw upon his shoulder, "It has simply receded, gone deeper, my friend. I can see it in you, like I can see a cold coal in the morning, after it has popped out of the stove during the night, and know that if I break it open, it will glow red with heat."

Nic moved gently away, out from under Manuel's hand. He felt as if his skin were tender, raw at the man's touch, and he wondered why.

"There is only one consuming fire that does not destroy us," the man said in a low voice, leaning closer.

Nic frowned. "And that is?"

"God, my friend. If we give God our lives, then He will consume us from the inside out, but we will not be destroyed. We will become more than what we were, not less. Part of the fire."

"I see. God." *Excellent, just what I need. A monk masquerading as a coal man.* Nic lifted his chin and eyebrows and tried to keep the derision from his expression. "May I get back to work now?" he asked evenly.

"Si, si," Manuel said, puffing on his cigar again. He released him with a wave of his hand, but his eyes held him, followed him all the way back to his position between the other two, who never looked their way, continued to do what they had been doing their entire shift: *dig, lift, toss.*

It was just Nic's luck, he decided, as he entered into the rhythm of his *compadres,* giving in to the slow beat of those who worked on either side of him, that the coal boss fancied himself a theologian.

And that he had at least twelve more days before he could jump ship.

❁

"You have to sell the land. Sell a couple hundred acres," Robert said to Bryce after supper.

Odessa glanced over at the men, across from each other at the table.

"I've been back over the books," Robert said. "You have to sell the land. Now." He was pressing his brother, Odessa could see, provoking an argument.

Bryce frowned and ran a hand through his hair. "I think we should wait. See what the men find, if they have to go as far as Spain to bring back more horses, see what the auction brings in from the paintings."

Robert let out a scoffing sound. "You're being naive, little brother. Shortsighted."

"Now wait a minute—"

"No. I've been here long enough," Robert said, thrusting his chin out. "I can see that you need some guidance, and I'm giving it to you. Sell the land."

Bryce shook his head, shock in his eyes. "You know as well as I that if we sell that land now, we're not likely to get it back. And the land that my buyer will want is the land with the water rights. Land that Odessa's inheritance went to purchase—"

"It doesn't matter! Stop being stubborn and do what you must. If you failed your wife, you failed her."

Bryce rose, slowly, his hands clenching and unclenching. Quietly, Odessa set down her clay pitcher, preparing to get between them if it came to fisticuffs. "You've crossed the line, brother," Bryce said lowly.

"I guess I should've crossed it a while ago. I can't sit around here forever, ignoring my own business to try and help you with yours. You need a kick in the—"

"Robert!" Odessa cried in alarm. "Bryce. Stop it, both of you. We will find a way. Find a way out of this mess."

"I think you should be on your way, Robert," Bryce said, seething. "Tomorrow. First train out. Get back to your precious shipyard and stay out of my business."

"Fine," Robert bit out.

"Fine!" Bryce said. He turned and stormed out, throwing open the door and not bothering to close it.

Odessa looked to Robert as his face softened.

"Pack up that crate of paintings, Dess," he said wearily. "I'll do my best by you, by Bryce. I'll head down to the bunkhouse, tell the men to pack and get ready for the journey tomorrow."

"You couldn't have found another way out, Robert?" she asked in exasperation. "You had to provoke an argument?"

"How? What would be my excuse for such a sudden departure?"

She stood there, considering him. He was angry at Bryce, wanted to punish him … over her. Her.

"We'll make amends later, down the road," he said feebly, pausing in the doorway. "You really will need to think about selling the land, Dess. Sooner than later. I don't see another way. Regardless of where the money came from, you'll need it back."

"We'll see to our affairs," Odessa said, standing straighter. "As your brother said, it's best you move on and see to your own."

He stared at her a long moment. And then he turned and was gone.

❧

Bryce had ridden ahead of them on the way to Westcliffe, making for a long, silent, tension-filled ride for Odessa in the wagon with Robert.

Doc, Dietrich, and Tait tried to maintain a quiet banter but obviously could feel that the McAllan brothers were at odds. Odessa was glad that Bryce had refused to let Tabito go—claiming he needed him, more than ever, as foreman—because if he had been here, the short man would've demanded they all make their peace and be done with it.

She didn't want what drove Robert to this to come out. Not here. Not now.

When they got to the train platform, Robert hopped out and helped her down. She caught sight of Bryce striding toward them, and Robert followed her gaze. Bryce came up to them, sighed heavily, and then reached inside his pocket for a thick wad of bills.

Odessa gasped. "Where—" But then she knew. He'd cashed in the gold bar.

"Take it," he said, holding it out to Robert. "The men will need some of it to get by. Who knows if my paintings will sell as well as you think they will. Then you see to it that they have enough to get to Spain and back with at least a few horses. All right?"

"But Bryce, that was to see you through the winter—"

"Never mind that. Take it. That's our business, not yours."

Robert accepted the money, tucking it into his own jacket pocket. "All right, Bryce. I'll see to it." He glanced down at Odessa. "The paintings will bring in enough," he said. "You'll see."

Bryce stared at him and then her. Did he suspect something?

"I think I'll check for telegrams while we're here," Odessa said. "Since we're waiting on the train," she added. "I'll be back in a moment." Without waiting for a response, she climbed down the steep stairs from the platform and hurried off down the block to the small wooden building that served the county telegraph operator.

"Saved us a trip," the man said, as Odessa walked in the small office. "This just came in for you last night, Mrs. McAllan. And this one, the day before."

Odessa reached for the telegrams, glad to be away from the stagecoach platform and the tension running between Bryce and Robert. Thinking of them, she shook her head and opened the first telegram. It was sent yesterday from the detective Bryce had hired. "All as normal in Leadville," was all it said. As did the other two, all dated within the week. Reid was settling in Leadville, beginning a new life, as Bryce had suspected. It seemed a distant concern, considering what was transpiring right before her.

"May I send another telegraph?" she asked the kind man at the counter.

"Certainly. To whom would you like it addressed?"

"This name here," she said, turning the telegram around. "In Leadville."

The man nodded. "Go ahead, I know his name and location."

"Do not let your guard down. He operates in shadows."

The telegraph operator glanced up at her as if she might want to change that last sentence.

"He'll know what I mean," she defended. "Please, send it as I've said it."

"Good enough," he said, immediately acquiescing. He turned to the telegraph table.

"I'll return after I see my brother-in-law off on the stage. I'll pay my bill then."

"Good enough," he said, waving her out, already tapping in the message.

She left the building, a small bell ringing above the door with her exit. Robert pushed off the wall where he had been waiting and edged closer, cautiously. "You don't have to wait until the train arrives, Odessa. You can say good-bye now."

"Robert," she said coolly, hoping he didn't see how his presence unsettled her. "We'll wait. See you off properly." She dared to meet his eyes, and he stared back at her intently.

"I made my excuses to Bryce in order to catch a moment with you," he said. "I want to apologize again—"

"No. We've been through it. Now we just have to get past it. It was a weak moment, for both of us. I should've never invited you on that ride and—"

"No, Dess. You should've been able to invite me without a second thought." He turned away from her and ran his hand through his hair. His face was awash with pain as he looked over his shoulder at her. "I'm your brother-in-law. You should be able to trust me." He shook his head as if disgusted with himself.

As angry as she was, Odessa didn't want him to leave still punishing himself, berating himself for years to come. "It's over," she said softly, moving forward to stand beside him at the boardwalk rail. "You'll return to Maine and find yourself a lovely wife, and we'll laugh about this when we're old."

He glanced at her, a measure of hope in his eyes. "Think so? Someday we'll laugh about it?"

"My father always said that time gives all things perspective. So yes, I'm confident we will."

They stood, side by side for a while. Robert cleared his throat and said, "Will you tell Bryce what I did?"

She considered his question for a minute, then said, "I don't know, Robert. Bryce and I strive to hold few secrets from each other. But this … I do not wish to harm your relationship. And if it never happens again—"

He turned to her and smiled, the hope now wild in his eyes. He shook his head. "It won't. Never again. I crossed the line. Forevermore, I'll be the most trustworthy gentleman in the room with you. I don't wish to risk my relationship with either of you or to not know Samuel as he grows up. Bryce would … And this …" He paused and sighed, staring at her. "Bryce would cut me off from you—from you all—forever. I couldn't bear that."

She studied him. "Go home, Robert. Do find yourself a good woman, someone who can give you the love you seek. Have a family. Then this, me, all of it will be behind you."

He nodded and smiled. "Because of all my time at sea, I'd thought I shouldn't marry. But maybe you're right. Maybe a good woman will cure what ails me."

She smiled back at him. "You'd be surprised."

He hesitated.

"Robert," she said, seeing him not as the man who had tried to steal a kiss but rather the man who had taken care of her baby in the depths of night. "Please. I've heard your words. Give me some time to remember them in my heart. You have done much good for us here. You're doing good by us, organizing the auction, seeing the men off on their voyage … it will be all right in time."

He gave her a half smile, twisted his hat in his hands one more time, and then set it on his head. "Until next time then."

"Until then," she said.

# Chapter 24

Sheriff Chambers circled around and brought Daniel up short. Both were astride horses. "Where do you think you're going?"

"After them," Daniel said. He paused and looked up to the sky. It was after noon; daylight was burning. And he had not one bit of strength to spend on anything but finding Moira.

"Daniel, you're wounded. Leave this to us."

"I would, but a promise is a promise." To Gavin. *I'll protect her.* To Moira. *You won't be alone.*

"I say, when a man suffers a gunshot wound, he gets a little leeway in fulfilling his promises," the sheriff said as one of his deputies rode up beside Daniel. Behind him, a snow-covered mountain range met a deep blue sky.

"If I couldn't move, I'd agree with you, Sheriff," Daniel allowed. "But as you can see, I'm getting along fine."

"Fine until you keel over from blood loss. Come now, Daniel, come back to the doctor's. We'll set out after Moira Colorado and Bannock at first light."

"At first light?" Daniel said in disbelief. "Look! We have half the day left. The trail will be cold come morning. We start now or I go it alone." He studied the sheriff. Did the man think he had imagined it all? Bannock stealing off with Moira? Or had Bannock paid him off, foreseeing a possible chase? Considering her injuries, Moira couldn't be traveling fast, not if Bannock hoped to keep her alive. "Get out of my way, Sheriff."

The sheriff swore under his breath. "You don't know who you're dealing with, Daniel. I did some checking on Bannock. He goes back with those folks near Westcliffe. He killed one of their ranch hands." He shook his head. "Not to mention the detective the St. Clairs hired."

Daniel's eyes narrowed.

"There's something big transpiring here, something bigger than us. We need a posse to go after them. Bannock was seen riding out with three men and Moira. He might be meeting up with more. We're not going after him—two of us and you, half-baked."

"I'm going after them now, Sheriff. Now I'll tell you again. Get out of my way." His horse shied left, antsy because of the men's raised voices.

The sheriff shook his head. "I've got my hands full here, man. Two dead from the opera house—"

"And a kidnapping victim, three steps farther away every moment we sit here, yammering on!" Daniel cried.

"I'll get a posse together. We'll set out in a couple hours."

"And I'll be a couple hours ahead of you," Daniel ground out.

❁

They were again on the move, every step an agonizing experience. Moira was atop a pack mule, which was tethered to Reid's horse ahead of her. She moaned with each footfall, despite her most fervent desire to keep from it. But when the donkey stumbled a bit and she lurched forward, every nerve ending in her burned body from ankle to scalp erupted in pain, making her cry out.

Reid pulled up and circled around. "Moira, really. Cease your dramatics."

She stared at him, aghast at his cruelty.

"Or do I need to gag you?"

She shook her head. "Does your hatred run so deep?"

"Deeper than you can imagine," he said lowly. "You stole my heart. Your sister and brother-in-law stole the O'Toole mine from me. Stole four years of my life. You will all pay for those injustices."

Moira groaned. Her stomach roiled, and her skin was a throbbing mass of pain. But she had to know what would end this journey, what he was ultimately after. "They can't give you what they don't have. The mine is nonexistent."

"There is something else that has been discovered in the meantime, the true treasure of which Sam spoke. I believe, Moira, that your sister knows the way to a hidden cave full of conquistador gold."

"You're mad," Moira said, shaking her head. "Unwell. You think Odessa would allow a stash of gold to sit out there, ready for anyone to pluck? If they've found it, it's in the Westcliffe Bank."

A rider came out of the shadows. "Boss, we have to keep moving. They can't be far behind us."

"So that is it?" Moira pressed. "Your price to end all this is the deed to the O'Toole mine or the conquistador gold?"

"I'm only interested in the gold now. I can't remain in the States after I accomplish this. I need portable wealth as payment. Be it gold or cash, the McAllans will pay."

"But what if they give you neither?"

Reid turned in his saddle to glance at her. "Then they'll pay me with their lives."

❧

Nic managed to avoid Alejandro for a while. He decided the captain had seen the tension brewing between the men and purposefully set them on separate shifts, in separate areas of the ship, day and night. Even when he wearily dropped into his hammock at night, Alejandro's, six nets down, remained empty. He dropped off to sleep, dreaming that Alejandro had fallen overboard and no one thought to look for him. He even began to feel a little sorry for the man, adrift at sea, calling, pleading for help, until the ship faded into the horizon.

But Manuel was more difficult. With the winds at dead calm, the ship was on pure steam power for three days straight. Manuel said nothing to Nic or the other seamen; he only brought in the bins of coal that rode along tracks from the stern hold and dumped them for each digger, grunting a brief greeting to each man. Nic never saw him without a cigar in his mouth; sometimes it was lit, most of the time it wasn't. He tensed under the bright gaze of the coal boss, expecting another sermon that he could not escape as he worked, but the man remained silent.

Until the fourth day. Nic finished the last of his pile of coal, placed his shovel upon the rack, and went outside. The two others still had half a pile each to shovel into the stove. Manuel followed him out and dropped the half barrel off the side of the ship to haul in some seawater. They stood, side by side, at the edge, watching it drag a moment. "You think about what I said to you?" Manuel asked him.

"About California?" Nic said, feigning forgetfulness.

"About God."

"Oh, yes. I thought about it."

"Good, good." Manuel moved the cigar to the other side of his mouth and hauled up the barrel from the ocean. He was burly, and the barrel swung on its rope above them within a minute. Manuel stopped its swing as Nic positioned himself under it. He was shirtless, but he kept his pants on—it was the only opportunity to get them somewhat clean—but he didn't know why he bothered; the coal dust seemed to stick to everything.

"It doesn't matter what you've done, Dominic. God can wash you clean."

Before Nic could respond, the coal boss dumped the cold water over his head, a steady rush of water that drenched him from head to toe. Nic sputtered and rubbed his eyes. He grimaced at the coal boss. "What if I don't want Him to?"

Manuel shrugged, and his eyes sparkled with a held-back smile. "Then He won't. He waits for us to ask it of Him." He pulled the cigar out of his mouth and gestured toward Nic with it. "But mark my words, God will chase you until the end of your life. Better to give in to Him sooner than later. Until then, you will have no rest."

He moved over to the freshwater barrels and dipped a smaller bucket into it. Nic took a coal-darkened cake of soap from a ledge and quickly lathered his hair and torso and arms with it. He doubted his fingernails would ever have a merchant's look about them again, between his fighting and sailing and now digging in the black. He refused to meet Manuel's gaze, not wishing the man to see it as an invitation for further conversation.

But Manuel paused beside him, holding the bucket of water at shoulder height. "Why do you resist Him, Dominic?"

Nic let out a scoffing laugh. "You mean God?"

"Yes, I mean God."

"I'll tell you why," he spit out, pointing a threatening finger at Manuel. Manuel seemed unperturbed. "Your God took my little brothers, one at a time. He let them suffocate from the consumption. Four of them," he said, shaking four of his fingers in the man's face. "Four. They were young, innocent. My youngest brother … he was three! What kind of God allows *that?*"

Manuel's face grew grim. "A God who wept beside you. A God who does not like death, and gave His own Son so that we might know life forever."

Nic let out another scoffing sound. "And was it *that* God that took my mother in childbirth? And the baby my mother carried? Don't tell me your God isn't about death."

Manuel let the bucket drop a little. He looked so sad that Nic was suddenly alarmed that he might cry. It made him want to hit the man, strike him. Nic wanted nothing to do with sorrow, especially on his behalf. He waved at the bucket with a shaking hand. "Get on with it," he snapped.

The coal boss let the fresh water flow, but Nic didn't bother to wash off most of the harsh soap sticking to his skin and scalp. He only wanted to be away from Manuel. To escape. He quickly rubbed his eyes and cheeks, then let the water rinse them before moving over to his shirt, which hung on a peg beside the entrance to the steam room even as the last drops ran over his head.

"Dominic, ever since the fall, man has known numerous woes. We no longer live with the perfections of Eden."

Nic laughed, sardonically. "Don't I know it." And with that, he left the coal boss's side, buttoning his shirt as he walked, his back tense with the urge to go back and pound Manuel until he stopped smiling as if he knew something everyone else did not.

It was unfortunate that as he was striding away, Alejandro passed by on his way to take his own shift in the steam room. He whispered an epithet in Spanish. Nic turned and roared. He tackled the wide-eyed man, who clearly never expected the attack. He went down, hard, with Nic on top of him, his face scraping along the deck's planks. Nic sat up and pounded at his face from behind, reaching around to hit each cheek, as the man tried to throw him off.

He didn't succeed, but a strong man lifted Nic away before his fury was fully spent. He writhed, almost freeing his right arm, but the man stubbornly clung to him. Manuel came over and assisted Alejandro to his feet, then helped him over to a bucket of salt water to clean the cut on his left cheek. Manuel's eyes, full of dread now, ran over Nic. The captain approached and Nic tried his best to calm himself.

The captain, about his father's age had he been alive, stood eye to eye with him. He stood there for a full minute, glaring at Nic. Nic wanted to glare back in defiance, but he knew that they had not even reached Mexico's Baja Peninsula. He needed to stay on this ship. A crowd gathered. He glared at them instead.

"You remember our agreement?" the captain said.

Nic remembered it. A paper that stated he would not drink or brawl while aboard ship. On shore was his choice. He dared to look the captain in the eye and nod.

"You signed your name, showing you have some education. A smart man," the captain said. "Not like most of these who signed their names with an X," he added, waving about them. He stepped forward and tapped Nic on the chest. The men who held him gripped tighter. "For a smart man, you are very stupid."

Manuel arrived at the captain's side and whispered for a moment in his ear. Nic could not bear the humiliation of what the man might be saying, that he might be trying to aid him. He wanted to owe the man nothing.

Manuel moved away, disappearing behind the wall of sailors. The captain stared at Nic for a moment longer and then looked over the starboard edge of the ship "We are too far from the coast to throw you overboard. It would be more humane to put a gun to your head. So instead, you will receive thirty lashes. Five from Alejandro, whom you attacked."

"Wait a minute. That man—"

"Ten from Alejandro," amended the captain evenly. "And once it is done, you shall remain tied to the mast until daybreak."

Nic clamped his mouth shut.

The captain edged closer again. "You are about to learn a painful lesson, Dominic St. Clair. You should have remembered your contract." He turned to the men who held him. "Strip his shirt and tie him to the mast. You," he said, lifting his chin toward another, "fetch my whip from the cabin."

The men did so, and Dominic did not resist. There would be some relief in the pain, the punishment. He thought about Manuel's words, about the anger within him that had driven so many away … How many had he failed? How many promises had he broken? He'd told his own mother countless times he would never fight again. His sisters. He had promised his father to look after his sisters, and he no longer even knew where they were, what they were doing, if they were alive.

The first whip strike made him feel as if he had been punched in the gut. He fought for breath, his mind trying to absorb the pain, make sense of it. The crew around him was silent. Only Alejandro laughed as he cast the whip toward Nic again. Nic gasped for breath at last, ashamed at the sudden tears in his eyes. But he could not help it—a third tendril sliced his back. He imagined he could hear the skin splitting, felt the warm rush of blood down his back. He gritted his teeth to keep from screaming and clung to the mast as if it were a lifeline, digging his fingernails in with each strike, concentrating on the feel of the damp, pulpy wood. He pushed his forehead against the mast, not wanting to give Alejandro the satisfaction of seeing him pull his head back in agony.

At last Alejandro finished his ten lashes. There was a brief pause as the whip changed hands. Nic felt distant, knowing he was losing consciousness. The next lashes came quickly, one after another, as if whoever struck him now only wished it quickly over. Probably the first mate. He lost count, wondering if this torture would ever end. And with the next strike, a wall of black rose up and claimed him.

He came to and screamed when two of the crew dumped a bucket of salt water over him. The other sailors dispersed, but Alejandro stood to one side, arms crossed, smiling as Nic focused on him. He tried to clamp his lips shut, cease his humiliating show of weakness, but his jaw seemed locked open—the stinging, raw pain in his back was simply too intense to do anything else.

Alejandro stepped forward. "Next time you will remember to

fight me face-to-face as a man," he whispered. "And if you are as smart as the captain says, on shore."

"Get away from him, go," Manuel said.

Nic closed his eyes and leaned his forehead back against the mast, trying to rise above the pain enough to think.

"The salt water is harsh," Manuel said sorrowfully. "But it will help your wounds to heal and not get infected. Here, I have some water for you." Nic turned miserably toward the coal boss and accepted the drink from the tin cup. Never had he felt so weak, so helpless.

"I will be back to tend to you."

"Don't bother," Nic rasped. He only wanted to be alone.

"It is no bother."

Manuel returned around midnight, as a sliver moon climbed higher in the sky off the starboard edge, and off to port, the brightest stars battled for their share of the light. In spite of himself, Nic was glad for his return because he was desperate for a drink. All the other sailors, by captain's orders, stayed away from him. But Manuel apparently had permission.

Nic noisily gulped the water down, and Manuel went to fetch more. After Nic finished the second cup, Manuel held up a pail of what looked like thick grease—sailor's balm. "I'll put it on your cuts. It will heal faster."

"Leave me be."

"I must. Captain's orders," Manuel said with a shrug. He disappeared around Nic's back. Nic shifted his weight to his left foot—or what he thought was his left foot, since his feet had fallen asleep an hour or so ago—and braced for Manuel's touch. He thought it would be almost as painful as the lashes, but it was surprisingly painless. In a minute or so, Manuel had covered half his back.

"The Christ suffered wounds such as this," he said.

"I do not wish to hear it," Nic said tiredly.

"He bore this, and worse, for you. So that you might be free."

"Manuel—"

"Our God understands our pain, reaches out to us through it. Whether it be a whipping or a loss—"

"Enough!"

"Yes," Manuel said, finishing covering the wounds on his shoulder and purposefully twisting his words. "It was *enough*. Enough for all. Enough for any. *Buenas noches, hermano*."

*Good night, brother*. Why call him brother? He was no kin to him. Why wouldn't the man just leave him alone?

# Chapter 25

Odessa had just settled Samuel into his crib for his afternoon nap, when Cassie—a neighbor girl who walked over on occasion to help—came running upstairs.

"Miz M, sorry to disturb you, ma'am, but there's somethin' goin' on with the boys. You better'd come quick."

Odessa peeked over her shoulder at the baby, who was turning over and whimpering in his sleep as she closed the door behind her. With luck, he'd go back to sleep, even if he cried for a few minutes. "Keep an ear out for him, will you, Cassie?"

"Sure 'nough, ma'am."

Odessa hurried down the stairs and out onto the porch. She looked to the stables, where it appeared all the men were gathering, facing Bryce. She muttered a brief prayer for protection and then groaned within. They'd just gotten Robert off and returned home. Couldn't they have a time of peace? Was there something wrong with the horses he'd brought in? Heavens, she hoped not.

She gathered her skirts and went down the stairs, then over the trail that led to the stables. She slowed her pace as she neared, not wanting to appear as if she intended to interfere, only support. She couldn't see Bryce anymore, just the circled heads of the men, all in varying heights. When a couple of men noticed she was coming, they turned back to the circle and whispered, and all of them turned to watch her approach. She paused, seeing for the first time the horror and sorrow on their faces. Slowly, she made her way inside their group, watching as Bryce rose, grim-faced.

On the ground were the broken bodies of Leander and Owen, two men who had been with the Circle M for more than two years. She gasped and brought a hand to her mouth. "Wh-what happened?" she cried, rushing to the men, kneeling beside them. Both were clearly beyond help, hours dead. She fought the urge to touch them, make sure there wasn't some horrible mistake—

"Looks like they encountered an accident in the Little Horn Valley," Bryce said, laying a comforting hand on her shoulders. "We think they got too close to the edge of the trail and some rocks gave way. They were found at the bottom of that bluff."

"That's a two-hundred-foot drop," Odessa whispered. She touched one man's shoulder and then the other, tears dripping down her face. They'd sat at her table, laughing and eating, just yesterday! Set out yesterday afternoon. "Why would they both fall?" she said.

"Maybe a cougar spooked the horses," Doc said.

Bryce pushed back his hair in agitation and placed his hat atop his head again. "Never seen a horse scared enough to do that. Cougar or not."

❧

Bryce looked down at the men. "Whatever happened, we'll never know. Please," he said, gesturing to four men on the end. "Take them into the stables. To the far end, where it's empty, so the stench won't upset the horses. You, Dietrich, head to town and fetch the undertaker. He'll see to the rest. We'll bury them on the hill."

Some of the men turned with Odessa to glance at Cemetery Hill, the spot Bryce referred to, a half mile away. There, perhaps twenty men and women and children had been buried over the years, victims of illness or accident or age. That was where Leander and Owen would be laid to rest. Forever.

Odessa moved away, crying now in earnest. Bryce fell into step beside her, again lacing his arm around her shoulders. "It'll be okay, Dess. Accidents happen. On a ranch this size—"

"Wh-what happened to the horses?"

"The men left them at the bottom of that valley. They're too heavy to move. We'll leave them to let nature take its course."

She nodded her agreement, then glanced back toward the bodies. "Family. We need to inform their families. I know Leander had a sister in Santa Fe. Did Owen have anyone?"

"Parents," Bryce said, his tone grim. "In Denver. I have information on all of them, in the study. I've always made a point of keeping a record on employees' next of kin, in case the time came …"

"In case they died," she whispered. She sniffled and wiped her eyes. "In four years, we've never lost a man, Bryce. Never. Not since Nels."

He paused and looked her in the eye. "Have we heard from the detective lately, up in Leadville?"

She knew what he was thinking. In losing Leander and Owen, and after sending the three others to Spain, they were five men down. She shook her head to stave off a shiver of fear. "Neighbors dropped off a telegram this morning. Reid is apparently the model citizen up in Leadville."

Bryce shook his head, as if he, too, were shaking off the eerie thoughts that Reid was behind this latest heartache, and they continued their walk to the house. "It's just a tragic accident, I guess." He sounded as if he was trying to convince himself. "We've been fortunate, this spate of years, not to lose a man. Other operations this size … Well, I'd say we've been blessed, in comparison."

"Up until now," she said.

"Up until now," he repeated. "The Lord gives, and the Lord takes."

"But that's hard, when He takes," she said, crying again. "There's been a whole lot of taking going on. The horses. And now these men. Bryce." She shook her head. "These were good men, fine men. I'm going to miss them."

He gathered her into his arms and kissed her hair tenderly. "Me, too. Me, too, Dess."

❁

Reid and Moira rode into a small camp, where six men sat around a campfire. As one, the group rose, hands on the guns at their hips, but relaxed when they saw Reid. They greeted him and Dennis and Smythe behind Moira.

"Who's that?" one called, nodding at Moira.

"Don't recognize her?" Reid asked, going to her and pulling her down off the saddle. She sagged against him, fighting the desire to fall into unconsciousness and escape, at least in some fashion, this nightmare as her body screamed in agony. "Why, this is Moira Colorado."

"Moira Colorado?" said the closest one incredulously. "You're joking. I've seen her poster. Moira Colorado is beautiful." He stepped closer and peered at her. "Looks like the Indians tried to scalp her and failed."

The others laughed and Moira could hear Reid try to cover his own chortle. "Now, now. Give her a moment and a bit to eat and maybe she'll give us a song. That'll show you."

She slowly raised her eyes to meet him. "I'll never sing for you."

His own gaze hardened. "Don't be so sure about that." He took her arm and led her to a log by the fire and sat her down roughly. "Give her some food."

As he strode away, Moira was careful not to meet the eyes of any of the other men. In a camp of eight men riding with Reid, her burns were the least of her problems. She could feel the heat of their gazes, enticed somehow, intrigued, regardless of how she appeared.

A man handed her a tin plate, filled with beans and a biscuit. She took a bite of the hardened bread, conscious she needed it to give her some strength to fight, but her stomach whirled. Reid sat across from her, eating and listening to the men tell him of their progress. They were a day's ride from the Circle M, and all was in place, they said. Three men had left with Bryce's brother on an eastbound train and hadn't returned. They'd killed two others and assumed those at the Circle M considered it an accident. So the ranch was down to seven ranch hands and Bryce.

"Good, it'll be an even fight, with a slight edge in our favor," Reid said. "We'll take out the lawmen as planned and there will be no one to ride to the McAllans' rescue."

Moira turned and vomited on the other side of the log.

"Hey, Moira Colorado," called a man, laughing. "You hate Jed's food or are you expectin'?"

The others joined him in his laughter. But as Moira dared to meet Reid's gaze, she saw that he had not. Fury washed over him and he rose, slowly, hands clenching and unclenching. He strode over to her, grabbed her arm and yanked her upward. She shuddered at the pain that shot through her tender skin, nearly causing her to pass out. He hauled her forward, and she could barely keep her feet. They rushed through the woods and in a moment were beside a small creek. He pushed her to the ground.

In agonizing pain, Moira turned to look at him and she screamed. He was coming at her with a knife. She tried to crawl away, but he was on her in a second, winding what was left of her hair around his hand and pulling her up short. She was crying and gradually knew he wasn't bent on slitting her throat, but instead on cutting her remaining hair away. "You had to go and do it, didn't you, Moira?" he seethed. He sawed at her hair. "You had to go and be that girl on the stage, instead of my girl. How much might've been different, had you only agreed to be mine in the first place? We might still be back in the Springs, married and raising a family. But instead, we're *here*." He finished cutting the hair and threw it to the ground before her, long, thick waves of blonde, no longer hers. She reached out trembling fingers to touch a few strands.

"Were you really married to Knapp? Are you his widow, saddled with child, or simply his whore?"

Moira was weeping so hard she couldn't respond. What was the truth? Had Gavin used her like a common harlot? Had she really allowed that? *Mama … God … help me …*

But then he was at her skirts. "You wanted to be a showgirl, you will be a showgirl. No more high falutin' Moira Colorado. You're going to be Moira St. Clair and get all the accolades you deserve for who you really are." He cut away her burned skirts, bringing it to a high V at the knee. She gasped in pain as he brushed past the burn on her leg, but he ignored her. He rose and pulled a kerchief from around his neck and then bent to the creek to wet it.

Then he took her chin and washed her face, gentling a bit. "Quit your crying, Moira," he said. "You don't look so bad. Just a bit like springtime sheep, shorn of their thick coats." He turned her face and rubbed some more, then looked down her neck. "Those burns will heal in time. You'll be scarred, which might hurt your business."

"Bu-business?" she said.

"When you go to the cathouse," he said, staring her in the eye. "Don't worry, you'll still be pretty enough to draw them in, despite your scars. Once your hair grows back, of course, and you're not fat with child." He gave her a false smile. "You didn't think that you'd resume your previous life, did you? Take a real stage? No decent man will have you now. You're used goods."

*He's right,* she thought desolately. No stage. No man. No future. Even Daniel, the last good and decent man she had met, her protector, was dead and gone. Because of her. She was alone.

Reid hauled her back to her feet. "Now you'll go back and give those men as many songs as I tell you to sing," he said lowly in her ear. "Or I'll give you a foretaste of your nights to come."

# Chapter 26

Reid hauled her back to camp and set her before the bonfire. The men laughed and taunted her, but she couldn't hear them clearly. It was as if they were a half mile distant, rather than several feet away.

Moira contemplated throwing herself into the fire, to finish what had begun four nights ago. To end this horror, to prevent Reid from using her to get to Odessa and Bryce …

"Give us a song," Reid demanded from the other side.

Moira stared at the flames. *Mama, I want to be with you.*

*Call on God, child. Only God can save you now.*

*God doesn't want me. I am nothing. No longer His. So far away from His …*

*He is the Redeemer. He is grace.*

*I AM grace.*

Moira sucked in her breath, hearing the deep, warm voice in her head, clearly no longer her mother's. More elegant than Jesse's. Deeper and lower than any bass. *Song*, personified.

*I AM grace,* He said again. *You are covered by Grace.*

*Not I, Lord. You don't know how far I've gone, what I've done … You can't cover me.*

*I know all. I have already covered you, through and through. I redeem all to those who call on My name. You are not alone. Call on Me.*

Not alone. Just as Daniel had said …

"Savior," she whispered. No man but He could rescue her now. "Jesus," she said.

Reid laughed. But he rose and there was no laughter in his eyes. "Shut up, Moira. This is not a church. Sing us a song."

*Sing them My song.*

His song? Moira's mind cascaded through time, through years of practice beside pianos across the world. Through bar songs, operas, and musicals, and back, back to the songs of her youth, to the songs that brought her first accolades, songs that made her father smile. Church songs. Hymns.

*Redeemer. Redeemer of murderers, slavers, thieves. Grace. He is grace. Amazing grace …*

"… how sweet the sound, that saved a wretch like me." Her voice, just gaining strength, cracked, and she paused.

Reid was moving around the fire, advancing on her. Lost, so lost. Just like she was. Blinded. For how long? Longer than she had been lost—

A man rose, as if to stop him, but Reid barreled past him, knocking him to the side. He reached out and grabbed her throat, but it was as if she wasn't really here. As if she were receding, melding into the wind that was kicking up, disappearing among the trees … as if she could see herself but no longer feel any of her pain, any of her sorrow, only her joy, her glory, her peace.

*It will be all right, Moira. Sing them My song.*

"A song, Moira. The first you were to sing in Leadville. The song you began—"

*My song.*

"I once was lost, but now am found—"

He struck her fast and she whirled, down to the ground, suddenly feeling every bit of her pain again. "Was blind, but now I see," she whispered and then, blessedly, gave in to oblivion.

❁

All was in place for Reid Bannock's gang.

He hauled Moira, tied and gagged, to a narrow crevice that allowed her a view of the whole canyon. "Watch and see a master at work. I'm about to show a man that no one keeps me from what I want."

She'd heard another say they were about five miles west of Westcliffe. What man was Reid talking about? For a moment, she feared that he spoke of Bryce, but then she saw a stagecoach rumble around the corner. "First Colorado Bank" was painted on the side, and there were two armed guards atop it, rifles at the ready. Now the bits of conversation she'd heard over the last couple of days made sense. It was a trap; they were laying a trap.

"Not yet," Reid muttered, holding up a hand, eyes on the stage below them. Moira looked down the rim of the canyon and saw the two men lying down, keeping the stagecoach in their gun sights. Two others emerged on horseback from the woods below, shooting and hollering. A guard sitting beside the driver fired back at them, but they pushed on, riding low in their saddles. "Wait," Reid whispered.

Moira could almost feel the two riflemen's frustration. One glanced Reid's way, wondering if he had missed his boss's signal.

"Not yet ..."

"There," he breathed through a smile as Sheriff Olsbo and his two deputies closed in, riding hard to catch the men who were attacking the stage. "Perfect. Wait … stick to the plan."

The plan. Moira knew this part. Wait until the lawmen were right before them, then kill them all.

Two more of Reid's men emerged from the forest, now sandwiching the lawmen between them. The first two turned from the stage and fired at the sheriff and his men.

Reid brought his hand down and his riflemen each squeezed off a shot. Moira gasped. Both guards atop the stagecoach fell, one to the ground, the other against the driver, knocking him to one side.

The men took aim again.

*No, no, no,* Moira moaned inwardly.

"Now they'll take out the sheriff and the deputies," Reid said in her ear. He was grinning. She could hear it in his voice. But she couldn't tear her eyes from the awful scene playing out below.

Both men fired again. Again, two men fell below.

The second deputy, surrounded, put up a hand in surrender and pulled to a stop.

Another Bannock man, one gifted with horses, closed in fast on his own mount, shot the driver, then climbed atop the nearest of the bank team and gradually brought them to a halt—even before they reached the end of the canyon.

Reid laughed. "Perfect," he said, rising and clapping. "Bravo!"

Moira watched as the larger lawman, wearing a sheriff's badge, clearly injured, rolled on the ground and reached for his revolver.

One of Bannock's men shot him in the head.

The two others who held the surrendered deputy looked up the cliff face, searching for Reid. When they spotted him, he nodded. Once. And then they shot the third lawman.

"Perfect," Reid said again. "You two, go down and help them ransack the wagon. Make sure it looks like a robbery. And of course, bring the money too. You all get a share of it."

He climbed up a step and then reached down. "Come along, Moira. You shall be key to our next step."

❁

Bryce's smile was fading and he was running his hand through his hair as a messenger rode away down the dusty trail. "Bryce?" Odessa said, staring after the man as she came out onto the porch.

He glanced at her and gestured to the two rocking chairs. "You may want to sit down."

She froze. "Nothing good ever follows that direction." She remained standing.

Bryce licked his lips and moved to brace a hand against a porch post. He stared out at the hills for a moment, then back to her. "Sheriff Olsbo and his two deputies were killed yesterday."

Odessa sank into the chair then, in spite of herself, Samuel suddenly as heavy as a lead weight on her shoulder. "Sheriff … Olsbo?" She pictured the man, big and lumbering, like a circus bear. With keen eyes, and a caring heart. And his wife—Odessa reached up a hand to her heart. "How? How'd it happen?"

"A bank coach robbery. Sheriff got wind of it, tried to head it off, but he and both deputies were killed. The bandits made off with the money, leaving them and the coach driver and guards all dead. Six in all."

"A robbery," she repeated. Six lives, lost. Six families, now grieving. All for a meager sum of money. She sighed heavily and glanced at Tabito. He sat on the porch rail, listening to the conversation unfold. Then she looked back to Bryce. "What did the messenger want?"

"To tell us what had happened, and beware that there might be highwaymen about. And now, the county is largely unprotected. It will take a while to find a lawman to fit Sheriff Olsbo's shoes. Some folks in town—they wanted to know if I'd be interested in filling in, temporarily."

Odessa looked at him with alarm. "What did you say?"

"Said I had enough to look after here," he said. He paused, watching her and Samuel. "I'm not going anywhere far from you, Dess."

She breathed a sigh of relief. "Thank you for that." She rose, then, feeling the need to busy herself, make use of the nervous energy that ran through her body. "Will there be a memorial service? I imagine there will be."

"Tomorrow afternoon."

"Then I'd best be baking, to take something to the families. Sheriff Olsbo and his men were well liked, well respected."

Tabito rose suddenly, hand going to his holster. He looked down the road, and Odessa's eyes followed his gaze. There was a large man, with dark, wavy hair, coming down the lane. He was hunched over, as if ailing—

"Go inside, Dess," Bryce said, moving slightly ahead of Odessa.

Tabito hurried down the stairs and then ran down the lane. The man pulled his horse to a stop, about two hundred yards away.

The men spoke for a minute and then he resumed his approach, Tabito trotting beside him.

Odessa and Bryce could tell by Tabito's face that this man was not a foe but rather a friend in trouble. She stayed on the porch.

Bryce walked down the stairs and took the man's reins when he pulled to a stop. "What troubles you, man?"

He gave them a weak smile. "I came from Leadville." He panted, reaching for his shoulder, that they all could now see was bandaged. Blood seeped through the thick gauze. "Name's Daniel Adams."

"Leadville?" Bryce asked. "That's a five-, six-day ride."

"Three if you don't stop …" He moved to dismount and then faltered, obviously terribly weak. Bryce rushed to take his arm and assist him down, and Odessa hurried inside for a glass of water and a couple of hard rolls.

When she returned, the man was in her chair on the porch. He took a long drink and then closed his eyes for a moment, before studying her. "She has your eyes, your sister," he said.

"M—my sister? You know Moira?"

"I do," he said. Sorrow tinged his eyes, and Odessa felt a shiver of fear. "My name's Daniel Adams. I met your sister and her beau on a ship coming from England."

"She's here? In the States?"

"She's here, in Colorado."

Odessa held her breath. Clearly, he had something else to say and from the expression on his face it wasn't good news.

"She took the stage name of Moira Colorado, and had been singing in small mountain opera houses across the Divide. But then she came to Leadville—"

The name of the town finally connected, and Odessa drew in a sudden breath as Daniel's eyes met hers. He nodded once. "She and I were reacquainted. But she also came across Reid Bannock again."

"Bannock," Bryce whispered, looking to the valley.

"But Moira is all right?" Odessa asked hopefully. "Up in Leadville?"

Daniel shook his head. "Bannock has her. Worse yet, she's injured. Burned in a fire, then kidnapped. I'm hoping you can tell me what Bannock wants with her."

It was Odessa's turn to shake her head. "But we got a telegram yesterday. Reid's still there, in Leadville."

"A telegram?" Daniel asked. "From a detective named Bell?"

Odessa eyed him and nodded once as dread settled.

"Bell's been dead for a week. Somebody's been sending you telegrams in his name. And there's only one man who would benefit by doing that."

"He could be here now," Tabito said, studying the valley with Bryce.

"Why's he after you, McAllan?" Daniel asked.

"Oh please, God, no," Odessa said, ignoring him. "Moira. The sheriff … Reid killed him!" She turned away, her knuckles against her lips. "And Owen and Leander." She looked to Bryce. "It was no accident. They were too fine, too good as horsemen to get chased off that cliff. They were murdered, Bryce. We are under attack. He is here. Reid is here."

Bryce's eyes met Odessa's. They were obviously thinking the same thing.

"He found out about the conquistador gold," Odessa said.

"He thinks we have it," Bryce said.

"Or know where it is," Odessa said.

But then they looked northward, to where they could clearly hear gunfire.

"Dess," Bryce said in exasperation, "get back to the house. Lock all the doors and windows, take my gun and hole up upstairs with Samuel. We have to see what's happening up north. If they take out our boys up there, we'll be down to three men." He looked to Daniel and then ran down to his horse, pulling his rifle from his saddlebag. "You'll stay with Dess?"

"Afraid I'd just slow you down out there. I'll do my best to keep her and your baby safe."

"Thank you, friend." The two men's eyes met, as if making each other a silent promise.

"We could ride for the neighbors," Odessa said desperately. "Go for help."

"There aren't enough neighbors to help us fight these men off," Bryce said grimly. "Our only hope would be to get someone to Westcliffe, but if he has the manpower to take down a stage and Sheriff Olsbo and his deputies, I'd wager he has the road to town sealed off." He took her by the shoulders. "We have to see this through ourselves, Dess. Please, go inside. And pray like everything we get out alive."

She pulled him close for a quick kiss. "We'll be waiting for you, Bryce McAllan. I love you."

He cradled her face in both his hands and stared into her eyes. "Odessa McAllan, I've never loved another as much as I love you. I'll do everything I can to get back to you. You know that, right?"

"I know it," she said, staring back into his eyes.

He broke away then, running to the stables. Daniel opened the door to the house with Odessa right behind, moving as fast as they could. Once inside, they went around, closing and locking every entry. Daniel pushed a chair beneath the handle of the front door, making sure it was braced, then did the same with the back. Cassie, white-faced, watched them in confused silence. She gave the baby to Odessa, and Odessa ran upstairs, looking from one window to then the next, trying to glimpse the men … or the invaders.

For the moment, she could see none of them. But then the gunfire began again. She ran around to the other bedroom, and Daniel joined her at the window. Sweat streamed down his face, likely more from his injuries than their fortification efforts. They watched Tabito and Bryce break away from the stables in a gallop, whipping their horses as they headed north. "Stay to the side, Mrs. McAllan." Daniel eyed the baby. "Can you put him down? He'd be safer in his crib."

She nodded, feeling foolish for not thinking of it herself, and hurried into the nursery. She moved the crib to the corner, away from either window, and then set the baby inside. He rubbed his eyes sleepily, blissfully unaware of what was happening outside. From in here, they could clearly hear the gunfire at the north end of the ranch, about three miles distant. Were the men hurt? And how would they ever get back? Could Bryce and Tabito get there in time?

Daniel walked to the window at the end of the hall and looked back at her as she emerged from the nursery. She shut the door, willing the layer of wood to become steel. "Mrs. McAllan. Come here."

She hurried over to him and slid alongside him to peer out the glass panes.

"One of your men?" She could tell he hoped she would say it was.

She squinted to see better against the high noon light, watching the two on horseback approach. She gasped then. "That's Reid Bannock," she whispered. She could see he had a woman before him on the horse, his arm around her shoulders. Her hair was oddly shorn, blonde—"Oh, no. No."

As if in a nightmare, Odessa looked to Daniel, who stared outward in rage, then back down to Reid, who had dismounted, right before the house. He gruffly pulled Moira from the saddle to stand in front of him. She let out a cry of pain. It came as a muffled whimper through the glass.

Lifting his gaze to where Odessa stood, Reid cupped his hands and shouted, "Come out, Odessa, or your sister will die in front of your eyes." He drew a revolver from his holster and put it to Moira's head. Moira was weeping.

Odessa could see Daniel moving below, outside already, gun on Reid. She hadn't even noticed he'd left her side, so intent she'd been on the horrible vision below her. Odessa felt her breath quicken as fear turned to panic.

The men were shouting at each other, but it was as if Odessa's ears were full of water. As if in a nightmare, she turned and walked down the stairs. Cassie was standing in the kitchen by the back door, wringing her hands. "He's outside, ma'am. Outside! Don't go out there. Please, don't go out!"

"I know, Cassie. Go up and sit with Samuel while he sleeps, would you? Put a chair under the doorknob, and don't let anyone in except for me, Bryce, the newcomer, Daniel, or one of our men. Understand?"

Wide-eyed, Cassie nodded and hurried up the stairs.

Odessa opened the back door. Daniel and Reid were still exchanging words. Moira was crying. But it was Moira. Moira! Odessa stumbled out toward her sister, ignoring Reid's gun, ignoring Daniel's shouts, her eyes only on her little sister. Her lost, injured sister. Four years, four years since she had seen her … a year since she had heard from her.

"Mrs. McAllan," Daniel warned, still keeping Reid in his gun sights. She took another step and he reached out to grab her arm. "Stop. *Stop*."

❀

Reid laughed. "Ah, sweet emotion. It makes for such perfect manipulation."

"Leave her alone," Moira growled, hating that Reid had put them in this situation, that he controlled even this, *this*.

"You, my dear, are in no position to make any demands," he purred in her ear. He kissed her, right below her ear, then. "I've enjoyed our brief reunion, but I'm onto the prize." He looked up and stared over at Daniel.

Daniel.

Moira still couldn't believe he was here. That he was alive.

That he'd come after her, despite his injuries.

"Adams," Reid called. "You obviously came here for Moira. Here she is, though she ain't so pretty now, is she? You can have the whore. Just give me the other sister in exchange." He pushed Moira forward, closing the gap between them but carefully keeping her between himself and Daniel's gun.

Moira lifted a hand to her face. "Don't look at me, Dess. Don't look at me, please. I'm a monster. I'm so sorry. So sorry Reid is using me—"

"Sh, shh," Odessa said, reaching out, as if she could touch her across the twenty paces that now kept them apart. "You are not a monster. You are alive, Moira, alive, and you have no idea how—" her voice cracked—"how happy it makes me. I've been afraid … when I didn't hear …"

"Too busy living in sin to write your only sister?" Reid asked Moira, his face a mask of mock dismay. But Odessa's eyes remained on her, full of longing and love.

"Mrs. McAllan!" Daniel cried, as Odessa stepped forward.

Reid eyed his men coming from the north, three on horses, one trailing behind. "No more time for games," he said. "When my boys get here, things will get infinitely more complicated. Keep it simple, Daniel. Throw down your gun, or I'll shoot Moira right now."

"You shoot Moira, I'll shoot you."

"But you still lose her."

"And then you lose your life."

Moira's eyes flicked from Daniel to Reid and back again. She could not make it if Daniel died here. Not here. Not now. Not because of her or her family—

"Daniel, let us go," Odessa said. "It's the fastest way through this. I know what he wants."

"No. No! He'll kill you! This man knows no boundary."

Reid grinned and pointed his revolver in Odessa's direction. Once he had her, he threw Moira to the ground before him. Moira was weeping again, shoulders shaking. She reached up to her sister, wanting to touch her, just once more—"Odessa."

"Moira," Odessa said, her heart in her eyes. "I love you. I've always loved you."

Reid hauled Odessa away then, toward his horse. He climbed up in one swift motion, keeping his gun trained toward Odessa's ear. "Tell Bryce and his men that if they try and leave the ranch or come after us, our sharpshooters will cut them down," he called over his shoulder. "They'll show no mercy. I'll return the woman when she gets me what I'm after. Maybe."

Reid reached down and Odessa accepted his arm. He hauled her up behind him, even as he turned the horse, so that the only exposed back to Daniel's gun was Odessa's. They galloped off across the field, thick clods of sod flying behind them. Up ahead of them, three men edged out of the trees toward them, guns drawn. Bannock's men, come to claim him, protect him.

"Odessa," Moira wept, a hand stretched in the direction they went.

"We'll get her back, Moira. Trust me." Daniel bent to help Moira to her feet, his gun still before him, even after Reid and his men receded into the trees on the far side of the field, Reid's reference to sharpshooters clear in both their minds. Slowly, they backed into the house. Once inside, with the door locked, Moira turned to him and he enveloped her in his arms, careful not to touch her burns. "You came for me," she said. "You came after me, Daniel."

"I made a promise," he said.

"Thank you," she said softly. "It's been a long time since a man kept his promise to me." She withdrew and looked up at him. "You were shot. I saw it."

He lifted his chin and tried to smile. "Winged me. But didn't kill me."

"You rode all that way … wounded?"

"So did you."

A girl peeked around the corner of the hall. "Mrs. McAllan, he took her?"

"He took her," Daniel said with a groan and slid into a kitchen chair. "Come in here, please, Cassie. Sit down, Moira. We need to find a way to save your sister."

✿

Manuel said nothing more to Nic after that night tied to the mast, but his words echoed through his mind as clearly as his father's. At last, the northern territory of Baja California dominated their view, a long and desert-like peninsula in Mexican territory that would go on for days, by all reports. Giant sharks inhabited these waters, and Nic was glad for the ship's shallow draft, not eager to hit a reef here. The sandbars and coral raced upward and descended just as quickly. It stole Nic's breath when he dared to watch, but the captain stayed at the helm, unperturbed, under full sail, the steam engine silent. They were blessed with constant, steady winds and, the captain obviously preferred the free wind power over that which cost him in coal.

The men relaxed, half of them given leave to rest in their hammocks, half on deck dangling from their sitting positions across the lanyards or against the deck walls. Some whittled wood, others told stories. Some sang. Others, like Nic, only gazed out at the peninsula, willing it to pass by more quickly. He dreamed of that moment when he would stand again upon steady American soil, remembering how he would likely still feel the swell and release of the sea for days as he acclimated to life on land.

Alejandro, clearly bored, trolled by on occasion, trying to get a rise out of Nic by calling him names. But Nic ignored him, thinking about the wounds on his back still healing and why those were there. They were scabbed over by now, but once in a while he would move in such a way to break one open, and his shirt would become soaked with blood. Healing was a long process, one he was not eager to begin again. But if Alejandro ventured ashore in California, then he could give him everything he had without threat of a captain's repercussions. The man passed him, whispering taunts, and Nic's eyes went from him to the captain. The captain saw it all, absorbed it, looked past what he could, addressed what he had to. Nic was determined not to force him to address his behavior again. All he wanted was his pay for the voyage and to be off, back in his own country.

Nic looked over the starboard rail, watching as a pod of dolphins raced the ship, gleefully jumping in graceful arcs, then diving down to gather speed again. The dolphins always made him feel lighter, somehow, like watching children play. They didn't have a care in the world. Nic glanced back at the captain and returned to his thoughts. *He looked past what he could and addressed what he must.* He seemed a reasonable, peaceable sort. Could Nic do the same—address only what he must? What was Alejandro to him once he was on shore? He would likely never see the man again. Could Nic walk away and not look back? He had never been much good at looking past things that irritated, angered, or frustrated him. How did one do that? Was it inborn or something he could learn?

Manuel passed by him, and Nic quickly looked away, not wishing to engage the man in conversation. But he caught the smile in Manuel's eyes, the sense of peace about him. Was it his faith that gave him that? The coal boss thought he had it all figured out. *Give in to God—until you do, you won't find rest.* How did he know that it would work for Nic? Nic hated people who were so smug about their faith, as if they lived in the light and he was in the dark.

He looked down at his hands and slowly unclenched them. He considered all the men he had punched with those fingers. Even on nights he had been severely beaten, afterward he would find a moment's rest, a bit of the peace he sought. His mind, his body were spent, and he could sit in a place of nothingness for a while, sleep without dreaming. He wished he could stay in that place, day and night. Calm, at rest. Yet it was impossible.

"You are wrestling inside," Manuel said, leaning against the rail beside him.

Nic looked up to the sky, trying to mask the irritation he felt. He had not invited the man to stop. Could not the captain decide to set the steam engine to work again and aid the sails? Then, at least Manuel would be down in the hold, attending to the coal rather than up here, idle, with nothing to do but pester Nic.

"You are a passionate man, Dominic," the coal boss said. He bit off the end of his cigar and spit it out to the sea. He left him for a moment to go and light the cigar in a hatch lantern that always remained lit. Nic braced himself for his return. "The key to passion is to find the appropriate outlet."

"Yes, women," Nic said with a grin.

Manuel laughed, and Nic softened a bit toward him. "A good woman, a wife, is a good place to put some of that passion to work," he said, waving his cigar at the ocean as if he were talking to the dolphins as much as to Nic. "But God can take our passion and give us fulfillment."

"See here," Nic said, straightening, "I'm not in the mood for another of your sermons."

"I don't blame you," Manuel said, still leaning on the rail. "If a man is on the run he does not wish to pause for instruction."

"I'm not on the run."

"Aren't you?" Manuel squinted at him over his shoulder, blew out some cigar smoke, and looked back out to sea. "You don't belong here, aboard ship. I believe you didn't belong in Argentina, where you began your journey. How far back did you cease to belong?"

Nic frowned and rubbed his face, trying to get hold of his rising anger. "I don't know what you're talking about."

"Oh you do, you do, amigo. You know exactly what I'm talking about."

"How far back did I cease to belong? What does that mean?"

"When did you lose your way? When did you begin to fight anyone who threatened you in the least bit?"

"I was a kid. A hotheaded kid." Nic leaned against the rail again, this time with his back to the waves.

"So … soon after one of your brothers died?"

Nic thought back to the first time he ever scuffled with another boy. There had been skirmishes at school here and there. But the first time he punched another until he bled? Scrabbled until he himself bled? That was the day after little Clifford, the brother he had felt closest to, died. Nic clenched his lips a moment and then said, "It means nothing."

"It does," Manuel said softly. "If you are not on the run, then you are adrift. You are like a ship without a mooring, weathering one storm after another."

"Isn't that life? Don't we all make our way through the storms, hoping for calm weather ahead?"

"No, life, life as God intended it, is sailing in a certain direction, with good bearings. Yes, there are storms. Sometimes there are shipwrecks. But we sail with a goal in mind. Before you were shanghaied—"

"How do you know I was shanghaied?"

"Because a man such as yourself does not sign on to sail unless he's forced to it. Before that, where were you going? What were you doing?"

"I was in Buenos Aires, fighting in the ring. Making a pretty good living at it too."

"And did you intend to stay there? Do that forever?"

"No one fights forever. They get too old, too broken."

Manuel took a deep breath and let it out slowly. "So what did you intend to do then, when you became too old or too broken?"

"I don't know," he said with a shrug. "See what captured my interest next."

"Adrift. Passion without an outlet." Manuel turned to lean his back against the rail beside him. He watched a few sailors pass by, nodding in greeting. "You are like this ship, with sails lashed and coal sitting in a pile. You are pent up, waiting for something, wishing you could move. Who is your captain? Who will give you the direction to haul sail or feed coal to the fire? How do you know which direction to point your ship?"

"You don't know me," Nic said, turning to face him. He wished he could knock that knowing expression off his face, but Manuel remained at ease, leaning back, puffing on his cigar and scrutinizing him. "Why not go and bother someone else? Why me?"

"Because God is after you," he said, gesturing toward him with the cigar between his second and third fingers. "And my direction is to follow God's direction. It is what keeps me from being adrift. It fills my sails with wind, keeps my steam engine's stove with burning coal."

Nic considered him for a moment. "How is it, Manuel, that a philosopher became a coal boss? Did you lose your way at some point?"

"I have lost my way on occasion, yes. But God always leads me home."

"Why did you not give your life to Him then? Become a priest?"

Manuel grinned. "I loved my wife too much to ask for an annulment."

"You are married?"

"Yes, yes. Twenty years or more, now."

"She does not mind that you go to sea?"

Manuel shrugged. "It makes my homecoming all the more sweet." He studied Nic a moment and said. "Listen, I do not wish to bother you. I will not say another word to you about this after today unless you ask. But, Dominic, when God sets His sights on someone, it always goes better if that someone learns to accept Him and appreciate Him. Like our captain there." Both men glanced to the man at the helm. "You can follow him the easy way and enjoy the voyage. Or you can ignore his orders and suffer the consequences. But one way or another, you will do as he says." Manuel stared Nic in the eye. "You think you were put here on this earth by happenstance? That God has no particular interest in you?"

"I don't know," Nic said. "I've never really thought about it."

"Think about it. God has a particular interest in every person on this ship."

"Even Alejandro?" Nic said.

"Even Alejandro."

# Chapter 27

Reid handed Odessa a mug, filled with strong coffee, from the scent of it. She took it from him without comment and sipped at it, knowing she needed to keep up her strength if she was to make it through the battle ahead. The man sat next to her on the log, and Odessa fought the urge to move away, reviled by his proximity. Instead, she stared at the fire, wondering what was happening at the Circle M. Who was injured? How were they all faring? Who was caring for Samuel, who would feed him? Her breasts seemed to ache in response.

"I take it you know where the gold is," Reid said, leaning down to rest his forearms on his thighs and look back at her.

She scoffed. "You think if we knew where it was, we wouldn't have come up here to get it?"

His mouth settled in a grim line. "So you *think* you know where it is."

"I have an idea, yes."

"And how have you come to that idea?"

Odessa stared at him. Did he think she'd give it up? Give him their future, their hope? Even if she did know how to find it?

"Odessa, we're an hour's ride from your house." He looked up at the men, lingering nearby, listening in. "I'll send my men back. Daniel will be no match for them. They'll kill him, and they can do what they please with Moira and your kitchen girl. And your baby … your baby, why, I think I'd have them bring him back to me."

She stared at him, hard. Clearly, they'd been watching the ranch for a while. Knew far too much about what happened there.

*Bryce, you and I have no future if either of us dies. Forgive me …* "Remember Louise O'Toole's cabin?" she finally said.

He gave her a wry look. "I have a fair recollection of it, yes."

"Inside the old Bible, in Genesis, there are markings in the center. Comparing it to our Bible in English, we think they're markings near every reference of 'gold.'"

"All right …" he said, in a warning tone, as in, *You better have more than this.*

"The first time gold is mentioned in Genesis, the description includes plants of bdellium and onyx stone—a true black rock—and a land called Havilah."

"Go on."

"There's a valley where they take the horses in high summer, and several small canyons. One is called Avilla Canyon."

"Havilah, Avilla. You're assuming they're one and the same."

"But Tabito and Bryce already went up there, looked around for days, searched a hundred caves. And found nothing. There were other clues—onyx, a black rock, and bdellium, a gumlike plant. They found a black stripe in the rock, but nothing more."

He stared at her a moment, his face eerily shadowed by the flickering light of the fire. "That's it. That's all you have. A valley name similar to what you found in the Bible, and the thought that there is supposed to be black rock about."

She stared back at him. "That's all I have."

He studied her a moment and then moved so suddenly, she didn't have time to react. His hand was on her throat, pinching in hard. "You better pray, Odessa," he hissed, "that when we reach that canyon, we find the right cave, or your baby will end up an orphan."

He released her then, tossed his cup aside and rose, striding away. The men looked from their boss to Odessa with curiosity and concern, but none moved. Odessa struggled, gagging still to catch her breath. She went down to her hands and knees, praying, calling to God for help.

But He was silent.

❁

Moira sat next to Daniel on the front parlor settee, watching the door, as the day, and the gunfire, faded. She leaned her good cheek against Daniel's uninjured shoulder and willed the knob to turn. Cassie was pacing with Moira's nephew, sweet little Samuel. Cassie kept going upstairs to look for approaching riders. Where was Bryce? Why had he not returned? Moira wanted to fight her weariness. Honor her sister by staying up the whole night, thinking about her. Praying for her. It had been a long time since she had considered praying. *I don't remember, God. How to pray. The right words. Do You even hear us, in the midst of all this madness?*

*I hear you. I am here.*

Moira remembered then, a prayer her mother had taught her. *Father God, keep in Your tender hands … Odessa and Bryce and all the others. Grant them Your tender mercies. Cover them with Your tender care. Be tender with us all, Lord God. For we are Yours.*

Those last words rang in Moira's thoughts, like distant echoes of a time long past. What did it mean, to belong to God? To receive His tenderness, rather than His wrath? She drifted off to sleep then, unable to think it through anymore, other than muttering a plea. *Please let Odessa live, Lord. Please. Please …*

It felt like seconds later when she heard the baby crying and Cassie calling, "It's Bryce! Bryce is coming!"

She glanced at the clock. She'd been asleep for an hour.

He burst through as Daniel opened the locked door, Tabito right behind him. Grimly, he looked from one to the other, then set aside his gun to take the screaming baby. He patted Samuel on the back and then reached out to gently embrace Moira. "Welcome home, Moira. I'm glad you're safe. But Odessa … How long ago did he take her?"

How did he know?

"Not two hours past," Daniel said. He rose and pointed to the west. "They disappeared across the fields."

"There were gunmen," Bryce told them, "to our north. They had us pinned down all this time. One of our men, Holt, the traitor, took off with them. They kept us pinned down until now. And then they disappeared among the rocks."

"A spy," Moira said.

Bryce nodded and ran a hand through his hair as he paced. "So we're down to four men, five, counting Daniel." He studied the newcomer, a shadow of accusation sliding across his face. Did he think that Daniel, too, was a spy? Sent to infiltrate them? "How was it that Reid got Odessa?"

"She gave herself up," Moira said, stepping forward, "for me. I'm so sorry, Bryce. I tried to stop her. Daniel did too. But Reid had men with him. We might all have died had she resisted. Dess seemed to guess that sooner than we did."

"Sounds like Dess," he said, staring up at the ceiling, still patting his crying child.

Cassie came and took Samuel from Bryce. She glanced shyly up at him and then away. "My family, they'll come lookin' for me, now that it's dark. I never've stayed this late."

❀

Bryce stared at the girl and closed his eyes as he drew in a long, deep breath through his nose. She was right. And if Reid was telling the truth, his men were liable to shoot anyone who came down their lane. He took a step left and then right, then paused, looking upward, his hands over his mouth. *Lord, I need some help here.*

"Send me," Tabito said lowly from where he sat.

Bryce glanced down and studied his foreman.

"I know this place," Tabito said with a shrug. "I can sneak out and over the hills, tell the girl's kin what is happening here. They can go for help. Bannock won't know we've raised a flag of alarm."

Bryce thought his words over. He was desperate to grasp any measure of hope. But to risk Tabito, his friend, his foreman … one of the few men he had left. And yet, he would be endangering Cassie's family if he did nothing. Had he not just asked God for help? He could not bear it if something terrible happened to his friend.

Tabito reached out a hand and rested it on his arm. "I will go, Bryce. Let me."

Bryce studied him a moment longer, then he nodded. The men reached for guns, handing them to Tabito, but he shook his head. Bryce knew his belt was laden with knives, knives like those he had taught Bryce to throw … with deadly consequences. On a quiet night, under watch, with so many of Reid's men in wait, knives would be their best defense. Silent killers, one by one.

"Go with God, friend," Bryce said, as he watched from the window as the older man padded quietly up the hill, melding with the dark in seconds. "God help us all." He closed his eyes, aching at the idea that Odessa was once again in Reid's hands. He couldn't stand the thought, choking in frustration that he hadn't been beside her, right when she needed him most.

Daniel joined him at the window. "She would've gone, even if you had been here," he said, seeming to read Bryce's thoughts.

"I wouldn't have let her," Bryce countered. Deep within, he knew Daniel had been powerless to stop it.

Why had Bryce not seen this coming? How could he have fallen into Reid's trap?

"What does she have that Reid wants?"

Bryce shook his head. "An old legend, nothing of substance," he moaned. He paced to the far side of the room and told Daniel all he knew about the mysterious O'Toole treasure. "The legend says that several troops got separated from the rest of their regiment. We don't know what kept them apart—weather, Indians, what. It was hundreds of years ago. They holed up in a cave, and there they died. All that's left of them is their remains and hundreds of thousands of dollars worth of gold. Gold that apparently Reid Bannock is bent on obtaining."

# Chapter 28

They rode for hours, starting at daybreak, and by midmorning, Odessa's breasts were aching with the milk intended for her baby. Even the thought of him, close to her, set the milk to flowing, dampening her bodice in two wide spots that grew as they rode.

Reid's men made lewd comments, which she ignored. But after a while, Reid pulled the train of horses to a halt, turned and rode his horse back to her. He looked her over slowly, waiting until she returned his gaze. "Find me the gold," he said, "and you return to your son … and husband again."

They climbed and climbed, until spots of the deepest snow lay in patches around them, the last vestiges of a hard, brutal winter. How deep had the snows been here, when the valley below had been so laden with white? She'd only been up here twice over the years with the men. And it was almost in a dream that she remembered Tabito talking about the Avilla Canyon as they passed. But they'd poured over the maps so long she felt like she had memorized every creek and canyon on their property.

If only it hadn't been Reid Bannock. It burned, the idea of Reid seizing such riches and fleeing for Mexico. He would live large, and long, with such funds. Odessa wanted him to suffer. Die for what he had done. So much hurt, so much haunting. The memory of him bringing Moira to them, injured, tossing her to the ground, made her want to leap from her saddle and take him down to the ground. She wanted to strike him again and again. Bite him.

She looked up to the ridges around them. She hoped Bryce and his men were behind them, closing in.

And even though she knew it was wrong, she hoped that when Reid died, he would suffer.

❁

Bryce rode out under cover of darkness, emboldened by the five men who came back with Tabito and Cassie's brother, mostly a group of neighbors, but good men. They had miles to gain, and they must do it quickly if they were to catch up with Bannock and his men. They had to be heading toward Avilla Canyon, their only clue.

They pushed their mounts to their limits before pausing at daybreak, halfway to the canyon. There, by a stream, they let the horses rest and drink their fill to cool down, relieved temporarily of their riders' weight.

They'd left Daniel behind to guard Cassie, Moira, and the baby. But Bryce's instinct was that the battle was ahead. Reid cared not for the inhabitants of the Circle M—only in how they might aid him in finding the gold these mountains held captive. He undoubtedly planned to seize the booty and ride out southward, past the border of Mexico, deep into her recesses where no lawman would follow. He probably did not even care what became of the mercantile and house that he had left behind in Leadville. With the promised wealth of the conquistador gold, he could purchase ten of the same, with money left over, even after he paid off his men.

His men. A man such as Reid Bannock did not often abide by splitting the spoils. Would he do the honorable thing and pay them off, or would he turn on them, take them down? Bryce hoped for the latter. If they turned on one another, it would make his success in fighting them off—and freeing Odessa—more likely.

❁

They paused and circled in the clearing, gazing up at wide, glacier-carved walls that surrounded them like a bowl. Odessa studied the striations of rock. There in the midst of the salmon pink and rose hues were stripes of gray—and a thin line of black. "Onyx," she said, pointing up at it triumphantly. She was half relieved, half aghast to be exposing this clue to Reid.

Reid eyed her and then the men around them. "Set out in twos, men. You're looking for a plant that gives off a gumlike resin." He smiled thinly. "The Good Book called it bdellium. I call it bread-crumbs, breadcrumbs that will lead us all the way home. Anyone who finds anything you think fits, call out. Sound will carry a good distance in a canyon like this. I'll come by. If I agree we're on the right trail, I'll call the rest of you in." He looked up to the canyon's edge. "Bryce McAllan won't be far behind us. But we have scouts out. They'll warn us when McAllan comes. If we're still looking, the task will be to take out Bryce and his men, then return to the search. Understood?"

One of the men let out a low whistle. "Could be more than a hundred caves in these parts, Boss."

"Yes there could be. And maybe cougars inside," he tossed out with a grin. "Keep a close eye out for signs of 'em. You won't find much gold if you're mauled into bloody ribbons."

The men laughed, but some of them were clearly nervous. Odessa had a hard time not hoping there was a cougar in every cave they encountered.

Reid passed out hunks of bread and cheese, then reached into his saddlebag and pulled out apples that he tossed to each man. "Good hunting, men. The man who finds our cave will get an extra portion, but all will share in the bounty, just like with the bank stage. Today, we'll all become richer than we ever dreamed. Move quickly and stay alert."

They moved out, disappearing down the trail and up into the hills. Odessa studied the canyon and striations, how the thin black line was on either side, moving northward, but how in a small side canyon, it seemed to pick up again, on the other side, at the same level. She glanced away, not wanting Reid to see what she was thinking, but it was too late. He was studying the rock too. "So, you think it might be back there?" he said.

She didn't respond, only looked at her hands.

"Here," he said, rising and crossing a few steps toward her. He handed her an apple. "Come on, take it. You need your strength to climb."

She took it and ate, casting aside the guilt from taking food from her captor. "Where're we climbing?"

He smiled. "You know where we're going. You're leading the way."

She rose and immediately walked in the opposite direction. In only a few steps, she knew Reid was not following her. When she turned to look at him, he gestured for her to come back, as if patiently dealing with a stubborn child. She frowned and returned to him.

"I've been a gentleman with you so far, Odessa," he said, cocking his head. "Trust me, you don't want to see my more ungentlemanly side. Come." He gestured ahead into the side canyon.

"Is that what happened to Moira?" she spit out, over her shoulder. "Are you responsible for her burns?"

He chuckled, and Odessa fought the urge to turn and slap him. "No, she did that all on her own. It's tragic, but perfect in a way, isn't it? The beauty loses her beauty."

"I see nothing good in it."

"Ah. But I do. Retribution is beautiful. Moira made poor choices. Now she sees what those poor choices have led her to. A life as a maimed, forgotten woman alone."

"She will not be forgotten or alone. She will be celebrated, loved by us."

He remained silent, and Odessa hated that her words sounded hollow, too defensive because of his lack of response. The two of them turned a corner on a goat or deer trail, climbing, already panting hard. Ten minutes later, she slipped on the loose shale and began sliding. Reid reached for her and missed, but Odessa grasped for a passing bush and came to a halt. Reid sidestepped down to her and offered her a hand up.

Odessa spit out the dust in her mouth and wiped her forehead with the back of her hand, ignoring his. It was then she noticed the gummy substance. She opened and closed her fingers, then opened them again, watching the strings pull apart like taffy.

"Bdellium," Reid murmured. His mouth fell slightly open.

"Probably not exactly like the biblical plant," Odessa said, rising. "But close enough." They looked to the right, where there were more of the plants, growing along a deep ravine that probably ran with a thin stream of snowmelt into June.

Reid pushed forward. "This is an old riverbed."

"An old river," Odessa muttered, thinking. She knew Bryce and Tabito had searched the next canyon over. Had the No Sip River once run on this side, instead of that one? Had it been diverted at some point, changed direction by avalanche or erosion?

Reid studied her. "Is this a clue?"

When she didn't respond, he reached out and grabbed her arm, yanking her to his chest. "Tell me," he ground out. "Hold nothing back or I'll send four men to go and collect your baby."

"The riverbed," she said, lifting her chin, but keeping her eyes on Reid, as if he were a deadly rattler about to strike. "We figured out another clue—the No Sip River, was Pison, spelled backward. But it runs over there, back in that last canyon, now."

Reid smiled and let her arm go. She rubbed it. "You think it got diverted at some point," he guessed.

"I wondered, yes."

He didn't summon his men, but it made sense to her, then. Reid didn't want to share the treasure if they found it. If he could find the cave, mark it, and then return to it later, it would be all his. She smiled thinly. If that was his plan, he was a fool. She knew from holding the one, just how heavy those gold bars were. He'd need a whole mule train to get them out. And there was no way that Bryce and the men would ever let that happen.

Reid laughed then. Odessa, curious in spite of herself, rushed forward. He looked back at her and then forward again. "See it?"

She did the same and discovered the faint outline of a path, carefully marked with the same size stones. Most of it had washed away, but it was clear that someone had once tried to mark it for reference. Louise O'Toole? Sam? He pushed away the scrub oak that had encroached over the years—and completely covered the cave entrance.

Here and there were cougar tracks, but they were old, imprinted in the mud.

Reid slashed away some branches with a huge knife and, with a powerful heave, broke off a leafy branch of the oak that blocked their route. He stood back, gazing at the black hole, panting, wiping his mouth with the back of his hand. Then he looked back at her and laughed. "I think, Odessa, you should leave your husband and marry me. I'm about to become the richest man you know. Look around for me, would you?" With that, he clamped down on her arm and threw her toward the cave entrance. "If there's a cougar in this one, I want him to discover you first."

❁

Tabito nodded, and Bryce and he threw their knives at the same moment. Both men went down silently, and they rushed them, intending to tie them up and leave them for later. But both were dead.

"You'll need to teach me how to throw like that," Dietrich said in an undertone. The three men continued on, working their way to the second pair they'd seen from the ridge, just five minutes distant. Even now, men from the Circle M would be quietly gathering the Bannock group's horses and leading them away. Bryce intended this to end here and now. There would be no escape for the interlopers who had dared to attack his men, his wife, his sister-in-law on his land. At least not on horseback.

They swiftly took care of the second pair, surprising them as they had the first. Bryce lifted his head as the sounds of a fistfight echoed through the canyon and then all was silent. Had any of Reid's men heard it too? If so, they'd be alerted now, wary. Their whole plan hinged on taking the interlopers out, two at a time. If they were discovered, it would mean an all-out battle.

But Bryce and Tabito had just eliminated four of Reid's men. Now it would be easier to capture the rest. What bothered him now was that Odessa and Reid had disappeared from the clearing.

Bryce stood where he had seen them an hour before, turning slowly, looking and listening for his wife or her abductor. They were in the middle of Avilla Canyon. Where could the two have gone?

❀

Odessa let out a little scream when she struggled to rise and realized she was atop a human skeleton.

"Shut up!" Reid hissed, rushing to her, lifting her partway and shaking her. "Shut up!" He hauled her to her feet, his hand clamped over her mouth as he glanced out to the bright round of sunlight that came from the canyon. There were no questioning shouts, no gunfire responses. Only silence.

He turned to the back of the cave, moving her forward as if she were his shield. There were two more skeletons, one on either wall, clearly once guards at the entrance. Reid bent down and lifted a sword, wide and ancient, from the dust and gravel that covered it. He raised it to the light and smiled as her eyes met his. "This is ancient … not forged in my lifetime, or even my great-grandfather's." He set it aside and peered into the darkness. "Go see what you find back there," he instructed.

She turned and frowned. She knew what he feared. A mountain lion, leaping from the dark recesses of the cave where she sheltered cubs. "You want the gold?" she said, backing away and shaking her head. "Then you go find it for yourself."

He reached for her but she dodged him, which only made him more angry. He lunged again, and again, she narrowly escaped him, scrambling over a pile of rocks.

"Get away from her," said a man at the mouth of the cave, gun drawn.

Odessa's heart leaped with hope. *Bryce.*

Reid slowly rose, his hands clenched.

Why was he not afraid? Bryce entered the mouth of the cave, drawing closer to them.

"How is it you escaped my men, McAllan?"

Bryce ignored his question. "You won't threaten me or mine again, Bannock. It ends here."

Odessa edged away toward Bryce, but Reid reached out fast and grabbed hold of her wrist, pulling her back to him. "No, no, no. No reunion for you yet." He threw a handful of rocks and gravel at Bryce's face, blinding him so he couldn't see Reid coming. Bryce called out for Odessa to run but Reid took him down to the ground. He pounded his fist into Bryce's face, but Bryce managed to avoid the second blow.

The men rolled and Bryce pummeled Reid's belly.

Odessa moved along the edge of the cave, back to the conquistador sword. Three feet away. Two feet. She reached out.

The men rolled again, knocking Odessa to her knees.

Reid was atop Bryce, choking him. "How's it feel, McAllan? To know you're about to die and I'll be free to do as I please with your wife? Then return for Moira, do her a favor and kill her, put her out of her misery."

"No," Odessa said, standing behind Reid with the old sword. "You won't."

And with that she plunged the sword down.

❦

Reid's face went from spiteful glee to terror. He stiffened as Bryce pushed him away, off of him, and he fell to the side, in the center of the cave. He seemed paralyzed and he struggled to catch a breath. Bryce rolled to his feet and moved over to Odessa, taking her in his arms.

Tabito arrived at the mouth of the cave, panting, knives drawn, but he slowly turned to keep watch for Reid's men. Bryce took Odessa's trembling hand and led her into the dark recesses of the cave. He reached down to lift a gold bar, identical to the one they had once hidden in their kitchen. He blew the dust from it and then smiled over at Odessa. She was too shaken to return the smile, and Bryce's own grin faded. He strode back to Reid and put the bar inches from the man's face, so he'd be sure to see it. "You found the gold. But you're about to lose your life."

"Kill me," Reid panted. "End it."

"No," he said, shaking his head and leaning closer. "I'd use the seconds you have left to make peace with your Maker, or you're about to enter a prison where no man is ever given parole."

Bryce rose and reached for Odessa. "Let's get out of here. Com'on, you're safe, sweetheart. We've taken out most of his men." He eyed Tabito, silently telling him to keep watch over Reid. And then he brought Odessa out into the warm sunshine.

He sat her down on a small boulder and took her trembling hands, kneeling before her. "It's done, Dess. He's never going to hurt us again."

"I-I killed him, Bryce."

"You defended me. Even if I hadn't found you in time, he would've had the gold. You think he would've turned you loose at that point? It was self-defense."

"I k-killed him," she repeated.

"Dess," he said, stroking her face, staring at her until she met his eyes. "You wounded him. Now it's up to God whether he lives."

They shared a long look. They both knew Reid would never leave this cave.

"It's been a lot," Bryce said. "I know. It'll be okay. Can you make it?"

Odessa stared at him a moment, as if seeing the fateful moment when she struck Reid again in her mind. But then she focused in on him. "Don't leave me, Bryce. Don't leave me alone."

"Never," he said, pulling her up and under the crook of his arm.

# Chapter 29

The remnant of Bannock's men—the four who survived—were ushered down out of the mountains, bound and pulled behind the men's horses. Every Circle M man and the neighbors who had come to their assistance carried a gold bar in their saddle pocket. Tabito had loaded the rest on two of Bannock's mules and led them in a line down the curving trail.

At Odessa's request, Dietrich rode ahead. Moira spotted him first. She ran down the porch steps and over to him, taking his reins as he dismounted. "Is it over?" she asked the man anxiously. "Is Odessa safe? Bryce?"

"They're all safe, ma'am," said the man, averting his gaze as if embarrassed to look upon her burns, her hair. Moira ignored it. She was too relieved that her family was all right to care about it now.

"Bannock's dead," he said. "His men all captured."

"Dead," she repeated in a whisper. She turned and ran inside the house. "Daniel, Daniel," she said trying to elicit a response. He lay on the couch, hot, as if with a fever, and didn't move. He hadn't moved in the past hour. "He's gone, Daniel," she whispered, leaning her head into his chest. She gently pulled the rifle from his hands. "It's over. Now we just have to take care of you."

Cassie moved in with a bucket of water and cloths, as if Daniel were a spill to clean up. But Moira was too weary, too weak to do any more herself. She sank down on the floor to watch. Cassie unbuttoned Daniel's shirt and pulled it away.

Moira gasped at the blood-soaked bandage beneath it, but Cassie turned to her and said, "Ma'am? Can you come and help me?"

Moira moved, and held the unconscious man as the girl indicated so she could unwind the bandage. When it was off, Cassie peered over his shoulder and grunted. "Wonder if he stayed put long enough to let a doctor fish it out, or if he took off after you."

"After me," Moira said dully. Shot because of her. Risking his life to come after her again.

"Lay him down, Miss Moira," Cassie said.

Moira did, trying to ease the big man back, but he was heavy, and he fell to the settee with a groan. "Do me a favor, Moira," he said, his eyes still shut, "and never become a nurse."

She laughed, so happy was she to hear his voice again. "I'll do my best," she said, "to try and avoid that."

"Is the bullet still in there, Daniel?" Cassie asked.

He waved her off. "No, no," he mumbled. "It's out."

"Good. At least the man showed some sense." The girl dipped the cloth in water, wrung it out, and then washed away the blood, the farthest away from the wound first, then moving in, dabbing as she got closer. He fell unconscious again, but moaned when she was directly atop the bullet wound.

Cassie reached for some strips of cloth, couldn't quite reach them, and then looked again to Moira. Moira moved over and handed her the cloth. "How do you know how to do this, Cassie?"

"Five brothers. Two of them have had bullet wounds."

Moira frowned and looked her in the eye. "How'd that happen?"

"Tomfoolery. Mother says that it would've served 'em right, dying. She didn't mean it, o' course, but boy, she was mad. 'Specially with the second one. But that was a hunting accident." She looked at Moira doubtfully. "Think you can hold him upright again?"

"I-I think so," Moira said. She reached around to hold Daniel around the torso, keeping him upright. His head hung to the side. He was so broad and finely muscled …

"He'll live, Miss Moira," Cassie said. "Gotta get the doc out here, o' course, but he'll be okay. He's just weak from loss of blood. And his wound is festerin' a bit, givin' him the fever."

Moira nodded, taking strange comfort in her words. If anything happened to Daniel … on account of her—

"Fine-looking man," Cassie interrupted her thoughts, still wrapping. "Lift up your arm there. That's it. Now I got it. This 'un yours?"

"Mine?" Moira asked blankly. "Why, no. I have no claim on him."

"But he came all this way to get you back from that Bannock?"

"He did," she said softly, easing back to look at him and giving Cassie room to wind the bandage around again. "And more. He did much more for me," she whispered. She thought of Daniel's many kindnesses to her, how he had saved her aboard ship, always treated her with respect, even after she had told him of her indiscretions and her pregnancy.

They had just covered him with a blanket when Odessa and the rest entered, a mass of excited conversation. Bryce and the men were intent on taking the prisoners to Westcliffe. "There's no sheriff or deputy, but there's still a jail. They can sit in there until the judge can get to us," Bryce said.

Odessa was moving across the floor to Moira, and Moira to her. The sisters embraced. Odessa, weeping, reached back for her husband, pulling him into their circle. "Oh, Sissy, do you know how I've longed for you? Missed you? Wondered about you?"

"I'm so sorry, Dess. Sorry about Reid, about everything. There's so much I have to tell you—"

"And there will be time, plenty of time," Odessa said. "You aren't going far from me again, not if I can help it."

"It's all right then, if I stay a while with you?" She held her breath, fearful of the answer. After all she'd done … not done …

Odessa lifted her head and looked at her, still holding on to her as if she'd never let her go. "Don't you know, Moira? Having you here, the thought of being together again … it makes my heart sing."

*A singing heart.* Moira puzzled over that a moment, then felt her own skip a beat at her sister's wide, beautiful smile. Odessa loved her, after all this time. Regardless of where she'd been, what she'd done. Regardless of how she appeared or what she did in the future. She was loved. Could she learn to know what a singing heart meant? Perhaps, in time.

But for now, this feeling of homecoming, the first step of restoration, made her want to hum. Hum a song her mother had taught her as a child.

*Do you see us, Mama?* She imagined their mother, standing on the stairs, looking down at them. She had been so beautiful, but remembering her now, Moira thought the most beautiful thing about her was the love she always held in her eyes.

*I see you, baby. I'm so glad you're all right.*

*But we're not all right, Mama. We're damaged, injured. Hurting.*

*Best you're home now, then. Where you can heal.*

*But I've lost everything that you and Papa worked for. All the money.*

*It wasn't the money we worked for. It was for you. Remember that. Your father and I loved you. Stay with Odessa. Remember how you were raised, what you were taught. Rest in the memory of love.*

*Rest in love.* Moira looked to Odessa, wincing as she squeezed her again, forgetting her burns. And she glanced to Daniel, blinking back to consciousness again, smiling shyly at the sisters, the sorrow in his eyes momentarily gone.

And for the first time in a long time, she remembered what it was to have hope.

Date: 10/26/2019 3:47pm
Member: JOANNE R BURKE

| Title | Author |
|---|---|
| Due | |
| [BOOK] Anna of Kleve, th | Weir, Alison |
| 11/9 | |
| [BOOK] The bookshop on t | Colgan, Jenny |
| 11/9 | |
| [BOOK] The cafe by the s | Colgan, Jenny |
| 11/23 | |
| [BOOK] Lake Silence: the | Bishop, Anne |
| 11/23 | |
| [BOOK] Last ones left al | Davis-Goff, S |
| 11/23 | |
| [BOOK] Ribbons of scarle | |
| 11/23 | |
| [BOOK] Sing: a novel of | Bergren, Lisa |
| 11/23 | |

Total items currently out: 7.

Wow! In 2019, you have saved $1183.

Our records show that you owe $10.00.

*Try texting a librarian at 703-520-2484
*Renew your materials by text by texting 'renew all' or 'renew due' to 703-520-2484
*For information about our renovation visit:
www.fallschurchva.gov/libraryproject

Date: 10/26/2019 3:47pm
Member: JOANNE [illegible] BURKE

Title
Due

[BOOK] Anna of [illegible]ve [illegible] Weir, Allison
11/9
[BOOK] The bookshop on t Colgan, Jenny
11/9
[BOOK] The cafe by the s Colgan, Jenny
11/23
[BOOK] [illegible] St[illegible] the Bishop, Anne
[illegible]
[illegible] l once left al Davis Goff, S
[illegible]
[illegible] Ribbons of scarle
[illegible]
[BOOK] Sing, a novel of Bergren, [illegible]
[illegible]/23
[illegible] items currently out: 7

[illegible] 2019, you have saved $1183.

Our records show that you owe $10.00

*Try texting a librarian at 703-520-2484
*Renew your materials by text by texting
"renew all" or "renew due" to 703-520-2484
*For information about our renovation visit
:
www.fallschurchva.gov/libraryproject

**... a little more ...**

When a delightful concert comes to an end,

the orchestra might offer an encore.

When a fine meal comes to an end,

it's always nice to savor a bit of dessert.

When a great story comes to an end,

we think you may want to linger.

And so, we offer ...

**AfterWords**—just a little something more after you

have finished a David C. Cook novel.

We invite you to stay awhile in the story.

Thanks for reading!

Turn the page for ...

- **An Interview with Lisa T. Bergren**
- **Discussion Questions**

# AN INTERVIEW WITH LISA T. BERGREN

Q. This is mainly Moira's book, but you also focused on Odessa's growth and relationship in this novel. Why'd you think that was important?

A. Moira seems to steal every scene she's in (Nic too!). But I wanted to show how Odessa, now physically healthy, still has some emotional growth ahead of her—like we all do. We're all continually evolving, learning, changing.

Q. Is that why you were so tough on these characters in this book?

A. I think it's easy to be a Christian when things are good. You show what your faith is made of—and possibly discover new depths—when you encounter the bad. Or you walk away. I was glad to see these three getting closer to God, but Nic obviously has a ways to go.

Q. You talk about the characters as if they have minds of their own.

A. [Laughing.] They do! That's the fun of fiction. I have one idea, but then a certain spin occurs and casts them in a different direction, and I discover new things with them as if I'm riding along, observing. I always start with a rough outline, knowing some key things that will happen, and the ending I'd like to see, but I leave it to the characters to take it from there. When I'm

invested in the scene, feeling it as if I'm in their skin, sensing their emotions and mind-set, the plot often turns.

Q. Why the title?

A. We often sing contemporary songs at church that make me think—phrases like "I will sing in the troubled times" and "praise You in the storm"—a pretty big challenge for most people. But learning how to do that makes the good, easy times even sweeter, and the rough times somehow bearable. It's so important that we all find that deep assurance that God is with us, regardless of what is happening in our lives, good *or* bad. And when we do, the only proper response is to sing praises in His name. There's a reason that heaven will be full of singing. They already understand what we're still trying to get, down here.

Q. We're in 1880s Colorado. It surprised me when we got to the conquistador gold—what inspired that?

A. The third novel I ever wrote was a romance called *Treasure*, in which the heroine was seeking Spanish gold as a nautical archaeologist. I think if I'd had half the chance, I would've loved the opportunity to be a treasure hunter myself. *Indiana Jones* and all that, you know. Childhood fantasies. So I always note treasure-ish things I come across, and I read about an actual legend of lost conquistador explorers, who left behind a bounty of gold when they got separated from the rest of their troops in

the Sangre de Cristos. Reportedly, two lost hikers came across the cave in a snowstorm twenty years ago, marked it when the storm ended, intending to come back, but could never find it again. They spent years of weekends searching for that cave. Isn't that fantastic novel fodder? Love stuff like that.

Q. What can we expect in *Claim*, the third book in this series?

A. Resolution is always nice, though I don't like things tied up in perfect little bows. Life isn't like that. But I'm striving to leave my readers satisfied and hopeful, right along with the St. Clairs. I think *love* is the key for all three. That's all I'm telling ya. You'll have to read the big conclusion for yourself.

# DISCUSSION QUESTIONS

1. Do you think that God answers our pleas at times with thoughts we don't recognize as guidance? Why, or why not? Have you experienced this?

2. Consider how you might have felt toward Reid, were you a character in this novel? Is it ever right or justified to wish pain, or even death, upon another? Why, or why not?

3. Scripture encourages us to sing God's praise, every day, regardless of circumstance. Do you think we must praise Him, even when things are bad? Why or why not? How do you tend to react when faced by adversity?

4. What lessons do you feel Odessa and Bryce were learning in their marriage?

5. Have you experienced division in your marriage? Have you ever thought you were on the brink of separation or divorce? If so, what brought you back together?

6. What should someone do when faced with the temptations Odessa and Robert faced? Do you feel it was right or wrong for Odessa not to tell her husband of his brother's advances? Why?

7. All three siblings are seeking something. What do you think each one really is hungering for?

8. Manuel told Nic of his need for God—has anyone ever done the same with you? What was that like? And if not, how would you respond if someone spoke so plainly to you about your faith?

9. Moira imagines her mother in the room with her, time and time again. Why is that? Who do you think her mother represents?

10. Why do you think Moira fell in love with Gavin? What impact will her scars have on her future?

MORE GUARANTEED
GOOD READS
GOOD READ
GUARANTEED
PEEL ME!
MELODY CARLSON
A NOVEL
AS YOUNG AS WE FEEL
THE FOUR Lindas
WELCOME HOME!
CHOSEN
THE LOST DIARIES OF QUEEN ESTHER
GARRETT
As Y
Melo
ett
KATHY HERMAN
THE RIGHT CALL
SCREEN PLAY
Chris Coppernoll
heading home
a novel
renée riva
The Right Call
Kathy Herman
Screen Play
Chris Coppernoll
Heading Home
Renee Riva
Learn more at DavidCCookFiction.Blogspot.com
800.323.7543 • DavidCCook.com
David C Cook
transforming lives together